A DESTINY STRANGER THAN YOU CAN DREAM

Mystery, passion, horror—it's the incredible chronicle of Senruh, slave on the planet Naphar, a history holding as much terror and bloody action as a nightmare . . . as much wild and savage desire as a forbidden dream. A journey to an unforgettable adventure, Senruh's quest for freedom takes him into the realms of enchantment and to the strange caves of the Off-Worlders, where his fate will be decided. And by his side is the handsome boy, Pell Maru, an enigma of raw sensuality and naked courage, ready to fight, even to die, for the new companion he has pledged to call Friend.

QUARRELLING, THEY MET THE DRAGON

QUARRELLING, THEY MET THE DRAGON

SHARON BAKER

AVON
PUBLISHERS OF BARD, CAMELOT, DISCUS AND FLARE BOOKS

QUARRELLING, THEY MET THE DRAGON is an original publication of Avon Books. This work has never before appeared in book form. This work is a novel. Any similarity to actual persons or events is purely coincidental.

AVON BOOKS
A division of
The Hearst Corporation
1790 Broadway
New York, New York 10019

First Avon Printing, October, 1984

AVON TRADEMARK REG. U.S. PAT. OFF. AND IN
OTHER COUNTRIES, MARCA REGISTRADA, HECHO EN
U. S. A.

Printed in the U. S. A.

WFH 10 9 8 7 6 5 4 3 2 1

Chapter One

THE OLD MAN squatted in the dust, joy smoke wreathing his head. Blind eyes half-open he bent, inhaled fumes boiling from a pottery bowl, and resumed his chant.

Beside him, Senruh leaned against his absent master's redfruit stall, customers forgotten. The sea breeze cooled his back as he gazed at the purple fire mountains behind the city and listened, his lips moving with the old scribe's.

". . . vanquished by the Great Worm's fire,
Dargon sought out great-thewed Ekt
And forced him from the wilderness.
Quarrelling, they met the dragon.
They raised their swords, they entered peril's tempering flame.
When they emerged—scorched, blooded—they stood united
And the dragon lay behind them, slain . . ."

The old man paused to suck in more of the sweetish smoke. It seethed over the pot's sides, gray against Senruh's dark robe.

The boy frowned and darted a look down the busy alley. He scarcely saw the press of small slaves, a red-robed priest striding through an herb woman's drumming, tootling retinue, or the soldiers pursued by street musicians clacking finger shells while brandishing their other instruments. Scrutinizing each tall ruler looming above the passersby, Senruh glanced at the white head and seamed brown face by his knee. He clicked his tongue,

"Go on, old man—" He broke off, his gaze on the shaking hands that clutched the pot. Sighing, the boy looked away, past the bazaar's awnings and smoking braziers to the heavens' thick blue where the goddess's flying lizards rode the wind. He squinted. In the city's center their vivid wings clustered above the temple's golden dome: pulsing red, green, turquoise, flaring yellow. From their midst a rare orange half-breed shot toward the sun.

The boy's impatience faded while he watched the little lizard flee, as he could not, toward the bluff where the white and amber city clung, and rainbowed spume blew in from the Western Sea. He tensed. Almost caught by its half-brothers, the flyer veered to skim back across Qaqqadum. Near the city's hub it circled nobles' courtyards loud with fountains, Senruh knew, and bright with flowers belying summer's end. There the little creature could descend the sky to safety, become a cherished pet. The boy held his breath.

The half-breed lizard rose high, scattering the colored flyers, to hurtle east toward the smoldering volcanoes. Beyond their slopes where wild men roamed lay the highlands, rich with myth. Perhaps there—? The scalloped wings checked. Like a swarm of brilliant petals, the others followed.

Glowing against the smoke, the orange lizard banked and arrowed north. As its shadow flitted over city walls bristling with guards, its fellows wheeled in a fluttering column, then drifted back to their nests in the goddess's golden eaves. Not for them the fissured plateau, the hills sheltering the gods' abandoned pleasure gardens and their meeting place or, beyond, the forbidden spaceport.

The small fugitive dwindled; throat tight, Senruh memorized its unique and lonely beauty. What would it find? A loyal companion, a place to belong, a home? Or death. He looked down from the dazzle to the scribe crouched over his bowl. The boy prodded him with his sandal. The high wood sole smeared dust on the faded robe.

"Hurry, old man. Finish. My master left angry this morning. I—I haven't brought much coin lately. He can't stay long at the grog shop."

"Oh, my son! One moment till the pain lifts." The scribe breathed deep of the fumes, his wasted hands groped upward. "In the meantime, my child, have you tablets prepared? You do well with the off-worlders' mathematics."

The boy leaned back. He pulled the slabs of clay from their hiding place beneath the counter, shoved between the paving blocks he lifted each morning. Wails cut through the market's chatter. He paused.

"Make way! Slaves to market!" a rough voice shouted, followed by the deep crack of a longwhip. A ragged sleeve brushed Senruh's hem. In the dust the old man covered his ears.

"Slaves! Always more slaves fed to the maw of this city when outside its walls off-worlders give release from such misery. Why? Why do not all our poor bonded creatures—you, Senruh!—run to their freedom?"

"Hush! You'll get us both Sacrificed!" The boy glanced around but no one seemed to be listening. He stooped. "Because maybe the misery isn't so bad. Not for me, anyway. I can handle my master. And I've saved almost enough for my freedom and that partnership he promised me. Then there's my lady . . ." He smiled reminiscently. She had visited him only that morning. "Anyway, your precious spacers are no better. They're madmen, killing for no reason!"

"My son, do not let a childhood memory distort—"

But Senruh had stopped listening. Dropping the tablets in his teacher's lap, he peered toward the city gates and the sound of keening slaves. A line of little captives snaked through the bazaar's jumbled shade, a tall slaver beside it, his black beard and eyebrows filmed with dust. He hauled on the rope knotted to his prisoners' tied hands.

"Step along. Faster! Sooner I get you to auction, the sooner I can wash your stink off me!"

The lamenting slaves' bare feet raised a haze of powdered clay. As they passed, the boy covered his nose. He doubted they had bathed in sennights. His mouth curved. Before he met his lady he would not have noticed. The scribe tugged at his arm.

"Are there many?"

"Fifteen, twenty. Young, older. Mostly undersized halfbreeds."

"Oh, poor children!"

"Well, they're only little emptyheads, old man, not humans. You know the saying: 'They live to get too many babies, need orders to eat and make dung.' " Squaring his shoulders, Senruh looked down on them. Their gazes were fixed on the ground as they filed by; most of the captives only reached his waist. None came above his shoulder, he saw, pleased. Not one glanced at him.

He wondered if they had understood him. Bazaar wisdom said not; their seeming speech was only mimicry. It scarcely mattered. For a crust or a kindness, a small body would warm his pallet, give him relief. That was understanding enough, the other half-breeds said, and laughed. But Senruh avoided using the little creatures much. He disliked the crawling sensation of shame when they cried.

"Senruh, Senruh," the scribe was protesting, "you must not speak so. I have told you the tales. We are all children of the gods."

"Hush your tongue! Listeners—!" The boy glanced up and stared.

The last of the prisoners had stepped into the open. Sun blazed on a tangle of straw-colored curls. Above an unbleached robe, eyes blue as morning glowered into his. Slouching, the boy—about his own age, Senruh thought—passed by his shoulder. Senruh turned to watch the narrow back. The captive's tousle glowed as bright as a flag of battle until shadow extinguished it.

"Senruh? Are you by me, my child?"

"Still here, old man." The boy touched the white straggle. "I was watching one of the slaves. A true goldenhair, eyes the color of heavenstone. First I've seen except for our high priestess. And even she has those red streaks. My master likes them. That one's too thin, though." Senruh flexed his chest and arms. Their breadth and his clogs made him more the size of a tall ruler, he thought. All the half-breeds developed their strength as he did, and saved for the high sandals.

"Ah. Fair. From a distant land, no doubt. Have I ever told you . . . ?" The scribe's voice dreamed into silence. Wispy head bent over the tablets, his fingertips raced across them, pausing now and then to flick a calculation with an uneven fingernail. Senruh glanced from him to the growing press of bazaar strollers.

"Tell me what, old man?"

"Mmm." Clouded eyes looked beyond the boy as the scribe clunked the blocks into a stack. Senruh took them.

"Have I ever told you of Dargon and Ekt? How the brave companions journeyed across the Western Sea and what they found there?"

Eyes on the first tablet, Senruh patted his robe for a stylus. He grinned. "Not recently." He thumbed a number, blurring it, and scratched a new one as the old man's chant began.

Soon, thoughts bright with adventure, the boy set the blocks behind him. The sun neared the zenith, its searing mantle tightening across his shoulders. His mouth dried. With an unfocused stare at the crowd's swirl and break as a tall ruler pushed toward the stand, the boy reached for a redfruit. His hand passed through a man-shaped shadow.

With a whir and a sound like a dropped melon, a fire-crystal knife thudded between his fingers. He stared. Black, translucent in the strong light, the blade poured its hollow shadow across his knuckles to the glowing fruit. Behind him he heard a growl, smelled old sweat and the grog shop's stale scent. The hairs on his neck rose. "M-master?"

As the growl strengthened, a dusty breath at his knee whispered, "I go, my son . . ." Senruh glimpsed the old man scuttling away and wondered briefly who hid him during these convenient absences. The boy's finger nicked the blade. His teacher forgotten, he turned. His arm bumped a portly midriff swathed in a free merchant's striped robe.

"That could have killed me! For one redfruit?" Still unreliable, Senruh's voice almost broke. He swallowed, shaded his eyes and stared upward. A square beard and waxed shoulder-length curls were black against the sun. "I . . . Master?"

The snarl turned to a roar. "Yes! Your master! Who can slay his nameless, tribeless, half-breed slave for one redfruit or for nothing! You're not your own, not yet. Nor your lady's, however she may praise your 'curls like carved fire-crystal,' your eyes 'dark as a moonless night'! " The merchant's tones minced.

"You listened." Flushing, Senruh kept his gaze steady. "She paid you? She said she had."

A large hand slammed a coin beside the knife. "A single silver piece! None afterward! And this, her first visit in two sennights!"

Senruh turned away, becoming very occupied in tidying the redfruit. "One and a half. She explained. She's been very busy."

"Busy! You're not pleasing her, scum! I heard you refuse her. And not for the first time."

The boy gave the counter an unnecessary swipe. "What she wanted, it would have hurt. I just told her. She didn't ask again."

"Nevertheless. Next time you satisfy her, even if you bleed for it!"

Senruh's mouth tightened.

"As for listening, how could I not? Along with half the bazaar! You shame me with your noise behind those thin walls." He jerked his head toward the back of the stall where the boy's pallet lay by his own beneath the great clay ovens. "It was better when she called you to her. If you're to make a fool of me in public and lose me my silver besides, I wink at no more pilfering of my stock. Or time. Legends, reading, numbers. . . . !" He spat.

"They help you! You used to keep accounts with a notched stick!" Surreptitiously the boy spread his robe before the counter and slid his tablets out of sight.

"No! They help you! But if you think to leave me for that wrinkled rutting female lizard, you're deceived! It's your lowness excites her, scum. You think she wants you a scholar, protected by her tribe, acknowledged in her palace?" Snorting, the merchant folded massive arms and shook his head. Behind him the sky's intense blue stung Senruh's eyes.

"That's not true!" he said, blinking. "She cares, she said . . ."

"Today?"

"No."

The merchant snickered, black eyes knowing. "Pallet promises. You're a fool, scum! I've warned you. Don't believe that sentimental lizard piddle when they drivel it to you and don't go babbling it yourself—upsets the customers. And . . ."

The boy stopped listening. He knew the rest. *Only perverts show they like it; if one wants you doing something back get the coin. Before. Lose a customer by talking or grabbing and I'll beat you for a fool!* Once the merchant had added, *Start tearing pieces off yourself for them and soon you won't have anything left,* but no such gentleness touched his voice now. He stooped low.

"Cost me coin and I'll sell you. To the butcher priests!"

Cold rippled down the boy's sides even as he held his breath against the reek. But he was no longer a child; he had friends. He flung back his head. "Since you bought me you've threatened me with Sacrifice! When I'm your partner—!"

His master's eyes bulged. "You! Speaking so to me! Kneel, scum!"

The boy stared into eyes like black stones. He would not. He must not. The gaze bored into him. Pulses thrumming, muscles protesting, he bowed his neck.

"Not enough," the merchant husked.

Back stiff, for a long moment Senruh endured the other's stare. Then ten cycles of discretion bent his knees. The dust felt hot through his robe. A muscle jerked in his jaw. Above him, his master's voice shook.

"I've never liked an insolent slave. Or a scheming one. You'll look elsewhere for your partnership. And tribe!" Senruh's joints turned to water.

"But you promised! I wove baskets, carved kitchen tools, got up before dawn to make farmers' rolls! And at night before I met my lady, I, you . . ." Swallowing nausea, he made himself flutter his lashes and grasp the thick hand. He pressed it to his cheek. It snatched away.

"Don't be indecent, scum!"

"So partnership was another pallet promise?" The boy's voice broke into falsetto. Behind him he heard a titter. He glanced over his shoulder and saw two little slaves hand in hand, watching. Eyes widening, Senruh missed the descending broad palm. It cracked against his head.

"Promises are for men! Purebreds! Not a little half-breed scum of a robe tosser!" The huge head tilted; Senruh pulled it into focus, his head buzzing, eyes swimming with angry tears. The deep voice dripped syrup. "Though if you asked me nicely—as nicely as I've heard you speak to your lady—I might reconsider."

The boy scrambled to his feet. "I've earned that partnership—and my freedom—six times over! But you take my coin—commissions, food, new robes so I won't shame you with an ankle showing! You'll reconsider if I— You just want to do free what the lady buys for silver. When you can do it at all. Well, I—" Loud laughter interrupted him. He swung around.

Behind him stood an appreciative crowd: towering Rabu rulers like his master, small Kakano slaves less than half their size, and a few half-breeds like himself, the free adults chest high to the Rabu. Grinning, the spectators nudged each other. The boy followed their gaze to the merchant's contorted face. "No!"

A huge hand grasped the neck of Senruh's robe. Lifting him, it slammed him against the counter. He braced himself. The merchant pressed harder. The boy's elbows buckled, his back arched. His shoulders smacked the counter, his head knocked wood. The sun burned white fire in his eyes.

"We'll see how the nobles like their pretty toy altered," the deep voice snarled. The boy's sandals left the ground. A fist like a boulder choked him. "You'll never grow to citizenship without your feet!"

Panting, Senruh's master felt for the knife. Chipped from a single crystal forged deep in the mountains' fires, it would sever bone.

"Help!" Surely someone—? But over the merchant's shoulder the boy saw the watchers press closer, avid stares on the blade and his bared ankles. Above him the huge arms and chest surged; the merchant's grip shifted. Air whistled into the boy's lungs.

His hand darted to the glassy knife handle. It felt hot. He yanked. It came free. His master jerked away. For an instant his fingers loosened and Senruh dove under his arm. Landing in a crouch, the boy waved the knife. It flashed with sunlight.

"Don't you ever again—! I'll take this!"

The merchant flinched back. The boy whirled and plunged through the onlookers. As he wove between slaves' small bodies and rulers' large surprised knees, he yelled, "I won't be back! Try running the stall yourself, you diseased dung lizard dropping!"

A little Kakano screamed. A wide hand ripped at Senruh's hair. Wrenching free, he bolted across the Way of the Southern Gate and into an alley. He scooted under an empty booth, squeezed between it and another to the next street. Dropping the blade into his robe's chest pocket, heart thumping, he slowed and merged with the throng.

He was checking behind him for pursuers when his toe caught on a bundle of rags and light warm bones. A hand grasped his ankle. Hopping, he glanced down into hazed eyes staring up into a private dark. In a trembling palm the scribe held out two redfruit.

"For you, oh son of my heart. I think you go now to a destiny stranger than either of us can dream. But my tales go with you." A tear leaked from one rheumy eye.

With quick thanks Senruh grabbed the offering and shoved it into his pocket with the knife. Behind him his master began a wordless bellowing. The boy took a running step, paused, and clasped his teacher's shoulders. "I'll be back, old man."

White locks fluttering, the scribe shook his head, denying him. Across the way the merchant's gabble turned to words.

"Be back by sundown," he bawled. "I'll have the longwhip waiting. And if you stay out and the curfew catchers find you, I'll give no coin for your ransom, not even your own. The butcher priests can have you!"

Senruh pushed deeper into the crowd, a chill spreading down his spine. Sacrifice. Or the longwhip. He had seen its victims' backs. Those who survived.

Chapter Two

IN THE ALLEY of the Metal and Jewel Carvers, Senruh eased out of the crowd. He leaned against a stall. His master's rages were getting worse, he thought. Forcing himself to breathe evenly, he ignored the nearby guard and picked up a golden head circlet. In the vertical sunlight, it glittered like the curls of the captive he had seen that noon.

The boy flicked a carved leaf and it bounced on its tiny spring. Once his master, flushed with pleasure, had promised him such a bauble. In those days the merchant had spoken too of moving from the bazaar, buying more slaves, as some of his neighbors had done. But none of it had happened, as his master had no knack for accumulating coin. Or keeping friends.

The tall guard interrupted the boy's thoughts. Chain-mail jingling, she eyed him and edged nearer, her hand on her dagger. Senruh dropped the fillet and crossed the alley to a jewel carver's stall where he pretended interest in a scooped-out green needle's egg. But there, too, he was not let alone.

Behind the counter a clear-eyed young slave woman pointed to the egg, babbling happily of giant insects that lived in the highlands sky, lighting on its cliff tops only once each spring to deposit their great green eggs. A child's tale, Senruh thought, and looked at her more closely. It was as he had thought—her vacant smile proclaimed her one of the goddess's Innocents. Minds wiped of

11

memories for a cycle, they were like children in their curiosity and credulity. Senruh gave her a long look, wondering what intolerable thing she had done or had had done to her. She rewarded him with a smile of pure joy. Chilled, he looked down at the leaf-colored translucence she had put in his hand.

The egg had been hollowed into a miniature cavern palace like those in the volcanoes' slopes—abandoned homes of the gods, so the storytellers said. It was like his master's world, the boy thought, and abruptly put the egg away. He pushed into the throng. If he partnered the man he must share that shrunken copy of a life.

Senruh halted, the strollers eddying around him, and looked up to the sky. The winged lizards hung and glided there; he remembered the orange half-breed's flight. But human half-breeds had no wings; they could not skim the city walls. And tonight he must return to the longwhip. The scribe, as always, could not or would not help. Senruh had no one else.

A Rabu noble brushed through the crowd. Like grass before a random wind, the smaller people knelt. When Senruh's turn came a bordered hem grazed his face, exuding the scent of costly oils like his lady's. His lady! She loved him, she had said so; her visits might be less frequent but she had explained that. Surely she would not want him hurt!

The noble passed; the boy jumped to his feet. But would she still be in the city? Afternoons she rested in her villa outside Qaqqadum. With a falling sensation in his middle, Senruh glanced up. Shamash the Sun God's fiery eye still burned in the center of the sky. No one traveled in the heat of the day; if he hurried he might yet find his lady in the Avenue of Precious Delights, shopping and trading news with the other well-born.

The boy breathed deeply of the bazaar's familiar smell: charcoal smoke, dust, excrement, and incense—the scent of excitement, of something hidden behind the next booth about to happen. He headed north then west toward the sparkling line of the sea.

Used to merging with the bazaar's tides and their flotsam and jetsam, or to traveling in his lady's wake, Senruh did not at first notice the disapproving stares. Weighing how much he could explain and still make his lady want him, he had just entered the Region of Government and Temples to the Lesser Gods when his phrases tangled and stuck. He looked up from the swept clay and watered plots of green, and his gaze met that of a merchant woman.

The tall striped-robed Rabu stood under the portico of the Building of Just Measures. She inventoried Senruh's lack of size, his aloneness, his dark slave's robe, and she nudged her companions. When the whole group—men and women rulers and their small slave attendants—stopped talking and turned to look, the boy flushed and hurried by.

Just before him a noble issued from a guildhouse followed by slaves bearing jeweled caskets and planning scrolls. Senruh dropped. The aristocrat glanced at him, kneeling by a master smith's statue, then peered beyond him to the shower trees that shaded the building. Their ferny leaves whispered and their great brown pods, swelling in the sun, creaked like thieves' footsteps. In a high fearful voice the noble called his small servants close.

Senruh stared after them. As they passed, even the little Kakano slave had drawn her skirts away.

He glanced across the double-rutted street. A young priest stood there, one foot on a shrine's entrance ramp, his gemmed and embroidered surplice flashing in the sun. He watched the boy, his expression troubled. Senruh scowled. Shoulders hunched, head hanging, he rose. Then he remembered his lady. Forcing his chin high he paced forward, looking through the towering rulers of Qaqqadum.

* * *

Sharon Baker

The streets emptied. Rabu merchants, soldiers, aristocrats, and priests lazed in temple pools and public and private baths, or sat in shady gardens gossiping over steaming cups of 'seq. Might his lady do the same? Surely she would not vary her habit and join those napping in their city homes or shops, or explore the still-open bazaar! The boy's steps slowed. Even if he guessed right, perhaps he should not seek her. Seasons ago his lady had forbidden him the Avenue of Precious Delights. She wished him to be her secret joy, she said, kept for her alone in the stall's back room or in her home. But of course she would not risk his life for that whim!

Ashy dust powdered his clogs. He entered the Area of the Merchants. Somnolence hushed the affluent homes. How much should he ask for, he wondered. Often the words had fluttered, almost spoken, on his tongue: buy me. Please, give me my freedom. Sponsor me. One look at her unblinking golden eyes and the pleas died in his throat. But now he must speak. She would want him to, if only because he would be no use to her, after. Besides, she loved him!

Holding the word like a talisman, he looked about. On the merchants' high walls, yellow and green lizards scurried; behind them, trees cast coin-shaped shadows in the dust. He breathed in the scent of hot clay and relaxed a little. He need not decide now. A breeze sighed agreement in his ear. Stirring the leaves above him, it whispered of fountains, and shade, and trellises nodding with flowers.

Someday he would own such a place, the boy thought. Then no one would dare threaten or look at him askance; they would not even notice his height. His smile twisted. *And stones have wings!* he thought. But if he had enough coin others might ignore his size.

His high wooden soles clopped onto the paving stones of the priests' and nobles' inner city. He looked down a long avenue to Qaqqadum's pivot: the Ensai's palace and beside it, the wide gold-domed column that was the Temple of Sassurum.

Senruh's heartbeat quickened. Before the goddess's wide-flung doors, a bronze statue well-known to every half-breed in Qaqqadum shone in the sun. It was a life-sized image of Nargash, the first Ensai to ally himself with Sassurum and her high priestess, thus ending a hundred cycles of civil strife. The figure's dress was in the antique style still affected by old men at court. Below, the tubular unpleated robes gleamed like pale gold. Higher, they darkened until the metal lay black with tarnish on the shoulders and proud uplifted head.

The boy squinted. He could see the points and curves of the Order of Twin Rule in the center of the Lord Nargash's chest. Against that order, once each cycle, a winding line of barefoot half-breeds measured their height. Top it and they might be citizens, adopted into a tribe, allowed property, even a voice in government.

But fall short and a half-breed proved he had inherited his Kakano parent's inhumanity. Too small in brain and strength to rule others or even himself, he could only be a slave.

The old dread lifted the hair on Senruh's arms. What if he did not grow?

Swallowing, he made himself shrug. Then he would truly need a loving mistress! Besides, the scribe called the whole thing nonsense. With practiced ease the boy put his thoughts away and looked past the figure to the entrance pools leading to the temple's interior.

Clotted with shadows, its altars held huge translucent blood basins, freshly scrubbed. Sunlight filtered onto painted god masks set around the ceiling; glints from their gilding skipped across the ramps spiralling the inner walls.

Did Sassurum listen there as her priestesses claimed? Senruh thought of her sacred messenger with its rare orange wings and its lonely exit from the city. Perhaps if the goddess gave it her protection she guarded other half-breeds as well. He muttered a prayer then looked around, ashamed. How the scribe would smile. Praying to a goddess who probably did not exist when he could seek a living protectress!

The boy set out once more toward the sea. And as he neared the Avenue of Precious Delights his mind tumbled with memories of his lady; their first meeting lay more than a cycle in the past.

Chapter Three

IN THE DAWN that now seemed so long ago, Senruh had been helping his master with the morning's fresh-picked fruits and vegetables. The boy was crouched beneath the counter when his master hissed with surprise. Senruh stood and looked. An unmarked sedan chair approached: scrolled with gold, it set the street beneath dancing with colored lights from the rainbow stones trembling on its sides. The boy stared. Wealth seldom penetrated to his corner of the bazaar. He went back to emptying the farmers' tall baskets. The produce was wet with dew.

Stowing any damaged goods beneath the counter for timid or careless customers, Senruh started brushing the white roothairs of pyramided purple crunchroots into a swirl. His master poked him. "Smile, scum."

Startled, the boy looked across the alley. Four tall half-breed bearers held the chair quite still. Its gold-threaded curtain twitched, revealing a sleeve with an aristocrat's wide border. Senruh stiffened. A noble, scum viewing after a night of revels in the inner city. His master had speculated on such a chance.

The merchant's heavy hand descended onto Senruh's shoulder. "Smile!" the Rabu repeated between his teeth. Pulse quickening, the boy obeyed. The curtains separated further. His master nudged him.

"They're interested. Show 'em more!"

Senruh glanced around for a purity priestess or the scribe. Only bazaar strollers, tall merchants, their small

17

bondsmen, and a few roll and sausage women yawned in
the horizontal light. The boy stepped into the sun. Heart
thumping, he slid a foot forward. He tightened his robe,
accentuating his broad chest, the strong curves of his hip
and sex and, shamelessly, the line of his leg.

The strollers snapped their fingers in approval, a few
chirring like rutting he-lizards on a summer night. Senruh
flushed, more pleased than not by the attention. A thin
weathered hand parted the curtains. Crusted with sparkling knuckle rings, it beckoned. Above it veils fluttered.
The boy's eyes widened.

A Bearer of Children! Those who opted at their Time of
First Blood to be Protectors of the Unborn must be different, finer, he had always thought, than the brash women
he knew who chose to work unveiled and forever barren in
the sun's full glare. Waxed curls brushed his neck.

"Remember! Get the coin, first!"

"I always do, don't I?" Scowling, the boy wondered if his
master would be so cool if it were his robe that was going to
be tossed. Taking a deep breath, he sauntered toward the
conveyance.

He smelled dust in the thick, glinting curtains. The age-
spotted hand plucked at his sleeve, drawing him forward.
Expressionless, the chairmen steadied the litter as he
clambered into the stuffy, crowded dark.

He found no place to kneel. Crouching, head bowed, he
breathed in costly body oils, scented joy smoke, and drink's
sour fumes. The tall cocooned figure sat on heaped cushions; more glimmered behind her, smelling richly of soft-
tanned manskin and the salty incense of trapper-fish silks.
He swallowed. What could one like her want with such as
him? Perhaps her secluded life made her curious but shy
and she wished only to question him . . . ? He bowed. His
hair brushed a lanky shrouded thigh. High above him, the
woman drew a harsh breath. Senruh's scalp prickled.

Her ringed hands darted through a sunbeam. They
flattened him against the chair's end. They groped his
shoulders, his arms, kneaded his chest and belly, they ran-

sacked him. Shy! The boy drew a ragged breath, remembered his master's words, and fought to school his body as well as his expression.

The muffled form bent. Head close to his, she grunted impatience. She yanked up his hem. Sharp-nailed, she fumbled at his loincloth. Her bony fingers began to work. Shock ripped through him. Men could be in such haste, but in his experience women seldom—! Her hands grew more urgent. His body answered, its pounding excitement quickening his breath. His lips parted. Eyes shutting, rules tossed to the winds, Senruh reached for the veiled head.

"No!" One-handed, she slapped his wrists aside.

"Please!" Wrung from him the word died, stillborn, in the hot gasping silence. Gauzes nuzzled his bared skin; the woman's head turned. Behind her red and amber mantles, eyes gleamed. They fixed on his face.

In her pupils he saw himself: half naked, dark eyes slumberous, hungering . . . His cheeks flamed.

Stripped of his last privacy, he clutched the litter's sides. His knees shook. His heart and breath were wild in his chest, and the boy's awareness shrank to a stranger's dry hands and his exploding senses. His last restraint burst. He arched, threw back his head, and cried out, thrusting and plunging into those demanding palms. They tightened, he shuddered and shuddered again. The chair shook.

"Steady, scum!" The hoarse voice was sharp. The conveyance righted.

Hardly noticing, Senruh slumped against its sides, the woman's hands still on him, his breathing rough. He wondered if she expected an apology. She should beg his pardon, he thought, his master had been listening. He glared at the tall wrapped curve, thinking of the beating her tricks would cost him.

A low chuckle came from behind the gauzes. His frown deepened. He had to obey all Rabu, but that gave them no license to mock him! Perhaps the scribe was right, this was no way to earn coin. Why, the lady had scarcely a veil out of place while he . . . Senruh looked down. His face heated.

With teasing slowness she released him. Skimming his belly and his rucked-up robe, the bony hand touched his cheek. He smelled his sex on it. Her fingers fastened in his hair.

Light from the slitted curtains struck his eyes. He tried to wipe all expression from his face but still her gauzes shook with her silent laughter. He scowled.

She smoothed a damp lock off his brow and leaned back, her breathing, like his, quieting. Palpable as a caress, her gaze traveled down his dishevelment. His flesh twitched. Her eyes crinkled, her thin spotted hand stole out. As he tensed, parchment fingers touched his. They pressed a coin into his palm. He had forgotten!

Her mantles fell to one side. She tilted her head and shook her finger. "Don't be greedy, my surly little ruffian, and I won't mention the coin you failed to ask for, or why. I'll only tell your master you pleased me. Very much." She ruffled his loose curls and whispered, "Bow your head, my beautiful! My sleek, lusty he-lizard."

Neck stiff, the boy scowled at the veils. But she was Rabu and noble. He had taken her silver. He lowered his head. A curfew permission tablet dropped, heavy, around his neck. She leaned away from him. Her draperies slid across his mouth.

"If you wish more of my coin meet my servant tonight at sundown by the Western Gate. My villa lies beyond. Do you wish to come to me there, my lovely, reluctant child?" She tipped up his face. "Or, if you do not," she whispered, "will that not make the night all the more entertaining for us both?"

A finger touched his lip. It traced down his chin and throat to the tablet's thong then slid around his nape into his hair. A chill chased down his spine. She wanted him! The coin proved it. She praised him, half-offered to protect him. Perhaps she even loved him a little? Unable to hide his triumph, he looked up. And remembered that if he went to her, he would walk outside the city walls. There, away from runners, rebels, and the superstitious, noble and spacer exchanged scrolls and knowledge as they did in Qaqqadum only at the Royal Academy. Perhaps, protected from the off-worlders' insanity by this lady, he might learn more than the scribe—! Swallowing, he nodded.

"Good." Her voice was flat. She straightened, her coverings billowed, giving out the scent of age and desiccated flowers. "My head bearer will settle with your master. Ras!"

"I hear, lady." The gravelly voice came from outside.

She bent. Once more veils drifted around him. Breath hot in the boy's ear, she whispered, "I am the Lady Ariahnne Addiratu. Think of me today. As I shall be thinking of you."

Addiratu. Princess. The boy's ready tongue deserted him. "Thank—thank you, lady. I will." Clothing disordered, legs aching, he wondered if he had been dismissed. She reached out. He stopped breathing. She flicked him with her nails.

"Go, my little wanton! Nap. I want you fresh for tonight!"

Crumpled, scarlet-faced, he stood in the full dazzle of the early morning sun. A crowd gathered around him. He looked away, not yet ready to strut and wink. His gaze met the head chairman's.

Above his broken nose the older, taller man's thick-lashed eyes were expressionless, as was his sculptured mouth. His arms bulged in his loose sleeves, he shifted to balance the chair. It was then the boy realized: each bearer had felt his weight's every transfer, had, unseen by him and forgotten, shared each tremor. He gave them a shaky smile. They did not return it.

He sat hunched on his pallet in the stall's back room. Shamed, aroused, Senruh listened to his master haggle over his services with the chairman whose harsh face held a ruined beauty. And when the shop was silent once more the boy's mind jangled with thoughts, as the lady had ordered, of the night to come.

As he had promised, Senruh went to the Western Gate at sunset, the permission tablet slung around his neck. The guards eyed him, exchanging jokes that made him flush.

A tall hooded servant came. Beckoning him to follow, the muffled form led him through the sentry niche and across the plateau to a villa perched high above the sea. Trees nodded behind walls glimmering blue in the afterglow. Entering through an arched side door, Senruh and his guide followed a dark corridor. They passed a barred timber door—all the rest had only curtains—and Senruh eyed its winking brass fittings, speculating as to the riches within.

In a torchlit courtyard the servant gestured for him to wait, and departed. The night darkened. As the sea wind blew stronger it filled with jingling off-key melodies underlaid by softly hooting song. In vain he looked for instruments or their players.

Senruh worked his bare toes inside his heightened sandals. He had braced himself for more indignities, even felt an unwilling excitement at the thought, but he had not expected neglect! Fidgeting, he watched the tip of Sassurum's Veil creep from behind the volcanoes. Woven by the goddess from a sun she exploded for her winter warmth, its first misty skein entwined a star. As the veil unfurled across the sky its crimson light scattered over the long entrance pool and fountain. The boy shifted his weight and sighed. He did not quite dare to sit, uninvited. He strolled across the courtyard to inspect the vine-hung walls for footholds. If this lady did not appreciate him, others would! He stopped short, eyes widening.

A straggle of pink-tinged flowers, luminous in the wash of veil and starlight, fronted the wall. His robe swirled as he halted and its breeze lifted the petals from glassy stamens that clinked and hazily reflected the sky. Nearby, a few pale lavender blooms lifted long mouths to join in with hoarse whistles. Crystal bells and windsingers—the gods' alarms! Bazaar wisdom placed them only in the sandy soil of the gardens of the gods, low in the sacred hills. One touch and they raged with melody. Senruh gave up all thought of climbing the wall. If he were caught—! Only Rabu might walk the plain unescorted. He wiped his palms on his robe and stepped back.

Behind him a rare caged lizard whispered into song. Its throbbing murmur spoke of loneliness, of solitary imprisonment in an alien land. Senruh's throat ached as he listened, afraid to move, afraid the music might stop, the magic break. Across the fire-bright courtyard, the Lady Ariahnne stepped from the shadow.

Her face was unveiled, her hair bright with gems and gilded braids. Garments streaming behind her, she glided toward him, her hands outstretched. He scarcely saw the creases about her lids, the sagging cheeks beside her turtle's beak of a nose. Instead he stared, incredulous, at the glow in her yellow eyes and the radiant smile on her thin rouged lips.

A handsbreadth from him she stopped, a column of tumbled mantles. He breathed in her heavy spicy fragrance. The tall head bent; her arms closed gently around him. She cradled his cheek against her breast, he felt her husky voice's vibrations

"Welcome, my treasure! I waited, I tried to summon the will to send you back. But I stole just one look at those great dark eyes, these curls . . ." She mussed them and held him away from her. "Softly, my small wild creature," she whispered. "I can feel your heart racing! I only wish now to touch you like this . . . and this . . ." She smoothed his lids and his lashes, then, smiling, she dropped a kiss on the end of his nose. She drew him, disarmed, to the edge of the pool.

"Now, my lusty one, since we have already settled your capacity, let us become acquainted! We have all the night, after all." Her smile invited him to share her amusement.

He forgot to drop to his knees, he did not press his head to her sandal as her station required. Instead, dazzled, he found himself sitting beside the great lady while she offered him sweets with her own hands and poured a sparkling blue liquor into his ritual masculine cup, gemmed and knobbed with gold.

She sipped from her feminine crystal vase and questioned him. He was very beautiful, she said. Was he good as well? No? But surely he never required a beating! Oh, really? Sometimes? She clasped her hands. Oh, poor, poor child! Her eyes were bright. And how did it feel? Was there pain? Much? Where was it worst, precisely?

When at last the boy stared, silent, at his toes, emptied of the last scrap of shamed memory, he wished he had kept silent. He mumbled, "I always was bad. If I'd been better, I might have . . ." What? he jeered at himself. Been loved?

"Nonsense!" the lady said. "You're perfect! Have some more fermented songfruit. Your master is a fool."

As he emptied his cup she lifted a finger. The torchlight danced on her rings and her feral eyes. "Or at least—you are tribeless, are you not? Have you a sponsor, a court connection?"

Flown on the drink and the praise, he gazed at the flash and glow of her hair and, flinging his master's advice to the four directions, answered, "No, lady, I'm crèche-bred. No parents, no record of a tribe, not even inherited slave rights. Or sponsor! If I lodged a complaint it would be a cycle before a judge even looked at me, let alone heard my case."

His phrases hung on the air. He bit his lip. How could he have exposed himself so? Unwanted from his beginnings! He put down his cup, afraid to see the scorn in her eyes. But she only poured him more drink and laughed.

"Better and better! I have discovered a waif! No one going nowhere. Almost I can forgive myself for what I will do to you!" She caught her breath. Voice harsh, she added, "Still, my dingy scrap of heavenstone, you shall have the goddess's Choice. If you wish to leave, go now. Otherwise . . . I know myself."

Danger breathed across Senruh's shoulders. But as his skin roughened he thought of returning early with small reward—and of his master's face. He remembered, too, those he had served in the back alleys by his stall and the Avenue of Precious Delights. How much more variety could there be? Last, he looked at the courtyard where glossy red-tinged leaves stirred in the breeze, starred with white flowers whose perfume drugged the senses. Behind them, the exotic singing flowers whistled and tinkled. He scanned the courtyard's fittings.

Torchlight glinted on brass and crystal and gold. Muted by distance came the talk of servants at last meal. Movement caught the boy's eye: deep in the leaf shadows by the pool, the small gray lizard stirred. It blinked at him from its cage scrolled with gold.

Even the scaled crawlers do well here, Senruh thought. He glanced at the dish of sweetmeats. He liked sweets. He shook his head. "I'll stay. I can take care of myself."

"Very well." With an almost shy smile, the lady snatched a honeyed fruit and popped it into his mouth just as he was shoving in a choice of his own. He choked, chewed, and swallowed hard. She laughed, voice soft with pleasure and victory.

As Senruh sucked his fingers in noisy satisfaction, she loomed over him. Her eyes swam with light. "Now you are mine, tell me of this!" She gestured around the courtyard, then at herself. "Have you visited others as you do me?"

He looked at her through his lashes. However he answered, she would not like it. They never did. Wary, he shook his head.

Lines dragged down her mouth. "No? Then where do you ply your trade? Certainly I am not your first! You know the rules too well, my scrubby little songboy!"

He gave her a hurt look and stared at his toes.

"Ah! It's a sensitive little bazaar scuttler." Scrawny fingers forced his chin up. "Tell me! In an alley? Behind your stall?"

Faced with those blazing eyes, his will shriveled. "Both," he admitted.

"Wonderful. Low. Perfect! And what did they do to you? And you to them? Say!"

Goaded, he told her a little and watched her breath catch and quicken. When he had exhausted his own experience, which seemed scarcely to whet her interest, he drew on that of his more adventurous acquaintances; he had no friends—with his industry and his learning and his hoarded coins. As she prodded him for more he repeated the stories, probably untrue, that the other half-breeds and apprentices snickered over when no Rabu master was in sight.

After those accounts too failed to satisfy her, he extrapolated from tales told by shabby travelers for coin late at night when curfew was revoked for the Feasts of the Fertile Fields. At last, warmed to his task, he let his imagination fly.

He invented secret forbidden rituals carried out at times and places to defy belief, as well as tastes and contortions to strain the most inflamed of acrobats, all featuring himself as participant-in-chief.

His well of invention dry, he grinned up at her. He could almost hear his master's voice: *Tell 'em what they want to hear, scum; that's at least half of what they're paying for!* His smile wavered.

Ariahnne's eyes had darkened, her breath came fast through parted lips. "If even a fraction of that is true—!" With a growl she was on him, her nails fastening in his shoulder like claws.

Startled, he found himself flat on the red-tinted stones by the pool. There she took her pleasure of him in full view of the veil and the stars, the gods, and any of her servants unwise enough to observe.

As the boy's senses began to riot in reply she whispered fiercely to touch her here, and here! and showed him how.

He caught his breath. She hissed that he must cry out if he wished. It was no shame to let another see his abandon and if he did, she would pay!

After, as he lay back, hoarse, sweating, dazed, she stroked him, calling him her darling great pocket stone. Such talent, such flawless flesh as his must be hers alone until she had taken a surfeit of him. Her head bearer would speak to his master in the morning. She leaned on her elbow and gazed down at his face. "I warned you," she murmured. "You could have escaped."

Before he could think of a reply she was on her feet gesturing for him to rise. A new set of lessons began: different from the scribe's, but no less absorbing.

Her initial thirst for him slaked, Ariahnne led the boy to the great blackstone entrance pool and motioned for him to climb in. A salt breeze rustled through its encircling black-green leaves, and ruffled the dark water awash with reflected crescents of fire. A bony finger nudged him; reluctant, the boy stepped in.

To his surprise the water lapping his knees felt warm as blood. He looked up. Ariahnne was dragging a chest from beneath the bushes.

With growing suspicion, Senruh watched her set sponges and brushes and what she said was foaming sand on the lip of the pool. Bare, hugging himself, the boy protested that she would remove his protective coating and he would die of the first sickness to sweep the bazaar. He almost despaired when she laughed, doused him, and scrubbed.

He was tingling all over when she stepped back, panting a little, to shake out her bedraggled draperies. "You may emerge now, my overvigorous jewel. Let us see what lay beneath that matrix of grime."

Glowering, Senruh stepped to the paving stones. The torches turned his splashes to liquid fire. The lady handed him cloths. He turned them over, mystified, looking for a sleeve, a hem . . . Clicking her tongue, Ariahnne whisked them away.

"They are for drying! Has your master never taken you to the baths?" She rubbed him briskly.

"He says the public fountains are good enough for me. Because they don't cost, is my guess. I don't like 'em much, though." He flipped back a lock of damp hair. Her eyes were hooded as she dropped the cloths and surveyed him.

"Pity. You launder well." Motioning for him to pick them up and finish, she turned her back. He heard her crooning and watched her force sweetmeats, then her bony fingers, into the gray lizard's cage.

"And will you sing for me tonight, my sweet, my golden-throated precious?" Her voice dropped to a murmur.

Dry, Senruh arranged himself in the torchlight. If she wished to see him, he was ready. It was what she had paid for, after all. But she seemed to have forgotten him.

The torches sputtered. The sea snarled, gnawing at the cliff's base. The breeze grew stronger until the blossoms clashed far out of tune and Senruh shivered. Abandoning his pose he glanced about him. He hid one leg behind the other, he spread his large square-palmed hands over his thighs. She could at least have given him proper covering for his legs, he thought. If she did not want to look, others might. He began to wish he had accepted his chance and left. Even now . . . he took a step toward the wall.

She whirled, veils wide around her, and grasped his arm. Shoving him downward, she stretched him on his belly across the stones. Indignant, struggling, he opened his mouth. A sandal jabbed his ribs.

"Do not. Your whining no longer amuses me."

He froze. It was her courtyard. She was Rabu and his owner for the night. She could kill him here. A coin to his master and no one would dare ask questions. He waited. Every finger-width of his nakedness quivered, open to inspection, to hurt. Her sandals slapped toward him.

Lightness dropped over his legs. He glanced back. She had covered him with a drying cloth.

Inside him a taut string broke. Choking thanks, he buried his face in his arm. Gauzes whispered, her fragrance enveloped him.

"Look this way, my small frightened turtle. And remember this moment. If you are wise you will always fear me a little. But no more than that. You must not let yourself be too easily conquered. Now, see how we will replace that precious coating of yours!"

Afraid not to obey, Senruh wiped his eyes with his fingers and turned his head. Ariahnne knelt by his shoulder, her long rouged nails interlaced around a wooden casket bound with bronze. She lifted out a crystal pot. As she rubbed oil from it onto her palms, its aromatic scent overpowered the dank smell of fresh water on stone. Bony fingers slipped around his neck.

"You're tense as a rock scuttler, my own. Relax. I will tell you a tale, one I've related often enough to my own offspring, to calm them for . . . well, for something other than what lies in store for you. But the account will be new to one of your sort. First, know that the pool you bathed in is called an apsu."

Senruh swallowed a shaky grin. With the scribe he had collected two hands of creation myths, all long. She could not be planning his immediate demise.

"That's better." Her palms moved down to knead his shoulders. "The apsu reminds us of Membliar, the great sunless sea where life began and where it will all someday end."

Confidence almost restored, Senruh assumed a wide-eyed stare. "That is wonderful, lady!" He set his cheek back on the cooling rock. As she swirled oil down his spine he ventured a child's question. "And did the gods spring from there, too?" Through his lashes he saw her look of annoyance.

"I was coming to that. Only the goddess, Sassurum the Unending, is of Naphar. She stood in the whirling dust of space when our world began; she will watch over it still when it rolls, a lifeless frozen pebble, through endless night.

"The other gods, my little lizard," Ariahnne said in more normal tones, "were colonist gods. They came millennia ago in their silver ships from a world that ended when its sun flickered out on the thin-starred edge of the galaxy. You know galaxy?"

Without thinking, Senruh nodded. Her hands paused; she frowned.

Customers don't want brains in a robe tosser, scum, Senruh's master repeated in his memory. *It spoils the pretty story they're telling themselves—them high, you low. They'll give you small coin for that! Start bragging about your learning and I'll see you don't lie on your back or sit for a sennight!*

Cursing himself, Senruh looked limpid-eyed at Ariahnne. "Is—is galaxy stars, lady?" She gave him a sharp look.

"If you were one of mine, I'd swear—!" Her gaze swept his length and she shook her head. "No little bazaar sweeping could—" She drizzled oil onto her hands. With langorous slowness, her palms slid down his sides. He shivered, he made sure she noticed. She gave a low laugh; he relaxed a little.

"Now, my moonstruck gift of the night, listen and I will tell you more." Her fingers trailed upward; the hairs on his skin stood on end. She chuckled and began.

"The stranger gods—giants, even to those of my stature —found Naphar much as it is now. Seas filled with shelled creatures and fish, lands alive with insects, snakes and lizards and our first primitive mammals; you know mammals?" Cautious now, Senruh shook his head.

"They are warm like us in all seasons. They are the large-eyed hiders in the trees and grasslands, oh gem of ignorance; they are also those who fly, naked-winged, beneath the moon." As her voice dropped into a chant, Senruh gave himself to the phrases and the feel of her hot dry palms.

"In Naphar the gods found a world much like their own; they made it more so. And Sassurum was patient; she extended her second chance even to those who, in their arrogance, would not accept the Weavers' Time of Ending for their world or for themselves.

"But Naphar was not their world, nor our sun their cooled one. Its rays aged them too soon; it marked and killed their few children. When they ate our native life, they sickened and they died. For know that our soil is rich in a certain metal that settles in the stems of plants and the shells of seeds. When our creatures eat them, the metal weights their flesh. It does not hurt them. But it killed our gods.

"The gods made machines to erase the poison." She paused. A fishy wind wrenched at the flames, sending the shadows leaping, clashing the crystal bells by the wall. The paving stones sharpened under the boy's chest and thighs. Ariahnne's knowing hands slid lower. Tremors ran through the boy in waves. Her husky intimate voice held a smile as it flowed on.

"The new gods retreated to their cavern palaces deep in the fire mountains. There they mixed their seed with our first mammals' to create servants in the gods' own image, servants who could live off the land and toil in the sun's full light. Many conditions of men sprang, new, from their hands and their machines. The large Rabu who rule—my people! And the small Kakanos who serve. Yours, I think, my small craven lizard?" Her nail tickled Senruh's neck, her words pierced the sensual syrup cloying his brain. His mouth tightened.

She had no right! he thought. She might have bought him for a night; she had not hired the right to call him coward and Kakano! She leaned near, her lingering strokes caressed him. Thought died.

"As it happened," she continued as if there had been no pause, "we, the gods' bastard children, do well enough in sunlight. But otherwise the gods failed. We inherited their own inconvenient digestion. We could eat native flesh and

grain only after it passed through their engines—for which
life-giving miracle we of course insisted they keep a share.
Divine chance, ordained since the first dust and gasses
that would be Naphar and its sun began to whirl then
glow; or so say the priests. But I think . . . the gods
would not be alone in keeping cherished minions by them
through fear, would they, my prize?"

After a heartbeat she added, "It is whispered that beyond the fire mountains, in the stony highlands, Kakano
nobles and rebel slaves practice a purified, stern religion.
With forbidden philters, they reverse our sacred order: the
large are drugged into obedience and ruled by the small.
What say you to that, my mutinous little lizard?"

Heart speeding, Senruh—who had heard it all before—
answered quickly, "That there are no highlands. And if
there were, half-breeds would be misfits there too." Peril
uncoiled and slithered away. She chuckled.

"True. Though you have your uses." She stared past him
to the sea where starlight washed the heaving horizon and
Sassurum's Veil poured its scarlet mist halfway across the
sky.

"They say also," she went on, "that you little half-
breeds and Kakanos have inherited the gods' own eyes,
eyes that saw for a million cycles by the scant red light of a
dying sun. And that we Rabu have our native diurnal
mammals' vision; to us the night is dark and we are blind
to the myriad stars that crowd our sky, high on this galaxy's
spiral arm . . .

"But that is absurd." Her nails twisted his skin. He
fought not to wince. Voice hard, she said, "The veil is only
a trace of pink before moonrise and no one sees without a
sun or a moon or a torch to light the way."

Prudent, Senruh said nothing, though all around him
red light dripped from fountain and leaf and stone, and
stars shouted their silver-white presence. Feigning drowsi-
ness—he was getting her measure now—he said, "You are
very learned, lady. I scarcely understand one word in a

handful. I only wish . . ." He fluttered his lashes and smiled sideways into her eyes.

Her nails released him. Her palms opened like flowers; they stroked him. As he shivered with pleasure she nudged him onto his back. His hold began to slip on his training; in self-defense he tightened his mouth, he hid his eyes with his arm as, with a delicate touch, she brushed small stones and grit from his chest and belly. For a long silent moment she looked. Then the cloth settled on his legs once more. She began to oil his throat.

"Do you like this? Shall I go on?"

"Yes, please, lady," he husked. Heavy warmth flowed into his loins. From under his forearm he saw her smile like a house lizard that has eaten a scuttler.

"My story pleases you so much? Then I will continue! Soon the restless gods, making Naphar their extinct world's reflection, tampered with the winds that race between sky and sun. The goddess watched. Still she did not strike. For she is a patient goddess—she would wait until the final instant for the gods to take her second chance and accept their destiny, their death.

"In that pause the earth shook. Great cracks opened. Here, the cliffs fell and the sea rushed in." She gestured toward the plateau, ragged with fjords. She took more oil. Her strong fingers pressed and smoothed the sinews cording the boy's shoulders and chest. As her hands worked downward his blood began to fizz. He lowered his arm. He watched her through his lashes. Her lips curved in a secret smile. Voice smooth as jellied honey-sweet, she continued.

"Their tools failed. The gods consumed what stores they had. Then, hungry, they demanded our children for their tables.

"At last, Sassurum grew angry! With rocking lands and lashing seas, she flung the despoilers back to the stars. She cursed them; never might they or their machines return.

"Abandoned by our creators, we ate untreated flesh and seed; we paled and weakened, staggered, convulsed, and died. Blinded mothers wept for stillborn monstrous babes.

We stopped the hunt, we husked our grain. Until, denied that nourishment, a new death found us. We grew lizard skin, our hair striped and loosened, we bloated and again we died. Then Sassurum whispered to us the gods' own cure. We learned to eat each other. Through ritual Sacrifice we regained our discipline, our strength. We lost the useless, the defective, the rebellious slave . . ." Gauzes trailed across the boy's chest, warm breath moistened his ear. Fear shivered down his sides. Ariahnne laughed and straightened.

Her hands spread, digging into the muscles lacing his belly. It jerked. He held his breath and watched her face, now in shadow, now in light. Her fingers worked until his heartbeat choked him. At last she rose.

"Theology has its effect on you, I see." She motioned for him to stand. She watched him tuck the cloth around his waist, she moved into the shadows.

Rigid, he waited beside the pool, its black water mirroring shattered flame and stars. With his skin he tasted the apsu's flat breath. It mingled with the sticky salt breeze and the sweetness of the flowers. Behind him strange music chimed. His fists clenched, his blood thrummed with wanting her. Her voice whispered from the night.

"The firelight gleams on you. Your eyes are pools so deep I could dive in them and drown." Hoarse, she said, "Come. I need oil, too."

In the empty courtyard the caged lizard began to sing. Its impassioned trills followed them down the corridors past the heavy brass-bound door until, pushing aside a curtain, Ariahnne led the boy into a long low chamber.

There, while melody soared above the surf's distant roar, Senruh lay with his lady on softest fluff-flower coverlets among cushions of sea-born silk, sweet scented but sharp with salt. Their glimmer lit her face, blind now with desire. He watched in wonder as, with increasing skill, he brought her to incoherence. Writhing, she yanked his moist curls and gasped he was her clever beautiful boy, her brave hunting lizard with a double-forked tongue. Then came the words he had not known he waited for: arching her back, she shook, clutched him to her, and cried out he was her own dear love.

Delighting in her and his new powers, Senruh labored over the aging flesh until, through the windslits, he glimpsed morning's silver misting the horizon. The mute appeared.

Weary, astonished at all he had done and felt and seen, the boy rose and dressed. The servant led him from the room.

They plodded across the wasteland where a sharp breeze sparkled salt rime on sere grass and above them, dawn drowned the stars in light. He passed through the gates.

Alone, skin pulsing from his lady's touch, Senruh wandered the waking city's long blue shadows, stumbled at last into his stall's back room, and dropped toward his pallet, already plunging into cool green tides of sleep.

That first night made a pattern. Again the Lady Ariahnne sent for him and again she gave him no chance to kneel. And when, sated with his flesh and lips, she wished to vary her pleasures, she encouraged what she called his gift for mimicry. She taught him manners and courtesy and the art of verbal swordplay. Soon he knew court speech and its attendant formalities, as well as how to survive an all-night banquet with health and modesty intact.

To test his new knowledge, she smuggled him into feasts and entertainments, quizzing him later on his near unmaskings, on the seductions they had planned—if they pleased her she laughed and gave him a coin—and on the purses he had lifted. Some she "found" and returned, others she let him keep. Those he took back to the city. He would not ask to use that bolted inner room and though she looked at him thoughtfully once or twice, she never offered.

Thus Senruh's freedom hoard grew, though more slowly

than if he had lived solely at the villa. Much went to his
master. "Expenses, scum," the merchant would growl.
"You're not available now." But the boy scarcely noticed
the complaints. His thoughts were with his new life, and
Ariahnne.

Once, after a glittering evening in a noble's city palace,
they returned alone to his lady's villa.

"You're like a camouflage lizard, my treasure!" she
said. "I can set you down anywhere and you blend! How I'd
like to show you off to my dolts of offspring. But they never
visit. I'm too disreputable for them. *You* never disap-
point me! If they possessed even half your capacity—! She
laughed then, and beckoned him to her.

Later as he lay beside her only half-waking he spoke of
the size and silence of her villa. She was quiet for some
time. Then, eyes closed, she said in a flat tone that it had
not always been so. Once it had been filled with the voices
of her children and of her mate.

". . . one day to be my life mate, I thought. I did not
know then that love ends, that usefulness finishes, and
that I—who am as I have always been, unchanging—could
be left alone.

"For as my partner assumed his honors, and his offices
and absences increased, he grew to curse my public sport-
iveness that once he loved and indeed, had been more inventive in than I. 'I must have dignity,' he said. In private
I must further his tangled plots, must—" Her voice faded.
On a breath so small she almost could not be heard, she
said, "must not love him so exclusively . . ."

In the breathing quiet Senruh lay very still. Turning to
her, he pulled her bony length close. He stroked the head
that lay heavy on his shoulder, stiff with braids and gems
and royalty's hard red paste.

"But, lady, forgive me!" he said. "There is always the
goddess's second chance! Another life, another partner if
you wish it, and truly, I have seen—"

She twisted in his arms, her yellow eyes flew open. "So!

My unlettered he-lizard spouts theosophy! And judges me besides!" Her smile as he flushed was not kind.

"Do not speak so to me again. Greater wisdom than yours, by far! has tried to change me. But I shall not change! If I am not acceptable as I am, then I never was. If I cannot have my old life back in every detail, I want none of any other. I only wait. For their return. For once I was loved. I remember . . ."

Her eyes grew distant. The narrow lips curved softly and Senruh held his breath. Her expression altered. Propping herself on an elbow, with one finger she traced designs on his chest.

"But I have discovered ways of passing the time, have I not, my potent, squalid little morsel? You have even found them reasonably satisfactory, as far as I can observe. You would not really wish me different, would you?"

Heart beating faster, the boy shook his head.

Her slow smile as her gaze devoured him did not reach her eyes. Then she was coiling and twining about him, her dry hands hot and urgent. Into his mouth she murmured, "Ah, gods! Forgive me but I love you! I'd never hurt you! Not you, not this time, not—! You drive me half-mad with the craving!"

Her excitement kindled his own. Forgetting his hurt, his singing blood repeated her gasped endearments, his pulses raged in his ears. She loved him, she had said so and he—
She cared for him, sheltered him in luxury, dressed him, fed him, gave him freedoms; she was old, but he—

Struggling to define his joy, his tenderness, his unease, the boy drifted into sleep, her rouged nails sharp on his shoulder.

Chapter Four

In the Avenue of Precious Delights silken awnings glistened in the sun. Senruh's memories of Ariahnne faded—he watched perfumed smoke roll from the scenters' brass pots, enveloping those small boys' bright robes before it curled about the nobles' brocades and borders, a merchant's stripes, and the plain folds of the few priests and officers making up the sparse noon crowd. It touched the ragged hem of a street child dodging an Evictor of Unpleasantness. Senruh grinned. A cycle ago, before he met his lady, that child might have been he, on the lookout for an unwatched bauble or a customer.

The boy looked from the firecrystal entrance posts—tall prisms of turquoise, black, bronze, and lavender—to the street's end where parked litters, coaches, and chariots waited with their Kakano and half-breed teams. Nowhere, there or on the tiled walkways, did the boy see Ariahnne or her wrapping of sun-colored veils.

Could he have missed her? If nothing intrigued her here she might well have defied custom and the heat and returned to her villa and its amusements: her book scrolls and living pictures, some of them copied from the Royal Academy's spacer collection; her sentient jewels from Naphar and the stars; even the secret pleasures she pursued in the locked room at her house's center. But he would not think of that. Or there were her chairmen. She liked to dally with them. Then, if Senruh were there, she would discard them for him, laughing at their jealousy.

Once the head bearer had dared to say . . . But he was gone now. Another had taken his place.

Senruh scanned the shops again wondering, if he found Ariahnne, what form her compassion might take. He missed the first brushing touch on his robe. The second was stronger.

"Boy?"

Senruh looked around. A thin-bearded young noble jerked his head toward the alley.

Senruh considered. He could use the silver. It should not take long. And the noble resembled the young men and women his lady picked for him now. But hidden away, he might miss Ariahnne. And if she saw them together without her permission—! Pretending to misunderstand, Senruh smiled, eyes vague, and crossed the street.

The noble followed.

The boy walked faster, hoping for an Evictor of Unpleasantness. Blamelessly sent away from the avenue, Senruh could sneak back and look for his lady. No evictor appeared. Beside him, with a furtive look, the aristocrat reached into his robe's chest pocket. Senruh did not want to be tempted by extra coin. Resolutely he examined the shoppers, but saw no trace of Ariahnne or any veil-cocooned Protector of the Unborn. The beginnings of despair slid, small and cold, into his middle. In his vision's edge, something glittered.

He swung around. Gems. Sharp, faceted, they studded the black lash tips of the noble's cloisonné handwhip.

Abruptly Senruh lost interest in the man's silver. He would never like pain; those who did frightened and revolted him. When Ariahnne hurt him—by accident!—and with a tiny smile ministered to each cut and swelling, he did not like it, though he made no complaint. And if he happened to hurt her he winced as if he too had been struck. Though Ariahnne did not seem to mind. Indeed, once she . . . He pushed the memory away and strode as quickly as he could from the noble.

Outdistancing him, the boy dodged around a knot of officers, knowing himself conspicuous in his dark slave's robe. Caught, he must obey. It was only afterward that a slave could protest to the tribal courts, and he, sponsorless, could scarcely expect the goddess's vaunted same-day justice, accuser and accused eye to eye. He glanced back. Rounding the soldiers, his pursuer winked and waved.

Almost running now, the boy passed a booth heaped with flasks of costly oils in dark red, amber, and green. Beside them lay crystal coffers scintillating with powdered aphrodisiacal gems. Breaking into a trot, he spared the last stall less than a glance. Hot 'seq's bitter aroma breathed around him along with the warm one of new pastries soaked in fruited honey. Behind the shop, motionless trees dozed in a tiny walled garden.

Senruh burst into the road's terminus with its jumble of chariots and carrying chairs and the gaming, gossiping teams. Skipping around a scythed war chariot's wheel, he looked over his shoulder, caught his high sandal on a small leg, and went sprawling. The racing Kakanos set up a cry. Strong hands caught him. He looked up—into the face of the Lady Ariahnne's new head bearer.

The young half-breed set the boy on his feet. Slowly he let Senruh go, then nudged one of the three older chairmen. They looked up. They rose. Arms folded, their faces expressionless, all four watched Senruh. The boy had never been alone with them before. But that was ridiculous! He was not alone. The teams, the noble—! He glanced around. The tall aristocrat stood poised above him. Grinning, the young man reached out.

"Please! Where's my lady? Ariahnne! Or—tell him I'm *hers*!"

But the bearers only looked from the boy to the noble and began to smile. Beside him, his would-be customer touched the handle of his whip. Its surface of black lacquer, decorated with copper-edged translucent flowers, slid aside. In its place golden pincers gathered the sun and threw it in Senruh's eyes. The noble held them up. He clicked them open and shut. They rang like golden bells.

And with that dulcet sound the boy could hide from memory no longer.

He had heard it before, half a cycle ago, in the early spring. Senruh had glowered into the setting sun, kicking his heels in Ariahnne's courtyard, forgotten again. For four days and nights she had sent for him at odd moments, only to let him sit so, ignored. Or worse, when she was with him she would break off, rise without explanation, and disappear into her house. Much later a servant would arrive, inform him he was not needed at present, and escort him back to the city.

Hurt, angry, the boy scuffed rocks and bits of moss at a garden shrine set in the courtyard's wall. Some dropped and set the flowers jingling. If Ariahnne had tired of him she should say so, not fob him off with obvious lying tales! He was not yet too old to attract another wealthy patron!

She wished him to lighten her tedium since she could not travel for a while, she had said. "For you know how I dislike an unbalanced litter! And my head bearer is . . ." She paused, tucking a smile into the corners of her mouth. ". . . engaged. In activities so absorbing, he finds himself literally chained to my villa!"

At Senruh's scowl she touched his shoulders, then his arms. "You are not yet large enough to replace him, my beautiful, though someday . . . The pay for what he does is excellent. And he is freed, did you know it? Perhaps in time you will wish to be in his position. Or, perhaps not." Looking almost frightened for a moment, she soon wandered away, not to return that night.

And now she neglected him again. Did she think him a fool, unable to guess what, and who, took her attention? Senruh kicked viciously at the vines trailing from the Green Goddess's niche. He was rubbing a throbbing toe when he heard the sound. A single musical tone, then silence. It had come from within.

He took a quick look around. He crossed the courtyard to glance into the corridor. The timbered door of the inner

room stood ajar. A chance at last to see inside Ariahnne's
treasure chamber! For that is what he had decided it was.
If he were to be dismissed, perhaps a loose coin or jewel
might sweeten the parting. For a moment a chasm of loneliness seemed to open within him. Refusing to acknowledge it, he stepped into the cool tiled hall. A moment later
he was revising his ideas. A strongroom would not have a
large sun hole in its ceiling.

A dazzle of horizontal amber light flooded one wall.
Above it, shelves held transparent bottles of murky fluids
and changeable rainbowed ones; bundles of leaves and
powder packets sat, neatly labeled, beside them. Senruh
recognized a few. He had brought them himself from the
bazaar herb women. One or two strengthened desire,
others forced wakefulness, at least one enhanced sensation. Below them on the work surface were strewn soiled
instruments of gold and silver: tongs, needles, knives;
chased and inlaid, their handles carved in fantastic
shapes. The rest of the room seemed empty.

Disappointed, wondering if he dared filch a golden
needle or two to sell in the bazaar, Senruh crept closer. An
ocean breeze swept through the roof, stroking his face with
invisible silk. He stopped dead. Its salt carried a medicinal
odor as well as the foetid ones of Sacrifice. He turned to go.
A groan came from shadows opposite the counter. Through
the half-opened door, he looked beneath the slash of sunlight.

Ariahnne. With her back to the entrance, she knelt and
drew something toward her. A jeweled handwhip caught
the light. She shut its base's dripping tongs. Their clink—
the same the boy had heard from the courtyard—sang
through the room and hall. Veils whispering, she stood.

Then Senruh saw by her gold-toed sandals, shackled to
rings in the floor, a man's naked foot, arm, and shoulder,
topped by a tangle of black hair that was ropy with perspi-
ration both old and new. The head turned. Sweat sheened
the head chairman's ravaged, once-handsome face. A run-

nel of crimson trickled from beneath him to a central drain.

Ariahnne set down a tiny ritual vase. Its deep green crystal rang on the stone like a distant bell. She wiped her mouth; she placed her sandal on her bearer's throat.

"Now do you acknowledge your insolence to me and my right to chastise you?" Her voice throbbed, dark and deep.

"I do, lady." The chairman's whisper roughened. "I am worthless beside you. Yours to dispose of as you will. Punish me more." Straining, he raised his head. He pressed cut and swollen lips to her sole.

Ariahnne's smile held a feral tenderness. Her handwhip swished high; exultation flooded the bearer's face. He arched in his bonds, gave a deep whispering scream.

Ariahnne dropped the whip. Scarlet spattered the stones. "Later," she purred, and laughed. "Wait for me." Incredulous, Senruh saw an answering gleam in the chairman's flat black eyes. Fixing her gaze on the man's jerking body, Ariahnne began to turn.

Loose-kneed, wide-eyed, Senruh had just enough wit to stumble backward into a curtained alcove.

When he joined Ariahnne by the apsu, its quiet waters reflecting the thin gold and pink of the spring sunset, he pretended he had just arrived. She nodded, her face becomingly flushed, her eyes dark gold as they dreamed. She smiled in welcome. Red smeared her teeth. She prayed him to excuse her, she must change her robe. Her dribbled hem and sleeves swung, heavily wet, as she crossed the courtyard; her sandals left dark smudges on the paving blocks.

She was unusually gentle with Senruh that night. Protesting at last that she loved him and had been causing him too much broken sleep of late, she brushed her mouth across his hair and wished him a pleasant rest and freedom from dreams. Then, abstracted, she dismissed him to his master before the sun rose.

The following evening they shared a late supper of hot spiced meat and purple-blue songfruit pressings ashimmer with flying lights. Senruh ventured an indirect question about the bearer.

Ariahnne gazed, smiling, into the darkness. "He is gone," she said. She glanced at their meal. "Though in a way, he will now be always with us."

The boy's stomach lifted and pushed on his throat. Surreptitiously he set his dish and bread scoop down; he ate no more that night. And soon a new chairman came to assist Ariahnne through the city and without, in her restless pursuit of pleasure.

Senruh stared at the new bearer now, squinting through the past-noon sun that, like everything else, seemed a little brighter, a little clearer, on the Avenue of Precious Delights. Younger than the others, the new man had less control of his face. When Senruh heard more melodious clicks behind him and pleaded, "Where is she? Tell me!" the chairman's glance flicked the nearest stall, fragrant with hot 'seq and pastries.

It was enough. Following his gaze, the boy saw tall, gauze-wrapped pillars filter from its entrance, talking and laughing, their veils in constant motion. One of them wore yellow. It lifted a bony finger to gesture. Familiar knuckle rings glittered beneath long rouged nails.

Fear, his dependence on his lady, shot the boy through the traffic and onto the walkway. On his knees he skidded across the tiles toward the dark yellow veils; this would be the first time he had knelt to her, he thought in fleeting surprise.

"Lady, I need you; the noble, my master, the longwhip and Sacrifice—" Forgetting his reservations and his rehearsed phrases, the boy reverted to his childhood's obeisance. Face in the dust, he laid his forehead on her sandal.

The long narrow feet stilled, though above him her husky voice continued as before. Bored, she related a maliciously amusing tale. Behind the boy, heavy soles slapped. Senruh peered over his shoulder. Deep in the folds of a bordered robe, golden pincers snicked.

His skin seemed to shrivel. Glancing at Ariahnne's head, lofty against the sun-whitened sky, he wondered if she knew him. If not, should he retreat now, go with the man, get it over with, then return when his panic had lessened and his thoughts and words could fall in better order? But the noble's whip, his sharpened tongs! And after, if Senruh missed Ariahnne, he faced the longwhip and the red priests' knives. Surely, once she knew his need, she would succor him! For she loved him. And, as he had reassured himself on sleepless nights, his lady only punished the guilty, those for whom she cared little, or those who begged it of her.

Heart battering his breast, he said clearly, "Lady. Ariahnne. It's Senruh." Still she made no answer. Beside him, the noble leaned close. Senruh could not delay much longer.

He stared at the sandals he had fastened only that morning; desperate, he thumbed the high wrinkled arch remembering how, when he touched her so, she would draw up her knees, kick at him, then, screaming with laughter, tumble him about their pallet.

At last she broke her story. High above him, surrounded by amber veils and backed by empty sky, yellow-brown eyes looked through him. Stranger's eyes. Her gold toe protector nudged his shoulder. Dust smeared his black robe. "Go, scum." He did not move. She paused, tension in her stance, and looked down at him. She turned. She clasped wrists with one, two, three other women, the only ones also in bordered gauzes. Skirts shushed past him, ashy dust puffed in his nostrils, loose veils started small scented whirlwinds about his face and arms. Laughing, chatting like a colony of nesting fliers, the Bearers of Children left. Only Ariahnne remained.

Senruh's legs were beginning to stiffen. Stupid of him, he thought. Of course she would not acknowledge him before her friends. But in private she was so lawless, so open; she gave him such freedoms! He blinked. It must be the dust that made his eyes sting so. "Lady?" he whispered.

The noble's shod foot slid under the boy's nose. Large fingers dug into his shoulder, hauling him to his knees.

"Mine, I think," the man said. "I'll see he doesn't trouble you further." He looked from Ariahnne to his whip and giggled.

Hot with sudden fury, Senruh flexed his arms and shoulders; the noble's grip loosened. _I could take him!_ the boy thought. But he stayed as he was. Slaves who resisted nobles died. As the man tugged at him, Senruh gathered an insubstantial handful of Ariahnne's hem, pressed it to his face, and blurted, "Lady, buy me! I'll repay you! In coin, in service! I never told you, but I read, I write and figure, in the common tongue, the southern and central ones, trade talk too! And at night I'll never rest, I'll do all you wish, even—even what I wouldn't before!" She trod on his fingers.

Silenced, hand and arm aching, he looked up. Yellow fires seemed to obscure her eyes. Through the blowing face veils, Senruh watched her sharp teeth catch at her lips; her red pointed tongue moistened them. "At last," she breathed. "In full knowledge of what I will do to you, you deliver yourself to me!" Her unfocused stare moved to the noble.

"This little scum of a robe tosser needs a lesson," she said. Her voice was deep. "When my men have finished with him, you may have him. Here. Where I can see. Then, leave him. For he is mine!" Gaze bright as a stalking lizard's, she gazed again at Senruh and snapped her fingers for her bearers.

Numb, the boy bent his head.

And the four brawny chairmen strode toward him.

Chapter Five

SENRUH DRAGGED HIMSELF to the city fountain, sourness burning in his throat. He swallowed. He knelt on the tiles by the pool's lip; sharp under his knees, the mosaic proclaimed a past Ensai's generosity.

Before the boy, water frothed over stacked whitestone blocks and circles. He stretched out a shaking hand. Keeping the other clenched, he splashed his face and robe. He choked and knuckled his eyes. Biting his swollen lip until it stopped quivering, Senruh took a long breath and, ignoring the market women's jeers, he climbed into the basin.

Cool water slid through his robe, lapped his chest and burning back. He shut his eyes and breathed in the moist vapors, waiting for the cold's erasure of feeling.

All four bearers, he thought. Then the noble. While Ariahnne watched, brilliant-eyed, in a growing cluster of observers. Senruh's face flamed. Glancing at the women behind him, he separated the fingers of his clenched hand. Gold shimmered between them, a pure rich disk of it, stamped with the Ensai's likeness on one side, the goddess's on the other. Payment. Enough to buy the freedom of a skilled slave like him, with enough left over for the feast and new freedman's robes. This morning, possessing it, he would have been ablaze with joy. Now he wished only to fling it away. Shame, then helpless fury, gathered like bundled firecloth inside him. As his thoughts touched it, it leaped into flame. Unable to push it from his mind any longer, he remembered his public humiliation.

* * *

Senruh had knelt, head bowed, in the Avenue of Precious Delights, his shock at Ariahnne's betrayal slowly ebbing, sharp resentment pricking through it. What did she mean, he chose this? He would never ask for hurt and she knew it! He ignored his just having done so. For hope lurked in him that he could soon coax her back to gentler pleasures. And perhaps his brief capitulation might intrigue her into wanting him enough to give him a home, protection, freedoms. He looked up, arguments sharp in his mouth. She was gone.

He twisted. Ariahnne and the noble stood behind him. They looked over his head to the street's end with its parked chariots and waiting teams. There, intent clear in darkening eyes and quick-lifting chests, the bearers' strides lengthened. Two circled toward his sides, two approached from the front. Senruh's heart stuttered.

No! To use him here as bazaar half-breeds might abuse a Kakano slave in a back alley! Thoughts of flight, of appeasement, vanished abruptly in crude hot rage. A hand taller than he, these chairmen were still half-breed like him, and slave. His legal prey. Senruh flexed his shoulders and dropped into a crouch.

The chairmen closed on him. Stepping off the tiled walkway, the boy met them in the street. His fists then his feet smacked hard chests and bellies. Behind him Ariahnne cooed with excitement.

A broad hand slammed his ear; another backhanded his face. His head spun. Blood filled his mouth. He hit out. Cursing, the four bearers piled onto him. Senruh's horizons contracted to deep voices, blows from rough-skinned palms, breaths that rasped in his ear and, clamping his hips and head, muscular arms and thighs slick with sweat and arousal.

With a cry of triumph the bodies vanished. Robes shook into place. Sun flared in Senruh's eyes. Hardened hands clutched his wrists and ankles, spreading him face up, over the road. The boy flung himself at one man, then the next, seeking to rend and bite and maim. How dared they! How dared any of them! His body, his affections, were his! Not cheap rags to be thrown from one to another for sport or to scratch an itch! He paused. The scribe had said such things, but Senruh had laughed at him for criticizing the source of such easy coin.

For the instant that the boy hung unmoving between his captors, the spectators exclaimed. The panting bearers grinned down at him and snapped his arms and legs wide. Senruh cried out and lunged at them. Panic nibbled at his rage when they only laughed and cuffed and played with him.

At last, arms shaking and useless, his breath a knife in his chest, defeat wormed through his belly. He lay unresisting in their hands; he submitted to all they ordered and did.

Dully, as the bearers prepared him for their final assault, Senruh listened to the crowd. Some tittered, one cried shame and stalked away, here and there a few took bets while others passed connoisseurlike remarks on his parts and reactions. The men's callused fingers dug into him. Hope gone, only wanting it finished, the boy set his bared legs where they pushed them. Ready to vomit in self-disgust as they loudly lined up behind him, Senruh tried to reassure himself that it could not be much worse than once or twice in the bazaar.

It was. One, another, yet another battered and tore at him while those waiting, growing impatient, wrenched up his head, forced open his jaws . . .

He retched. In a brief respite the boy spat and spat again, longing for handfuls of stomach-steadying chewing leaf, gathered in abandoned courtyards, and quiet woods beyond the city walls. Quick footsteps hastened toward him.

New hands grabbed him. Long, soft, unsteady with eagerness, they hauled him from the chairmen's rough palms. The men shouted objections. Senruh blinked upward—into the noble's thin-bearded face. The boy began to tremble.

In an alley's hot sepia shadows a jeweled flail gleamed. Ariahnne's husky voice scolded, laughed. Terror and agony crashed through him. Then beneath it something alien budded, unfurling its strange dark leaves into a fierce blinding joy. Shaking, writhing, cold with horror, the boy bit back sobs of gratitude even as he found absolution for cycles of striving, of difference, of beatings and his master's and customers' contempt. Pain like lightning seared him; he arched and screamed and heard himself beg for another, more . . . Then through a haze of fire, he dreamed he heard Ariahnne's imperious tones. And umber night fell on him.

Consciousness and pain returned. Senruh lay on his back half out of shadow, heat and light a weight on his face. Zitters whined around him, their quick stings burning his skin. He sighed and rolled his head away from the sun. Pebbles rattled, many-layered veils brushed his arm, disturbed the dust. As the fine powder settled on his lids and parched mouth it wafted the heavy scents of costly oils and of age. Ariahnne. From long habit the boy turned to her, thankfulness washing through him like well water. Memory pounded back, his eyes stared open.

The noble was gone. The boy released a held breath. But at the street's terminus the bearers stood motionless by his lady's gold-scrolled chair. Its crystal drops shot uncertain rainbows onto the short-shadowed clay. Except for the stains on their robes the men might never have shouted, fought, clasped him . . .

Heart threatening to shake from his body, Senruh uncurled his fingers toward Ariahnne's. "Lady? Is it over? Am—am I punished enough?" The words blurred on his thickened tongue. His eyes prickled. Wanting only to hide in her and weep, he waited for her to whisper her love for him, her pity, her promise to carry him to her villa, to nurse him. He swallowed. Where were his insulating humor, his bazaar swagger, his pride? He lifted lashes heavy with dust and tears to look into her eyes. And began to understand.

Like a greedy child's, Ariahnne's sulfur gaze roamed his sides with their swellings and cuts. It paused, gloating, on his skewed robe, his smeared and bloody haunches. Flushing beneath her single face veil and her rouge, she fumbled in her purse and leaned down. That was when she pressed the gold coin into Senruh's palm. New-minted, sharpedged, it glittered like a miniature sun. He stared at it. Why was it there? He had not served her. And anyway, she never gave gold. "From—from the noble?" he croaked.

"No! From me." Her whisper shook. "You were a revelation, my treasure! Spirited, uninhibited—" Her gaze burned upward to his mouth where blood's metallic sweetness dribbled. She dabbed at it, she licked her finger and smiled as her gaze drifted lower. "A fine first payment. And only a drop in the flood to come! For this, my own delight, is how you will pay for the sweets, the robes, every fine for your seductions, each stolen purse! I have tallied them all. For you are only a rented slave, you know, not mine. Your debts are your master's responsibility. As to how he chooses to pay them . . ." She shrugged, sighed luxuriously, and moistened her lips. ". . . I know not. But in my opinion, you are his greatest wealth, my jewel. And so I shall tell him. Also that I shall be more than generous when you willingly enter my inner room."

Senruh stared at the stranger wearing his lady's face: Ariahnne whom he had thought too enamored to more than applaud his activities. And he remembered the plain brown trapper fish that swam in the Western Sea weaving fantasies of light, of the half-witted victims that blinked their fishy eyes and flirted toward that enticing tensile loveliness, and of the wide white-toothed jaws that awaited them. Too late, the boy recalled he should know nothing of Ariahnne's locked chamber. "In-inner room, lady?"

Ariahnne's smile curved downward. "Ah, do not pretend

ignorance with me, my filth-smeared gem! Did you think only you could look through a door?"

"Who—?" he blurted and stopped. If she had not been certain she was now.

"Why, Ras saw you. My bearer before this one, stupid child! His debt was once as great as yours. Greater! But he has paid it, and lavishly. As will you."

She leaned close. Her breath was spiced and hot. The zitters whined away as her yellow eyes and veils replaced the sky. Her dry touch pushed Senruh's robe aside; it brushed his shoulders and arms. His skin crawled. "To think that I fought this," she breathed. "I no longer remember why." Her gaze swept his length. "You are almost ripe for a bearer, my lovely. Will you like living with me— and them?"

Looking in the dark caves of her pupils, the boy seemed to glimpse a starved clawed lizard god. Beside it a spring worshiper, visited by the goddess's frenzy, whirled and tore with dripping nail and tooth at the new cycle's first Sacrifice. Senruh blinked. The silhouettes vanished.

Ariahnne's yellow gaze dimmed and the boy glimpsed her old humanity, though no trace of the sardonic humor he had loved remained. Haltingly she said, "I told you not to come. And you never abased yourself before! You boasted of learning, learning greater than mine. You had to be punished!" She shook her outer veils over her face and stood. As she did so a passing merchant gave her, then Senruh, a curious glance. Neither heeded the striped-robed figure. Ariahnne beckoned her bearers. "It's not as if you mattered," she told Senruh as they approached. "You're only half-breed, after all. And slave. I can buy another." She glanced at the gold in the boy's numb fingers. "And—I've paid!"

When Ariahnne and her chairmen had gone, Senruh waited for his heartbeat to slow. He frowned at the heat that shimmered on the road like white-metal mirrors. So. Ariahnne had never loved him. For people did not hurt those they loved. Nor did the sane relish their own pain.

Did they? He remembered her knowing smile. His newly budded desires were no secret from her. He had nothing left to withhold to keep her wanting him. He shuddered and closed his eyes.

Later an evictor dragged the boy deeper into the alley. Brushing dead zitters from Senruh's robe, the man said, not unkindly, that the boy might stay until he could walk. Then he must leave. For the merchants paid well to keep all unpleasantness from the Avenue of Precious Delights.

Remembering shut away for a while, Senruh tightened his fingers around Ariahnne's coin of waxy gold. He drank deep from the fountain, then stared at the dimpling water beneath, full of brown and red swirls. They looked like veils, he thought, thin but sharp-edged. Or clouds.

He gazed upward. Day's blue coverlet hid the stars. Perhaps there, somewhere, mankind was different; the scribe insisted it was so. The empty brightness cut at Senruh's eyes and he glanced down, shaking his head. There was no kinder land. Not for him. The old man's tales of homecoming, of valor and selfless friendship, were only tales, kin to those of odd-colored dragons. Real people did not love. They took. Tremors racked the boy as he remembered the day and its gift of self-knowledge. For a moment of intense sensual memory, Ras's transported face, filmed with sweat, filled Senruh's vision. Envy like sharpened nails scraped in the boy's belly.

At last the fountain ran clear. Sick with self-loathing, Senruh stepped out, holding on to a phrase of the scribe's—*A scholar does not refuse wisdom, oh child of my mind*—as if it were Dargon and Ekt's storied key to the first of the interlocking Treasure Chambers of Learning. But, Senruh had asked the scribe, once the scholar had his knowledge and did not want it, what did he do with it? The old man had not replied.

The boy wrung out his robe. Water lisped onto the tiles and he stared at the sunlight fracturing on the golds and

browns and blacks of a dead Ensai's face. He could not stop
shivering.

The old women shouldered him aside, eager to fill their
pitchers; others plunked mounds of clothes in the basin
and began beating them clean. Still clutching his coin,
Senruh hobbled toward the city's center. His sandals'
wood platforms clunked on the clay, leaving dark spatters
in the dust.

His own section of the bazaar might be unsafe for him,
but Senruh knew its dangers and deceits. He could burrow
there until the evening trumpets sounded and he must return to his master and his uncertain future.

Chapter Six

KNEES WOBBLING, hungry, his gold coin sharp in his fist, Senruh turned into the Alley of the Web Spinners. It should be cool there, he thought, though when the wind blew seaward from the fire mountains it mixed their sulfur with the stench of the nearby Slave Pens.

Today, however, the breeze was in the opposite direction. Only Iammu the Sea God's moist breath exhaled across the bazaar's southern quarter. It tossed a bit of cheap soft sea paper into the alley's rippling shadows. Aching, searching for a place to hide from the gossips' smiles, Senruh followed it.

Like a spring leaf the scrap of paper winked from columns of sunlight into shadows cast by squares of silk two man-lengths high, stretched overhead on poles. The vibrant blues, yellows, and greens were of spider silk, the boy knew; beyond them lay the trapper fish's pale rectangles, bellying in the wind like the sails of airy ships.

A moment later, dropped by the breeze, the curl of sea paper skated down the layers of charcoal smoke and incense to vanish in the crowd. Small plain-robed Kakano slaves trampled it underfoot; the taller half-breeds scuffed it into the air again. It fell. The shod feet of looming Rabu priests, nobles, and merchants trod it into the clay. Laughing, calling like festival-goers, Kakano, half-breed, and Rabu alike flocked toward the alley's center.

Senruh hesitated. He had wanted a quiet place to rest, but in this crowd he could more easily filch a length of cloth to staunch his bleeding or a chewing pod and a bit of honeyed fruit to ease his hunger.

"Auction! New slaves for auction!"

That explained the crowd, Senruh thought. This late sale would probably be the last one before the winter snows set in. The boy joined the mob. Buyers and onlookers at a slave selling would take little interest in a lone, battered half-breed, so plainly owned by another.

Senruh's wet robe flapped about him as he pushed into the throng. He slid toward an opening as, behind him, a slave dealer cried, "New clean imports, some fresh from the highlands!" Somewhat revived by the shade cast by the silks flying above him, the boy peered between tall shoulders.

He saw a wide platform set throat high between two silk spinners' stalls. Senruh hardly glanced at them though the sight usually intrigued him: the great furry red-eyed spiders astride the shoulders of their small boy partners, spinning endless threads of silk onto the reels in the childrens' hands. Instead he looked hard at the scuffed dais before him, empty but for a center slave post and its rope trailing toward the back. The early afternoon sun flooded the platform's near edge; behind lay filmy shadows cast by the bright silks.

Beside the boy the crowd shifted, protesting. Still crying his wares, the auctioneer shoved through it and climbed onto the stage. He yanked on the rope. From below the platform, her head bowed, the first captive mounted the dais. And at that moment the auctioneer's word struck Senruh. Some of these slaves were from the highlands!

The boy grinned, winced at his swollen lip, and continued his smile inside. What audacity for the auctioneer to claim he offered a slave from the fabled highlands! Where small Kakanos ruled large Rabu, indeed! Senruh had not told his lady on that first night, but he knew the old chants that told of the highlanders' descent from vanquished Kakano nobles, priests, and soldiers. Fleeing across the fire mountains to the soil-poor highlands, they preferred scratch-

ing a living there to a life enslaved in the warmer, more
generous lowlands.

There were children's stories, too: of little people who
came at night to spirit away Rabu babies from the Rock of
Sacrifice before death or the butcher priests could find
them.

Dreams! Senruh thought. As soon believe in a pink-
spotted dragon, soon to waddle across the dais with a leash
around its thick neck, green wings folded and rustling.
Highlanders and dragons lived only in the scribe's tales
alongside mythic heroes who always spoke truth and were
loyal and selfless in friendship. Nevertheless, Senruh wel-
comed any distraction from the pain and rage he dared not
show. He wriggled forward.

When the boy leaned against the platform's edge he
*hmmm*ed in disappointment. The tied prisoners straggling
into place looked like typical end-of-summer dregs. Droop-
ing, obviously untrained, most were undersized half-
breeds. The young ones would probably not grow to Rabu
chest height; the adults certainly would not. They would
be a burden on their owners forever. And not a fancy
among them. Unless . . . A bright head topped the stage.

Senruh blinked. It was the glowering goldenhair from
that morning, and looking much cleaner. The slaver had
evidently led his charges to the baths. But the small captive's scowl was as surly as ever. His blue gaze searched
the crowd, lit on Senruh, withdrew, returned.

Hand more or less hidden in the folds of his robe, Senruh
glared back and curled his fingers into the averting sign.
The last time that captive had scowled at him, Senruh had
ended with a knife between his fingers. The blue eyes
glanced downward—surely he could not see Senruh's hand!
The captive's mouth curved in a supercilious smile before
he looked away.

Flushing—he was not superstitious, Senruh thought,
only careful—he opened his fist and remembered the knife.
He touched his chest. Yes, the black crystal blade still lay
in his central pocket. Beside it, through the damp cloth, he

felt bulges. The old man's redfruit! Senruh could eat one now and still have another for later. He was fumbling for it when he glimpsed a large striped-robed merchant elbowing his way toward the platform. The Rabu hauled himself onto the dais, waxed curls scarcely moving on his massive shoulders. He glanced around.

"Master!" Before his lips had stopped forming the word, Senruh had his head down and was squirming backward through the packed bodies. He stopped behind a Rabu to peer around a large scarlet sleeve.

On the stage the tall merchant headed straight for the goldenhair. Senruh swallowed as he watched his master reach down and rub through the captive's pale tangles. With his other hand, supposedly hunting a faulty tooth or an old owner's tattoo, the merchant pried open the boy's mouth and, faintly smiling, explored deep inside.

The prisoner swayed under the slow fingers, his tied hands strained behind him by the communal rope. Jaws at their widest stretch, he gagged a little, face draining of color. The soles of Senruh's feet seemed to curl. His master could only keep one servant. Yellow hair drew him. Senruh's pallet beneath the ovens might soon belong to another.

Feeling ill, the boy fingered his lady's coin. Could he dash to the Slave Courts, somehow beg a hearing from one of the twelve tribal judges, exchange his gold for a freedom tablet, and still be back at his master's stall by sunset? And what of his debt? Even if he did overcome all difficulties, how likely was it that the merchant would sign agreement? The man could smash the tablet, claim the gold, then sell Senruh for what he could get. Perhaps—perhaps to Ariahnne. Fear and . . . something else . . . squirmed in his loins.

The boy massaged his neck, whipped shoulders burning as they flexed. Weakness shuddered through him; in the silks' shadow his wet robe sent tremors along his sides. Whatever he did, he must rest soon and dry off.

Before him the wide red shoulders moved; they ceased to

screen him. White-metal calipers swinging at the Rabu's sides—as much a mark of his trade as his Sacrificial knife—the butcher priest joined Senruh's master on the dais.

Senruh crouched. He limped backward through the press of bodies. His clogs struck a pile of refuse, he kicked free, the back of his neck prickled as if someone watched. He turned.

On the platform, sky-colored eyes glowered over his head. The merchant pulled wet fingers from the boy's lips, he stooped and grasped the captive's hem. Senruh made himself shrug and keep going.

Free at last of the crowd and its reek of tear root, stale scent, grog, and sweat, Senruh loitered by the booths looking with growing desperation for a place to hide and rest and eat.

A vendor strolled by carrying a tray of the cycle's first hot fish crisps. Sparkling with salt, they reeked of sour songfruit's hearty tang. The boy's mouth watered. As the seller passed him Senruh trailed a sleeve over one edge of the pile. He had his fingers around hot brittle edges when the man glanced at him, then at his hand. At the same time the boy's high sandal rolled on something rounded. Off balance, he dropped the crisp and kicked at the shard of a broken crock, arms flailing the air. The vendor dodged around him and scooted into the crowd, singsonging the freshness and safety of his wares, now summer had ended and the poisonous spring floods had been leached from the fish.

Senruh took a hopping step toward a pair of vacant booths, grabbing for support. His fingers brushed a row of furled awnings that leaned against them. He snatched at one, fell inward with it. The boy jerked back, glimpsing brightness in back of the cloth-wound pole. He peered behind it.

A parallelogram of sunlight warmed a broad space between the deserted booths. A forgotten storage area, Senruh thought. Perfect! He glanced around. His neck prickled again but he caught no eye watching him. He slid through the narrow opening and replaced the awnings.

Alone, no longer needing to pretend unconcern, his teeth began to chatter, his knees to shake. Abruptly, he sat and gave himself to Shamash the Sun God's fiery kiss. He covered his face with his hands. Time stopped.

Till, simmering with heat, the muscles in his torn back unclenched and Senruh straightened, no longer afraid he would howl aloud his outrage, suspicion, and fear. He rubbed his face; he squatted gingerly on his heels. Blood slicked his legs.

Sighing, the boy hauled up his robe, listening to the sounds of the growing crowd. Tearing strips from his loincloth, he bound his wounds and leaned against the sunny wall. He reached for the first of the scribe's redfruit.

Sharp sweet juice filled the boy's mouth; smooth pulp slid down his throat. As the gentle stimulants revived him, a rope ladder of knots seemed to unravel from his chest to his thighs and he planned.

When the auctioneer called for bids on the goldenhair, his master's attention must be there. Senruh could slip away then, and . . . Find a kindly judge to help him to his freedom? Coax Ariahnne into forgetting his debt? Discover that the bitter, heart-stopping pleasure he had found in the Avenue of Precious Delights had not existed?

A stray breeze touched the boy's robe with tender fingers. As Senruh hovered, somnolent, between dreams and reality, the sound of the crowd changed. Loud voices yelled rude remarks. Muttering, others scuffed or stamped away.

Curious, still holding the last bite of his redfruit, Senruh climbed to his feet and peered between the stacked awnings to the platform. They were stripping the slaves.

The boy's nostrils pinched. It was a shabby practice! Instead of decent private showings, the auctioneers stimulated a sluggish market by displaying the better-looking captives to any and all passersby. Even Senruh's master scorned . . .

His master. The boy swallowed. As if drawn, his gaze

slid down the stage past the few prisoners, male and female, who stood, bare as peeled sandmelons, in the harsh
hot light at the dais's edge. Behind them lay the communal rope still attached to the other slaves.

Hardly noticing the captives' untied hands, clenched or
limply hopeless at their sides, or the crowd's shouts as to
each slave's potential in the fields or on the pallet, Senruh's gaze skidded to the platform's end. There, a
lone butcher priest and Senruh's master rummaged the
stripped goldenhair with their eyes.

Pale as a root, the boy stood in the restless shadow, robe
and loincloth heaped behind him. In the booths by his platform, small boys continued winding their silk, murmuring to their red-eyed spider partners. The boys looked up as
the black-bearded slaver prowled toward them and the naked boy, his whip's lash twitching behind him like a thin
dark snake.

Its black tongue licked out. It coiled around the goldenhair's ankle. The slaver's hand jerked; the boy stumbled
into the sun.

Blue eyes glared at the slaver, then, in the sudden quiet,
at the crowd. His straw-colored tangles burst into pale fire.
Senruh caught his breath. Pale as sea froth where his robe
had touched him, the boy seemed to be made of gold and
sky and cloud. The onlookers murmured. Senruh's gaze
roamed lower.

The sun's white flame edged a rounded chin and throat
with light, it lapped across unbroadened shoulders and a
chest just deep enough to shadow a flat belly and narrow
flanks. The slaver loomed over the boy; the little goldenhair pulled back. Sun streamed over his shoulder to gild
the curls about his long swinging sex. And below . . .

Hastily, Senruh looked away. Even a shameless little
emptyhead should have his legs covered, he thought un-
comfortably. One bared them in the baths or in war sports,
but to display them here, in public!

On the dais the red priest stepped in front of the boy. The
crowd chirred and screeched, complaining obscenely about

their obstructed view. The Rabu ignored them; the scarlet robe draped in graceful folds as he knelt, calipers in hand.

Above the priest's ordered curls Senruh watched the goldenhair move on order, muscles sliding smoothly under the flawless skin. Senruh's gaze sharpened. Not a sore, not a scar from old illness marred the boy, nor could he see starvation's protruding bones. Why, then, had the goldenhair not developed his strength as Senruh had, as all lowlands slaves did? Well, perhaps he was not bright.

As Senruh widened the space between the awnings, acrid dust puffed from them. A sneeze swelled in his nose. Nostrils flaring to stop it, he set his watering eyes to the gap; they widened. The blond boy's chin jutted, his lips were white-edged. He looked angry, outraged, Senruh thought, he had been all along!

But emptyheads had only shallow emotions; everyone knew they thrived on prurient attention. Senruh drew in a quick breath. For a moment the blue eyes had seemed to glitter into his. He drew back and replaced one of the poles. A tack, hot from the sun, burned his finger.

As he sucked it he watched the priest shut his calipers and motion impatiently for the goldenhair to turn around. The blue eyes flashed but he did as he was told. Senruh's master crowded closer, looking down at the boy with bright black eyes. Impersonally, the butcher priest stroked then squeezed the boy's buttock. The goldenhair started; someone in the crowd laughed. Grinning, the tall merchant reached down and did the same.

The goldenhair's teeth showed in a snarl. Whirling, he dropped into a crouch and raised his hands' cutting edges. A bystander cried out. The throng jostled, blotting out Senruh's view. A whip spoke on the platform one, twice, again.

In the spinners' stalls, the small boys, paling, stroked the red-eyed spiders on their shoulders, calming them, while the boys' fathers emerged from the stalls' back rooms to hover anxiously beside them.

When Senruh could see the stage again, the slaver bent the writhing goldenhair in a bow, one slim wrist pulled high between jutting shoulder blades. The Rabu bent, his beard moving as he whispered. The goldenhair jerked away; after a moment he nodded tightly.

In spite of himself Senruh winced at the twist the slaver gave the boy's arm before he released it. The goldenhair's mouth tightened. His arm dropped to his side to hang there, slack.

While the crowd jeered and pelted him with refuse, the boy turned on command, lips shut, slim body rigid as a priest's puppet. He submitted, white-faced, to the men's large inquiring fingers.

Senruh looked at his rival with grudging sympathy and rotated Ariahnne's coin. He knew he should put it in his robe for safety, but once he did it would signal acceptance of Ariahnne's bargain that was no bargain at all. He watched the goldenhair's muscles tighten in throat and chest. The little emptyhead had courage, he would give him that, Senruh thought, but he brought the need for it on himself. He should joke, wink. Or if he could not manage that he should do as the others did, hang his head and look docile. No one but a red priest hunting young tender meat would buy a slave who looked like trouble.

Then even the priest rose, shook his head, and moved toward a large-breasted broad-hipped young woman, calipers snicking wide. Only Senruh's master remained by the fair boy. The merchant gave him a hooded look, stooped to run a hand through the golden curls then down a straight bare leg. As the mob hooted, the man stepped off the platform. Senruh clung to the awnings, feeling ill. He had seen his master signal the auctioneer.

At the end of the dais the slaver nodded to the boy and pointed to the only remaining heap of garments. The goldenhair dove toward them. Senruh's eyes widened at his haste in whipping the loincloth into tight folds, his hurried struggle into his robe. Fading back into the shimmering shadow, the boy edged toward the stage's end, slim fingers flying over the neck thongs, lacing them high despite the day's heat.

Modest! Senruh thought. Where could an emptyhead slave have learned that? And no wild half-breed, snatched from the fire mountains' lower slopes, would care!

At the other end of the platform the auctioneer began to cry virtues; the sale began. Rustling, spitting, loud with raucous comments, the throng jammed toward him, giving Senruh a clear view of the fancy. The slaver's knots about the boy's narrow wrists looked hasty and only a loop of rope connected the young prisoner to the tied line of slaves. Senruh expected the man to secure the knots. Instead, shoving his whip in his sleeve, the black-browed slaver turned his back on the boy and strode toward the auctioneer.

As the man moved away, his captive stepped behind a neighbor. Under the robe, slim shoulders moved. Blue eyes flashed a look at the platform's end; the thin body tensed. The ropes tumbled to the floor—the boy leaped off the dais.

Behind the awnings Senruh crouched forward, sweating in the hot light. The crowd parted, exclaiming. He saw the little goldenhair stagger in the platform's shadow then run, pebbles spurting from under his bare feet. He circled the far edge of the crowd, dodged a hand, and sped down the empty alley. The slim form darted between two booths and with a flip of the light-colored hem, it vanished.

A small slave piped, "Escape! Catch him!" A few half-breeds joined in. Only then did the tall slaver turn, drag his whip from his sleeve, and stroll toward the end of the stage. Senruh watched impatiently as the man squatted there. He seemed prepared to listen to each shrill emptyhead and half-breed in turn. A few merchants crowded around him, gesturing to the alley, the stalls, and the street behind them.

At last the slaver jumped off the stage. The noise about him increased. In the spinners' booths, red eyes swiveled, furred legs scratched for new holds on their boys' backs as the silk spiders caught the throng's excitement. A few spinner children rose and, helped by their fathers, moved to the backs of their stalls. The slaver pushed into the mob and questioned a noble, then another. Each shrugged and also pointed down the alley.

Movement on the platform caught Senruh's attention. With no slaver or whip to direct them, the captives milled in the luminous shadows. A few lunged after the golden-hair. The ropes attaching them to their more stolid neighbors yanked them back. They crashed to the floor, pulling the others with them, in a tangle of arms and ropes and kicking feet. Howls rose from the dais; the more enterprising in the crowd began taking bets on potential escapes.

Next to the busy stage, still making his unhurried search, the tall slaver peered into one spinner's booth, then another. As he ambled down the dusty clay, shutters crashed, awnings rattled shut. Within, Senruh knew, fathers were helping sons gentle restive spiders they had themselves once partnered, offering them shallow dishes of sweet numbing fluids. For if the long-lived arachnids became too distressed, one sting could end a generations-long symbiosis for them all.

In the alley, small Kakanos in ragged robes pelted after the slaver. "Escape!" they cried. "There, catch him! He went that way!" More little slaves joined them; some squeezed through the stalls into the next street where they filled the hot breeze with shrieks.

Shamash the Sun God drew wisps of steam from Senruh's robe. Beneath it the boy's skin crawled. Through the crack between the poles he saw the bearded slaver turn. The Kakanos' dusty heads bobbed around the Rabu's waist as he started up the alley toward Senruh's hiding place.

The boy tensed. If he had to run would his legs carry him over the back of the stall? And would he leave a trail of blood?

As he crouched, eye to the slit, Senruh's heart seemed to pound in his ears. Through it he heard a stealthy brushing sound. A lizard, he thought, nesting in the empty booth. But, haunches tight, weight on his toes, he knew.

Sobbing breaths rasped through the wall. Senruh heard scrabbling noises. He glanced up. He raised his hand—

He had time for one sharp cry as a broad shape poised on top of the booth. Then, black against the sky's sharp blue, robe fluttering, a body hurtled downward.

A fist struck Senruh. He tottered back. Heels gouged his belly. Senruh's hand shut around the gold coin as he fell backward and cracked his head on the clay. Powdery dust rose and sifted onto his face. The sun split his eyes. A hard body, all muscle and bone, slammed onto his chest. The breath whooshed out of him.

Chapter Seven

LUNGS PUMPING, eyes shut, Senruh sucked air. A slim strong hand glided up his sleeves, patted his ribs, his chest; it dove into his robe's chest pocket.

"Ha!" a boy's voice said. The weight bounced on Senruh's belly, dislodging his last bite of air. When at last he snatched another he opened his eyes. Above him the afternoon sun lit tangles pale as scorched hill grass. The escaped goldenhair. Senruh's mouth twisted. He had been right to make that averting sign.

"Get off me!" he wheezed. His throat moved against his own knife blade. "And give that back!" The sharp pressure changed to a sting. Warmth trickled down his neck. The blond interloper leaned forward.

"One more sound and I'll slit your gullet!" He smelled of sweat, dust, and fear. Above him a dark yellow banner rippled across the sky. Fixing his eyes on it, Senruh stilled. The goldenhair relaxed infinitesimally.

"Thanks for the knife, by the way. And for showing me this place." His accent, strange to Senruh, slurred the words' endings. Outside, the throng jeered the auctioneer. His high-pitched quick talk began.

Under its cover Senruh breathed, "Let me go!" When the escaped captive said nothing Senruh tried again. "I can't raise the alarm. My master's out there and I'm—"

"Master! You're slave?" The boy's weight shifted on Senruh's belly, the shadowed face loomed close. His breath smelled of grain. "Black eyes, black hair, like the pictures

67

in the mountain shrines of the Old Blood . . ." His eyes widened and the boy's knife hand moved as if to touch Senruh's hair. *No!* Senruh thought, skin writhing with memory of the bearers' rough palms, the noble . . . He winced away. The blade settled again, keen, on Senruh's throat. "You don't look like the dust-colored louts at home. Are you sure you're slave?"

Carefully Senruh nodded. A pulse in his throat jumped against the blade. *He's mad,* he thought. *I look like every other bazaar half-breed.* The boy glanced at his hand just below Senruh's chin.

"All right! I believe you. A noble or a scholar would have a metal knife." The goldenhair swallowed, then bent so close Senruh could make out the dark shade of the sea's horizon rimming his eye's light-filled depths. So blue! He had never seen . . . The other's eyes flickered. Hard knees clamped Senruh's arms to his sides. Senruh tensed his haunches.

"You're not going anywhere! You treacherous lowlanders! Our priests said— I saw how those other slaves chased me. Small people! Like me!"

"That's different. They're jealous. They'll always be small and slave. We half-breeds might grow into citizenship." With the muscles across his shoulders and belly coiled and ready, Senruh watched his captor.

"We! I'm pureblood, small!" The goldenhair flourished the knife. "My father acknowledged m—"

Senruh whipped up his knees, he arched his back. The boy shot over his head. Fair hair flew as the other somersaulted toward the entrance. He landed on his feet, toes gripping the powder, crystal haft clenched in his upturned fist. His other arm dangled at his side.

Senruh bounced up. He whirled. His bruised leg cramped and he jarred onto one knee. Pain shot through his rump, blood warmed his bindings. He fell forward onto the fist shut around Ariahnne's coin. Edges bit his palm.

The goldenhair flung himself on Senruh's back. Senruh grunted, bracing himself on all fours. The boy's callused

fingers slipped down Senruh's arm to his wrist and yanked
it up. Off-balance, Senruh dropped. The boy jumped off him
and kicked him onto his belly. Grit mashed between Senruh's lips and teeth. A hand grasped his wrist, twisted it
high behind him. Still holding it, the goldenhair pounced.

"Agh! No!" Tears spurted from Senruh's eyes. He lay
unable to move as knees rotated on his back and buttocks.

"Blood?" His captor's voice sounded blank with surprise. "No wonder you didn't put up much of a fight. What
happened?"

"None of your—" Senruh spat dust. "I had a bad day."

"Well. Don't tell me if you don't want to!"

Senruh grinned weakly into the dirt. As the boy's offended silence lengthened, the bidding outside crescen-
doed. The auctioneer screamed triumph and approving
fingers snapped up and down the alley. In the sun-bright
space between the stalls, the escaped slave scooted up Senruh's back. Keenness slid like ice along his collarbone and
Senruh lost all interest in the sale. Knees thrust into his
spine and the weight was gone. The knife stayed in place.
Senruh turned his head. He blinked. Only finger-widths
from his nose, the sun blazed on a nimbus of blond ringlets.
The other's breath fanned his face.

"Get up. Slowly. Or I'll cut you an extra mouth."

Heart thumping, Senruh crawled to his knees. He
squatted on his heightened sandals. "You fought me. A
little Kakano emptyhead. Who fights!" Anger lit its slow
small fire in his belly. *Outwit the little zitter-brain,* he
thought. "That was my master up there on the dais with
you and the red priest," he began.

"Hush down!" the other hissed, as outside the auctioneer praised the sinew and durability of the next captive. The onlookers hooted. Facing Senruh, the other
whispered, "That? That greasy oaf was your master? I
thought at least— He stinks!"

Senruh squashed an impulse to grin and agree as he
would to a friend if he had had one. This boy was no friend.
He couldn't be. Not with Senruh's knife in his hand. And

he was Kakano. "Nevertheless," Senruh said after a moment, picking his words, "he wanted only you. Now you're gone he'll have left, so I can too. I won't tell you're here. I can't. I'm out without permission. So—" He stood. *Confidence,* he thought, *those little emptyheads give in to it every time. It's their nature.* The other boy's pale robe belled. He planted himself before the entrance.

"Try leaving and I'll kill you." Senruh froze. Eyes bright as summer skies glanced up from the dark blade. "I'll kill you like I'd have killed that slaver if I'd had this! Filthy lowlander. He made me— After he'd taken my gold!"

"Gold!"

"We sew a little in our hems in case of raiders. Or to bribe slavers. If my father knew I let him live and me, too—" The boy clamped his mouth tight. Above him deep yellow spider silk echoed his bright ringlets as it rippled across the sky. A green banner unfurled beside it. Senruh looked from the glowing cloths to the boy, puzzled. "Why . . . ?" Then he choked on a laugh. "You mean you're upset just because you and he—?" With one hand he made a graphic motion. The boy reddened and gave a stiff nod.

"Well, everybody knows you little creatures live for that, the rougher the better! I bet you loved it but now you don't want to admit it."

The blade whipped upward to prick Senruh beneath the chin. "I didn't! Only perverts can't keep their hands off you big louts! Anyway, in my highlands no one but life friends, battle companions . . ."

"Highlands! Oh, *faugh!* Next you'll tell me you flew here on a pink-spotted dragon with green wings." The blade rasped around Senruh's jaw. Sweat crawled through his hair. *Again!* he thought, fury zinging through his head. Ariahnne, the bearers, his master, now this mad little Kakano, all had made him afraid. Well, the others were out of reach. But this one! He'd show him. He'd show them all. A plan bloomed, rich in detail. He cleared his throat.

"Now, little fellow, you don't want to hurt me. I can help you out of the city, show you how to get to the spacers.

They're just north of here—they'll free you for nothing even if that slaver did cheat you out of your gold."

"Cheat!" The knife swished downward to point at Senruh's belly. A ball of sunlight bounced from the dust to Senruh's dark robe. He rubbed his throat. His fingers slipped in blood. His anger burned higher.

"Yes, cheat! That's a work-slave auction out there. Now summer's over the smallest gold piece buys two, three! untrained slaves like you. No more merchants chancing snow in the passes, harvest's in, from now till spring you'd just eat and take up space. Even the butcher priests are overstocked. That slaver diddled you out of your coin and your, ah . . ." Senruh raised an eyebrow and grinned. With satisfaction he listened to the boy's teeth grind. His plan was working. For good measure he added, "And a puny one like you would go for even less. Of course you couldn't be expected to think of that, not with that zitter-sized brain."

The interloper scowled then looked, lip curled, at Senruh's broad arms and chest. "I wouldn't want to be a block of brawn. At home I direct brainless lumps like you." Robe billowing, the boy squatted to frown at Senruh, knife poised. *Know when to stop talking,* Senruh's master repeated in his memory. *Too much and you'll spoil a sale.* Senruh waited.

Charcoal smoke drifted into their cell, curling through the line of shadow and wide oblong of light. It brought the sizzle and spice of sausages. Outside, the auctioneer's quick talk vied with the sausage woman's lusty call. As she haggled with customers her voice dropped and the auctioneer's rose. He shrilled the strength and endurance of a pair of field slaves. The bidding grew spirited. Haunches aching, Senruh watched the little goldenhair work his toes in the tan powder and think. The blue gaze fixed on his. For an instant Senruh stared, surprised all over again at the color.

"I hadn't thought of the spacers," the boy said. "Even in

the highlands they say they're to be trusted. Can we go now? Over the back?"

Senruh rounded his eyes. "Sunset's better. I'll guide you to the Western Gate. I know some of the guards there, they get careless at harvest time. No runners. When the farm carts go out at curfew you can nip between them, be out like that!" He snapped his fingers. Inwardly he chortled at the gullibility that made these creatures natural slaves. He took little notice of the blue eyes fixed on him. Kakanos weren't clever enough to distrust anyone.

Shamash the Sun God's incandescent palms spread across Senruh's shoulders. Their ache and sting eased. In his mind Senruh added the city's reward for the boy, the bonus for taking him after curfew, and the temple's bounty on a machine lover caught going to the spacers. He figured in the largest sum his master would squeeze out for the little goldenhair for, as informer, Senruh would own the boy. Relief weakened his knees. It was enough! If he added his savings he could buy his freedom, membership in one of the lesser tribes, and still have a large first payment ready for Ariahnne. Surely with a tribe and its judge to back him, she couldn't insist— Senruh looked up into sky-colored eyes.

"Why not after sundown?" the goldenhair asked.

"Gates are locked. Only exit's through the sentry booth. And that's guarded by two soldiers twice your size, another on the wall."

"I could stay here, hide . . ."

"You don't know the city. The slave finders would have you back with the slaver in a lizard's lick. As he probably planned. Now you've run you don't have a category. You're just—his! He can sell you as anything. Probably a fancy—with your coloring you'd bring three, four times what you would as a drudge. Maybe you should do it! You'd be famous," Senruh needled. "Songs written about you:

'Your eyes of flame hurl darts of love,
You're the hair of spring, the light of the earth,
the torch above . . .' "

he intoned soulfully and grinned at the other's expression. "Favorites get their names on cups, vases, mirrors, shields . . . Sell better that way," he amplified. "One even got his carved on a finger of Lord Nargash's statue. By the sculptor, so they say."

"No! Not without my consent!"

Senruh shrugged. He brushed at the dust smudging the front of his robe. It puffed into the slanting light. "Who'd care if a tribeless foreign slave hadn't filed a consent tablet?"

"I have a tribe! My fa—"

"Here? Identification? Proof?"

The boy's lips compressed. He shook his head. As he moved into the light his curls swayed like tide weed. Green shadow tinged them.

An oblong of the goddess's sacred color of growth and renewal spread, rippling, across the baked clay floor. It lapped at Senruh's feet. He looked up. The earth had tilted away from the Sun God, pulling a lens of flying green silk before Shamash's fiery eye. Outside a roll seller cried his wares. Spiced with ground redbark and honey, the warm yeasty fragrance wound through the verdant shadow. Senruh's mouth filled with fluid. He heard the other boy swallow.

"When did you eat last?" Senruh asked.

"Yesterday," the boy said reluctantly. "And a handful of cracked immer before we got on the platform. For good behavior." He reddened.

Abruptly Senruh thought of Ariahnne's caged lizard. At least it had occasional privacy. And got fed. He slid his hand in his pocket. The fair boy tensed. Carefully, Senruh withdrew his hand. "Here," he said gruffly. He held out his remaining redfruit.

"If I take it, I still won't let you go."

"You won't make the gates if you don't eat something. Go ahead." *I'm protecting my future coin,* Senruh told himself, *nothing more.* The goldenhair snatched the fruit.

As the boy reduced it to sharply fragrant juice that trickled down his chin and set him to licking the backs of his hands, Senruh listened to the auctioneer call for a young female to demonstrate her charms. The spectators snapped their fingers, others chirred the hunting lizard's mating call. But Senruh heard no joking remarks or coy laughter from the girl to indicate she too enjoyed the moment. He squirmed. He ran his thumb over Ariahnne's coin. The gold felt soft and slippery. He remembered how he had wanted to throw it away. He recalled too how the blond boy had hated the smell of Senruh's master. Outside the ribald comments grew louder.

Frowning, Senruh poked at a pebble caught in his clogs. What he planned was not really betrayal, not of an insane emptyhead who wasn't even human. And he was a stranger besides, ready to knife him . . . Senruh shifted. The bleeding had almost stopped. His backside ached down to his toes. The other boy cleared his throat.

"I'll do it," he said. "I'll go through the gates at curfew."

"Good." Not as jubilant as he had expected, Senruh got to his feet and strolled to the entrance. He could look for slave finders in the bazaar, and if he didn't come upon any gossiping there . . . A light robe swirled. The boy and the black crystal blade barred Senruh's way.

"Not yet!" Summer-colored eyes glittered upward, unreadable. "We leave when the auction's over. Together."

Senruh hesitated. He could hunt the slave finders after he hid the boy. He had to heal somewhere. He nodded. But the goldenhair's mouth was tight with suspicion. Thinking to reassure him, Senruh said, "Fine!" and gave him one of his best smiles. The fair boy blinked. Involuntarily his mouth curved in response and for an instant he looked dazed. Senruh flinched as he had from memories raw with the bearers' wrenching touch. He had seen that look before.

* * *

The Lady Ariahnne had worn it when, eager, believing himself beloved, Senruh had come to her in her courtyard one night almost a cycle past. Recovering, she had whispered, "That smile lights you up like a lamp in a secret cave. Come here, my sleek strong little lizard!"

Yellow eyes glowing like twin mountain fires, she leaned down to pull him close. Behind her the torches sputtered, harsh-scented with salt and tar. As her long rouged nails glided over Senruh's face, his throat, and slowly untied his robe's thongs, he shivered, his pleasure spiced with fear. Until, lips parted, blind, he lifted his face to hers.

The Sea God's breath skewed the flames and the shadows; it ruffled the sacred pool filled with stars. And lost, deep in the inky dark, the caged lizard began to sing.

Remembering, Senruh's skin roughened. Gone! he thought. More, Ariahnne's delight in him had never been. Even in remembering, his belly ground with pain. Dimly he heard the auctioneer's screech of victory. "Sold!" In the heartbeat of silence Senruh heard the girl catch her breath in a sob. Then the noise of the bazaar and the throng swept across her weeping. Senruh lay down.

"No book scrolls, nothing else to read, might as well rest," he muttered. And, blanking out the boy, the knife, and his world, he slept.

He startled awake. A hand shook him. Anxious blue eyes looked into his. His lashes fluttered down. When he focused again the other slouched, face shuttered, in a shaft of dusty light. Beside the boy, the entrance lay in shadow.

"You cried out. Someone might have heard," the golden-hair said.

On his back, more than a little asleep, Senruh listened to the shuffle of sandals, the murmur of passersby, and the distant grumble of the sea. "Auction over?"

"Awhile ago."

Senruh yawned and rubbed his face. It felt like it was

covered with drowsy webs. Memory edged back. "I thought I was finished with that old dream."

"It must have seemed real. You were . . ."

"Well, it was real. I'd barely lost my first milk tooth when a spacer tried to flame me." Relaxed, still wandering sleep's unbarriered lands, Senruh did not notice the other's sudden stillness. "I was just out of the slave crèche, new to my master, to the bazaar—I thought it was the most wonder-filled, exciting place on all Naphar—I was exploring under a barrow full of baskets. I saw silver feet— spacers' boots. I crawled around the barrow to see the rest, the man was still walking forward, and he tripped over me. He grabbed his laser pistol—you must have seen one in the guard niche when you came in—silver, rings around the barrel?"

"Yes."

"I watched him roll the charge wheel, his trigger finger got white, I couldn't move . . . Then another off-worlder came fast from behind him, he rammed him with his shoulder. That whole barrow—baskets up to the sky!—glittered and vanished. No ash. Just a little smoke. It should have been me.

"Its owner started yelling, jumping up and down. But the man in the silver boots only stood there, staring at the pistol. The other off-worlder paid the merchant. And me. Said—I could hardly understand him, his accent was so thick—his friend was nervous, just back from a war. But since, I've wanted nothing to do with the spacers! Killing, for no reason—!" Senruh stopped. What was he saying? He glanced at the boy through his lashes and tried a smile. "Anyway, that's how I earned my first freedom coin."

"So. Those are your spacers. Who will free me."

Senruh stared at the little goldenhair. The boy had made the connection! He did not fit anything Senruh knew of Kakanos; even his coloring was wrong. And he was bigger than most. Nearly . . . Senruh spoke as he would to an equal or to a friend if he had ever had one.

"You don't have to go to the spacers. You can do what I

do. Submit. Earn. Save if your master will let you. Buy
your freedom in a few cycles, maybe."

"Thinkers don't submit. But, buy—?"

Senruh watched a flimsy red pennon dip into the yellow
sunlight. Someone rolled it around its pole; soon it pointed
like a dark finger at the sky. Behind it a heavier square of
trapper-fish silk glimmered like displaced moonlight. Soon
it too stood rolled beside the wall, a luminous ghost in the
shade of late afternoon.

"Buy? Where does a slave get coin?" the boy's slurred
accent prompted. Senruh changed position on the cooling
clay and winced. Surreptitiously he pulled his robe free of
dried blood.

"You get coppers, sometimes silver, for running er-
rands, making things to sell, letting merchants, nobles,
ladies . . . you know." He gestured.

After a long moment the other said in a strangled voice,
"You mean you toss your robe?"

Senruh glanced sideways at round blue eyes. He
flushed. "Sure." He stared upward. The tight-wrapped
banners speared a deepening sky. Soon its color would thin
and he could see through it to the stars.

"Bold women who touch your— Men? The—the small?"
The goldenhair took quick breaths through parted lips.
Senruh paid him scant attention. He shrugged.

"What difference does all that make as long as they
have coin!" He took a long breath and stared at the sky,
trying to explain something he had never fully thought out
even for himself. "You know when they give silver they
want you, that you're really— They'll shake sometimes,
can't wait, start whispering how they— Well. When Rabu
do that, half-breeds are forbidden so much, they make you
feel, I don't know, powerful! And they can be so gentle, try
so hard to . . ." He broke off. "Of—of course, they're not always . . ." he faltered and stopped, raucous voices and
laughter loud in his memory, his body alive with tearing
hands and hurt and a final letting go with its own dark un-
bearable delight. His stomach lurched. Pulses racing, he

wondered if he could ever earn his coin in the old way
again, if instead, now he had found this new pleasure . . .
Cold to his fingertips, he glanced into the dusty light, saw
the other boy's face, and came fully awake.

"Don't!" he blurted. "I'm no dung grub!" Babbling
again. Senruh could almost hear his master's jeers. How
dare a Kakano—one he had thought to help—look at him
like that? He would pay him back in his own coin: shame!
Propping himself on one elbow, Senruh gave the goldenhair a long slow look from under his lashes.

"As for the small," he murmured, his seductive tone vibrant with fury, "you little creatures never have any
silver. I pay you. Why, did you—?" Invitation in every line
of his body and tilt of his head, he smiled with perverse
charm straight into the blue eyes. They darkened, then
flew wide.

"I—no!" The boy's glance skidded away. Bright flags
flew in his cheeks.

Senruh suppressed a laugh of angry satisfaction. He had
seen purity priestesses with that horrified but arrested
look. Generally, after their once-a-cycle sweeps through
the bazaar shaking their fingers at wrongdoing, one or
two returned to him, alone, flushed, often afraid, but with
their coin ready . . . Could this boy also—? No. *Conceited!*
Senruh told himself. Dismissing the priestesses and the
boy from his mind, already a little ashamed of himself, he
began exercising his aching body. He was flexing his still-
painful shoulders, getting ready to sit, when the other boy
leaned over him. He smelled warm, his ringlets fired with
light.

"Where I live, our holy teachers may be fools or hypo-
crites or both, but they do teach us to touch only where we
love! While you—" The boy snatched a breath and hurried
on. "You're like the night toads: croak, shake, and thrust!
At least they do it because they can't see, but you! You
don't even care! Rocks, other males, pairs that are already— Even the s-small, like me! I couldn't, not with the
large, not ever! And don't you ever again—"

Senruh's mouth tightened. His impulsive revenge had worked to his advantage. Only a fool would fail to use it. "Well," he said evenly. "Then you'd better go to the spacers, hadn't you?" In the taut silence, his sinews warming and their stiffness easing, he finished his stretches and contractions.

Outside, apprentices laughed as they stacked away the great bolts of silk. Behind the rear stall two voices haggled. While, hunched in the sunlight pooled before the rolled awnings, Senruh's captor sat, seeming bodiless, just folds of pale material topped by a tousle of light. Eyes the color of the sea at noon watched Senruh. "Thick body, thick head." He thumbed the serrated blade.

Senruh lifted an eyebrow. "Jealous?"

"No! And I never believed that about the scrolls, either. You louts don't read."

"Not if we're smart." Senruh eased his weight off the worst of his bruises. "And you Kakanos can't read. Your little eyes won't stretch to fit in a whole word."

"Well, I read!" The goldenhair's chin jutted. "Everybody respects a scholar."

"Liar. And put that knife away before you cut yourself. You emptyheads don't kill. If you'd ever meant to, I've have been dead right after you got here." Senruh looked over the boy's head. He estimated the bright rays slanting across their shared prison. He breathed deep of warm dust and the bazaar's pungence, cooled now by the slow breathing of the sea. He stood. "Time to leave if I'm to get you to the Western Gate and me to the Southern Gate by curfew. *I'm* not going to the spacers!"

The goldenhair rose. The black knife flashed upward, catching the yellow light. "Oh, yes you are. Did you think I'd sit tamely in a hole of your choosing while you ran to the slave finders?"

Senruh's knees loosened. He sat. "But I—my master—if I'm caught out after sundown he won't ransom me, I go to Sacrifice!"

The slighter boy shrugged tense shoulders. "My own

life's in danger. Compared to that— It's not as if you were human!"

"No lowlands emptyhead would ever talk like that," Senruh whispered. "You really are from the highlands aren't you? Where they pervert the goddess's laws, turn them upside down, and the small rule the large?"

"I said I was! And you're the pervert—corrupt like the priests say. You lowlanders are all diseased, ugly! Though *you're* not. You look all right." Flushing, the boy broke off and stared upward. The evening trumpets were sounding.

Atop the temple's golden dome the player priests' dark robes were dots against the fiery dazzle. Their brass horns lifted to the sky as if, in a last passionate farewell to day, they drew lengths of the sun, molten, into their eager hands and mouths. Senruh, who had seen it all before, glanced away, anger and panic jumping in his belly. He leaped up.

"By the gods, who are you to judge me, throw out my life? You're undersized, stupid—didn't even know your own price! You wouldn't last a day here where I've earned a name and a place. As for pervert: *You* lay with that slaver, and not for love either! *You* stripped down in public, not me! And if you fought either time I didn't see a mark on you. Anywhere."

The blond boy's face drained of color. "I'll kill you for that," he whispered. "It's different for me."

Senruh snorted.

"I don't touch." The goldenhair's voice was low. "Not since I grew my first meat tooth and had to move to the men's house. My mother died then. My father never . . ." His glazed eyes focused. "I can't talk like this to a lout. You just—obey! Like the slaves at home!"

Senruh ignored the almost pleading glance. Instead, looking from the blade to the boy's opposite dangling arm, he slid a sandal forward. He tensed his shoulders. Across from him blue eyes narrowed. The other dropped into a crouch . . .

Senruh remembered the longwhip. He flexed his aching

body—even a little Kakano had added to its pains. In his mind, the afternoon's voices whispered through his resolution.

The goldenhair's: *It's not as if you were human!*

Ariahnne's: *You're only half-breed, after all. And slave. I can buy another.*

His master's: *Promises are for men! Not a little scum of a robe tosser!*

His own: *You can do what I do. Submit.*

For a long painful moment Senruh hesitated. Then, avoiding the other boy's glance, he sank stiffly to the ground. His captor expelled a ragged breath. Cooking fires, roasting meat and grain scented the ocean breeze. Savoring the homely smells perhaps for the last time, Senruh looked up, memorizing the ending day.

The light thickened to poured honey. Through it, like a swirl of gemmed leaves, the sacred lizards sped homeward from the volcanoes' violet dark and the green translucence above the sea. He scanned them for a flash of orange. He did not find it. *Dead?* Senruh wondered, *or free?*

As the pods on the shower trees cooled, creaked, and exploded galaxies of spinning suns into the brilliant dusk, evening's hand smeared the sky with crimson. Its dark fingers opened; scarlet poured from the heavens to the Western Sea.

And the sun set.

Chapter Eight

STRIPED AWNINGS flapped in the deserted bazaar. Beneath them distant torchlight scrabbled, thin-fingered, at the shaking dark. Senruh eased from the gap between the stalls.

With every pore he tested the air. The wind scuttered a chewing pod; the boy's stare jerked to the shadows. As the breeze flicked the pod again he released his breath and looked up.

Stars burned above the volcanoes' fire-cobbled slopes. Behind the black cones scarlet tinged the sky. Soon Sassurum's Veil would rise . . . Senruh's gaze sharpened. "The veil! Sassurum's Veil! I never thought—!"

"Shut your teeth!" Cloth rustled behind him. A knife pricked his spine. "Calling the slave finders, thickhead?"

"No, listen!" Heedless of their being captive and captor, Senruh grasped the other's shoulder. Scowling, the boy twisted free. Senruh scarcely noticed, his words tumbling out. "Look! We have a chance! Because of the veil—you do see it, don't you?" When the other glanced at him as if he had run mad, Senruh hurried on. "They don't. The Rabu, I mean. I'm almost sure! Once in the Feast of the Fertile Fields—curfew's revoked then—we 'breeds were back late. No moon, but the stars were out, and the veil. Red light everywhere. We were climbing a wall, sneaking home, when a Rabu master came out to relieve himself. We froze. He finished, went inside, he never saw us!

"Someone said he couldn't! That we 'breeds and you

little Kakanos see by the veil and the stars but a Rabu needs the moon or a torch. That's why they're so strict about curfew. They're at a disadvantage at night. I laughed but later my lady—" Senruh swallowed. For a moment he seemed to sprawl again on the stones of Ariahnne's torchlit courtyard. Ghostly fingertips walked his spine, a husky voice breathed in his ear. Lamely he ended, "Uh, another Rabu mentioned needing a torch or a moon. She didn't seem to see the veil. Or the stars."

The other boy stretched out his hands. Starshine silvered them. "So that's why . . . Our full-blooded louts never were any good in the dark." For a long moment he gazed upward to the constellations shouldering across the sky. "They miss all that?" A red wisp crept from behind the volcanoes. It snared a star. Senruh's heart jumped.

"The veil's out," he said. "If we chance it, we leave now. By midnight the veil's set and the moon comes up. By then we'd better be safe inside the space station! We won't have time to reconnoiter like we planned; people awake, guards fresh, I don't know . . ." The distant torchlight leaped. Stones and ruts threw long shadows. Senruh glanced up the alley. "Get back, they're coming!"

But the goldenhair had darted into the glow. "Oh, don't be so timid," he said over his shoulder. "Let's do it, get it over with!" He lunged toward the street, pale as a candle in his captive's robe.

"Timid! At least I think!" Senruh snatched at the departing folds. Jerked backward, the other whirled, crouched, and brought up the knife. It gleamed; a polished slice of dark.

"By the brown-mouthed dung lord," Senruh rasped. "Between you and the curfew catchers! Look down. That torch makes you bright as a bolt of trapper-fish silk. And that's no friend of yours holding the torch, either! There's our first test of their eyesight unless we go back between the stalls."

Shaking his head, the blond boy looked where Senruh pointed.

A few intersections away, two figures—one short, one very tall—wavered toward them. Their burning brands held high, they paused. Black robes and head mantles swayed. The pair bent over a smoking bowl; they breathed deep. The smaller one's giggle drifted toward the boys.

The goldenhair pressed against the stall beside Senruh. "I—I could wrap up in dark spider silk."

"If you can steal some, you mean! So you're not so holy after all." When the other glowered Senruh motioned, grinning, across the alley to the silk sellers' booth. "Those shutters are locked. We could force them, but the smallest sound and our sacred curfew catchers will be here in a lizard's lick. Tell you what. I'm dark. So is my robe. When they get closer you hide behind me."

After a pause the boy said, "You'd shield me? After—"

Embarrassed by the emotion in the other's voice, Senruh shrugged. "Ready?" Taking the goldenhair's silence for assent, he raced toward the corner stall. Panting, he melded with the shadow beneath the broad overhang. A moment later, the goldenhair pelted up. "Next time you wait! I give the orders!"

"Why? Who knows this city, anyway? Not you, whoever you are!" Senruh glanced out. The two night priests were straightening from their bowl. In a moment there could be no time to talk, to breathe. "What is your name, anyway? If I'm going to die with you I'd like to at least know that. I'm Senruh." He held up his wrist.

The other's arms stayed down. "I'm Pell. Pell Maru. But I—my father—I can't clasp wrists with a half-breed lout. Or a pervert."

"Pell." Hot-faced, Senruh turned away. *Who cared what emptyheads thought? If they thought at all,* he told himself fiercely. Light filled his eyes.

His heart banged against his breastbone. One row of booths away the curfew catchers hesitated in a pool of smoking light. Senruh glanced around for a door niche, a gap to hide in; he met flush boards and, by his shoulder, wide blue eyes brimming with firelight. He hesitated, thrust Pell behind him.

The wiry body struggled. "I can't touch louts! My fa—"

Senruh twisted. "Oh, yes you can! What sort of place is your highlands that it never taught you anybody is capable of anything!" He turned away to stare blindly at the dark.

What possessed him tonight, he wondered. He never took the lead or spoke his thoughts except to the scribe. It was not safe, not for a slave, not with strangers. But there was nothing safe about tonight. And Pell did not feel like a stranger.

Against Senruh's back the boy's chest rose and fell, protest in each breath. From the street a low laugh shivered toward them. Pell stiffened. Just a man-length away the veiled pair stopped. Entwined, they bent over the dish. With a vacant titter, the smaller figure glided toward the alley opposite the boys, cradling the bowl, trailing a hazy scarf of smoke.

In the road beside them the giant partner swayed. Torch extended toward the road, thrusting the boys into shadow, the huge form shambled toward them, black mantles quaking, anonymous as retribution and death. Senruh squeezed his eyes shut. Not a gleam should give them away. Then the giant was beside him.

His world shrank to the musty scent of the curfew catcher's coverings, the burning brand that spat and smelled of pitch and sounded like rain, and the Rabu priest's hot breath, rank and sweet with joy smoke. Skin tingling, Senruh mouthed a brief prayer. "Let me be right, goddess. Let him not see . . ."

Sandals shushed. The feeling of presence eased. Through slitted lashes the boy saw the towering curfew catcher's back. Across the street, the smaller partner emerged from an alley. The huge night priest moaned and hastened forward, garments streaming into shadow. Senruh exhaled and relaxed his shoulders. Pell wriggled from behind him. Together they huddled beneath the overhang, watching the pair merge and breathe deep of the billowing smoke until, veiled heads as one, they exchanged a last caress, parted, and stumbled toward another set of alleys. Pell swallowed audibly. He flapped his sweat-damp robe.

"I—thanks." His gaze would not meet Senruh's. After a moment Senruh replied.

"We were lucky. Even joy-dazed, the Kakano would have seen us." Signalling Pell to follow, he sprinted across the street.

The boys paused in the shadow of a great squat building. Starshine silvered broad ramps concave from the tread of centuries of feet now dust. Red light washed the stone façade, black slashes marked its infrequent windslits.

Pell moved closer to Senruh. "What's that? We've got nothing above two man-heights in the highlands. It stinks!" Putting his hand over his nose the boy winced as murmurs and muffled shrieks came from inside. Whip cracks rent the restless night.

"Slave Courts. Pens are in back. Why? Didn't the slaver bring you here to register?"

"Should he have? He just dunked us and sold us . . . C'mon! I don't much like it here!"

"You should. It's all the protection a slave's got. But if your name and bond terms aren't scribed here you don't exist, legally. Anyone could take you, sell you, use you any way he wanted . . . It must have been an owner-pay-fee sale, only you escaped before— Look out!" Senruh slid in front of Pell. With practiced ease the boy curved around Senruh's back. Above them at the twin ramps' apex, a shaft of light broadened. Heavy doors swung wide.

Lamplight spread like beaten gold across the slanting walkways; it lit the trampled clay where the boys huddled. A court-robed Rabu stood silhouetted in the radiance. He paced downward, stiff pleated robe swaying against the light. A small slave followed him, torch held high.

When the sound of their footsteps had faded and the receding light only dusted the Slave Courts' stone, Senruh pulled away from Pell. "Judge, leaving late," he said. "Clerks will be right behind. We'd better go. Now!"

Light-footed, they circled the building and its reeking pens. Hands reached out from the cages' bars, more thrust through gratings sunk in the ground. Voices cried for buyers before the red priests took their toll at dawn.

Shaken, the boys expelled held breaths as they sidled between white-plastered buildings. Cool grass and flowers clung to their feet. With Pell close behind, Senruh stole onto the swept clay of the Region of Government and Temples of the Lesser Gods. He looked down. Light nudged his sandals.

It came from a temple's inner shrine. Beyond entrance ramps and thick-based pillars twined in red and black, braziers flared. They shot fitful light and shadow over deities fat and thin, many-legged, lizard-headed . . .

The narrow beams turned the entrance ramps to triangled porticoes seemingly risen from the ground while the rest of the buried temple pushed from beneath the packed clay, a shrine in the silent city of the dead.

Senruh imagined the foreign gods' sacrificial victims whose clean bones lay beneath the road: transparent, blind, they roamed through mold and hard dry dust, clamoring, vacant-throated, for release. The hairs on the boy's arms rose. Down the way a torch appeared.

Pell dove for a ramp's inky shadow as beside it Senruh swarmed up the pedestal of a canopied statue. A stone snake gazed, blank-eyed, into Senruh's face as he crouched behind cold painted draperies. His wooden soles slipped. Loose stones clattered. The torchlight jumped.

"Who goes?" an old man's voice quavered. Shadows swerved; a tall watchman shuffled toward Senruh's hiding place; he waved his dimming torch at the shadows. "Can't see . . . Little scum of a partner would choose tonight to cast off a friend. River of Death! River of Joy's more likely. And with his brother's mate again, too! Tsk!" Muttering, the elderly Rabu started around the statue's base. The light strengthened, seeking Senruh's face and hands. The boy rolled forward onto his toes.

From beneath him came a lizard's hiss, then the delicate patter of clawed feet. A final sibilant scold, and he heard a scaled body rustle between stones. The torchlight withdrew.

"Lizards! Think they own the city! All the same, this is the last time I cover for that strutting little he-toad!" When the watchman's thin stooping form had gone, Senruh joined Pell beneath the ramp.

"Lucky about that lizard," Senruh said.

"Luck!" Starlight gleamed white on Pell's teeth. "That was no lizard, that was me!"

"But—"

"You know bazaars, I know lizards. And snakes. And bugs. My father didn't believe in the goddess, so without gatherings to go to, and no real friends, all I had to talk to were louts and liz— Never mind! Let's go! That way?" Scowling now, the boy shot Senruh an uncertain look and pointed. Senruh nodded, surprised both at the confidence and at the boy's urgency. When Pell sped away, Senruh followed more slowly.

Their flight became a sharded mirror reflecting fragments of black and silver flooded with crimson. Above, the veil slid through the crowding stars tangling them in its webs of filmy scarlet. Beneath, the boys raced its passage.

As they crossed the city, lamplight spilled through windslits while inside children called. In the empty streets below an occasional Rabu passed, followed by a small entourage. Watchmen and slave finders prowled the city; in its byways the boys glimpsed others who, like themselves, preferred to remain unseen.

As each new danger lay behind them, thwarted, Senruh's mind sang with the battle lays of warrior companions. He did not question why.

At last they left the city and entered the fallow lands; the scent of the sea was sharp now. Dry grass crackling un-

derfoot, they avoided the furtive gardens of the poor and
the soldiers' practice circles and ran, bent, toward the
gnarled orchards ahead. Senruh pointed to the dusty-
leaved trees. "That's the last defense ring before the bazaar and the city walls. We can rest there. And plan."

The boys squatted, panting, in a moving lace of black
and silver inundated with crimson light. In its radiance
Senruh scratched pictures in the dust.

"I hope you were an observant child. And that laser pistols haven't changed." Pell's tense shoulders belied his
grin.

"So do I. I'd do that part but with your arm . . . Just so I
can use the knife. I'm still stiff. And I know some of those
guards. I wish—maybe the first plan will work and we
won't have to kill."

"I want to." Pell's voice was low. "You should, too, after
what they did—"

"They're all right." Senruh did not look up. "They don't
mean . . . They just don't realize . . ." He swallowed. The
words came hard; the boy would not understand. He
glanced up feeling shamed and resenting it. Blue eyes
looked into his with regret, he thought.

"You really don't want to go, do you? I didn't realize—oh, a lot."

"I do now," Senruh said. He stood. "Better give me the
knife. I may have to use it in a hurry."

Pell did not move. White-knuckled, he poked at their
plans with the black knife, embellishing them. "Later."

Hand out, Senruh stared at the pale curls hazed with
white, tipped with red. He knew their softness, their scent.
In their dash across the city, the other's body had become
almost as familiar to him as his own. Like a brother's if he
had had one. Or a companion's.

"Pell . . ." When the other did not reply, Senruh lowered
his hand. He pressed it to his stomach. It felt weightless, as
if he were falling.

Pell glanced up at him, face contorted. "I'll give it to you
in a little while, thickhead! Don't you trust me?"

"Yes. I did." The exhilaration of their escape drained away. *Fool again!* he told himself, throat tight.

"Oh, for—! You don't have to look like a wounded tree hider about it!" Pell jumped to his feet; his bare heels crushed weeds. The broken stalks gave off a pungent smell. A glassy handle slapped into Senruh's palm. "There! I trust you! So now what?" Pell's deepened voice sounded breathless.

Senruh stared at the firecrystal knife. A star balanced on its point. He thumbed the blade's sharp, tiny scallops, looked from them to Pell, and hefted the weapon.

The other boy dropped into a crouch. Defiance raised his chin. Without thinking, Senruh drew a chest-expanding breath and straightened. At his throat Pell's eyes widened. They stared at each other in mutual recognition until, grinning, Pell straightened and Senruh slumped. Senruh dropped the crystal blade in his chest pocket.

"So nothing! We go on as we planned—idiot!" He circled the other's shoulders in a brief hug.

Pell's answering chuckle was shaky. Stepping back, he hesitated. Then he flung his good arm around Senruh. For a moment the wiry body strained close, grip awkward. The boy's shoulders dug into Senruh's upper arm. Flushed face averted, Pell let go. His eyes shone. Surprise held Senruh motionless.

"I thought you didn't touch!"

"I—" Pell gave a lopsided smile and shrugged. He turned. He blundered toward the next tree. Senruh stared after him. Then, warmed, the night's ebullience restored, he stifled a laugh and followed.

"Yes, I did." The exhilaration of their escape drained away. Find Merof he told himself, thrust right.

"Oh, for— You don't have to look like a wounded fron—"

Chapter Nine

THE MUSTY THATCH scrambled with lizards. Inside the abandoned hut, stale joy smoke and urine tainted the air. Senruh took short breaths half-wishing Ariahnne had never educated his nostrils. Beside him Pell, kneeling, raised his head to peer out. Torchlight wavered through the windslit. It turned the boy's bright curls to fire.

"Get down!" Senruh's hands clenched. "They're still talking. If even one guard sees that hair—!"

"I'm tired of waiting! Look at them, they're just over-sized work louts! Lumps that big wouldn't notice if we strolled through the sentry booth, let alone ran. So let's go!" Pell started up. Orange light flickered on his face and chest.

Senruh lunged. His fingers sank into warm springy ringlets. He shoved downward.

"What— Keep your hands off, you big lout!" Pell twisted and hit out.

"Shhh!" Senruh launched himself. They scuffled in hard-breathing silence, no noisier than the lizards scurrying above. Pell yipped with pain. Senruh rolled off the boy's useless arm; the wiry body heaved then lay still beneath him, panting.

"Listen, you imbecile," Senruh whispered, "Those are five Rabu out there—three more than I planned on! And they're not drugged slaves, they're soldiers! I don't know the two night guards, but the day guards have campaigned in the north, and the wall guard! I've seen her stab a man just because she didn't like his jokes! We've got to run, not kill! These crystal knives are brittle; ours could break. And I'm not sure I can . . . So wait. Think. All you little emptyheads feel first, regret later!" He glared downward at wide eyes that gleamed in the darkness. Pale curls spread across the noisome floor like captured light.

"They're not human, Senruh." Pell's voice was a breath. "It's like stepping on a dung grub. But I keep forgetting you're only a lout; my responsibility. I'll do all of them."

"Oh, for . . . I don't need you! Anyway, you can't, not hurt like that. I only meant, the scribe talks about us all being children of the gods . . . and I've never defied . . . Oh, forget it!" With a harsh sigh, Senruh released the other boy and stood. He looked out.

Paving blocks with their twin carved ruts flickered with torchlight. Beyond them lay the city wall. Brands wrapped in firecloth and daubed with pitch were stuck just above the timbered gates. An onshore wind blew their flames. Light skittered over the two day sentries' open clinking vests, and the latched mail of the other three guards. The torchlight stretched tentative fingers toward the unmanned sentry booth.

Scooped from the wall's mud bricks, its opposite side lay open to the blue glow of the plain and the sea. Within, a single stone lamp laid petals of light across account scrolls, the day's travel sheets, swords, pikes, a half-eaten redfruit, walls striped with scurrilous graffiti and, on a shelf, the silver shine of a ring-barreled laser pistol.

"It looks the same," Senruh said. "Think you can use it?"

"Yes." Pell swallowed. His breath was moist on the back of Senruh's neck. "How's the veil?"

Together they turned. They looked toward the hole between the rafters where they had crawled into the hut from the back alley. Through the gap the volcanoes' dark cones seemed to support the night. Their flames licked the veil's red swirl as it slid toward its nightly laving in the Western Sea.

"Even a thickhead coward can tell the red light's going," Pell prodded. "Once the moon rises they can see us, follow us all the way to the space station. What's that?" He spun around. Senruh followed his example more slowly.

Across the way the wall guard swung up the footholds to the city wall's top. She complained of the heat.

"Take your mail off, then," a day guard called up to her, "or undo it. Not an army in a season's journey and no runners till winter."

Fists on hips she shook her head. "I follow regulations. Carelessness kills, as you'd do well to remember." The men hooted. She frowned, banged her pike on the clay-daubed bricks and marched into a net of leaping shadows. Below, the four day and night sentries laughed and settled down to a serious gossip.

For a long moment Senruh stared at them. Then, beckoning Pell, he eased toward the door. He paused at the windslit. "In case I— Just in case, there's where we're going." He pointed toward the sentry booth. Through its opening the boys looked to the north where, rooted behind low hills, a fan of white light erased the stars. "Spacers' beacon. Run there. Remember?"

Pell nodded. "All right, you showed me. Now let's go!"

His gaze on the wall guard's progress, Senruh murmured, "Not yet." The hot flavorless scent of cooking oil floated into the hut. It mixed with charcoal smoke. A breeze crept in. Redolent of the wet stones and tide weed beyond the walls and plateau, it fingered Senruh's hair. And what would it find of him to touch in a few moments, he wondered. His heart beat faster. The wall guard's mail gleamed then faded into the breathless dark.

"Now!" Senruh whispered.

Pell behind him, he scuffed across the littered floor. He drew the knife from his pocket and hid it low in the folds of his robe, serrated edge upward. He stepped into the road. Skin prickling as if exposed to a thousand suns, he moved into the torchlight. By the wall a day guard stopped scratching inside his open vest, yawned, and glanced up.

"Ho!" he called. "Who comes?" Senruh lifted his free hand and kept walking. "Oh!" The guard's chin lifted. "Well, look who's here. The bazaar's own insatiable he-lizard! This morning wasn't enough for you, eh? Going for a private repeat performance?" He turned to the other sentries. Through bursts of laughter Senruh heard him say, ". . . bazaar crawler I was telling you about . . ." Forcing a knowing smile, Senruh kept going. The day guard interrupted another's murmur. "Well, they don't feel pain the way we do. Like it, in fact! Why, I've heard . . ." Out of the corner of his eye, Senruh caught Pell's questioning glance.

Mortified anger sang through Senruh's head until mercifully he could hear no more. As he made himself swagger, his hand tightened on the knife. For the first time he felt he could use it.

As if by accident he paused by the guard niche, Pell a few steps behind. Beyond the lamp's gold shimmer, purple night pressed. In a moment they could be in it, running . . .

The day sentry pushed away from the wall. Head and shoulders above the boy, he lunged toward him. "So tell me, scum, what have you and that tireless lady lizard of yours got on for tonight?"

Senruh choked on a breath. He summoned a leer. "No plans. Just asked me to bring a friend." He jerked his head toward Pell. "Tonight we'll only, ah, feel our way. I'll know more by dawn." Heart thumping hard, he slid a sandal toward the niche. His calf muscles bunched. A hairy wrist shot in front of his nose.

"Just one instant, songboy. Where's your permission tablet? And your escort?"

Senruh stood very still. Behind him, Pell faded toward the shadows. By the wall the other day guard shrugged out of his mail. It clashed to the paving stones with a sound like untuned bells. Rubbing his sides he said, "Caught a desperate criminal, have you? Delay our friend here, and we'll have the Lady Ariahnne in a rage. Likely swallow her teeth then blame us when they bite her so she can't sit down. Or worse, give the boy a nip just as he's halfway to giving satisfaction!"

The soldiers laughed. The now-unarmored sentry dropped a heavy hand on Senruh's shoulder. "This is no runaway. He doesn't like spacers, do you scum?" The hand spread under Senruh's chin. "C'mon, little tosser, where's your pass?"

Senruh hesitated. When he and Pell had made their second plan, Senruh had glossed over how he would distract the guards. He shook himself. Who cared what a stiff-necked little emptyhead thought! Anyway, he had no choice. He gave the tall soldier a heavy-lashed upward glance. Smiling, he edged away from the sentry box. His questioner followed. Good, Senruh thought. His heartbeat quickened. "I didn't put the tablet around my neck; it's somewhere else. Think you can find it before the lady's servant gets here?"

Beyond him the night guards straightened, roared with laughter, and gave the hunting lizard's mating chirr. The first day guard, behind Senruh now, shucked out of his mail. It jangled against the wall. "Don't look too hard," he hollered at his partner, "I want a turn, too!"

Chuckling, the second guard bent low. Senruh smelled sweat mingled with clay dust, honing oil, and lamp smoke. It took him back to the days before Ariahnne when he had sat by this man and others like him listening to their tales of far places, of the battles they fought, and their discussions of how best to kill and maim. The scribe protested such things, but the old man disapproved of so many of Senruh's pleasures . . .

Now Senruh's palms slicked with sweat. He couldn't! Perhaps even now, if he pleased the men . . . But Pell! Flushed, agitated, the boy breathed faster.

The guard set his mouth against his ear. The man smelled of tear root. "So those bearers really got you hot! Now I know what you like I can show you a wilder time than they ever did." The big hands reached for him.

The bearers, the dust, his humiliating self-knowledge, treated by this man as a joke! "No!" Senruh whipped the knife from the folds of his robe. It blurred upward between the sentry's outstretched hands.

Its edge jagged with broken flame, the knife plunged into the guard's chest. Blood gushed, wet, warm. The handle turned. The soldier jerked upright. The knife slipped. Trying to yank it free, Senruh sliced downward instead. The blade cut through the man's belly. It slipped out.

The laughter drained from the soldier's face. "Why—?" His glazing eyes stared into Senruh's. Bemused, the man looked down. Blood fountained across his robe. Cloth and skin parted. Gray, glistening, his insides spilled. Both hands out as if to cradle a child, he caught them. He sank to the ground, his back to his approaching partner and the night guards by the wall. Beneath him a dark pool spread toward the twitching shadows.

Senruh forced his gaze away. He caught a flicker of movement by the sentry niche: Pell's hem. Only a little longer . . . Sandals slapped behind him. Senruh whirled.

"Why didn't you—?" The second guard's eyes widened. He reached for his dagger. Holding the dripping blade in both fists, the boy rammed it upward. The massive sentry fell on the knife. His weight jarred Senruh's arms to the shoulders.

The man grunted; the sound whispered into a bubbling sigh. Blood sprayed over Senruh's face and hands. He tried to pull the knife away. Slick, it twisted; it squeaked on bone. The man toppled. Jumping to one side, the boy snatched the blade free. Curses came from behind him. He spun around. He could not see Pell.

From the shadows by the wall both mailed sentries strode toward him, daggers drawn, helmets sparked with torch and starlight and the red mist of the veil. One tossed his dagger into his other hand. His gaze never leaving Senruh's knife, he drew his sword.

"Pell. Help!" Senruh's cry was the mewling of a nesting lizard. There was no reply.

The men's harsh lined faces loomed above him. Little gold lights twinkled in their mesh coats. Despair twining through him, Senruh dove for their feet. Even if he crippled them he could not dispatch them, not with a firecrystal knife. Only lasers cut metal.

"He's down! Get him!" A sword blade threw light in Senruh's eyes. Breath rasping, he slashed at an ankle. A studded sandal kicked his side. Senruh gasped and rolled. "Pell!" Louder this time, his voice cracked. Still no answer came.

"Who's he calling?" a guard asked.

"There was another one. Get him! I'll finish this one."

"Later. He nipped into the booth. Long gone. Make an example of the one we've got. Guard killer!"

The sandal thudded into Senruh's ribs again. He caught his breath at the pain; he tried to rise. A heavy foot pinned his haunches to the sharp paving stones. His wounds there reopened. Blood warmed his loincloth. He struggled. While the first guard immobilized him, the second hunkered down.

"Know what we do to guard killers, dung lizard dropping?" The soldier's voice was flat. In the pause Senruh heard the torches sputter, a harsh gasp from one of his victims, and in the distance an infant's thin monotonous crying. He shook his head.

The crouching man took the boy's arm in a delicate thumb and forefinger. Tracing with his dagger's point, he said, "First we take a slice—here. Then one there, inside that thigh. Another here, from your other arm. That knife hand goes, a joint at a time. As for the parts your lady likes best . . ."

Pell was gone, Senruh thought. Fool, not to have foreseen another betrayal! Well. He might yet trick the soldiers into a quick kill . . . Loins fluttering with dark anticipation, he heaved upward.

The guard with a foot on him hopped. Senruh scuttled out from under him, crawled toward the amber rectangle spilling from the sentry niche. Under his nose the square stones blurred. Close up, the bordering grass blades became a multitude of green and black sentinels. He glanced over his shoulder. In two strides the huge guard was on him. The man raised his sword.

"No, you don't!" The deep voice came from behind. The guard whipped his head around to stare behind him, face blank with shock. Senruh followed his gaze.

A long black shadow divided the light. Pell stood in the booth's opening, his tangles changed to lit, tarnished gold. A sea breeze ruffled the edges of his robe. In one hand he held a laser pistol. While time stood still he raised it, aimed, thumbed the charge wheel.

A crimson ray ribboned, transparent, over Senruh's head. It glittered on the night guard's mail and uplifted blade. It rained sparkles on the soldier hunched behind him. Effervescent with light, one man then the other winked out. Gray wet smoke drifted past Senruh's face. Feeling as though he waded through an old dream, he wobbled to his feet.

His senses clamored with messages: pain, the feel of dust on hands sticky now with drying blood, the pungence of smoke and of the butcher shop drifting on wind tinged with the tide's salt, the stench of opened entrails, of cooked flesh . . . Behind him someone—Pell?—retched. Metal clanged on stone, skidded, and stopped. Above him Senruh heard a steady tramp.

"Hurry, Senruh! The wall guard's coming!" Pell's whisper danced with urgency. But Senruh could not wrench his gaze from the drab mists, already dissipating, that had been two men.

"Human," he said, unaware that he spoke aloud. "Like me. Even if they didn't know it."

Iammu the Sea God puffed at the twin wisps. They spread, mingled, became a diaphanous tapestry of yellow torchlight laced with black shadow and the veil's crimson. Then even that was gone.

A callused hand tugged at Senruh's arm, then his sleeve. "We've got to go! She's almost here!" It thrust him into the sentry box's cozy glow. Above him the measured tread paused, then thudded faster.

"Ho!" a deep contralto called. "Halt!" The wall guard blew a single note on her battle clarion. "To me!" she cried.

Breath sobbing in his throat, Pell tugged Senruh toward the dark. A cool breeze wrapped them, clean with salt and the scent of sun-dried grass. Senruh took a long breath and shuddered. Then, fumbling the blood-slimed knife into his pocket, he ran

Chapter Ten

GRASS WHIPPED Senruh's ankles. Beneath his pounding sandals the blades released their dry fragrance full of memories of summer and the sun. Its incense blended with the salt flow of the breeze. Senruh pushed at his hair; his hand came away wet with sweat. Numbness gone, his ~nses pulsed, giddy with returning life. He gave a breathless laugh and glanced at the fair curls tossing beside him. The veil tipped them with crimson.

"Where *were* you?" he asked Pell. The boy glanced up, eyes purple in the thin red light.

"Right where I said I'd be. In the sentry booth. I just couldn't—!" Pell hopped, grimaced, and concentrated on the loose rocks wobbling underfoot. Senruh clopped over them sending pebbles clattering. Pell dropped behind. When he caught up, the boy's gait was uneven, his mouth tight. "I heard you call. Twice."

"I didn't! I don't need—" Senruh broke off. Denial did not fit the night. "I did call. I was afraid you'd left me."

Pell looked up at him, intent, started to speak, then frowned and looked away. Silent, they fled on.

For Senruh, time shrank to the smooth flex of muscle in back and arm and thigh, the heat of Pell's nearness, the boy's gasping breaths that rasped in rhythm with his own, the complex clack and thud of feet and wooden soles on clay. Then, behind the sounds came voices; Senruh looked back.

The sky, thick with stars, rained silver light on the volcanoes' flame-hatched cones. In their laps the city lay, lamps and torches flickering here and there in its concentric rings of streets, domed palaces, and towers. At its nearest edge the Western Gate bloomed with light. A scatter of tall silhouettes spread from it across the plain, lanterns and brands held high. Calling, their voices dimmed by distance, the figures stumbled into a run.

The boys' glances met; they increased their speed.

Pell snatched a breath. "Couldn't find the pistol's charge wheel!" He frowned at the pale stems and cracked soil unrolling beneath their feet. "When I thumbed it, it stuck. Had to tip in lamp oil. Then the marker beam wouldn't fire. When I got that working, you were . . . I had to wait for you to get clear."

He ran a little further. With difficulty he said, "I take back what I called you. You thickheads aren't cowards."

Fingers of pleasure strummed Senruh's neck and belly. He laughed. "Don't! I was so scared I almost filled my loincloth. Still am. But we're alive!" In a burst of delight with himself, with Pell, with the night, he said, "I never once refused any Rabu. In my whole life! But tonight—four of them. And when they looked at me, they were afraid! Of me!"

Pell stared at Senruh. "Of course they were. You were their death. So was I." He swallowed and looked back at his racing feet. "They weren't good men," he said. "I've read, argued ethics. They'd have used us, killed us. It should have been all right to kill them. But they weren't evil, Senruh! And I—the blood—that smell! I didn't know!" He retched and tried to cover the sound with a cough.

Senruh glanced at the other's set face. So he had not been alone in his revulsion. "You never killed before, either?"

"No!"

As they followed the dark line of the cliff, feet skimming rocks and the weeds' dry bones, warmth tickled Senruh's haunches. Scarcely conscious of his opening sword cuts or of the wounds the chairmen had inflicted, he ran on, wetness trickling down his legs. It oozed into his sandals. His feet slipped.

They neared a fjord. The phosphorescent sea's glow reached deep into the plain. A second fjord lit the plateau beyond, doubling the crash and suck of waves and distant rattle of stones. Glancing at the lights in the villas huddled at the nearer chasm's edge, Senruh angled inland toward the hills mounded beneath the off-worlders' beacon. Behind him Pell stumbled again.

". . . dung-eating rocks!" the boy muttered.

Senruh paused, half-turned, and caught Pell's arm, lifting him along. "I forgot! You're barefoot. Let me—"

Pell yanked free, tripped, then found his stride. Senruh slowed to accommodate him.

"Where I come from we don't touch!" Pell said. "In spite of tonight. In spite of . . . not unless . . ." He glanced at Senruh, scowled, and stared at the hard-packed soil.

Puzzled, Senruh felt some of the night's elation slip away. He grew conscious of seeming daggers in his lungs, of his wounds' sting and ache, of the blood-wet robe that slapped his legs. Behind him, he heard a shout, then a gabble of sound. He glanced back. Shock tweaked his ribs.

On the wide tilted plain between Senruh and the city, streaks of light and shadow careened from a central brilliance; above it tall shapes bent, gesturing, deep voices mixing with strident contralto and soprano. The cluster bulged, a figure emerged. Linked mail glinting, upheld torch streaming black and yellow banners of smoke and fire, the soldier ran. Straight toward the boys.

"Bloodstains!" he whooped. "We got 'em! This way!" The rest leaped up and followed.

Senruh veered away from the beacon, making for the second fjord. Pell ran on alone. He glanced back. Limping, cursing, he swerved and caught up to Senruh.

"What are you doing! The spacers are over there! Lunk!"

"You go. They're following me. I'll—wait! Pell, have you still got your loincloth?"

The blue eyes snapped wide. "Why?"

Senruh looked over his shoulder—their pursuers were making great strides—and gave a gasping laugh. "I'm not being obscene! I need it. For bandages. That's my blood they're tracking. I was going to try the sea, maybe find a sewer outlet, but if you—"

Pell was no longer beside him. Senruh halted and circled back. Chest heaving, the boy stood, hem tucked under his chin, fumbling with his loincloth. His legs were twin white glimmers in the night. Hastily Senruh looked away. Bobbing torches and lanterns filled his vision. Just behind him dry grass rustled.

"You'd drown," Pell said by his shoulder. "Here." Cloth bundled into Senruh's hands. Still warm, it smelled of the boy's skin. Senruh started tearing it into strips. "Besides," Pell said, "the sewers are guarded. The slaver told me that much." Inner thongs retied, his robe whispered into place. Senruh watched a soldier's lantern, another, join the torch that flared and danced in the lead. He held out two lengths of material.

"Bind your feet. Or they'll follow your blood trail, too."

The boy knelt, whipping the bandages into place. "How about you?"

"Later. And—thanks. I'll meet you in those trees." Lungs pumping, throat tight with unexpected tears, Senruh pointed to one side of the spacers' fragile wedge of light. "Pell? If I . . . If we miss each other, I—" His voice stuck. On the distant plain the guards seemed to leap toward them.

"You what?"

Senruh gulped and found no words. "Nothing!" he said. "Just—good luck. Now go!" He turned, expecting to see Pell's retreating back. Soft curls brushed his jaw.

Senruh stood very still. Darkening eyes stared up into his. Between thick short lashes, stars gleamed and the last misty folds of the veil.

"I'm going with you," Pell said.

"No!" Senruh stepped back. He gave the wiry body a push; it resisted. He swallowed, summoning reasons.

"We're safe as long as those lights don't hit us, but let them catch us once—with that hair and robe you're bright as a sun follower—and they'll get us. Besides, you can't keep up." He looked pointedly at the other's white-wrapped feet. *And I want you safe,* he thought. A vast astonishment filled him.

Pell looked stubborn. "But I—"

Confusion, shock, burst into the safety of anger. "Get going!" Senruh said. Over the boy's shoulder he watched their hunters string into a wavering necklace of fire. "You little emptyheads are all alike! Can't think straight, always arguing, just do as you're told for a change!"

The dark blue eyes flickered. Pell whirled. Over his shoulder he yelled, "All right!" and raced for the hills' black bulk as if chased by all the demons of Arob Shamsi.

Chapter Eleven

FEELING INCOMPLETE without Pell's footsteps thudding beside him—but it was only the sound he missed, not the boy!—Senruh neared the second fjord. The glow from the tiny organisms in its warm water pulsed dark then light, across the salty grass. As the Sea God's breath strengthened, Senruh pulled in great drafts of air flavored with tar and weed from Iammu's drowned palace gardens. He ran steadily, conscious now of his seep of blood, his temples' thumping, a thin keening in his head; he shook away dizziness and listened for the guards.

Behind him they called to each other, their voices chaining like a war song. They drew nearer.

Ahead of Senruh a crack glimmered in the plateau, sharp-edged with shadow. The fjord! He leaped for it, skidded to its edge and looked down. Good! The shallow ravine at his feet ended in a cliff plunging sheer to the sea far below. He snatched a look behind. His raised dust blurred the guards' lights, turning them to hazy golden jewels. They were still distant. He had time.

The boy balanced forward. Gritting his teeth, he sat and bumped down the side of the ravine. As he bounced toward its narrow spray-wet base, pain clamped his muscles, his sight, his hearing; rocks tumbled before him, powder smoked into the air, sudden dark blindfolded him. His feet hit stone.

Vision then breath cleared. He got up. Knees shaking, he stumbled the twenty man-lengths from the gully's shallow beginnings toward its abrupt end high above the waves. As his feet disturbed the phosphorescence in the puddles of fallen spray, they winked with trails of light. His sandals sank into loose ground. Here? Senruh peered downward.

The earth looked raked by minute fingers. Sun followers. They must have been here recently. He pictured the yellow flowers massed on the hills beyond Qaqqadum, spreading their petals to the sun while beneath the soil their roots whispered and called and moved, drawing the colony toward ever greater heat and light. He glanced around but could find no sign of them, shut and pulled half-underground for the night. Instead he saw his trail, its red spatters shining on the stones by the light of the veil. It was very long. And wide.

Cold crept into Senruh's middle. Feverishly, he hauled off his robe, dropped the remains of his loincloth, and bound Pell's tightly around him.

As he dipped handfuls of grass into the pooled spray and scrubbed, the bleeding slowed. Shaking the last tiny suns from his fingers, he put on his robe again and found a large rock. He wrapped his blood-soaked loincloth around it and sat down at the edge of the precipice, his heart beating a little faster as he memorized footholds on the gully's far side. When he heard the guards they could hear him and it would be time to carry out the rest of his plan.

A hiss blew toward him on the wind. He had thought the first one part of the shush and scrabble of the surf but it came again and with it the rush of quick-fanned air. He looked up. Out of the chasm's blackness sailed a little body on scalloped wings. A sacred flying lizard!

Throat tight, Senruh watched it bank and turn, light from the veil and the stars sheeting skin like polished metal, not gold or silver but rare precious orange. It floated nearer.

"So you did escape!" the boy breathed. "And is this your new home? Or do you go north to the Unknown Lands?"

It spiraled low. A bitter pungence whooshed past Senruh's face. Startled, he thrust up his arm. The lizard darted high, chirring and scolding, forked tongue flickering, tasting him even as it fussed. The boy held up his wrist. "Come back. I won't hurt you."

Chattering, it circled downward and hovered. Round black eyes stared into his. Set beneath high bony brows, they brimmed with stars. The triangular head tilted, a wild simplicity touched the boy's mind. He felt no invasion, only innocence—and recognition. He laughed aloud and held his fist high.

"So you're truly a messenger of the gods. They said you spoke in your own way. I thought it was a lie. Come?"

The creature shrieked and skated upward, chattered, then dove. Senruh held firm. At the last moment it braked. Warm, dry, fragile-boned, its toes touched his wrist and closed. He tensed, supporting the sudden weight.

He raised a finger to the gleaming neck. The little lizard trod up and down, kneading Senruh's skin with fine pointed nails. Murmuring to itself it sidestepped up his arm.

Gently Senruh touched the blunt head, smoothed the brilliant back. "A companion to princes," he breathed. "I never thought I'd—!" The flyer chirruped. It stretched its pulsing throat over Senruh's hand and peered upward. For an endless moment black eyes gazed into his. An alien sweetness flowed into the boy like strength. He caught his breath.

"You beauty!" he whispered. "I wish I could give . . . Wait!"

Back straight to balance his passenger, he knelt in the earth turned by the flowers and sifted its coolness. The small creature worked its way up toward his cheek; the forked tongue explored it. "That tickles!" Senruh rubbed his jaw and laughed. Beneath him the waves seemed to brawl with angry voices. He shook the dirt off a handful of pods and wrigglers.

"Grubs. And seeds!" He held them beneath the lizard's broad chest. The little flyer cocked its head.

"Take them! Or do you only drink the goddess's nectar?"

The lizard hissed, teeth grazed Senruh's palm, and the offering vanished. Gulping, the sacred lizard fluttered, regaining its balance, and snuggled beside the boy's ear. Its heart beat fast against his neck, its clean pungence mingled with the wet smell of spray and rock and a whiff of smoke. Thinking to find it shelter, Senruh glanced to the end of the gully where he had entered. He saw no shelter. He saw torches. Abruptly the angry voices separated from the ocean's roar.

"He's veered!" a soprano shrilled. "Making for the sea! Head him off!"

The flying lizard started, its heart bumping Senruh's jaw. Then it screeched and shot upward.

How could he have forgotten even for an instant! Fumbling in his haste, Senruh picked up his weighted loincloth. He wrung it. Blood splashed the ground at his feet. Good. It looked as though he had stood there awhile, summoning his courage. Then, with all the strength of back and arm garnered from cycles of lifting heavy paving blocks to increase his girth, Senruh heaved the rock into the sea. Beneath its long trajectory red spattered the cliffs and beach and waves.

"Aghhh," he called, turning toward the guards, artistically fading his cry. The rock splashed. The stained loincloth floated free. He gave a loud gurgle, grabbed a breath, and balanced forward on his toes.

"He jumped!" a deep voice howled. "He doesn't escape us that way! Fish him out!" The lights separated. Some slid downward to leap toward Senruh, others bounded above him toward the precipice. In two long strides Senruh crossed the gully. Scrambling up its side, panting, he flung himself onto the plateau and glanced back.

Above the undulating glow of the sea the little lizard flashed through crimson and silver radiance. The tussocks by the boy's cheek turned black, damming a slide of lantern light. Footsteps shook the ground.

The lizard, wonder, exploded from Senruh's mind. He rolled. Out of the lanterns' and torches' glow, he scrambled to his feet and ran. A scream lifted his hair. Cold rippled down his sides and he raced faster. Then annoyed reassurance touched his mind and he almost laughed. Behind his eyes the lizard relived its objections to the guards' invasion. It screeched again, sounding like a man in agony. As he pounded on, Senruh heard the soldiers shout and run toward the sound.

"Thanks for the help, goddess," the boy gasped between strides. "Keep it up and I'll believe you really exist, complete with messengers, second chances . . ."

The words had scarcely left his tongue before a chill closed around him like a hand. Behind him he felt a presence as boundless and old as the sky.

He dared not look back, but with his skin and blocked breath he knew. Sassurum's black eyes stared down at him, her tossing curls blotting out the stars. Her great amber hands that destroyed as often as they succored reached for him, seeking, almost touching . . . Heart shaking in his chest, able to suck no air, he stumbled and fell to the ground.

"Goddess . . . Forgive . . ."

The presence eased. As the boy's skin warmed and his pulses steadied he felt a smile on the breeze, the ghost of a caress touched his neck. Shaken but obscurely comforted, he rose, shamefacedly sketched a bow, and plunged toward the hills.

Senruh's breath was a knife in his chest. His knees seemed weighted. Halfway across the plateau he looked back at the sparks clustered on either side of the fjord. Two parted from the rest. They jigged along the glowing chasm then sped toward him. Cursing the guards' longer stride and their freshness—they had just come on duty, he had been up since dawn—Senruh passed a hand over his robe.

Dry. No fresh blood had made a trail. They could not know he lived.

Now the off-worlders' beacon fanned above him, its incandescent center thinning to fragile edges. Below it the sacred hills spread their arms wide, ready to enfold him in the gods' abandoned pleasure gardens.

Senruh eyed them, nostrils pinching at the rioting scents of stems, earth, the skinlike smell of fungus, chewing leaf's cool clarity. Among the crowding fronds and branches, giant ferns' spores whirled upward. A wind drew whispers from the leaves, the empty pods of shower trees creaked and plopped to earth. Through the multitude of sounds streamed an eerie crystalline music and the resonance of flutes. What musicians played in utter dark? If there were any other sanctuary! Yet here was where he and Pell had agreed to meet. Senruh looked back.

Only a few man-lengths away tall shadows loomed. Deadly circles of light tilted toward his feet.

Thighs burning, breath sobbing in his throat, pain stabbed the boy's ankle as a high sole rolled on a hummock. He could stop, rip them off . . . No time! And without them no one would take him for anything but slave. He hurried faster.

Behind the boy a pursuer slipped. Pebbles scattered. He tried to match his strides to theirs. A deep voice rapped out a curse.

Eyes straining into the silver and crimson dark, Senruh saw masses of scarlet and glints of light in the undergrowth. They became ruffled petals and the slide of stars on moving prisms. Beyond lay beds of purple flowers, their trumpets lifted to the wind. Of course! Windsingers and crystal bells. So this is what they were meant to be, Senruh thought, not the straggle of jangling whistling noisemakers in his lady's garden. But still, they were the gods' alarms. Breath rasping in his throat, he angled away, snatching a look behind him.

Helmets loomed against the night. Swinging lanterns blasted white light in his eyes. He sprang.

He landed full-length in the woods. He rolled. Ferns showered him with spores, crackled and swished over him. They oozed sharp-smelling sap. Nearby he heard a tintinnabulation of bells.

"Who's there!" a gruff voice cried from the plateau.

Senruh froze. Wincing, he turned on his back, dazzled eyes futilely searching the dark. He scraped up loam and pebbles, threw them. Brilliant polyphony caroled through the air.

"Over there!" Heavy feet tramped away.

Mentally congratulating the vanished gods on their taste in flowers, Senruh turned onto his belly and squirmed into the ferns and vines. He fetched up against a shower tree's vast bole. Curled between roots thick as a soldier's waist, he tried to stifle his panting and listen for the guards.

"Must have been a lizard." Those deep hesitant tones sounded familiar. A pod crashed to the ground. The night shimmered with melody.

"Or a pod," the rougher voice agreed. "He can't be here. I heard him, saw the blood! Besides, maybe all the runners do head this way, but not him. The wall guard says he hates spacers. Known for it."

"Oh? Senruh, you said? From the Southern Gate?" After a pause the familiar voice added, "Well, his friend might not hate them. Let's keep the sirdar happy and search. But be careful. I don't want us burned or grabbing for our bowels. That was quite a little songboy, carving up two seasoned guards. And for no reason, you say? That doesn't sound like—"

"None! Oh, a little flirting, fooling around, but he was all for it until . . . Well, all those juicy little pallet thumpers are born raving or half-witted or both. It's to the good, I say! Makes them frisky! Inventive! I never was much interested in their minds, like you. It's the other end I—" He laughed. After a moment the other joined in. The two crunched away. The breeze that thinned their voices cooled Senruh's hot face and set the blossoms ringing. It

didn't matter what they said! Or what Pell heard or
thought if he were near, or that deep-voiced soldier, either!
For Senruh had placed him.

He had heard those tones nightly for a season, daily
when the man could steal off-duty. So enamored had he
been that he had spoken of sponsoring Senruh for adoption
into his tribe, of travel, schooling . . . Once the guard had
even tried to buy him, but in those days Senruh's master
had found him far too profitable to part with. Then the
guard's sirdar had heard of his intention, sent the man to a
distant post, and Senruh had not heard from him again.
Until now. His fingers dug into the shower tree's pithy
bark as he denied his younger self's memories, his hopes,
the old betrayals.

A breeze from the sea enveloped him in its scent and the
grass's dry breath. He heard a choking noise quickly strangled, a shuddering gasp. The sounds seemed near.

Pulling his damp robe from his sides, flinching as sweat
trickled into his wounds, Senruh put his old customer from
his mind and crawled closer.

Chapter Twelve

SENRUH HESITATED beneath a wind-tossed giant fern. Behind him a mass of purple windsingers fluted as the breeze riffed tinkling melody from the crystal bells beside them. Senruh gave them only a glance then looked again into the tiny clearing before him backed by a high pile of vines. A figure in an unbleached robe knelt before it. Pell.

The boy's head was bent. His fair curls blazed with the stars' silver light, the veil reddened their gold swirled with inky shadow. He retched, shuddered, wiped his mouth, and sat back heavily on his heels, cradling his hurt arm. The smell was strong.

In the seething darkness beneath the fern, Senruh grinned. Shaking his head, he tiptoed back to strip the chewing leaf creepers. *This should dent the boy's arrogance,* he thought as he stuffed the oval leaves in his pocket. Could his redfruit have been bad? He returned to the clearing.

Pell had not moved. He strangled, drooled a thin fluid onto the broken stems and grass, shut his eyes and swayed. In two strides Senruh was beside him. He put a steadying arm around the boy's shoulders.

Veined lids snapped open, dark blue eyes focused. "You!" Pell leaned into his embrace. Then he caught his breath, tore free, and crouched an arm-length away. "You're dead! I heard you scream, the guards—my fault. Well, I won't let you make me dead, too. I h-hate you!

Abomination! Begone!" Fingers clumsy, he raised them in an averting sign.

Senruh's mouth twitched, amusement overcoming a twinge of hurt. "Shut your teeth! They'll hear you. Soldiers. Followed me. And I'm not dead, not yet." As he jerked his head in the direction of the crystal blooms and the guards, the volcanoes flared beyond them reddening the eastern sky. An earth tremor shook music from the flowers. Senruh looked at Pell's hand. "I thought you didn't believe in demons."

"I don't." The boy's arm lowered. He leaned against the towering mound of vines, hurt arm loose across his knees. "Senruh?" Pell's voice was thin. "You're alive?"

"For now. But keep quiet or neither of us will be for long."

The other boy nodded, sucked air, and choked. Senruh jammed his hands in his pocket, touched crisp bumpy edges. When Pell finished and turned away, hiding his face in the vines' shadow, Senruh held out the leaves.

"Here," he said gruffly. "These will make you feel better. How long have you been doing this?" He glanced uphill toward the beacon then in the guards' direction. "Can you stand? Walk?" But they had to run.

The boy wobbled to his knees but they collapsed under him. Ignoring Senruh's offering, he shook his head. "Since I got here." His ringlets glittered like moonlit ice. But they wouldn't be cold, Senruh thought, they would feel warm and silky. He swallowed. Suddenly angry, he thrust the leaves again at Pell.

"These are chewing leaves, you idiot!" he said. "They settle your stomach. Don't you highlanders know anything? Just don't swallow or you'll throw up some more."

Blue eyes glared at him as Pell crammed the foliage into his mouth. The boy spat and muttered something.

"What?"

"The smell!" Pell burst out. "I aimed that pistol and they—they vanished! And then you— Coward, I'm a coward." His good hand clenched, knuckles turned white.

Relief shook a laugh from Senruh. "Oh, is that all! By the gods, I thought you were sick!" He gripped the boy's shoulders. Bone and sinew filled his hands.

"Haven't you ever heard soldiers talk? Even old campaigners, scarred, notches on their swords like saws, that first time they often . . ." He nodded toward the messes in the ferns.

Pell jerked free. Senruh's palms felt empty. *"You* didn't!"

Senruh remembered his exhilarating run across the plateau. "It took me differently. And I haven't had time to think. But at first—" He pushed back the memory of the gray mists that had been two men; he proffered the leaves once more. "Here. Finish. Make you smell better. Then we can go."

While Pell worked his way through the double handful, Senruh broke off ferns and pulled fresh-scented creepers from the sparkling sandy clay, his ears at the stretch for the guards' return. He crisscrossed green over Pell's spew. "No use hanging out a sign saying we've been by." Senruh jumped up. "Ready?" Dark veils seemed to tumble from the stars. He couldn't see, his ears hummed. He stumbled.

"S-Senruh?"

"I'm fine. Just got up too fast." *But I'm not,* Senruh thought. *And without rest I have to run again, support Pell . . . Help me, goddess!* Had he spoken aloud? Hastily he opened his eyes. But the other boy wasn't jeering, he huddled at Senruh's feet, teeth chattering.

"What—!" Senruh's knees lost their stiffness and he sat. Beyond them, voices growled. Every hair on Senruh's body rose. "The guards!" he whispered. "We've got to leave! Now!"

He helped Pell stagger upright, take a step, another; the boy stumbled and began to shake. "Up! On my shoulders!" But when he hoisted him, Pell was solid, heavy. He couldn't carry the boy all the way to the spaceport, not running.

He set Pell down. Senruh's glance darted around the

clearing, pausing at the tall fluttering vines. The voices grew louder. With a quick breath he raised his arm and propelled the boy, then himself, into the mass of creepers.

Leaves and stems swished behind them. Senruh turned. Frantically he interlaced vines while, behind him, Pell grabbed at branches to keep from falling. Their entry hidden, Senruh lunged at the other boy, pushing him into gray crackling twigs. The mound's outer lushness had been deceptive. Inside all was dry and hung with only a few leaves' crisp corpses. One dropped, clicking on the dusty stems.

"What was that!" The deep voice sounded nearer. And nervous. Senruh's heart banged his ribs even as he felt a small glow of pride.

"Pell!" he breathed. "Your lizard imitation!" But Pell had both hands clapped over shaking jaws. Light plucked at the clearing.

Beside Senruh, the other boy's knees buckled. He snatched at Senruh. Off-balance, Senruh fell with him, twigs slashing his face and arms, chattering in a hundred arid voices. The boys hugged the ground. Guards stamped through ferns. Just beyond Pell's feet they set the flowers chiming.

"Mott take those bells," the rougher voice said. "Can't hear a thing over them. Might as well carry a trumpet." Under the music's cover Senruh hitched them both along a rustling pallet of leaves. His shoulder bumped hardness. He groped along it. A ramp! He looked up. Were those columns in the middle of the vines? And a dome? The design . . . Remembered temple paintings floated behind his eyes. He put his mouth by Pell's ear.

"If I break through those stems, can you follow? I think this was a gods' summer bower. There's a superstition in the barracks about curses; most soldiers won't go near them. At least the ones I knew won't." He thought of the temple murals picturing the ancient gods, tall as young trees, strolling the shadowless dusk to pavilions such as this one. Other icons showed the gods, fanned by their

little favorites, sipping cooling drinks from thin golden
cups, heads tilted, listening to their created flowers' songs.
Senruh's mental pictures faded into the scratchy, rustling
dark.

Curls brushed Senruh's mouth. Pell had nodded. Skin
roughening, Senruh gave the boy a quick look then dropped
to his belly and wormed forward. He glanced over his
shoulder beyond the glimmer of fair hair.

Breathing curses, the guard Senruh knew followed his
partner through the melodious blooms. Between the
meshed branches Senruh watched powder sift like strewn
stars from the flowers' central prisms; it glittered on
smooth petals and thick dark leaves as the blossoms short-
ened their stamens, tuning themselves to each others'
choirs. He heard a ripple of flutes and the guards were out.
Senruh lowered his head and followed the ramp to the center of the vines.

When the boys could no longer maneuver between
trunks as thick as a man's shoulders, they crowded into a
corner made by the ramp and the ancient pavilion's curving wall. Curiosity jumping in him, Senruh got to his
knees.

A head-high floor perhaps three man-lengths wide
formed a base for red and black spiralled columns supporting a dome that erased the midnight sky. The dome
was lit by a gray glow from the floor. Through the
branches netting the entrance, Senruh could see the floor's
gray translucence empty of leaves, crawlers, even dust. It
illuminated a low circle of wall filled with images of the
gods, black-eyed and reed thin, in their narrow archaic
robes. As in the city temples, they did not look outward to
Naphar or upward to the stars. Instead they locked their
gazes forever upon each other. The mural seemed bumpy.

Outside, steps crashed. Light shot through the outer
leaves and inner branches. It slid over the figures. They
seemed to move.

Senruh's heart knocked his breastbone. He made the

averting sign as, below him, Pell yanked at his hem. "Get dow—" The command ended in a gasp.

There is no magic, Senruh my son, only those who prefer the ease of superstition to reason, the old scribe's voice quavered again in Senruh's mind. Pulses tapping, he forced himself to take a last hard look at the seemingly living gods. And saw that they were painted on the tips of finger-long cones; the play of light and shadow about the cones' bases gave the figures their apparent life. His fingers relaxed.

"Senruh!" He ignored Pell's urgent whisper, the lanterns' harsher light, the strengthening tones of the guards. The antique figures drew him. *Come,* they seemed to call, *we have the power to give you peace, safety, to free you from accountability; all we require from you is your will.*

He took a step forward. He reached for the curiously intact ramp . . .

Outside, the crystals jangled.

White glare touched his fingers. From below Pell yanked Senruh's robe, hard. As if felled by a spear, Senruh dropped. Dizzy, heart thumping, he hugged the goddess's earth. Beside him, Pell's teeth began to rattle.

Beyond the vines, the voice Senruh knew said, "Don't see anything, but we'll make a couple circles, carry my lantern, use yours as a marker. Daggers out!"

Light swayed across the dusty leaves. Senruh flung his arm over his eyes. By his shoulder, Pell shoved his good hand between clicking jaws. The boy retched and yanked it out; his teeth clacked together. They sounded very loud. Enormously dilated eyes stared into Senruh's. Pell sat up.

"—go!" he jerked out. "No use, take us both!"

For a moment Senruh basked in the promise of safety. Ready to nod, he glanced up. Pell's illness, the lantern's shadows, gave the boy's face a stark maturity. *I know how you will look when you are a man,* Senruh thought.

Pell wavered to his feet. Senruh's hand shot out. "No!" He jerked a fistful of robe downward.

Pell went sprawling, unguarded jaws clattering like a fall of stones, one arm swinging, his other hand and his feet scrabbling between the stems for purchase. Senruh leaped on him; they rolled, Pell gasped with pain. The boys' harsh breathing, the leaves whispering beneath them, and the soldiers' footsteps were the only sounds, except for the wind and the flowers' clamorous singing.

Heat tore Senruh's back. His sword cut had opened. With a gasp he pinned the boy beneath him. "We escape together or not at all!" he hissed. "Or don't you high-landers keep your word?"

Pell lay rigid, his teeth clicking like finger shells. Then, to Senruh's intense surprise, he lunged upward and buried his face in Senruh's neck. "Th-thanks!" Two hot drops splashed Senruh's shoulder. A callused hand gripped his back until he thought his lash cuts must force him to cry out. The hand felt cold. He looked; Pell's hands were mottled. But not entirely blue, he reassured himself, not yet.

Feet tramped near. Pell's face burrowed deeper. The lantern glowed brighter, then light blasted Senruh's eyes. Behind it a great head peered in. A timeless moment dragged by.

"Nothing. Bower. Bones. Columns intact, so the old defenses are still up. Sure as Mott, I'm not going in there!" The gruff voice retreated, the light withdrew, ponderous steps continued their circuit.

Senruh released his breath and loosened Pell's fingers. "Hurts," he breathed in the boy's ear. "Whip cuts." As the guards outside surprised a riffle from a stray bed of windsingers, he added, "Thank the goddess for superstition." Pell didn't answer.

Senruh glanced down at the curls splayed across his chest, at the strong young body shaking a scrupulous finger-width from his. Something stirred inside him.

He and the scribe had helped other little halflings who suffered as Pell did. Beaten, hardly used by half-breed gangs, they often shook like this. They were only Kakano, weak . . . but Pell! Pell, who had bickered and scuffled with him, killed for them both, feared to be touched . . .

"Ho! Broken stems!" The gruff guard's shout came from the ferns where Senruh had first landed. His old customer tramped toward it. A crystalline music glinted on the wind. "Bring that lantern!" the rough-voiced man called. "Gods-blasted wilderness, I can feel an eye in every tree. It's unnatural!"

Senruh's haunches bunched. When they found the rest of his trail . . . The other's steps halted.

"Broken stems!" said the voice Senruh knew. "You've got your big flat feet right in the middle of them! Blunder-foot! Make enough trouble and we'll get no pallet time at all tonight." As the other guard grumbled they moved away. A thin slide of lantern light swung through the bower. Senruh willed himself to release his breath, to unwind his muscles.

Leaves scraped as Pell drew up his knees. A bare toe brushed Senruh's ankle. It felt cold as winter. Murmuring, the boy rolled his head back and forth. Senruh's heart bumped. Pell would be babbling soon. Then, if the guards didn't find and kill them both, he would fall into a chilly sleep, fail to breathe, and die. *No!* Senruh thought. He could try . . . Beyond the vines the guards' voices faded into the wind. Arms stiff with self-consciousness, Senruh reached out to draw Pell near.

"Pervert!" The boy slammed his knee into Senruh's belly. *"Nobody* touches me like that!" Pell hissed through chattering teeth. "Not even my equals! And *you!* An oversized— Just because I let you h-hide me!"

When Senruh could seize a scrap of air, he grabbed Pell's curls and mashed the boy's face against his chest. "By Mott's demons!" he breathed, "you want to get us killed, shouting like that?" The other *mmmph*ed and struggled. "The gods gave us bodies, hands . . . What do you think they're for? And as for this—!" Anger—and something else—slid his fingers down the boy's back to the top of his hip. It felt firm, well-muscled. Senruh kneaded it. ". . . .

this is a pleasant pastime, no more . . ." He doubted the boy heard him; Pell was throwing his shoulders to one side while Senruh pinned his ribs. The leaves and twigs shattered loudly beneath them. ". . . and no less. Ow!" Pell sank his teeth into Senruh's arm. Recalled to himself, Senruh let go the curve of flesh.

He smacked a hand over Pell's mouth and listened. A sea wind rasped stems, stirring a breath of mold from the long-dead leaves. The guards' voices were faint. Senruh put his mouth by Pell's ear.

"You're not going to die for a stupid highland scruple! I'm only warning you, you fool, so you can run! And I, uh, I shouldn't have . . ." His voice trailed off. Pell had stopped tussling. Cautiously Senruh withdrew his hand.

Pell stared up at him. He licked colorless lips. "All right," he whispered. "Only war companions, heroes . . ." He gulped and stopped.

After the first halting words Senruh ceased to listen. Worried, he checked Pell's shallow breathing, lifted his mottled, blue-nailed hands. He could not waste any more time, Senruh thought. Already it might be too late.

Gingerly he lowered himself beside the boy. Feeling shy as he had not in cycles, he pulled the wary body toward him. It came. Enchantment flushed his veins like that he had felt when the orange flier first trusted him enough to touch his wrist. Against his chest, the other's heartbeat quickened. He reached down and hooked Pell's knees over his thighs.

"Pallet touch!" Pell started. Senruh snatched his hand away.

"The blood flows better when your, uh, feet are up." Listening to his careful explanation, Pell's rigidity and tremors lessened. Good. Above the beetles' click and lizards' scurry and the suspirations of wind and bells, the guards' voices were only a remote sonority. Senruh could risk more talk. Now what would the scribe tell him to say?

"We'll get out of this, Pell. Even with their lanterns

they're almost blind. And long before the moon rises you'll have stopped shaking, then you'll snap back fast . . ."

The boy's head lay heavily on his shoulder. Senruh's whip and sword cuts burned, the wounds the bearers had inflicted ached. Head buzzing, he tucked the boy's robe around his icy feet, turned him, and pulled him tight against him. Pell drew in his breath, as did Senruh. He had forgotten that beneath his robe the other wore no cloth.

Breathing a little harder, Senruh tried to shrug. He put his arm around the boy, sliding his fingers under the locks at Pell's nape to the tight sinews there. The other swallowed and scarcely seemed to breathe. Senruh worked lower, slow and impersonal as his lady's touch had never been, till Pell released a shuddering breath and relaxed against Senruh's chest and hip and thigh, attentive to his unceasing croon.

". . . and then I'll tell you what flew to me from beside the sea. Have you looked at the ocean yet, Pell? What our priests call Iammu's kingdom?" The boy shook his head. His curls stroked Senruh's throat. Warmth spread through Senruh and in sudden unreasoning joy he inhaled the salt breeze, the smell of old leaves and stone, and the scent of Pell's skin. His hand hovered above the straight strong back, the hair pale as moonbeams. No. The boy did not want that. He despised Senruh for what he was. He had said so.

Anger and remembered grief blew on buried, half-forgotten embers, spurted tiny flames. Senruh ignored them and continued his steady soothing. Beyond the mesh of stems and twigs and blackened swinging leaves, the wind rushed and set the bells to ringing. Beneath their high sweet song lay the distant thud of feet. They ambled nearer. Caught in dreams, Senruh scarcely heard them.

"You'll like the waves, Pell. They roll in forever from beyond the world's end . . ." His fingers drifted upward. As if by chance they tangled in the boy's hair. Pell stiffened. Outside, twigs snapped. Light ached in Senruh's eyes.

"Oops!" The gruff voice could have been beside them.

Senruh's pulses clapped together. He let Pell go, he pulled his feet beneath him, flexed them . . .

"That's right, drop the lantern, get us Campfire of the Cycle Award, I don't think!" The guard Senruh knew sounded farther away. Through latticed branches a white-metal blade spun miniature suns into Senruh's eyes. Senruh pictured the glittering blade slicing his inner arm, his living thigh. Outside, the gruff-voiced guard followed the other, grumbling.

". . . not a sign of them. These runners give me a pain in the backside. Murderous little scum! Catch one, haul a screamer back to the Slave Pens and you're asking for a knife in the ribs or for some citizen to call quiet and heave his slops on your head or both. Now, what *I* like is waiting for me back in those barracks. Best little pallet warmer I've had in two seasons! No, make it four. Lively, do anything!"

"Hush yourself! Remember those eyes. And ears to go with them."

"Oh, worry, worry! You can squirt blood that way."

Feet tramped through the ferns and the flowers' trilling harmonies until at last the voices moved uphill. As the lanterns withdrew, in the nook between ramp and wall and twisting stems, shadow overlaid the light. Only the bower's glow faded its black to gray.

Sweating with relief, awaiting his night sight's return, Senruh palmed circles across Pell's shoulders. The boy leaned against him, face hidden, his slow breaths fragrant with chewing leaf. He reached up; his good arm crooked possessively around Senruh's waist. Skin prickling, Senruh eased away. The boy muttered a protest; his grip tightened.

Shock jumped in Senruh's nerves. Then he smiled. Of course. Pell must be asleep. Senruh looked forward to twitting him about this! The boy's weight was warm and comfortable. Senruh's pulse beat a little faster.

Mind drifting, he gazed up at the leaves' changing fili-

gree that surrounded the bower's dome, a great poised gem
of night. Absently he kept his hands gliding over Pell's
smoothly muscled sides and back. Once the guards finished their circuit, he and Pell could head over the hill.
Then only the ruined meeting place of the gods lay between them and the spaceport. For the first time Senruh
thought he might live past moonrise.

On the crest above them the soldiers wrangled. The
gruff-voiced one declaimed:

"Oh, noble comrade, I swear to the goddess I'll keep
every last one of her curd-eating children from the off-
worlders and their accursed machines. For a single life
thread lost to the Weavers of Destiny changes the goddess's design irrevocably! And thank Sassurum that our
nobles selflessly take such evils only upon themselves,
thus keeping the abominations of off-world jewels and
scrolls and living pictures from besmirching us common-
ers' spotless innocence! How's that?"

"That mouth of yours is going to get us thrown where
they don't allow pallet warmers or much of anything else!
Now, about that robe tosser we're hunting. Did the wall
guard say anything more?" The sound of voices and footsteps diminished. Abruptly the hill cut them off as the men
descended its other side.

Senruh looked up. Only a misty swirl of the veil showed
through the twigs and leaves. Soon the evening moon
would rise. Then, when the guards had sight, could Pell
run? He glanced down. The boy had turned his head, the
bower's glow lit his cheek and eyes. Senruh's hand stopped
in mid-caress. Pell wasn't asleep.

His clear profile, as new and as old as a hero's on a coin,
wore an inward look of grave happiness. Involuntarily
Senruh's arms tightened. The lean form moved with them.
Senruh tingled from arch to groin. The boy was alive with
leashed untutored eagerness.

Perhaps that slaver taught him more than I thought. Senruh's eyebrows rose as he remembered Pell's scorn for how
he earned his coin.

He ran slow fingers down Pell's spine; he brushed them across his hip, naked beneath the summer robe. Pell shivered and pushed closer. Heat burned Senruh's face. *It wouldn't take much,* he thought. *Bring him to the point then ease off*—a technique Ariahnne had taught him to wring promises from frantic nobles at her feasts—*he'd be begging for it! From me!* Senruh's heart began to pound. Throat almost too tight for breath, behind him he seemed to hear a jeweled demon rustle pointed wings and whisper, *Try!*

His hand wandered over firm buttocks to the boy's thigh. Now, surely . . .

But Pell said nothing. His legs parted uneasily. Gaze fixed on the other's coloring face, Senruh inserted a palm. The boy swallowed and looked away. Through the flimsy robe, with increasing freedom, Senruh fondled long thighs, knees, tight-muscled calves; Pell sighed and slipped his arm around Senruh's neck.

Exultation showered like gold through Senruh's veins. He would show that little . . . show him . . . what? Breath sharp in his chest, Senruh pushed up the boy's hem, bared a cool ankle. It lay heavy in his palm. He lifted, stroked it. The boy allowed it. But Pell hated . . . Tomorrow he would rage, be ashamed . . .

As Senruh fingered thin-skinned projections and silky hollows, the other's breath quickened. Eyes hot, thoughts becoming only glints in a growing haze of heat and sensuality, Senruh heard a voice in his mind cry, *It doesn't matter! He's willing. They're made for this! Why should the slaver take his pleasure here and not me? And, besides, there's time . . .*

Pulses banging in his ears, Senruh smoothed the boy's robe, palms memorizing what lay beneath.

The busy night sounds resumed: the whisk and ululating calls of burrowers and climbers, the night flyers' rattles, a breeze shimmering through the crystal flowers drawing out the throaty song of the windsingers behind them. Senruh bent, pressed his lips to the salty tendrils

clinging to Pell's cheek, and whispered his story of the flying lizard and his first glimpse of it that morning. Now and
then Pell interrupted with a quiet question, factual at
first—those Senruh answered readily—but soon more
probing. Senruh's returns faltered. *Pallet babble!* a scandalized voice exclaimed in his head. But he ignored it and,
face hot, stammered a reply. And all the while, undis-
cussed by either boy, his hands grew bolder.

"Tell me!" Pell drew down Senruh's head. Shyly he
smoothed Senruh's lashes against his cheek. "Have you
ever loved as the poets do, or the heroes, or even . . ." He
stopped as Senruh teasingly explored him in detail. ". . .
even like that v-verse you sang?" he husked when he
found his voice again. "Fancies. Have you been with
many? Were they . . . ? They know more than I do, don't
they? And they can recite, argue philosophy, sing, besides
the—the other."

Senruh grinned. As if he owned it now, he cupped the
boy's throat, his fingers moving with its vibrations and
convulsive swallow. "Well, your arguing's fine and your
lizard talk back there was a lot more use than if you'd
burst into song." He spread his hand on Pell's chest, rev-
eling in his knowledge of the boy's every pulse and breath.
The wind gusted, crescendoing the flowers' phrases. Gently Senruh pulled the boy's hurt arm above his head, lifted
the other high, and stroked firmly beneath them. Pell
closed his eyes.

"No, but tell me, Senruh, have you ever loved?" His
voice sounded drugged with pleasure. "Not like this, I
know you've . . . I mean when you just see someone and
feel glad they're alive?"

"Well . . ." His hands grew busy. When Pell moved and
groaned, Senruh swallowed. He had meant to wait, hold
off. Why? No matter, he would remember in a while . . .
He walked his fingers up the boy's chest to lay them over
the heart that hammered there. "You first," he husked.

After a moment, Pell managed, "My mother."

". . . and?"

"My father. But he didn't want it, oh Senruh, I never knew—! And you make me laugh . . ." Callused hands found Senruh's, skimmed up dark sleeves, and dug into his arms. For a moment Senruh held the boy, smoothing the muscle sheathing his sides. Pell caught Senruh's hand and carried it to his cheek. "Don't! Can't think. A—a pot mender."

Pell's eyes opened. He licked his lips and continued. "He and his tribe came by our farm, barrows loaded with dented pans, buttons, laces. You've seen them?" He glanced up at Senruh who nodded and pushed moist ringlets from the boy's flushed face. Pell recaptured his hand. "If you want to hear—! That old pot mender always had a toy for me—my father didn't believe in them. Images, he called them. And when Father was out of sight, the pot mender told me tales. Later when I could read, he brought histories, adventures, songs . . . He taught me the little I know of the world."

Pell's eyes darkened. He drew Senruh downward until their breaths mingled. "Why don't we—? I can talk anytime." When Senruh did not answer, Pell frowned. "I used to get so tired debating my father's everlasting ethics and philosophy! But I'll argue some for you. Or recite poetry. If that's what they do, just so you'll . . . I want to please you." He turned his head, his lips moved against Senruh's palm.

Tenderness shivered through Senruh. "No!" he heard himself say roughly. He thumbed the boy's lips, cheekbones, jaw. "You don't have to do anything, just be . . ."

And for the second time that night astonishment opened like a chasm in Senruh. He hid his face in the soft hair. *What is this?* he thought. *Pell gave me no coin, I gain no advantage, so how could I? I've never once for—for love—*

Inexpert lips moved against his throat, callused hands roamed about him engulfing him in a flame of sweetness that burned away all thought, all desire, but to give pleasure, utter joy. As the supple body moved against him, hot cheek pressed to his, Senruh's loins tightened. *Now!* he thought, reached down, and with both hands grasped the other's compact buttocks. He tensed; Pell strained close, his breathing harsh in Senruh's ear. Senruh's fingers stiffened. Digging deep, he ground the other's hips and sex against his own.

Pell caught his breath. Heart shaking against Senruh's chest, he worked warm bare toes through the leaves to the other's sandal. "What—what do I do now?" he whispered.

"I don't know. Just tell me. Whatever you want!"

Earth tremors of protectiveness rippled through Senruh's loins. Gently he laid Pell down and straightened his robe and useless arm. "Nothing," he husked. "Just lie back and let me . . ." The boy gave him a hazy smile, darkened blue eyes soft with stars. Senruh caught his breath. His master's tones echoed in his head: *Don't do anything back, scum, that costs extra!* Even as his pulses thrummed, Senruh's lips twitched. If the merchant could see him now! What else had Pell wanted to know? Oh, he couldn't talk about that! But the boy had asked. And Senruh wanted to give . . . He cleared his throat.

"I have loved, Pell. The old scribe who taught me, my—my lady. More, if you count . . ." he began with difficulty. His face warmed with the telling. Beneath him the boy listened, eyes dark as midnight wells. His questions grew intimate. As steadily as he could, Senruh replied.

Till, talking ended, he held Pell close and caressed him. The boy shivered. Senruh felt the thrust of his desire. Senruh raised himself on an elbow and with slow familiarity slid a hand down Pell's robe, damp now and clinging. He nudged the strong thighs. They opened. The boy's flesh throbbed in his palm. The last rags of Senruh's calculations frayed and dropped away.

"Shall I finish?" he whispered.

Pell's movements gave him answer. And in that moment like so many others in the bazaar and nobles' palaces, Senruh's mind cleared. He remembered how he had started this and why. Throat tight, he recalled all the words the boy had coaxed from him. *He'll laugh like the others!* Senruh thought. *Fool!* and, *Fool again!* His hands moved and tightened.

"Ah! Gods!" Pell cried out. Beneath them the leaves released the scent of a thousand forgotten summers while above, the dying vines scolded sibilantly in a stray irresolute breeze.

"Say it!" Senruh hissed, his brief power acid on his tongue.

The fair head turned. His eyes dilated and shiny with tears, Pell looked straight at him. "Yes, finish. Please." His voice shook, then firmed. "I love you, Senruh." And he began the warrior's pledge.

Senruh's mockery died. As Pell chanted the antique phrases giving loyalty and honor to life's end and beyond, Senruh relaxed his hold. He gazed beyond the boy; through the stems and waving outer leaves he glimpsed a palm's width of the veil dragging a scatter of stars below the sea's horizon to Arob Shamsi, the sunset land of the unhallowed dead. No fear dwelt in that place, or delight, or remorse. Suddenly, passionately, Senruh wished himself there. For soon, by the pledge's austere requirements, he must tell the boy all the truth. Gently, he let him go. Pell murmured then looked up, questioning. But first, Senruh thought, just this once . . .

Eyes stinging, he smoothed the boy's hair, lowered his head, and kissed Pell on the mouth. Lips closed, the boy kissed him back. Like a child. He smelled of salt and foaming sand. He touched Senruh's cheek and lay back.

"You're beautiful," Pell whispered. "When I first saw you, the sun shone on you—I didn't know hair could be so black! Or eyes so dark. I couldn't look away. Then you saw me . . ."

"But you scowled."

"You remembered!" He gripped Senruh's arm, his mouth curved. "You stared through me. So arrogant. Sullen! I thought you were angry, that everyone gaped at you like I did and that you hated it."

"Idiot! I was admiring you." Senruh's voice was thick.

"Really?"

Senruh nodded. He must tell the boy. Now. His lips parted. In his mind his master gibed, *Pallet babble!* and *Only tell them what they want to hear, scum!* No sound came. Oblivious, Pell rushed on.

"I never noticed your size, your robe, nothing! I thought you were a visiting prince, a scholar. Then, later, when I saw— And you said you were that man's slave and that you lay with anyone . . ." Pell swallowed. "No, look at me!" He grasped Senruh's chin and turned it. "I felt betrayed. Jealous of everyone who had owned you. Touched you. I didn't want to feel that way. When you grow up with just lizards and book scrolls and huge drugged slaves, not much feeling comes your way. I didn't know how . . ." He gazed steadily at Senruh. "That's why I said what I did. And made you angry. I'm sorry. I was then, too. But now—!" A smile lit his shadowed face like flame.

Senruh's throat tightened. "Pell . . ." As he spoke he grew conscious of an ebb and flow in the voice of the breeze, a roughness beneath the windsingers' obbligato. The guards! He half-sat and squinted between thick columns and meshed branches toward the hill. At its crest, light grayed the night. The unevenness in the breeze's song became the soldiers' grumble.

"Pell, they're coming. Before they get too close I have to tell you—" The boy wasn't listening. Eyes intent, he unlaced the first thongs of Senruh's robe. He slipped his hand inside, he flattened his palm over Senruh's suddenly fast-beating heart.

"There's never—ever—been anyone but you," Pell whispered. "No real friends. That slaver"—his mouth straightened —"didn't count." His pupils grew large. "You know all of me now. You feel so good; I want to hold you, see all of you." His gaze dropped. Across his lids, black leaf shadow danced with red and silver chips of light. "I've never talked like that. Not even thought— But I feel I can with you. Only—don't you have anything to say to me?"

His voice broke and he withdrew his hand. He fixed his gaze on the swinging thongs.

"You can see, handle, anything you want!" Senruh had to clear his throat before he could continue. "Of course, right now I'm pretty battered. And sure, you can say whatever . . . I'll try to answer. But Pell, I have to tell you—" His thoughts skittered like trapped lizards between the guards—he could almost distinguish words in the wind and among the bells—and his confession. The scribe said the goddess's second chance existed if one had the wit to recognize it. He clung to that. "Pell, I—"

"Do I disgust you?" the other asked, low-voiced. "When I shouted at the slaver that this"—he ran a newly knowledgeable hand across Senruh's flanks and belly; Senruh sucked in a breath—"is forbidden between large and small, he laughed. But in my highlands!"

White light topped the hill and set the shadows swinging. The rougher voice spoke above the wind and the chiming, hymning flowers. ". . . still some pallet time . . . back to the fjord; they better be there or sirdar will have us searching under every rock and beetle!" Pell froze. His hand groped for Senruh's and clutched it. Senruh gathered his feet under him. Beside him Pell did the same. The leaves beneath them whispered then held their breath.

The voice Senruh knew grew loud. ". . . searched everyplace else . . . this time *I'll* have a look." Outside the shell of fluttering leaves a tall silhouette bent low. A lantern thrust into the sticks. They popped like burning wood, releasing an old dry scent. Senruh grasped Pell's arms and shoved the boy behind him.

"What—!" Pell struggled.

"Shhh!" Senruh sat on him.

The lantern swung in an arc, the shadows fled on either side. It dimmed the bower's gray glow, shot nearer, and pinned Senruh in a blaze of light. The man behind it caught his breath. "You! I'd hoped . . ." Senruh blinked, eyes tearing from the brightness.

"Please." Before he knew he was going to speak, his lips framed the word.

"You poor stupid scum." The other's voice was just above a whisper. "They'll catch you, you must know that. If not here, then at the spaceport. Why couldn't you have waited?"

"What are you muttering about in there?" the other guard called. "Those southern outposts got you talking to yourself? Or"—his voice sharpened,—"is there somebody in there?"

Senruh's old customer said nothing. The singing breeze carried the barracks' scent of honing oil and metal and sweat through the branches. Senruh felt weak with memory.

"Mmph!" Beneath him Pell bucked. Casually, Senruh leaned back and flattened the boy's knees. Outside, the man made a sudden movement.

"No!" he shouted to the other guard. "You were right." His head and shoulders turned, the light swerved then came back. Senruh squinted into it, wondering if the soldier had changed. As if the words were twisted from him, the man's hesitant voice breathed, "It was my career. I meant to—" The man withdrew.

"Nothing." Heavy sandals crunched through ferns, then hushed across the tussocks. The soldiers' murmurs faded into the sigh of wind and flowers and the deep quiet cadence of the sea.

Senruh cleared his throat, released a cross, disheveled Pell. "What was all that about? I can fight!"

Senruh grasped his arms, careful of the hurt one, and pulled him close. Pell leaned rigidly against Senruh's chest.

"We can go, now," Senruh said into his hair. He smoothed the boy's shoulders. His palms recognized their every contour. "We have to—they'll be back. But—" Pell relaxed against him, breath warm on his throat. "You don't disgust me," Senruh whispered. "You shame me . . . Stop, Pell, and listen!"

The boy's hand paused. He glanced up and grinned. "Just giving you something to remember me by in case— Don't look so sad! I won't if you don't want me to."

"But that's it. You wouldn't want—this—if, well, if I hadn't tricked you." Senruh fixed his gaze on a crust of leaf beyond the fair head. It was rimmed with the bower's gray radiance. The drab light overflowed the ancient stone. Lapping high on the columns, it rippled over naked stems to light Pell's curls. The boy looked up, eyes wide and still.

"Tricked?" he whispered.

Senruh nodded. "I wanted to show you you weren't above a little body fun. With me. I forgot what the scribe said, that you emptyheads can have feelings just like us, and the soldiers' talk, that after almost getting killed you say, do, things you wouldn't . . . Oh, Pell!" Throat aching, he watched the other's laughter die.

"Nobody ever wanted me before," Senruh plowed on. "Only the—the use of me." He swallowed. "So how could I suspect you . . ." No more sound would come.

Pell moved his head as if he shook off a dream. "Empty-head," he breathed. "You never forgave. I thought you wanted me. You didn't. Don't." The dark blue eyes looked blank. Senruh hardly listened. He was readying the last of his confession.

"Anyway, if we do much more, I'm going to hurt," he brought out. "Today, my lady's bearers—"

"I know. I'm not stupid, Senruh. I'm just a fool! I wanted to make it up to you."

"Oh." A sheet of hot blood rolled up Senruh's throat to his face. When he could speak again he said, "I wanted this too, if that helps. More than I ever—" He swallowed. "Later, if you still . . . Well, I promise, I—I'll do anything you like."

"Anything I like!" Pell twisted out of Senruh's hold to crouch before him, taut as a strung war bow. "That's not what I wanted from you! You're nothing but a priest's pup-pet, banging away like wood wherever you're told! I wouldn't get coin the way you do, not for all the Ensai's treasure! I'd rather have just a little and earn it! And save this for—" His face contorted. " 'Lively. Do anything.' And how did you plan to entertain me next time?"

Pell jumped up and shoved blindly through the dusty stems. Unable to move, Senruh watched the gray glow fade from the boy's robe and hair as the night's dark arms reclaimed him. With a crash Pell was out. Through dead branches Senruh watched his blond ringlets flare with light. They were unique, Senruh thought. Unique as the orange flying lizard. And lost. By his own doing. He dug his nails into his palms. Blood slipped under his fingertips.

Pell skidded back to him, almost shouting.

"Well, come on! We can't stay here! You heard that guard! Oh, gods!" The boy's voice cracked. "Come *on*!" He turned and ran.

Senruh got to his feet. The bower's uncolored brightness filled his eyes. He leaned against the pavilion's low wall and looked again at the thin strange gods and their secret smiles. They had power. It seethed, prickling, all about him. Was loss of Choice so much to pay? He reached up, gripped the ramp's sharp dustless edge, ready to heave himself upward. His fingers brushed into a lightweight heap, roughness . . .

Loose white objects, some round, some long, rattled down his shoulders and arms. He jumped back. Bones! Lizard, crawler, human . . . Shuddering, he kicked clear and thrashed into the path Pell had broken. The glow dimmed behind him.

And I thought that guard superstitious. The gods do have defenses. Only luck, and Pell, saved me. The scribe was wrong, Senruh thought as he battled through the dusty stems, *and wrong, too, about that second chance.* For the old man was aged after all, and blind. It was not his fault that when he could no longer see its ways the world had changed. Eyes stinging, Senruh hurled himself through the last cool-leafed vines.

As his fingers flew, weaving them together, he glanced back through waving branches to the plateau.

On the star-washed line between land and sea, lights clustered. Two lanterns bobbed toward them—the guards who had just searched the woods. The pair cast long shadows toward the sea; behind them, an edgy moonlight bleached the grass.

Senruh's head whipped around. From behind the volcanoes' fiery cones, Shirah, white-faced daughter of Asherah and L'h, peered down. Her stark white radiance gave the night-blind Rabu the gift of sight. Above the sea's deep rhythms he heard their distant welcoming howls.

Fear's old habit welled high. Brushing at his eyes, Senruh turned his face uphill, set it toward the spacers' beacon, and raced after Pell.

Chapter Thirteen

SENRUH PEERED out from behind a tumbled column. His skin seemed to draw up on his bones. So this was the fabled meeting place of the gods. Its paving stones and shattered pillars gleamed white beneath the encroaching ferns and trees. The weathered ruins stretched almost to the hilltop, last barrier before the spaceport and safety.

The boy gazed at the great square, its blocks broken and upended. He thought of the strange tall gods who had once strolled the night to claim the small mortals drawn here by their Time of Need. A need the gods built into their seed's seed so that, through the generations, when the Yearning clamored in their blood, small humankind grew blind and deaf to all they owed to tribe and city, work and self-respect. Aching to submit to a near-immortals' touch, they gathered here. And, chosen, became servants who could not betray, gaudy playthings who could not deny their gods' strangest pleasures.

Senruh squinted at toppled pediments, reduced by the moonlight to triangular glimmers choked with weeds. Flesh creeping, he scuttled along a fluted column toward the square, and its promise of concealment in the gaps between the paving blocks. As his hands and knees scuffed the cold earth, it breathed musty dreams of antique lives mixed now with the dust and forgotten. He squatted behind an elaborate capital, straining toward the friendly trees behind him, trying not to listen to his memories.

They whispered with the bazaar singers' voices, chanting the familiar ending of the gods. Deserted by their fellows for more forgiving stars and suns, a handful of stubborn, foolish, devoted gods remained. Cursed by the goddess they defied, they began to rot. As the huge bodies festered, their wills grew lax, their control of their small minions loosened. Through the long cycles of decay the immortals' thoughts worked on, undimmed.

Thus no thin haze dulled the gods' perceptions when, on a night like this more than a thousand cycles past, small mortals swarmed through echoing fire-mountain palaces, routed out their dying gods and brought them here, moonlight bright on blade and nail and tooth. Wild was the feasting on that night when, at last, the gods and their servant children merged.

Refusing to think of the blood and fear soaked into this ground, Senruh looked to the top of the hill. There the spacers' beacon spread dazzling wings across the night. Just below it, in silhouette, the blocks and pillars leaned—if he could squirm through it, the quickest, safest way to the spacers. In the city he and Pell had agreed to ignore superstition and take just such a route if they could find it. Pell must be in there! Senruh raced across the silvered open, skidded, fell into the dark.

Roots and dirt slid with him, clods and pebbles spattered his face. He grasped a block—his hand slipped and his nails scrabbled in earth; he jarred to a stop, glanced back, and listened. The rising wind carried the distant flowers' faint iridescent harmonies. Above his column, light sifted through a storm of leaves. It shone on the great stone head of a woman, her carved locks stirred by a breeze stilled a millennium past, her blank blind eyes fixed on the stars she would never reach.

Senruh glanced up at the sky she had contemplated for longer than his race had history. He thought of the galaxies unravelling before her gaze as, all about her, cities rose and language grew and the world changed.

He heard a shout, a tinkling chord; he whipped around. Far below in the sparkle and flash of the crystal-stamened flowers, spear tips tossed back the light. A contralto called orders, the jangle of mail and crash of sandaled feet divided to flow noisily around—but not through—the ruins. As he turned, breath short, Senruh glanced at the column he had left and the woman's head that was its capital. The branches above it rasped together, hiding the woman once more in anonymous moving shade. Senruh lowered himself between the paving blocks. On his belly, he squirmed into the goddess's bitter-smelling earth.

Crushed roots' pungence teased Senruh's nostrils; he lifted his head to stare into a span of black slashed by moonbeams. The light filtered through chinks between the jumbled blocks. He had wormed a long way on elbows, hips, and knees. They smarted. His wounds had opened. Where dirt was working into them they ached and stung. He wriggled further.

Senruh's hand closed on a chunk of cool, furred moss, its roots still damp. Someone—or something—had been this way. Recently. Senruh lay still, snatching at breath, great clawed lizards prowling behind his eyes, or the monstrous horn-footed guardians of the gods that lived on, and on . . .

Outside, the guards called: soprano, contralto, bass. Swords and lances thudded in the woods below while an eldritch nocturne tinkled on the wind. As its fluting tones ebbed, Senruh heard a grating sound just ahead. It stopped. He heard harsh panting.

His forehead bumped a root. Yellow and white comets shot behind his lids. He rubbed his head, tensed his haunches, and set his hand down. It closed on a warm bare foot. The foot kicked. Grasping it, Senruh pulled his feet under him, ready to follow around the corner. Sticky clots full of pebbles, then fresh blood, slipped in his palm. The foot jerked free. It whipped back to kick again.

"Pell, no! It's me!"

A mop of pale curls replaced the foot as the fair boy crawled into a patch of moonlight. "Oh. Where have you been? You could have warned me, thickhead. Or come a little sooner and helped." Pell gestured toward the blocks. The earth around them was disturbed. "Be careful!" he said as Senruh moved to follow him around them.

"Oh, I always bellow out where I am when I'm running from the guards," Senruh said as he eased around the leaning stones. "Of course, sometimes I just send a scroll with a map saying, 'Here I am, come and get me.' " He pulled himself into the space where Pell crouched. Senruh avoided the shadowed blue gaze, heaved himself to a sitting position, and looked around. They were in a chamber the size of a root storage bin. Overhead, stars winked between overlapping blocks wrapped with vines.

"What did you want help with?" he asked. "And what happened to your foot?" With the words he remembered bare toes on his, a cool ankle that lay, alive and willing, in his hand, the boy's breath warm in his mouth . . . He swallowed and leaned into the shadow.

"I walked on it, what do you think? If you're afraid I'll slow you down, go ahead! This should stop a few." Pell gestured toward the blocks behind them. Senruh looked from them to Pell, eyes narrowing.

"Oh, for—! You know what they'll do to us if we kill even more guards? And like that, so they can't go to the gods weaponed and fighting? Put it back—I'll help!— and let's go. They're cutting us off."

"I know. I did this while I was waiting for you. In case you needed . . ." Pell's voice was almost inaudible. For a heartbeat Senruh said nothing. He must have misunderstood. He made a great show of brushing himself off.

"Well, let's fix them then and get out of here!"

Pell turned. Overhead, weeds reached between the stacked blocks to trail dead white fingers across the boy's neck. He paused, brushed at them, and moved forward. They swung and dropped inside his collar. Again he halted and reached behind him.

"Hurry up!" Senruh reached over the boy and yanked at the roots. The stones they grew in rumbled. Like a gauze curtain, clay-smelling dust filtered across a moonbeam.

Close by a contralto cried, "Look! Movement! In the ruins! Double pay to whoever flushes them out!" Feet stamped, voices muttered.

". . . the gods . . . bad luck . . ." a soldier growled.

". . . more than bad luck to get the rotting sickness . . ."

"Oh, so you're a god, worried about the sacred illness. I didn't know! Shall I bow down?"

"Go ahead and argue. I'm going in! I can use that pay."

In the chamber's stony dark, night-grayed eyes glared at Senruh. "So you send scrolls, do you? And for special occasions you deliver full-sized tablets!"

"I just wanted to help—!"

"Well, you didn't. We can't stop to fix anything now. Come on!"

Senruh threw himself after Pell. Behind them came the crash of overturned stones and the guards' bellows. The earth shivered as great blocks thundered to the ground. Powder smoked down the tunnel.

The boys emerged just below the hill's crest. Before he dropped onto his belly, Senruh risked a glance over his shoulder. Most of the guards hovered at the ruins' edges; only a few pried up stones. Senruh looked forward trying to pinpoint the spacers' door? Shelter? Light blasted his eyes. He shook his head, blinded. Pell's bright curls floated out of the dark.

"They'll see your hair."

The boy shrugged. "If I pull my robe up to cover it they'll see my legs. They're just as pale. As you well know."

"I didn't—! I wouldn't look!"

"Never *mind!*" Pell's voice cracked. He bent down. With better control he said, "I can rub dirt in it." Dust wreathed his head. "How's that?"

"Well—duller."

"Good. Let's go."

"Pell. If we—" Senruh reached out.

"Don't! Scum. Robe tosser."

For one thump of his pulses Senruh turned his head and stared into the light. On the slope behind him voices snarled; the guards had found the boys' trail. They roared; someone had dived into the passage. When Senruh was sure he could keep his voice steady, he said, "You learned the bazaar cant fast."

"I always knew it!"

Behind them came the deep contralto. "Pincer formation to the top. Quick march!" On either side, feet thudded upward. Voices shouted, eager for the kill.

Senruh leaped forward, scrabbled toward the rim. As the sentries' promises repeated in his head, the hairs all over his body lifted. Pell's hiss followed him.

"I lied! I never cared, I just said all that to try you out. Like poking a dung grub. So when I got home I could tell them all about you: how a lout of a pallet thumper, arms bulging like a snake full of lizards, changed his mind. Saved me a trip to the disinfectant baths!"

Knees gathered under him, Senruh paused. Breathing fast, the guards' shouts loud in his ears, he plunged a hand in his pocket. His fingers closed on the heavy waxiness of gold. When Pell wriggled up on his belly, Senruh's hand darted out. He pinned the boy's good wrist to the cracked clay.

"Let go! Half-breed! Lout!" Pell twisted, his useless arm caught beneath him. Hot joy licked Senruh's veins as he felt the other's struggles weaken, watched the blaze of curls tumble fruitlessly over flushed cheeks, and eyes the spacers' light stained brilliant blue. So lifting paving stones had had purpose: it gave him mastery of Pell!

Senruh threw himself across the boy's back. His face brushed soft ringlets. Beneath him the wiry body heaved then tensed, panting, waiting.

Abruptly Senruh remembered his own submission to the bearers. He was no better, he thought, no better at all. Sickness burned his throat. Still grasping Pell's wrist, he rolled off him, pried the boy's fingers open, and shoved Ariahnne's coin between them.

Senruh's voice was thick. "There! That'll rent your next bazaar scum now you've got a taste for us. Just show it to him first, save a mistake. I told you! *I* pay you little empty-heads. Not that you were worth it. But keep trying. At least you're willing!"

He flung Pell's hand away and stared into the furnace of light, nerving himself for the last run. A rumble twisted him around.

Behind the boys in the shifting dark a handful of shadows moved among leaning white columns and stones. The guards above and below had almost reached Pell's unbalanced blocks.

Heart thudding, Senruh glanced at the chainmailed figures in the forest on either side. Out of formation, they watched as, in the ruins, cold radiance flared on a soldier's spear. He shoved its point between the unbalanced stones. Daggers high, a guard, another, jumped through the enlarged opening joining those below. The watchers cheered. The great blocks wobbled, the ones resting on them slid. Leisurely they fell. As they split and the sandy sparkling earth flowed down, Senruh heard a drawn-out roar that mingled with the screams beneath. The wails thinned, cut off; the stones crumbled into dust. Long wisps of powder curled into shafting moonbeams.

". . . cursed! Under the gods' protection . . ."

". . . still defended . . . magic! . . ."

In the forest on either side of the ruins the soldiers made averting signs and ran—a few to dig in the fallen stone, the rest into the trees.

"Forward! Quick marchers, go! Any deserters, I execute—here! And half-rations for the next cycle if you let those guard-killing scum escape again!" The contralto scream lowered to a mutter. "Peace-fat, careless, lizard-bellied . . ."

The soldiers formed ranks. The ground rocked with their marching. Senruh's haunches bunched.

"That made them afraid of us!" Pell whispered fiercely beside him. Senruh turned. The boy's eyes looked glassy, his face very white. He choked. "Oh, Senruh, all that dust in their mouths, their eyes . . ." His throat moved. Pell glanced at his fist, then at Senruh, then slowly uncurled his fingers. He stared at the coin awash with moonlight on his palm.

"Senruh? That's gold. A lot of it. Maybe enough for your freedom. Is it the one you got from—"

"So now it's enough for yours! Laugh with your friends about that!" Stiff-armed, Senruh pushed his knuckles against the clay. Furious tears prickled behind his eyes. How could he have told Pell so much! Fool! At least shame had silenced him as to Ariahnne's final bargain. Behind him the soldiers' tread grew louder. "Let's go. Now," he breathed.

Callused fingers touched his wrist. "Senruh—?"

Don't! Don't touch, don't look at me! For a moment Senruh feared he had spoken aloud. He jumped up. Light poured into his eyes, over his hands, it flooded his dark robe. From below, the woman blared like a battle clarion.

"Look! Up there in silhouette! Flame him!"

Senruh sprang over the lip of the mound. *Unveiled half-woman!* His skin shrank from an arrow, a scorching ray. *She can't give life so she takes it! Mine!* Pell behind him, he pounded down the slope, arm flung over his eyes against the light. Rocks and dirt clods loosened, slid under his high soles. He tripped over a bush, recovered, and plunged downward again. The pat and smack of Pell's bare feet stumbled, recovered, raced on. Senruh heard a grunt, a thud. Pebbles skittered by. He glissaded to a stop. Doubled over, he scrambled up the hill toward Pell. His eyes widened.

Twin crimson filaments crossed in the cloud of dust he had raised. Beside him sparkles bathed a stone. It vanished. Senruh glanced at Pell's hunched figure, shapeless in its pale robe.

"Go on! I can't!" Hand clutching his ankle, the boy's face twisted. Beside him a bush glittered, smoldered, then exploded into flame. As smoke billowed downhill, more uncolored rays crisscrossed it.

"No! Together!" Senruh lunged toward the boy. His fingers touched a sleeve.

From the hilltop he heard the woman's shout. "Widen beams, increase charges! Vaporize them, don't smoke them to death!"

Brilliance scintillated by his sandal. His fingers closed on cloth. He looked. Good. Pell's unhurt arm. He yanked. "No!" Pell rolled toward him. From above, the contralto came again.

"Marker beams on, you zitter-brains. So you can aim!" From the ruins and the hillside, voices grumbled.

". . . stuck!"

". . . can't see! Dark as the inside of Mott's backside out here!"

"Don't name the Death God, dung eater, not now!"

"I'm shooting over their heads! I don't want the gods after me, too!"

". . . rutting, lizard-eating, off-world junk! Give me a bow or a spear or a throwing stick anytime . . ."

Pell slammed into Senruh's knees. Bending, Senruh flung the boy over his shoulder. His lash wounds opened. Sickness rolled up from his knees and loins. Pell straightened and tried to slide down. More sparkles lit adjacent tussocks and bushes. They crackled with flame.

"Let me—! Go on, Senruh. You can't—!"

From her vantage point on the slope, the woman interrupted her steady cursing. "After this fiasco, I'm inspecting every laser every sennight, *and* marksmanship! One little curd-eating robe tosser, and you— Fail inspection and leave's revoked for the season!"

Groans erupted from the ruins and the trees. Senruh hooked his arms around Pell's knees and elbows and hurtled downward, silent death glittering all about him.

"Pell! The pistol! Shoot back!"

The other's chest and belly contracted against Senruh's neck. "Can't," Pell said. "Threw it away. By the city gate."

A laugh tore Senruh's throat. "I thought you were so

bloodthirsty! You're no more a killer than I am!" Something sizzled on his arm. He glanced down. From wrist to shoulder the dark cloth smoldered. He should hit it, beat it out. But if he let go, Pell . . . He raced on. The line fringed with flames. Cold sweat dripped into his eyes.

The slope ended. Senruh's wooden soles clopped onto a huge circle of seamless stone. He smelled singed meat. Pell exclaimed and twisted around.

"Senruh, you're on fire!"

Weak, hurt, nauseated, Senruh let his grip on the boy slacken. Pell jumped free. He hobbled in front of Senruh, stooping and zigzagging between the thin rays and sparkles while with his good hand he pounded Senruh's burning robe.

"Never mind!" Senruh said. "Where—" He peered around the fair head for shelter, a bolt hole. Nothing. In that vast featureless circle he saw just one anomaly—a black square. He veered toward it. Pell's hand slipped from Senruh's arm. The flames leaped higher. They spread. He smelled charred hair and flesh.

"Wait! I'll—" Pell barrelled into Senruh. They rolled. A hand thumped Senruh's burning arm. As earth then sky whirled before his eyes he glimpsed crimson ribbons netting air thick with smoke and dust. The earth shivered beneath him, rumbled. He glanced toward the fire mountains.

Behind Senruh, the contralto yelled, "Last chance! Miss again and it's laser drill tomorrow, sunrise to sunset, on curd and water! Hold your fire! Take careful aim . . ." The sound of stone grating on stone grew louder.

Yanking free of Pell, Senruh snatched the other boy's good wrist and bounded toward the square. He thought, *If it's just a mark, in the next instant we'll be dead.* Before him the rumbling stopped, a lighter blackness filled the widening oblong. A dark head poked through.

"Boys! Over here!" The voice was deep. A hand beckoned, inverted, the palm turned up as if to catch the stars.

Towing Pell, Senruh vaulted toward the opening.

". . . and fire!" the woman howled from above.

Sparkles danced around them. Overhead, three straight scarlet strands lowered toward their heads.

Chapter Fourteen

DRAGGING PELL, Senruh rolled the last man-length. Powerful hands grabbed his arms, climbed to his shoulders, and hauled him into a glowing dark.

Senruh snapped his feet under him. They thumped rock. Rumbling filled the cramped space, along with smoke and powder eddying down from the surface. Senruh glanced up. Off-balance, his wooden soles skidded over an edge. He tightened his grip on Pell's wrist, flung out an arm, and caromed off a rocky wall. As he grabbed it, bright pictures were printed on his eyes: of a narrowing rectangle of midnight sky faded by moonlight, of meshed red rays piercing clouds of dust and smoke, of Pell's tumbling body. The boy's light robe replaced the sky.

Knees slammed Senruh's ribs. Pell's head knocked his, the boy slapped on top of him. They bumped down more ridged rock.

"Ugh!" Head throbbing, Senruh grabbed for his belly and sides. The rumbling stopped. The guards' shouts, the crackle of burning weeds and bushes abruptly shut off.

"S-sorry!" Pell scrambled down, stuttering apologies into the hush.

" 's all right," Senruh said when he could get his breath. "Hardly noticed it this time." The acrid scent of burning thinned until it was swallowed by the cool one of clean dry stone. Nostrils full of the stench of his own sweat and burned skin and hair, Senruh pulled himself upright. Pell's curls, twisted around sticks and clogged with dust,

147

were below his chest. Senruh blinked into the dim radiance.

At his feet the light ascended a steep ramp notched into regular ledges. "Stairs!" Senruh exclaimed. Flushing, he shut his mouth. Pell, two levels beneath him, and the dark-faced man who had pulled him in and now stood another two notches below Pell, turned to look at him. "I, uh, never thought I'd see any," Senruh muttered. The scribe had told him of the awkward curiosities.

He looked up, wanting to ask a question, straight into the dark-faced man's light eyes. Though the spacer stood four notches below him, their heads were level.

Senruh's thoughts rocketed. A ruler and taller than his master! He glanced down at Pell. The boy had been wrong. Well, Senruh would take care of him. Senruh straightened on his high sandals and tried to look authoritative. The spacer's teeth flashed white in the muted light.

"Welcome, strangers! Your condescending visit does my poor palace great honor!"

Court speech—and to him! Senruh blessed his high soles. The spacer must think him noble. He bowed his head toward his knees as, below him, Pell hesitated then did the same. Senruh glanced up. The tall off-worlder pantomimed wiping his forehead.

"You two had a near relative in an incestuous relationship!" The man's indecent words seemed to echo. Half-risen from his bow, Senruh held very still. Pell twisted. Blue eyes stared into Senruh's. Both looked back at the madman's bland expression. Then Senruh swallowed a chuckle and touched Pell's shoulder.

"I think he means 'close call'!" he whispered. The boy twitched away.

"Oh? And how do you know so much about spacers? You do it with them, too?"

Senruh's inner laughter shriveled along with his pleasure in solving the puzzle. His glance darted to the tall man before him but the spacer seemed to notice nothing. He smiled again, turned, and stepped down a notch.

"Prithee, follow me," he said over his shoulder. The stronger light illuminated his robe.

Surreptitiously Senruh looked for a noble's border, a soldier's plain cloth. The man wore orange! The color for madmen and wild untaught slaves. The spacer took another step. His robe divided. It outlined his legs. Only the lowest pleasure slaves, dressed for very private parties . . . ! Senruh glanced sideways. Pell's mouth was tight.

"I'm not following—that!—anywhere."

Slowly, Senruh looked from Pell to the man who was watching him and thought: his lady's rules had been different from the bazaar's. Yet . . . The level eyes observing Senruh held a gleam of humor. They were green. Like spring's new seedlings. "He's tall," Senruh said, as much to himself as to Pell. "He doesn't act crazed. Or like anyone's plaything. And"—he nodded upward toward the heavy stone separating them from the guards' shining, sparkling death—"we can't go back. Maybe—" He broke off. The tall man was speaking.

"What?" Senruh could have bitten his tongue. He had forgotten to use the court's archaic language and courtesy. But with seeming patience the deep voice repeated itself.

"I said, if thou wilt remove thy foot apparel for the disinfectant baths . . ."

"Disinfectant!" Senruh's face flamed. First Pell, now this man! He should have known. The honorable greeting could only have been mockery. Tribeless, with just half a name, his slavery, his lowness, his easy availability must be a part of him now, like a smell. Dizzy, he groped for the wall. Darkness flapped black wings across his vision. Straightening with difficulty, he maneuvered his burned arm into the shadow. He would not show weakness! Below him Pell dropped into his old arrogant crouch.

"He will not go to the baths! He doesn't need them!"

Tilted green eyes measured the boys. "Thy pardon, noble ones," the man said after a moment. "Allow me to elucidate this misunderstanding. It is our custom here, forsooth, that all who venture outside remove from their person those parts of your glorious planet which might cause others here, from less favored worlds, to sicken or die. I, too, must be cleansed." He palmed the wall beside him. By his hand a cavity spiralled open. He bent, pulled off his thin foot coverings, and set them inside. They slid past the gap and disappeared. He turned and held out his hand to Senruh.

Senruh's fingers had twisted into an averting sign. He hid them in his robe. From his sight's edge he watched Pell do the same. "But that's—!" He stopped. As a supplicant he had better obey. He stooped and untied a thong. But would he receive the same courtesy if he were small? He paused. What kindness could he expect from those employing demons or machines? He glanced at the opening in the wall.

It must be machine. The scribe said they were neither cursed nor blessed but tools, and understandable given Senruh's learning. He eyed the hole's floor. A circular belt, perhaps, with rollers at either end? Run by slaves, or spacers taking turns, or possibly some kind of stored energy? The man snapped his fingers.

"Well, lord my brother?"

The honorific reserved for fellow princes! Giddy at the distinction, Senruh whisked the thongs from his other sandal. He pulled at his shoe, then he remembered the incest slur and stopped. Perhaps the spacer meant honor no more than he had meant insult. The scribe's voice echoed in his memory: *Every reality has a hundred faces, Senruh my son, each one true.* He glanced up, wishing for the old man's advice. Blue eyes glared into his.

"Oh, get on with it! Short or tall, it's freezing in here. Let's go someplace warm!"

Senruh whipped out the remaining laces. It wasn't until he was handing his sandals to the spacer that he realized how reflexively he had obeyed the command in the other's voice. Face hot, he tried to shrug. Once a slave, always a slave, he thought. The off-worlder swung the shoes by their thongs.

"Good boy!" he said.

Senruh's toes curled on stone. Raising his shoulders to his ears, he backed up a step. He felt as exposed, he thought suddenly, as Pell must have when the slaver exhibited the boy, stripped, on the slave platform.

The dark hand flung his sandals toward the cavity. Opening his mouth to call them back, Senruh's voice failed, his eyes widened. The spacer was running a casual finger down his robe's center. It parted. It dropped to the floor. With the unself-consciousness of a madman or a child, he stepped out of it and stuffed it, too, into the cavity. Hands on dark hips, he jerked his head, indicating the boys should do the same.

Senruh heard Pell suck in a breath. The man wore nothing but a stretch of material across his loins. It left his legs fully visible from hip to ankle. Senruh's gaze scooted to the ceiling, paused, and dropped to the dark face and quizzical green eyes.

"Come, noble brothers," the spacer said, lowering Senruh's rank several levels. Senruh suppressed a smile. "Let us doff our robes of ceremony and do that which will cause us to be disinfected."

In front of Senruh, Pell stiffened. Senruh leaned forward, relishing the scandalized look in the boy's eyes. Mouth just above the dusty ringlets, he whispered, "Crazed, lewd, or not much at court speech. Which do you wager?" His lips curved openly when, between the gold lashes, he caught Pell's answering glint of amusement. The off-worlder held out his hand.

Pell's half-smile turned to a frown. He crossed his good arm across his chest and shoulder. "I'm keeping my robe on!"

The big man raised an eyebrow. "Wear it farther and we'll have to burn it—this is our only disinfection facility. Then we'll give you standard issue like this. Understood?" He glanced down at his orange suit. Pell's gaze remained stony. The spacer looked from him to Senruh. "You?"

Senruh, about to echo the other boy, paused. He was re-

membering a moonlit courtyard where he had learned of
baths and other things. Once learned, those lessons had
taken him to nobles' archives stuffed with scrolls, their
pallets and their purses. He smoothed his robe. His fingers
caught on leaves stuck in crusted mud and blood. He
itched all over. "All right!" he heard himself say. Before
he could change his mind he bent, grasped the hem, and
pulled his robe over his head. He tucked it under his arm
and whispered to Pell's stiff back, "It's only skin!"

"That's the way!" The man grinned. *What happened to
the court speech?* Senruh thought belatedly.

"Good gods, son," the spacer went on in idiomatic bazaar
talk. "Why didn't you say something? Are you in that kind
of shape too?" he asked Pell.

Slowly Pell turned around. Senruh's confidence wobbled
as wide eyes the color of afternoon stared at his torso, naked but for the borrowed cloth about his loins. They
blinked. "What? No. No, I'm fine."

"His feet are cut." Senruh pointed to the smears glistening on the levels behind them. "One ankle's sprained,
maybe broken. That arm doesn't work. And his other
hand's burned."

The off-worlder stamped down the serrated ramp, seeming to swear in a strange, clicking language. "And you let
me babble on, playing the psychologists' games? That's
fresh blood on your loincloth, isn't it?" he asked Senruh.
"And that burn—up to your shoulder! I can patch the one,
but you . . ." The light eyes turned speculative. "I'm going
to get you a real doctor. Time she came out of retirement,
took an interest in something alive for a change." He
glided toward the wall, dusky body vague then gleaming
in the uneven light. He leaned toward the cavity and spoke
into it.

Watching him, Senruh thought, *Even bazaar herb wom-
en expected pay, but a spacers' physician, full of learning,
honor*— "No! Not a healer! I can't—"

"Hush yourself!" Pell hissed while the spacer talked
into the opening above the foot of the stairs. "You need

one! Maybe you louts don't feel pain like we do, but *you* look awful. My fault . . ." He almost swallowed the last words.

Scarcely listening, Senruh strained to hear the tall man's increasingly brusque tones. So, the healer did not wish to come. That would raise the fee and make forgiveness nonexistent. In Quaqqadum, Senruh knew, the mended bodies of coinless patients were forfeit to their physician. Slave, again!

"I don't want—" Senruh looked down at the other boy, then away. He could not ask for the coin, not after what he had said! He wiped his clammy forehead and breathed in quick shallow gasps. "I'll be all right!" he said loudly. But the off-worlder only nodded and turned, the cavity swirling shut behind him.

"Sure you will, son," he said. "Our Marget will fix you up. Just follow the tunnel, branch right. Seat at the end of the corridor—wait there. I won't search you. Can't be hiding much in that." He jerked his head toward Senruh's loincloth. "Even if you are, she's tough. She can cope. Little excitement should do her good."

The big man reached up toward Senruh. "By the way, I'm Li Tober Enkolo. Head of Mission. That means I tell the others what to do—sometimes they even surprise me and do it! My good luck to be on duty when the screens showed you coming in. Should have called our anth—uh, Studier of Mankind, but you looked like you were in a hurry. Besides, Grinelda can have her share of the fun once she's, ah, suited up. Always takes her awhile . . ."

As the deep voice flowed on, Senruh stared at Enkolo's pink palm. To clasp wrists with a ruler, as if they were equals, friends! Could the scribe have been right? Did a kinder world exist, and here? Hesitantly, half-expecting a rebuff, he reached over Pell's head.

Instead of his wrist the tall man grabbed his hand and yanked it up then down. "Your name, son?"

"S-Senruh, mas—lord. From the Southern Gate."

The man paused in his moving of their fists. He gave

Senruh a sharp look. "Senruh, eh? Glad you're here. And you're—?" He extended his hand to the other boy.

The blue gaze lingered on the orange suit. Slowly, Pell took the other's fingers. "Pell. Pell Maru."

"Pell." The man pumped the boy's arm then started down the curving tunnel. The light brightened with him, illuminating chiseled rock the dark brown of a frost-killed branch. Neither boy moved.

The spacer turned and motioned for them to follow. "Incidentally. If you answer our Studier of Mankind's questions as I expect, she'll ask you another. You might be thinking about your answer. Whether you want your freedom and enough coin to keep you in the city of your choice, or if you'd rather stay with us."

"Stay!" Pell exclaimed. Senruh echoed him.

"If you and we think you can adapt here we'll train you. We're always short-handed. Consider it." He took a step forward and lifted an expectant eyebrow. Pell, who was to go with him, stepped down a notch. Blue eyes glanced back at Senruh.

"I can't tell you what to do . . ." Senruh stopped. Pell wasn't looking at his face. Senruh's toes dug into cold stone. His memory flashed the feel of them, warm, buried in crisp leaves, while the other whispered that he wished to see all of him. Face heating, Senruh looked down. And found swellings over his discolored ribs, drying blood from the guard's sword cut, his red charred arm puffy now and leaking yellow fluid. Lower, bright and darker red stained his loincloth, his legs. He spread his hands over his thighs. They looked long, obvious. After Ariahnne's and her friends' praise he had begun to take an embarrassed pride in his body; now it was neither symmetrical nor smooth-skinned. Cheeks warm, he saw how little his hands covered and hugged himself instead, trying to hide the most disfiguring cuts and lumps. He glanced up through his lashes. Perhaps Pell had stopped looking, the other had not noticed. But the blue gaze still pinned him. A green one had joined it. For a moment he shut his eyes.

"Senruh? You're not well, son. Let us give you a hand. You can lie down in the health room while you wait for Marget."

Senruh thought of the man and Pell behind him, seeing the lash cuts of a slave, the noble's pleasure marks. "No! I'm fine! You go. Leave me alone! I got here, didn't I?" He wanted to dive back into his robe, but after his nonchalant removal of it, what if they laughed? A chill shuddered through him. He licked parched lips and willed the man to leave.

"Well. It's not far." Mercifully, the spacers' leader dropped his gaze to the other boy and Senruh felt a warmth as if a hand had rested on his shoulder. "Come on, youngster," the man told Pell. "Sooner we put you back together, the sooner we can return you to your friend."

Senruh watched them go. *Friend!* he thought. *Pell couldn't be that! Hadn't the man seen—?* Inside him a grieving child seemed to weep. He stared at Pell's departing back. The boy had not agreed they were friends. But he had not denied it, either.

Chapter Fifteen

SENRUH'S FEET slapped on rock. He walked alone in a dark
corridor. The floor's chiseled edges bit into his soles. He
had grown soft since his barefoot childhood, he thought; he
had forgotten how much better toes gripped a floor than
wooden soles one hand thick. Dizziness whined in Senruh's ears. Bare but for his loincloth, he tried to ignore the
heat that throbbed in his burned arm, the cold shivering
through him. He hugged the wall for support.

The corridor ended in a large vaulted cave. He blinked
at four unlit tunnels yawning from its depths. The smell
of earth and stone and growing things was strong. He
squinted toward the cave's other end to what looked like
carved double doors. Black curtains descended inside his
eyes. Lids shut, he swayed and leaned against the cool
wall. He wiped his forehead. After a moment, following the
spacer's instructions, he edged into the corridor to the
right.

Senruh found himself in a low tunnel. Several doors
pierced it but instead of the familiar curtained rectangles
of Qaqqadum, the openings were rounded triangles and
lopsided arches. Wood panels closed them. The boards
were stained the color of forest moss and sun-streaked
stone. As the boy moved farther down the corridor, its
strong light showed its end: a circle punctuated by a cush-
ioned seat. Someone had set the pillow in a knee-high
niche.

With a little tugging he got it loose. He put the cushion

on the floor where it belonged and squatted, working it
into comfortable contours with his toes. He leaned his head
back against the wall and waited for the healer.

The spacer had said she was retired. That meant she
must be too old to work but had been saved from Sacrifice
by someone who loved or honored her enough to support
her. Senruh pictured an ancient brown-faced woman like
the scribe. Wispy, sightless, a hand that shook—how could
one like that help? With magic? But the scribe had taught
him not to believe in spells. Or perhaps . . .

Senruh had heard whispers of the beings secreted here,
alien creatures originating not on Naphar but among the
stars: faceless, shapeless ones who neither saw nor heard,
others who breathed not air but water and who spoke without words. Need the healer be human? Even in Qaqqadum
only the bazaar herb women were certainly so. Senruh had
seen them often with their simples-carrying retinues, pre-
ceded by beating drums and wailing flutes. But the true
healers who always cured and always collected their high
fees were black-robed, masked, immensely tall, and only
came and went by night. Bazaar gossip had long speculated what rustled beneath their humpbacked cloaks and
hid behind those strange still faces. A chill rippled down
Senruh's spine. He glanced into the corridor with its
alternating shadow and pooled light.

Beyond the central chamber a tunnel's wide mouth
formed a deeper darkness. He shivered. Cloth rubbed beneath his arm. His robe! He had forgotten, so had Enkolo.
He shook it out.

Grimacing, Senruh tucked the dusty folds around his
shoulders and drawn-up knees. Anxiety crept from the
shadows. No. He pushed it away. He had seen little emptyheads who had bled as he had, cry out at invisible terrors.
He would not be like them. Tightening his mouth he widened his eyes and stared.

Beyond the main grotto in the opposite tunnel's depths,
something pale jerked from shadow to dim light. It dove
again into darkness. Fear caught Senruh's breath. He

watched the thing flap to the corridor's mouth, flutter into the main cavern and across; it entered his own passage and took form.

Senruh blinked. He almost smiled. It was a lone hurrying spacer woman shrugging into a white overrobe that was split down the middle from throat to toe. Even as he watched, it settled over her shoulders, and pink short-nailed fingers yanked it closed over the dark gown beneath. A night robe, Senruh thought. He felt giddy with relief. His eyes closed.

He dreamed he was in his lady's villa. She skimmed across her torchlit courtyard, veils fluttering, chin high and imperious as the spacer woman's. Warmth flooded him as he relived her smile of welcome. Long-nailed hands reached for him, he shivered . . . No! Ariahnne was not here! And even if she were, her seeming affection for him had been only mockery. He forced his eyes open. The roar of surf faded with his dream. He heard nothing but stony quiet and the spacer woman's steps. She was almost by him.

He blinked upward. She wore no rouge, no eyeblack, her hair was not braided or looped into curls. Cut too short for beauty, its beige almost as pallid as her face, the straight fair hair only reached her jaw. She came nearer. She had no fragrance. Ariahnne had moved in a cloud of scent.

For a moment Senruh longed for his lady, for her laughter, her dry hands on him, her whisper hot in his ear . . . No! He would not remember, would not trust, not again! Senruh swiped at his eyes and pushed his feet deeper into the long flat pillow. The foreign woman was staring at him over her short straight nose like a scum viewer in the bazaar. She seemed to expect . . . Experimentally, he fluttered his lashes.

The light eyes brightened. Then the colorless mouth firmed. She did not wish to be attracted, he thought. Maliciously, he tilted his head and sent her a gleaming look. Pink touched her cheeks. Surprise? Fear? moved in her face before her expression blanked. Senruh tired of the game.

Dizziness swept over him. He pressed his spine into the uneven wall and closed his eyes, wishing the healer would come. Monster, crone, pitiless creditor, at least she would rid him of this curiosity seeker. He could not serve anyone tonight. Even at the thought of urgent voices, hands, a trembling rooted in his middle. The foreign woman halted before him. She plunged her fists in her side pockets and scowled.

"Are you Enkolo's famous emergency?" Her accent drew out the vowels. Even angry, she gave the bazaar talk a singing quality.

Go away, Senruh thought, and pulled his filthy robe high under his chin. He gave her a limpid stare. "No, lady," he said.

*Hmmph*ing, she looked from his cushion to the shelf where he had found it. "Destructive barbarians!" she muttered and tapped her foot. He looked around for barbarians. He found none. But she did not go hunting them. Instead she glared at him, tan eyes bleak. They seemed not to see him, but a different scene in another time. Not a pleasant one, he thought.

"Enkolo," she said softly, "if this is your idea of a joke!" Her hand slid into her pocket. She pulled out a hammer. Silver, shining, it glittered as, in a hot brown alley, gold pincers had gleamed. She whacked it against the white folds of her robe. Senruh's fear slipped its leash.

Heart racketing against his fists and the gathered cloth they held, he twisted backward. He saw only wall. He whipped his head up. In the ceiling's rock, inadequate light leached color from the air. He sucked in a breath. Cool, bland, it had no savor. Above him long man-lengths of stone pressed, heavy, shifting, soon to crush him as the gods' sparkling earth had drowned the soldiers . . .

Senruh's mind flashed a picture of the world he had relinquished: the veil drifting across the stars and into the sea, below it a cliff top, its grasses rippling, pale against distant swells bathed by starlight. In the fjord below, waves crashed and glowed, their winking spume salting

the air. From behind those waves, arrowing from the inky
dark, orange wings burst into the light. They circled, tilting into red then silver radiance, riding the Sea God's
breath. Lost! Senruh had killed outside the goddess's law.
Gone from him now forever, put away by his own hand . . .

Traded for this off-worlders' hole. How could he have
hoped, even for an instant, that it was different here!

In the spacers' rocky tunnel Senruh blinked stinging
eyes. The woman's indifferent ones looked through him.
Still seated, weak, he clutched his robe before him like a
shield. She bent. Shadowed now, her pale brown irises became the color of autumn pools choked by dying leaves.
One hand held the hammer, she reached for him! Senruh
slid off the seat, rolled onto his knees. His robe dropped to
the floor. Naked but for his loincloth, he bowed his head.

"No, lady!" he choked. "Not again! I beg you."

In a soft rippling tongue she exclaimed. Her fingers
snatched at his burned arm, tearing it. "Don't!" she said,
"Get up!"

Pain seared him as it had when the bearers ripped at him,
when his master clutched his throat and reached for the
firecrystal knife . . . the knife! Already this evening it had
made other tall rulers fear him. With both hands Senruh
grabbed his robe. He pummeled it, searching. He broke
into the pocket. A haft rammed his palm. Crusted, sticky,
it fitted in his fingers. He yanked it out.

The woman's breath caught. She bent, her fine pale hair
curtained the light. She knocked his burned wrist aside,
grasped it and his elbow, and brought up her knee. He heard
a crack like snapped wood; aching fire seared him. He fell forward.

The knife shot from his fingers. With the harsh sound of
badly cast bells it shattered, its black fragments spinning
pale lights across the walls.

I have no choice, he thought. A dreadful gladness flared in
his loins. He crouched, laying his head on her shoe. He waited
for her will.

Chapter Sixteen

THE SPACER WOMAN clicked her tongue. She pulled her foot out from under Senruh's head, her heels tapped a short distance. Her robe rustled, broken firecrystal clinked. She walked back to him. Her voice was cold.

"I've got what's left of your knife. Now, you can stand up and walk into that room. Or I can put you out and have you dragged in. Choose. But don't think you'll get second time lucky. Come at me like that again and I'll hurt you so bad you'll wish I'd killed you."

Senruh opened his mouth. "I—" His voice broke. He tried again. "I'll walk." Fumbling for his robe, he draped it in front of him and climbed to his feet. His useless arm swung forward. He bit back a groan. Warmth gushed into his loincloth. Blood. The bearers' wounds, the sword cuts, all had opened. Black dots slid across his vision, merged, and seemed to swarm into his lungs. He could not get a deep breath. The floor circled beneath him, soft, inviting . . .

A shoulder slipped under his. He smelled clean cloth. A hand, intimate on his bare back, guided him across the stone. Head hanging, Senruh watched his naked feet swim into sight. Pallid thong marks crisscrossed them. He should have kept his sandals on, he thought. Tall, this foreign woman might have respected or at least feared him. He looked beyond his feet to a wall panel colored the green and dull gold of lichen on sun-dappled rocks. It slid open. Amber light spread toward his toes. Again the hand nudged him forward. The stone warmed under his feet. The hand's support left him. He swayed.

"Very good acting if you're faking. Now, drop that robe. Strip. Show me where it hurts. And it had better hurt a lot. Dragging me out of bed, pulling a knife . . ." The musical voice dropped to a mutter.

Senruh could not look at her. He remembered Ariahnne's greedy unfocused eyes, that first night's quizzing of his pain . . . He opened his fingers. His robe slithered to the floor. His legs showed. As if that mattered now! Would her first touch be gentle, only her nails . . . ? His skin roughened. He loosened his loincloth. It fell. A trembling took him. He waited for the hammer, the lash. Senruh heard her circle him, choosing her place . . .

"Oh," she said. He squinted through his lashes. She was behind him. Before him he saw a teardrop-shaped room, its muted light a wash of amber on stone walls dark as winter's leaves. Waist-high cabinets lined them, their tops the color of thick autumn sunlight. The teardrop's base lay behind him, he turned to see if the panel were closed. Vertigo roared in his ears. He crumpled.

Warm hands caught him. They dragged his good arm over a crisp-robed shoulder, then walked him to a barrier as high as his hip. Leaning on it, he dragged his eyes open. It was as long as a pallet, the same dark wood as that of the wall cabinets, topped with a yellow pad.

"On your back," the woman said. She helped him sit on the yellow pad; she hoisted his feet into place.

As Senruh lay down, fire raced through his lashed shoulders. Aching, he shivered. A cold mist seemed to pour from the light. He fell into it.

Senruh woke to warmth. A cone of hot yellow radiance flooded from the ceiling; he saw the room through its haze. He inhaled it as if he were a field of sun followers, their long spring migration ended, their thick gold petals open to heat and light on the summer hills behind Qaqqadum. He sighed, seemed to melt, and floated back into dreams.

* * *

Fingers pressed his wrist. Senruh's eyes fluttered open.
The foreign woman turned his hand over and looked at his
nails. If they were not clean would she bathe him in her
courtyard pool? He slipped into torchlight, a breezy dark,
Ariahnne . . .

Heart banging against his ribs he tore off memory's
sticky webs. He opened his eyes wide. The stranger woman's fingers darted toward them. Blinding! Senruh rolled
away. His head lunged off the pad, his shoulders; he slid,
he fell . . .

White-clad arms caught him. His charred arm crushed
against a shoulder and breast, broken ends ground together. A shout ripped from his throat. A storm of dry surf
roared around him. The black depths of Membliar closed
over his head. Membliar, the sunless sea where all life began and where it must one day end.

The dark wave carrying him ebbed, thinned. Golden
light filtered through. It strengthened. Senruh opened his
eyes. Beige irises peered at him. A thumb retracted his lid,
released it, and peeled down a lower one. His sight! Ward
her off—! Senruh tried to lift his hurt arm. It felt heavy. He
glimpsed it. It was tied to a shaped board. Its ache had
eased.

Could he have misunderstood, did she mean help? He
rolled toward her to ask . . . He could not. Bands cut into
his ankles and unhurt wrist. His breathing stopped.

For a vivid moment Senruh stood again in Ariahnne's
villa, looking through a half-open door to her inner room.
A man's naked ankles and wrist lay shackled to the floor,
blood trickled toward a central drain, a sweat-sheened face
turned toward him . . . Ras, the head bearer! Dead . . .

Feeling as though rags wadded in his chest Senruh
snatched at air, he jerked, hard, on his bindings. They
held. The face close to his frowned. Clicking her tongue,
the woman bent lower. She clamped his head between her
arm and her warm, many-layered side. She stared at his

eye, her breath fanning his face, then released his lid. He could still see! Sweat crawled through Senruh's hair. Frowning, his captor picked up a metal disk. She put it on Senruh's chest. It was cold.

"Don't," she said. "I'm not hurting you. Not yet. Ignorant brute." She looked at the coin-sized circle, dropped it in her pocket, and flipped a knob beneath the boy's high pallet. A chime rang through the air. The silence changed: it seemed to breathe and listen.

"Enkolo?" she said. She moved toward Senruh's feet and the cabinets beyond them.

"Marget? How's your charge doing?"

Senruh started. Enkolo's deep voice came from beneath him. He looked for the man, but the room was empty. Senruh snapped his hand into an averting sign.

But spacers used machines. Could one attract a voice through walls as, through cloth, a lodestone pulled bits of metal? And—Marget. He had heard that name . . .

Glass clinked. The woman set tubes and flasks in a row. They held crystals, colored fluids. He remembered other shelves lit by the sunset's rays, packets of herbs, flasks of potions to increase sensation, wakefulness . . . The spacer woman spoke. Like obedient demons, jars and bottles spun and shook themselves. Senruh made the averting sign with both hands, opened his mouth to shout for Enkolo . . .

"I don't know how he is, Enkolo," the woman said over her shoulder. "But I need help. Someone to take the retractors. Another to hold him down. I don't want to knock him out, I don't know Napharese dosages. Not for this kind, anyway."

Senruh stopped listening. So. This foreign sorceress shamelessly asked help from her ruler in her pleasures. At least in Qaqqadum, Ariahnne had found it expedient to keep her tastes secret.

". . . and I want that help fast," the woman's singing accent continued. ". . . too cold for him down here . . . shocky . . . exsanguinating . . ." Enkolo rumbled counterpoint.

"Hold your own retractors! And what do you think the

straps are for? I'm busy with his friend here. Everybody else is off now or has his own work to do."

"Senruh? Is that Senruh you're talking about? Is he— is he well?" Pell's voice—real? a dream?—made Senruh think of loss, shame . . . He fled into unconsciousness. Enkolo's voice followed.

"Have you tried explaining? He seemed like a reasonable youngster. Bright. Or are you still getting by on minimum contact, Marget? That boy may be Napharese, but he deserves better from us than that."

Marget, Senruh thought. He almost remembered. Glass crashed on stone. Quick steps clacked toward him. The pad he lay on indented. The woman's liquid accent exploded in his ear.

"Boy! That huge naked savage? Reasonable! When he attacks what he doesn't understand with a knife?" She snatched a breath as if she had been running. Startled awake, Senruh listened in deepening embarrassment.

"I've heard the priestesses talk, the nobles," she hurried on, "these half-breed slabs of muscle don't think, they don't even feel as we do. As for explaining, you don't explain to a brute! No civilized person could. There's no common ground. No humor, no logic, not even anything so rudimentary as shame. This one, for instance—he hasn't got the modesty of a—a lizard! Not even these coastal natives' leg fetish!"

Enkolo's voice cut across the woman's hard-breathing pause. "He has it. What have you been doing to him, Marget?"

"I! To him! Well, let me tell you, he—!" She stopped, then began again in a low shaking voice while, on the counter, carafes and coiled tubes spun and jiggled like an army of the possessed. "I've done nothing he didn't have coming to him. Deserving boy! Well, you can have your deserving boy and all his relatives! Who kill, lie, eat human fl—!" She rammed her knuckles into her mouth and turned away. Senruh stared at her quivering back, indignant. To blame him, when she was only undergoing Revulsion!

"Enough!" Enkolo's voice cracked through the room. "You have your intelligence in common! And more—your descent. I remind you of your own partner's theory: that Naphar is another lost prehistoric sister colony. Bigotry aside, your own chromosome studies show you and the boy share half your ancestors. He's as human as you are."

After a long pause the woman spoke, her back still to Senruh. "I—I'm sorry. Jien wouldn't—"

The silence hummed. Enkolo's deep tones slid into it. "Now was that so hard? Saying his name at last? The boy's bringing you back to us already, Marget." In a brisker voice he added, "No. Jien wouldn't. He loved the Napharese. As he wanted you to, as he taught your child to on those trips to the surface you were too busy to join . . ."

The woman's protest was half-sob.

"All right, Marget. But for Jien's sake and your own, you're going to know one Napharese well. Beginning now, you're this boy's sponsor. And no help. The others have carried you for a cycle. That's long enough! He's all yours."

Sponsor! Pushing all but the one word aside to ponder later, Senruh's heart tripped over itself. Just when he had given up hope he was being offered a place, a tribe, here, with all the stars to call home! He willed the woman to look at him, to accept him. If she did, he would willingly . . . He thought of Ariahnne's bargain and swallowed.

But the spacer woman kept her back to him. Leaning across the counter, she touched the base of a large dome set into its top. Little lights shot across its transparent surface when it flipped back to reveal glittering rows of knives, needles, pincers . . . Senruh turned cold. She reached toward them then checked, fists clenched.

"I can't, Enkolo! I'll treat him. But sponsorship! It's like adoption, partnering. And he's—he looks like the ones who sold Jien, butchered . . . my baby . . ." she whispered. Hands shaking, she took a white metal circlet from the table, opened it and set it around her neck. She fumbled in her hair. Senruh heard a click. Light radiated from the circle to glow about her head. She pushed her hands into two holes beside the knives.

"Anyway," she said over her shoulder, "I don't have time. There's my own research, language studies, Jien's notes to write up, his book to finish . . ." She took her hands out.

"It can wait. Jien's dead, Marget." Enkolo's presence wiped from the room. Marget did not seem to notice.

Bitterly disappointed at her refusal, Senruh was letting hope's brief clarity slide from him when she burst out, "How could I even talk to him, counsel him? It's been a cycle since I've said much more than pass the salt! To anyone!" The tray rattled. Through the cone of radiance the boy watched her set flasks and tubing on a shelf beneath her tools. His skin roughened and he closed his eyes. Her protests flowed on.

"I don't want even this responsibility. Goddess's interdict on machines!" She made the phrase sound obscene. At the word *machine,* a faint curiosity stirred in Senruh. "No regeneration tanks," she listed, "no scanner, can't take blood gasses, immunities, I've never even dissected a Napharese—I could kill him!"

Senruh's eyes flew open. She meant him.

"Enkolo?" the spacer woman said into the unresponsive silence. She jiggled the knob by Senruh's foot. "Enkolo! Answer me!" When the quiet remained unbroken she said something in a strange rippling tongue then caught her breath. She pressed her fingers to her mouth. "What have I been saying?" she breathed. "May you freeze in Niff l'Hime's dark forever, Enkolo," she grated and swung around. For the first time since the early moments in the corridor, Senruh thought she saw him.

"You heard all that, didn't you?" she asked him. "I just realized. Enkolo had us talking in your dialect. But it was none of your business. So forget it!" She whirled away. Then, seemingly uncertain, she glanced back at him.

That parody of a coy look coupled with her statement that his sponsorship, his death, were not his affair, were too much for the boy. Fear giving way to shaky laughter, he tried to stop his mouth from twitching.

Impersonally, she surveyed him. Her glance lingered on his burned arm, the swellings on his ribs, the cuts and bruises lower down, his dribbled thighs . . . Senruh's face flamed. He tried to pull one knee over the other, to bring a broad palm over his bare leg—the band at his wrist pulled him up short. He lifted a defiant gaze to hers.

"Why, you're blushing!" Eyes wide, the woman stooped, she dragged thick yellow folds from beneath his pallet. Looking away from him, she shook them out. Like a cloud, the coverlet settled over his naked ugliness. Senruh's muscles uncoiled one turn, the backs of his eyes ached.

"Thank you," he croaked. A drop of moisture, another, dripped down his temple to his ear. Arm tied, unable to swipe at it, he scowled at the woman. If she laughed—! But she was frowning at the blanket she wadded under his feet.

"Force is wrong," she said. "Even for a . . . Well." At last she looked at him. "If you'll promise not to struggle I'll take these off." Her hand slipped beneath the cover, closed on one bound ankle. He shivered at the pallet touch and what it presaged. But to die free, not like a bound, squalling hill man at Sacrifice! He nodded. "I promise."

With quick tearing sounds she released him. Replacing the blanket, she smoothed it over his chest. "You don't need this," she said to his chin. "The hot light's all we use. Body shame has been dead for centuries in most of the civilized galaxy. Except for my family's private satellite." She made a face. "My ancestors drummed in all the old myths and virtues: poverty, chastity, temperance . . . I still get twinges. So this is for me. And you . . . I've never yet treated a boy your age who wasn't at least a little self-conscious. Though you don't need to be. You're very—" She bit off the sentence and crossed to Senruh's other side. Cautiously, she lifted his burned arm in its hollowed board. For a moment no other part of his body existed. He hooked his uninjured elbow over streaming eyes.

"It's that bad? I'll fix the pain first, then." She bent over him, tucking the coverlet under his side, and reached beneath his pallet. "I'm, uh, sorry I didn't realize how young you were when we—met. But you're so big! Anyway, if I'd known I'd have tried not to do this." Her touch on his arm was light as a breath. She broke off and glared at him. "Not that I'm giving you license to act up!"

He shook his head, wordless. With newly free fingers, he wiped his eyes. Her short straight hair swung into the light. Gold streaked it. She seemed—kind. Could he have misunderstood? Spacers did things differently. She had no retinue, she looked ordinary, but could she be the missing healer?

As he opened his mouth to ask she moved to another counter. "Almost ready," she said over her shoulder. "Just waiting for my lasers to finish charging. I haven't used them in a—a cycle." Lasers! He scarcely noticed the palm-sized tubes she picked up with finely trembling hands. Gray smoke seemed to drift again before his eyes, all that was left of two men. And soon he—! Her low-voiced explanations continued. He could not bear to listen.

"They'll be all right." She turned a tube, fired it, and nodded. "Thank your goddess those priestesses let me keep mine. I couldn't operate with antiques like the ones they allow your guards. And I'll be all right too! I have to be . . ." She flexed her fingers, then shook them. Senruh's legs tensed.

But he had promised. And where could he run? He watched her pale cheeks flush as she counted over her sharp bright tools. He thought of what she would do with them. Anticipation twined through his belly. Horrified, he felt pleasure's heaviness warm his loins even as a clammy dew burst from his pores. Destruction loomed over him, dark, beautiful, compelling as a lover. His chest lifted faster and he looked within. In one day to become—this! He began to shake, retched, swallowed. When she did not approach him, slowly the cloying unwelcome heat receded. With a clink, the woman set down her last narrow tube.

"Enkolo's impossible!" she told it. "But he's right about explaining. I—" She turned abruptly, her eyes narrowed to brown slits fringed with gold. She squinted through the haze of light that bathed him. "What's your name?"

He remembered what, only moments before, he had yearned for. Had she known? He could not look at her. "S-Senruh, lady."

"Well. Senra." Her mouth sketched a smile that did not reach her eyes. "I'm Marget. Marget Tretten-Nagoya. I—the warning. I have to give it, it's your law and ours. Our words are going to a—a sort of scribe that sends them to our people and your priestesses. What we say here and my recommendations will help them decide, when they meet you, whether you stay here or return." She looked down at her ringless hands. "I'll try to be fair. As your healer, I—"

"My healer!"

"Why? What did you think I was?" Marget tipped her head. Her hair slipped, shining, over her robe's high collar. "Some odd spacer woman who picks up stray Napharese boys and tortures them?" She swept a hand toward her rows of instruments. A dimple appeared in one pale cheek; her eyes rounded. "You did!"

"The hammer." She looked mystified. "In your pocket," Senruh stammered. "There."

She drew out the silver mallet. Its handle tossed back the light as it had in the corridor. But now, in the health room's brighter illumination, its head looked porous, softer.

"This? It's just for testing reflexes! Here, I'll show you. No, let me."

Pushing the blanket aside, Marget slid a hand under Senruh's thigh and lifted. When his lower leg dangled she swung the hammer in a shining arc. When it tapped his knee, his foot kicked high in the air. He stared at it.

"Well, at least your responses are fine. But I knew that!" Grimacing, she dropped the blanket into place and patted her pocket.

Wings of darkness beat across Senruh's eyes. Those jagged lumps behind the white cloth were the remains of his smashed firecrystal knife. How could he have forgotten? He had tried to kill a healer. She had every right to demand his life in return.

Chapter Seventeen

STARING DOWN at Senruh, Marget choked on a horrified laugh. "You thought—! And yet you kept your promise and didn't move! I'd heard you natives were stoic about torture, Sacrifice . . . Or are your nobles right and you like that sort of thing?" Senruh's eyes flickered, but she had swung around. She could not have seen.

Heels loud on the rock floor, Marget strode to the counter, yanked open a drawer, and clattered instruments into the twin holes beneath the hood. She had thrust her hands there, earlier. She pulled the tools out, she fanned them on a cloth. They were all pincers. Large, small, handled, unhandled, sharp-edged, blunt-tipped, gleaming . . .

She is a healer! Senruh told himself. The woman walked toward him, eyes bright. Her voice lilted. Like Ariahnne's.

"On your side! You're going to be fine. The touch, the procedures, they're all coming back. Like light sailing, you don't forget. Though whether I'm doing you or anyone else a favor . . ." she added under her breath. Her sidelong glance was one Senruh had met before, in the Region of Government and Temples to the Lesser Gods. He shrugged, telling himself he didn't care, he hadn't expected anything else. He rolled onto his hip and unburned shoulder.

Senruh's scowl dissolved into surprise. The yellow pallet beneath him purred. It humped to support him. *It's not sorcery!* he told himself. Holding on to the scribe's teaching with both hands, the boy gleaned words from old lessons:

172

metal cogs, sensors, energy captured from the sun? waves?
storms? and stored . . . Slowly his fingers uncurled from
the averting sign. And Marget called the instruments to
her.

In the center of the amber counter, untouched, the transparent dome lifted. The tool-filled cabinet beneath it separated from the shining wood that lined the room and
rumbled toward them.

"By-Sassurum's fiery womb!" Senruh choked as the pincers as well as knives, drills, picks, saws, scissored twee-
zers, tubes, cloths, and pistol-gripped canisters and bags of
fluid trundled past. The woman glanced at him.

"Really! You'd think you'd never seen a voice-controlled
computer before."

"No," Senruh managed.

"Well it's not a demon! It won't hurt you. It's just a machine."

A laugh built in Senruh's throat. Demons were familiar,
almost homely, compared to a machine. And the fate
awaiting any Napharese caught using such a goddess-
cursed instrument! Well, perhaps this spacer woman did
not know.

"Yes, lady. Thank you," he said. She walked behind
him. Briskly she pushed away the blanket. Cold whisked
along his spine. She pinched him.

"Feel that?"

"A little, lady."

"Hmmm." The cold came again. "Now?" The pain
seeped away. From his rump, his sides, his arm . . . She
pinched him a second time. He felt only pressure. He had a
wild urge to weep, to shout thanks.

"Nothing, lady," he husked.

"Mmm!" she said, satisfied, and began.

Soon only the healer's sure touch tethered the boy to the
chamber. He had slipped into a waking dream of an orange
flier that swooped upward toward the sun. Beside it Senruh skimmed on hot summer breezes. They sang with Marget's rippling accent.

"Record: Subject is a well-nourished, well-developed, very muscular north Napharese half-breed adolesc—hmmm. Stop recording. Are you still growing, Senry?"

"Senruh, lady. I hope so."

"Sen-ruh. Sorry. You hope—? Oh. Oh, I see. That coastal caste system." She bent her head. Behind him the steady fingers snipped, smoothed, tugged. "Continue recording: . . . adolescent male, suffering from hypovolemic shock due to hemorrhage. Break and second and third degree burns on left arm. Sword cut . . ."

The boy yawned. She reached across him. Her robe smelled like sunlight. Peace stole through him as, for the moment, he gave up his strivings, his fears, and passed the threads of his fate into the healer's competent fingers. Through closing eyes he saw her sleeve catch on the knob below his pallet. The quiet altered. A soft chime sounded, almost lost in the clink of instruments. Pell's voice whispered in Senruh's ear.

". . . found out he was a slave, an oversized lout—!"

"Why were you ashamed of that, son?" Like a shadow spirit's, Enkolo's voice breathed through the susurrus of stone-cool air. Senruh blinked.

He looked over his shoulder to Marget. Surely she heard, would explain. She worked on, absorbed, a silver shimmer from her necklet outlining her head as she leaned into the thick gold cone of light. *I'm asleep,* Senruh thought. And, as if in a dream, he listened.

". . . liked him! I'd always wanted a friend, imagined one like him, I grew up so lonely!"

Enkolo's question was pitched low, Senruh could not separate the words.

"No," Pell's voice answered. "Our neighbors thought we'd contaminate them. My father believed in L'h, not their bloody goddess. I just saw them on market days. But mostly then I'd listen to the storytellers when my father wasn't around. They told about demons"—the boy's voice slid into singsong—"demons of dark and enticing beauty, who walk the earth as princes, sages, scholars. Only their ensorcelling charm, their inhuman comeliness, their size, hint to mortals in their toils of their disguise . . . their size," Pell ended, voice bleak. "I even caught myself wondering if Senruh could possibly . . . Me! And I don't even believe in L'h!"

At the anguish in Pell's laugh, Senruh's eyes opened. His nails curved into the spongy yellow pad. This was too real, Pell's dilemma too familiar! He glanced back at Marget. But still she seemed to hear nothing. Her face was intent, serene. Enkolo's voice whispered into the dark brown health room's silence. It sounded amused.

". . . huge size like mine, you mean?"

"I know it's superstitious nonsense—now." Pell's tone was stronger. Perhaps he had moved closer to the catcher of voices. "But—when everyone around you believes it . . . and the only oversized people you know are drugged into mindless obedience, and slaves—you can't believe you can talk to, much less lo—" Pell gulped. Senruh's ears seemed to stretch toward the voice as he listened, incredulous. ". . . so I'd say, oh, awful things, as if it was his fault he . . . I'd act . . . Then when I'd try to fix things, he'd be mad from the last thing I'd said, so he'd laugh at me and I'd snap back, and it got worse! Until now I've gotten him killed, and I never once told him . . ."

"Oh, I think we can trust our Marget. If she says she can fix him, then—" To Senruh's frustration, Enkolo's deep voice cut across Pell's. "In fact," the spacer continued, "let's ask her. What—!" Enkolo's voice was suddenly loud in the teardrop-shaped chamber. "Marget! Turn off your intercom!"

"Intercom? Didn't I?" Marget sounded like a dream priestess breaking from a trance. Senruh watched her as she got up and, eyes abstracted, walked around his pallet, then stared at the knob by his feet. "Why . . ." She bent and pushed it with her elbow. She frowned at Senruh. "Did you hear anything? Because I didn't. Of course, my hearing isn't good, especially with this." She motioned to her necklet and the aura about her head as she went back to his side. "Too many cheap commutes down to medical school, for one thing, next to the shuttle engines."

Not knowing what to believe, much less what to say, the boy shook his head and closed his eyes. Had what he heard been real? Was Pell lonely? As was he. Did Pell have no friend at home? Senruh did not. Then could Pell have lied about laughing over Senruh's . . . Face hot, the boy gave up his questions. He sighed, let the mists close over him, and for a timeless interval wandered Mott the Death God's gray and sterile lands. Marget's voice plucked him back.

"Senruh? Wake up. Talk! Tell me, oh, where you got hurt, what kind of bugs I'm dealing with. I've found dust, grass, picked out a few bits of metal . . ."

"Where I—!" The boy came awake with a rush. The dark safe rock about him seemed to vanish. In its place were heat and light and stinging zitters. Yellow eyes burned down at him from behind blowing veils. He cried out.

"What? Did you feel that?" Marget reached for a canister.

"No! Where it happened! Avenue of Pre—" Senruh stopped, mouth open. Only a creaking sound came out. And no breath.

The healer exclaimed in her strange tongue, slapped a pad under him, and rolled him onto his back. As, chest heaving, he struggled to sit, she supported him, pulling his head against her shoulder. He clutched at her.

"Shhh, it's all right." Her voice by his ear was steady. "You can breathe. Inhale through your nose. Hold it. Now breathe out. Slowly! Again." A heavy bag plopped into his hand. "When you can, drink this. There's something in it to relax you. May make you talkative."

The boy's trembling slowed. After what seemed a long while, she eased away from him. Reluctantly he let her go. He drank. The sweet liquid had a salty undertaste, a tinge of bitterness. He retched, put it down, and surreptitiously edged it toward the jumbled blanket. He glanced up. She fixed him with a stern, light brown gaze. He picked up the pouch and drank. When he had finished he stared at the

dark ceiling, afraid to close his eyes. The healer moved to
his side.

"I should have realized," she said. "You've been too
quiet. Of course getting those wounds must have been un-
pleasant, even for a—" Breaking off, she leaned into the
light. Her gold-framed hair flicked his chest. The ends
were soft. Honey-colored eyes looked into his. "Listen, Senruh. I made a mistake with you. I'll probably make more.
But I will help if you'll tell me how." She straightened until she stood out of the light. "If you can," she added almost
inaudibly.

Senruh found no mockery in her rigid colorless face. He
gave a slow nod.

"Good." She sloshed another bag down beside him.
"Drink. You need the fluids." She opened the dark wood
face of the cabinet, hustled her stained and bloodied tools
onto a lower shelf, and pulled out a new set.

"Don't look," she said. Her instruments chinked and
rang. Obediently he turned his head. He stared at the dark
chiseled cave wall, the row of cabinets, the play of light on
stone, on amber counters, on dark polished wood.

"Now tell me," she said. "What happened today? You
were lucky you had a friend along and that you both got
here. Weren't you?"

Friend. The word Pell had used. Not songboy or even
pallet companion. Like a child's dam of sticks at floodtime,
Senruh's barriers quivered then tumbled away. Haltingly
at first, while Marget cut and scraped and smoothed, he
spoke, soothed by a quiet broken only by the rush of air
like the sound of distant rivers, and at one point, a faint
bell.

". . . so I, I stopped. I should have known Pell would hate
me for that, too!" he finished. He had left out only his painful new self-knowledge. He flung an arm over aching eyes
while, blanket gone, Marget laid a flexible coolness over
him and smoothed it into place. Her sleeve brushed his
bare foot as she reached over him, her white robe brushed
her instruments. They clinked. One seemed to chime.

"I—I guess I deserved that!" He gestured downward, hating himself for how he looked, what he had become. "I've always done things wrong, gotten in trouble." He broke off. What was he admitting! Where was the silence, the seduction his master had taught him, or at least his bazaar swagger, his courage! Afraid of seeing the healer's contempt, he pressed his arm over his eyes. He tightened his mouth to keep it from shaking.

"Senruh." Marget's voice sounded thin with control. "What they did was not your fault. It was theirs. And it is they who deserve punishment. Not you."

She nudged him onto his belly. More coolness enfolded him, firm hands molded it to his skin. "Now," she said, and her tone was gentle, "tell me the rest. How did you get here?"

When Senruh stopped talking the room was very quiet. Eyes closed, he rested, feeling solaced as after a storm of weeping. He missed the healer's touch. It had been gone for some time. The deep lap of comfort thinned. Was she gone? Had she left from boredom? The need to laugh? He opened his eyes.

At first he did not see her. His blanket lay crumpled beside him. He glanced from a second skin, opaque and seamless, stretching from his chest to his knees, to the film encasing his hurt arm. It was rainbowed as an insect's wing with a thin green wire running its length. Beneath its covering, the flesh was red but healthy, the charring gone. Tubing cradled his arm, bending it stiffly over his belly. He heard cloth rustle, then a sniff. He turned his head.

Marget stood above him. A tear sparkled on her wet spiky lashes; it followed others' tracks to splash, gold in the light, onto his hand. Her mouth trembled into a smile. "Look what you've done to me! Leaking like a broken fountain. Most unprofessional. You poor child," she said, "I didn't understand—anything! Now, up! Time for the 'fresher.

"This demon-ridden planet!" she burst out as, shoulder

under his arm, she led him across the chiseled floor to the teardrop's point. "I have some influence with those priestesses. I can make sure you never again . . ."

Senruh scarcely listened. The healer, a ruler, had wept— for him! They stopped before a tall narrow panel. Marget touched the wall. The panel slid open and she stood aside.

"Go ahead!" She nodded toward the opening. "I won't let you fall. And your dressings will be all right. They're the same semipermeable membranes we use to visit the water dwellers. Let air in, keep water out." When a puzzled Senruh still did not move, she said, "Oh, of course. You don't know." She touched the stone inside the opening, then whisked the blanket from his shoulders. He heard the sound of rain.

The cubicle's rough walls had vanished beneath veils of spray and billowing mists. He reached out an incredulous hand. Marget's voice stopped him.

"Senruh, I—" Her gaze on his coverlet, she folded it into meticulous squares. "I shouldn't have said that about your planet. Your master, your lady, they're casualties that could happen anywhere. So can kindness. Even in that city of yours, if you know how to find it." She held the folded blanket tight against her chest. "But," she said with a quick glance at him, "please call me Marget, Meg, doctor . . . anything! Only not *lady!* All right? Now, get in."

"In that? But I'll drown!"

She clicked her tongue, reached up to grasp his good arm, and pushed him into the chamber. He scarcely noticed the heated waterfalls or the nozzled vapors or that he still breathed. She had reached up. Her tawny head hardly reached his shoulder. *Slave! Emptyhead!* The words clamored in his mind. But Marget was no servile plaything. The floor seemed to drop from under Senruh's soles. Pell was right, the small did rule here. Or, no, Enkolo was tall. Senruh remembered his dream of Pell exclaiming in a tiny voice, *Superstitious nonsense!* But that would mean . . .

Marget reached to him through the streaming warmth. The boy's whirling thoughts slowed, then drained away with the dirt and old blood as he gave himself to the healer's touch. Sexless, gentle, it made him feel a child again, his secrets mostly known and thought not so very bad. She slanted him a smile and pushed aside her moisture-beaded hair with what he saw now was a small as well as a capable hand. Senruh felt surprised all over again. The waters stopped. Heated zephyrs puffed around him.

"Senruh. Out! They'll be waiting for us." Draping him in the fluffy blanket, she followed the boy back to his pallet. "Look at you!" she accused; but her mouth curved. "Almost back to normal, and after what you've been through! Your butcher priests get results, I'll say that for them. Forced evolution! When I think of a planet full of people like you: healthy, strong, charming, bright!"

He blushed. "I'm not—"

She paid no attention. Turning her back, she rummaged through a drawer, muttering, ". . . billions stuck forever in hospital satellites, producing children we're pledged to save no matter how painful or empty their lives. Not one able to set foot on any planet and live. The backbreaking taxes just to keep them functioning. Which is the more civilized system? I wonder . . ." She hunched her shoulders.

"On your back!" she said loudly, and faced him. "Your regulator has to match your resting heartbeat. While we're waiting for it to slow down . . ." Obediently, Senruh flattened himself on the yellow pad, strange pictures of the world this pale small woman lived in darting, ill-shaped, through his head. Marget dropped a thumb-sized metal circle on his chest. She reached for his bandaged arm. She lifted it—he released a held breath. There was no pain. Carefully she tweezed the green wire through the film.

"Tell me more about your friend," she said. "Why are you so afraid of being close to him?"

"Afraid! I'm not afraid of him! He's only a little emptyhead like—!" When he stopped abruptly Marget's mouth twitched.

"Like me, you mean?" Speechless, Senruh reddened.

"You'll have to work out the importance of size and

caste for yourself, Senruh. I'm not allowed to—" Biting off the end of her sentence, the healer concentrated on her work.

The last connection made, she tapped the round bit of metal. "This gathers your body's electricity—you know electricity?" Without thinking the boy nodded. Marget's amber eyes glinted approval. Senruh's surprise flicked an elusive memory. Another had not been pleased at his knowledge . . . He did not retrieve it. Marget had lifted her hair to show him a similar disk.

"Mine activates our few machines, like this sterile-field projector." She indicated the metal circle at her throat. "While you sleep, yours will feed your stored energy into those wires to make your bone fibers grow straight and fast. Should help the pain, too. If that returns, tell me, and I'll increase the current, restimulate your endorphins. Now, drink. Rest. I have to finish my report. You're going to need your strength."

Reluctantly, the boy gave up his examination of the cell and wire, picked up another bag, and drank.

Senruh opened his eyes. Something whizzed over stone, the sound that had awakened him. Liquid curses accompanied it. He looked down toward the voice.

Marget knelt on the rocky floor peering into a wall cabinet. Beside her, orange squares littered the dark brown stone. "Ha!" she said. She slapped a bright oblong thicker than its fellows onto the rock.

"Lady, what . . . ?"

The healer emerged, hair disheveled. She stared at Senruh, announced, "You're awake!" blushed, and dove back into the cupboard.

"Yes, la—Marget." He began to smile.

"Clothes," she said from the depths of the cabinet. "You need long ones. There should be one more . . . Senruh! I must tell you . . ."

The boy lifted an eyebrow. "When you meet the other personnel tonight," she said, voice hollow, "they'll know about you from my report. They might—one might—try to take advantage of you. Don't let them! Understand?"

Advantage. What could he give a spacer that their machines and the stars could not? Senruh's smile dimmed as he shook his head. "No, lady."

She gave a sharp sigh. "Well, then! I—I'll explain." She cleared her throat. "It's not your fault, I don't think you even care either way," she began obscurely, "but your master and your culture have made you much readier than we are for skin-to-skin companioning. That is going to fascinate, um, at least one of us."

Skin-to-skin-companioning. Ah. Senruh hid a grin and politely waited for what he was sure was coming next.

"Daily, you enter what should be the culmination of the most intimate of relationships; it's heady, it's easy, you miss the problems, the joys that should lead up to it, that would have made you ready for your friend—" She broke off. Her clear gaze grew sharp. "Have other adults told you this? If so, I'll save my breath!"

Senruh tried for gravity. "The scribe, a little. A priestess now and then. But the others . . . Well, they would not."

Her eyes darkened. She looked at him hard, then away. "Oh!" she said. "Of course . . . You poor child! And you don't even realize what's been done to you!"

Dismissing her odd remark—of course he knew! Inattentiveness at such moments earned little coin and fewer favors—Senruh asked, "But if spacers do not companion, how do you pass the time? Surely you do not work day and night?"

"We talk. As you have to me. As you should to your friend, to the others. Or you haven't got a chance," she added under her breath.

"But that's pallet babble! I couldn't! It's indecent! The other, it's nothing, I don't mind . . ."

"It's not nothing! And talk isn't indecent. Not on any subject. My family sings an old, old chant. Jien, my—my partner, translated it into your tongue long ago. I—" She

swallowed. After a moment she began to whisper an eerie
half-toned melody.

> "My world is a song, my song's name is love,
> Touch is its geography, words are its air.
> Tear either one from me, and we can't live there
> Anymore . . ."

Her voice shook. She broke off. Her back was rigid in her
white robe. Throat tight, Senruh struggled onto one elbow.
He held out his hand.

"Marget, there are other partners, not as fine perhaps,
but others! And touch alone can be a comfort, truly! I—"

"That's not what I wanted to discuss!" Marget had
turned her back. The boy's hand dropped as he cut short
his tumble of words. He lay down again. "I have to tell
you . . ." Marget said with an effort. "Look at yourself, Senruh. I've arranged things so you can't do much *but* talk!"

He jerked his head up. He surveyed his length. The spacers' seamless new skin wrapped him from chest to knee.
His body was as sexless as a priest's puppet. His arm, en-
cased in a rigid tube, jutted before him, implacably guard-
ing any approach to his chest and belly. Certainly pleasure
would be difficult! After a moment's shock he began to
laugh.

Marget withdrew at last from her shelves, picked up the
thickest orange square, and walked toward him. Her
cheeks and the tip of her nose had turned pink again. Eyes
still slitted with amusement, Senruh held up his hand
then touched his mouth.

"You forgot to cover these!" When her flush deepened,
he straightened his face and asked solemnly, "Marget? If I
should eat or drink more than my body can hold in the next
sennight or two, how do I rid myself—?" He paused delicately.

She showed him then burst out, "You're still free to
choose! If you insist, I'll redo your dressings, but—" She set
down her package beside him and leaned into the cone of

light. It gilded her hair and eyes. "That you can laugh! Any of our men would be furious! If you were my son . . ." She stopped. In a low voice she repeated, "My son . . ." She assessed the boy's broad chest and arms until he wanted to grab the blanket and pull it up to his chin.

"You're very strong, aren't you?" she whispered. "You must eat a lot of meat." She made a strangling sound and turned away, both hands over her mouth.

"Marget! Lady! What have I done? I did not mean to laugh, I only . . . !" He stopped. "You had a son."

The healer shuddered and turned her back. "A baby, just—just walking. He was with Jien when your people took them, sold them to the—the butchers . . . I can't." Her voice was a thread. "For a while I forgot, I thought . . . Enkolo asks too much. You're too different."

Different. Pell had said that. And, in another way, Ariahnne and his master. But he did not feel different! Heart beating hard, Senruh protested, "But that's Revulsion, lady! It has taken you harder than most, but it passes!"

"You dignify—that!—with a name? It passes? I'd starve before I'd . . . But not you! You're well-fed as . . ." She swallowed convulsively.

"I did starve! But I was young, my crèche mother noticed when my belly swelled and I weakened. She laughed and explained and made me meat broth and hot spiced sausages . . ." Marget choked. Hastily the boy said, "I spewed them up! And that night I had my first Dream of Knives, and the other, the Dream of Meat That Speaks and Weeps . . . It's common. There's a joke—"

"Joke!"

Senruh caught his breath at the horror in her voice. The brown and amber room seemed suddenly empty, and he alone. But for a while she had almost seemed to care . . . Shaken to his roots, scarcely aware of what he did, Senruh dropped off the high pallet to the floor. Dizzily he set his head by her foot. "Please, lady! Forgive me!" he whispered. The stone's edges pressed against his face. The cool air flowed and shushed through the silence. After a time-less space, fingers touched his hair, retreated.

"Don't. You mustn't do that anymore, Senruh. Get up. I've hated too long," Marget said, as he obeyed. She helped him back to the pallet. He felt very cold. "Oh, not you, don't look like that!" He shivered as radiance and warmth enclosed him once more. She looked down at him. "You're caught by life, too," she said, and swallowed. She patted the bright folded square beside him. "Now get dressed. We're late."

Senruh picked it up, not seeing it. So that was why she would not sponsor him. It was nothing personal, just that he lived. Trying to smile at his joke, he focused on the stiff oblong in his hands. Orange. The color for unbroken slaves and madmen. He unfolded it, an awful suspicion growing. A collar appeared, long sleeves, a throat slit, the shame of a defined waist . . . The rest unrolled.

"I can't wear that!"

Marget looked up from her scroll of cheap sea paper. She moved a weight to one side, opening the scroll wider, and tapped its figures with her writing stick. "Nonsense! Everybody does. Standard issue all over the galaxy."

"But it—! They'll show!" He gestured toward his legs. Indignant, he watched her fight down a laugh. He shoved the offending garment away and snatched up the blanket. "I'll wear this!"

"You will not. Not for a formal Questioning!" The healer whisked away the yellow folds, bundled them into a drawer beneath Senruh's pallet, and shut it. A lock snicked closed. Senruh glared at her, then scanned the floor.

"If you're looking for the rags you carried in here, I tossed them in the incineration chute. Didn't Enkolo warn you?"

"No. Yes! I'll go like this!" He slid off the yellow pad.

"No, Senruh! Be reasonable. At least the worksuit covers you!"

Thinking unsayable things, he looked at the heaped

orange cloth with loathing. He picked it up with finger and thumb, turned it upside down, investigated the seams. It would not go over his head. "How do I—?"

Her cough sounded very like a giggle. "You step into it."

Holding the obscene garment as far from him as possible, he touched his bare toe to the front slit. Immediately, he noticed, Marget's eyes swiveled away from him. Color staining her cheeks, she stared down at her scroll. Modesty! Now? This time it was Senruh who hid a smile as he slid a foot into its cloth tunnel.

Well, he had never heard that the goddess required sense from those occupying her world, only that they be useful, and the healer was certainly that. He pushed his other foot into its confining cylinder, shrugged into the sleeves, and stretched.

He felt well, tired but supple inside his added skin. Marget had mended him. And he . . .

It was his turn now. He must pay. In coin, so the law said, or if he could not, with his freedom. Abruptly, Senruh's contentment vanished.

Chapter Eighteen

THE BOY SAT cross-legged on the high yellow pad, worrying at his orange suit's closure. He could find no thongs to tie it shut. When the edges touched, they clung. He stared. Had the suit been exposed to a sorcerer's lodestone, magnetized, as the scribe would say? Or could one side be a vacuum? His curiosity overcame his anxiety about payment. He looked up. "Marget, why—?"

"Not now, Senruh."

The healer had put her pale green sea-paper scroll away. Her lips moved as she counted her stained instruments. There were a great many of them. All for him. And she had expended time, skill . . . His coin gone, what had Senruh left to pay with but his freedom?

He sneaked another glance at Marget. Her forehead puckered. She began her count again. He wondered if she would be a kind mistress. He suspected she would be an exacting one.

She looked at him, one eyebrow lifted. "You're very quiet. Anything poking you? One's missing." She gestured toward her array of tools. Her hand brushed a crumpled square of cloth. Beneath it, metal shone. "Ha!" Stuffing the square into a box of used ones, she dropped the missing instrument on the tray with its brothers and told the table to return to the cabinet, sterilize and order its contents. Obediently it rumbled toward the gap in the counter.

Marget pointed to a row of squeeze bags and empty flasks beside it. "We'll pick these up after Enkolo and our

187

Studier of Mankind finish with you. I'll be waking you tonight to drink and fill those bottles. Can't risk your going
back into shock. Though you seem—much better." Something in her comprehensive glance made Senruh flush and
pull his legs beneath him. She clicked her tongue. "Do you
understand? It's that or artificial blood. It would take a
long time feeding that viscous stuff into your veins, and
it's dead white. You'd be pale for the Questioning. Besides,
I've never tried it on a Napharese."

"I understand, la—Marget." Not far from Senruh, the
table hummed beneath its dome. He understood that soon,
unless he thought of something, he might follow her orders
as automatically as that thing. Before he piled up debts
that would bond him past his manhood into old age, he
must tell her. "Marget?"

"Mmm." Back to him, she had taken up her scroll again.
A glowing tablet materialized above the counter. Senruh's
eyes narrowed. He had seen something like that before.

Early in his acquaintance with his lady, in Ariahnne's
long low sleep chamber, glowing people dressed in tunics
like flower petals had danced into being above his and his
lady's pallet. He started violently and made the averting
sign. Smiling, Ariahnne moved away from the box that until now she had kept hidden behind a tapestry, her long
stringy body appearing and disappearing behind her diaphanous night veils.

"These are not demons, my small dweller in blissful ignorance, they are spacers' pictures made of light, like the
beams from those pistols our guards are so chary of," she
said, as she walked through the posturing group and lowered herself to his side. She leaned back on a glimmering
cushion and traced the line of his arm with her nail. A machine! Shock slammed him.

"Spacers! You wish me Sacrificed?" Senruh turned his
head so he could not see the forbidden projections. Ariahnne's nail scratched deeper. In spite of his anxiety the
boy shivered.

"Nonsense!" she said. "We are beyond the city walls. Spacers and their inventions are not forbidden here, not to such as me. If I wish to show them to my minion, why, this is my villa and you are my creature. What I do to you is solely my affair."

But Senruh firmed his chin and would not look. Only that morning he had seen a slave Sacrificed for sacrilege; and for several sennights he had heard nothing from the scribe who taught that the gods were powerless, the spacers' machines innocent in themselves. The boy was beginning to fear his own curiosity about off-world knowledge and artifacts. His lady's nails halted their caress. They embedded themselves in his forearm.

"By our goddess's great toe, you are overpious!" Ariahnne's husky voice was loud above the slosh and sigh of the sea. "I bought this toy fairly of the spacers, with my cousin the high priestess's full knowledge. Oh, not for coin. It was an exchange of services. I am not without influence at court, or ears in the bazaar and elsewhere."

"But I am not you, lady! I am slave and half-breed! We are forbidden—" As he spoke Senruh hunted among the tumbled cushions for his robe and struggled to his feet. A bony hand yanked his ankle. Sputtering, he fell on his back.

Ariahnne straddled him, hissed in his face, "Listen, you stone-headed scuttler! The high priestess of Sassurum herself uses such things. Not as I do, but she uses them. Do you think she hides them like a nervous postulant each time a servant enters her chamber? Or that she would demand it of ME?" She sat back on her heels, a tiny smile curling her mouth. Senruh lay still, suddenly afraid to move, while above him phantom skirts, long strangely carved prisms, and unshod feet lifted and swirled and combined.

"Our high priestess," Ariahnne continued smoothly, "moves as freely among those spacers—with her servants!—as she ever did when she taught with them at the

Royal Space Academy." Experimentally, she reached out
and drew her nails across the boy's belly. It jerked. Her
thin rouged lips curved. "Recall, oh timorous one, she is
the Mouth of Sassurum, who in her turn is Keeper of the
Stars and all they breed. My cousin sponsors Naphar's off-
worlders, even to dispensing justice to any Napharese
among them. She is said to possess her own entrance to
their audience chamber. Even I, out of curiosity, have visited there. Neither of us has gone unattended. Now, have
you ever heard the smallest whisper of our priestess's sacrilege or impending Sacrifice? Or mine? Or our servants'?"

"Nnno"

"Then look!"

Cautiously Senruh glanced upward. He stared, eyes widening, at the long-haired men and women, at what they
did beneath their belling skirts, as they separated and entwined above the pallet he shared with Ariahnne.

His lady leaned close. She set her hand on his knee. The
intimate touch, her heavy-scented heat, and the visions ac-
complishing the impossible above him, stirred his loins.

"Watch closely, my skillful little lizard," she whispered.
"Do you think that you could . . . ?"

His senses whirled with the orgiasts overhead. "Yes!"
he husked. And, heart thudding, he arranged himself for
her among the cushions.

The sharp remembered pleasure made Senruh blink. He
focused on Marget's bright screen, watched her frown as
she checked its columns against the tallies on her scroll.
The boy studied her slim straight back. So, the spacers
sometimes exchanged services. And unless the dancers
were a lie, touch was not as forbidden among them as Marget had implied. He looked again at Marget, her hair, her
small fine hands. Surely beneath those layers of cloth,
even the fierce little healer kept a body, needs . . . And in
the corridor when he had first smiled at her, he did not
think he had mistaken her interest.

"Marget," he said. He made his voice soft.

She twitched her shoulder as if a zitter whined there.

The boy's mouth curved. To his surprise, regret welled through his amusement. He had liked the growing ease between them. After this transaction he doubted it would be the same. If, after all he had babbled to her of his feelings and history, he could bring himself to touch her . . . Of course he could! Any embarrassment, any discomfort was better than a lifetime of servility. And perhaps, if he pleased her, she might reconsider his sponsorship.

"Marget?" he said again, heart thudding. He felt a little sick. At last the healer spoke a command; the shining tablet vanished.

"What?" she said. "Ask fast, we're late. But at least I'm sure now you won't keel over during Questioning. And you've added a lot to our knowledge of Napharese physiology." She glanced around the rough stone chamber, tidy once more, then at Senruh, dressed now in his orange suit.

"In fact, ask me on the way." She picked up the sea paper, rolled it, slapped it into her other palm, and started past the boy on her way to the door panel's sun-splashed greens.

"No!" Senruh caught at her sleeve. She looked up at him, her eyes spilling over with golden light. Drums pounded in his ears. What was the matter with him, he had done this a hundred times! Swallowing, the boy ran a finger down the front of his suit, opening it. He leaned above her, breathing in her faint scent of clean cloth and warmth.

"I have no coin for this." He gestured down at himself. "But if you like . . ."

She looked up at him questioningly. He tried the lashes-fluttering smile his master had taught him, but under her clear gaze it went lopsided. He reddened. Were all spacers this dense? Anyone in the bazaar would have understood long ago. No wonder the spacers seldom touched!

"Coin?" Marget said. "The suit's yours, Senruh, for as long . . ."

"You don't understand!" He snatched her hand, plucked

the rolled sea paper from her suddenly lax fingers, pressed his mouth beneath her wrist, and ran his hand under her sleeve. Her skin felt firm and smooth. His heart thudded into his throat. He carried her palm to it. For an instant she left it there; delicately her fingertips explored his pulse. She tore her hand away.

"No!" She whipped around, breathing hard, and leaned stiff-armed on the counter. Her hair swung forward, hiding her face. "Didn't you hear a word I said, you randy little—?" She caught her breath. "Fasten your suit and let's go!"

"But I'm clean, lady! And I have no other coin!" Senruh's voice broke as a warm lump of grief gushed into his throat, threatening to overwhelm him. He touched the second skin she had wrapped him in. "And even with this, I can give you pleasure! Please, lady, it's all I have—I can't be slave again!"

Wordless, she shook her head.

Senruh looked down at himself. Bandaged, and beneath the dressings lay cuts, swellings—he was ugly. Of course she would not want him. No one would. His eyes stung. Furious with himself, he knuckled them. She turned around.

"Oh." The dark gold eyes widened as he glared at her, daring her to notice his tears.

"And now you're insulted. What a world!" A corner of Marget's mouth twitched. She walked toward him, reached up, administered a brief brisk hug, and stood back. "My fault. I told you, I'm out of practice explaining. And your fault too, Senruh! You know we don't have slavery. But I suppose you didn't believe it." She pulled out a drawer beneath the pad where he sat and handed him a cloth. She stared at the humming dome while he blew his nose. When he was finished she said, "Now I'll explain. I don't take pay for healing, Senruh. You heard Enkolo. It's my share here, like piloting a scoutcraft or fixing the machines. Besides, I took an oath not to mix medicine and pleasure. Not that kind of pleasure, anyway. Understand?"

"I didn't know." Senruh looked straight ahead. His eyes felt hot. Gently, she fastened his suit for him, right up to the chin. He tried to smile at her prudishness and could not.

"No. Because I didn't tell you." She patted his hand. Her touch was tentative. She looked away from him. "You only shocked me, Senruh. That was all. I haven't touched— companioned—since Jien . . . died!" she ended firmly. "If I thought you really wanted . . . But you don't, do you? I doubt you ever have. Isn't it time you started considering *your* desires for a change? And planning how to satisfy them? Look at me, Senruh!"

Reluctantly he lifted his gaze to meet her eyes. In the light's flooding radiance they shone like gold coins.

"You're a beautiful boy! Good brain, humor . . . To sell all that for a bit of silver or a few stitches and a splint— what a waste! I'd have gotten much the best of the bargain! Well. Lecture's over. Shall we go?"

But Senruh could only sit, throat aching. He snatched Marget's hand and squeezed it convulsively. "Lady, I . . . Thank you!"

"Now," she said. "Now, now." And pulled his head onto her shoulder. Very carefully he put his free arm around her. She felt pliant and dagger-strong. With light and tender fingers she stroked his hair.

For a long moment Senruh forgot his wariness; he no longer calculated the usefulness or danger of those about him. Instead he inhaled the scent of clean cloth and her hair and skin and gave himself up to peace, wondering if this were what it felt like to come home.

She helped him sit up. She switched off the amber light. "Now we really must go! They've been waiting far too long. If I wasn't sure Grinelda's taking her own goo' time—!" Marget's faint smile belied her tone. Her skin wore a becoming flush as she slipped a hand around Senruh's good arm and accompanied him to the door. The panel slid open; the lights in the teardrop-shaped chamber faded. Her dimple appeared as she sent a glancing smile upward.

"Enkolo was right again, rot him! Sponsoring you is going to be a lot livelier than my translations and lab work!"

Sponsoring! As they made their way through the shadowy cavern, the word reverberated in the boy's head. The healer stopped him in front of twin carved doors.

"Wait," she said. "It's only fair to warn you, they'll be observing you from the moment you step inside. And what you'll see may startle you."

"Marget!" he burst out. "Did you say sponsor? Adopt me into your clan?"

"Well, yes! Didn't you hear Enkolo assign you to me?"

"But you said . . ."

"I say a lot of things," she said, closing the subject. "And we don't have clans. Senruh—"

Reaching behind his neck, she pulled his head down. Startled, he turned to look at her. Aiming for his cheek, her pursed lips hit his. She stiffened, then with a little gasp her cool mouth opened, softening under his as she pulled him closer. Her fingers crept into the still-damp curls at the back of his neck. Awkwardly, his splinted arm between them, the boy supported her, questions ricocheting through his mind. He shelved them. His eyes fluttered closed and he sighed, aware only of her mouth, her clean breath mingling with his and, beneath it all, the warmth of her that, like a small bright hearth fire, kept the dark and the fear at bay.

A deep voice came from the room beyond. ". . . going to see what's keeping them!" Senruh opened his eyes.

The doors flung wide. Parallelograms of smoky green light fell across Senruh's arm, dimming its orange where it circled Marget's shoulders. In the pause that followed, the healer's gold-tipped lashes rose. She took a quick breath and pushed Senruh away. He straightened. Below her darkening eyes, her hand pressed against her lips. She stepped back. "That was for luck, nothing else!" She peered around him, her cheeks and the tip of her nose turning pink. "Enkolo! How long have you—?"

Turning, Senruh found himself staring at a lean orange-swathed midriff and chest. His gaze skidded upward past a dark muscular throat to leaf-colored eyes that watched Marget intently. The man's gaze ticked Senruh's, flicked away. Enkolo's face lost all expression.

"So, our frozen sleeper's waking," he said. He looked down at the boy. "You're a fortunate young man. I hope you appreciate it." For another long moment he stared at the two of them. He turned and flung the doors wide.

"Here they are! Soon as Grinelda arrives, we can start!"

Enkolo winked at them over his shoulder, and Senruh wondered if he had imagined the man's stillness, the danger that had seemed to pad, soft-footed, from the shadows. He darted a look at Marget. Color fading, she was smiling at Enkolo's nonsense. Senruh shrugged. He could only wait and see. The tall man threw his long arms around both of them.

"Late but not lamented!" he said to the room at large. "This is Senruh, arrived with Pell over there, had a short layover for repairs. Come on in, son, Marget; find a place to sit!"

The green-eyed man pulled them across the threshold. The great doors swung shut behind them.

Chapter Nineteen

SENRUH PERCHED on a low curving shelf, his orange-clad legs stretched out before him. He gazed through the green light at a cavern hung with flowers and vines. He was torn between wanting to scan the twenty or thirty forms clustered in its nooks, and wishing to sit on the floor, his legs and bare feet curled decently beneath him. He had started to sit that way but Marget had given him a warning look. He sighed, imagining every eye in the room covertly examining his legs, and wondered why he had not found Pell. If the boy was unconscious . . . Marget's liquid accent broke into Senruh's growing worry. She waved her hand at the many-leveled chamber.

". . . early feminist design, womb rooms they used to call them. Very soothing . . . reaction to men's straight lines and angles. Gaudi, Couelle, Vilaró . . ." She named some of the period's first male architects and Senruh stopped listening.

If he found Pell, what would he say to him? Or do? His gaze returned to a gray, almost faceless creature across the room, wrapped in an undulating construction Marget had told him was a sensory table. Cuddles, she had called the being. A nickname, she said, since the creature communicated by translating the room's sounds and sights to touch. All the colonists enjoyed trying to learn its language, Marget said, twinkling up at him. Senruh's mouth had twitched. So much for the spacers not liking personal contact!

Now his gaze slid over the other forms. Most were man-like, some dressed in orange suits like his, but none wore an unbleached robe topped by a mop of pale curls. If anything had happened to that argumentative, stiff-necked—! He felt deserted, he realized suddenly, as if he had lost a friend. Friend! His cheeks burned. He made himself listen to Marget.

She glanced up at him and laughed. "This must sound odd to you. You've always had equality between the sexes, haven't you?"

At the end of the cave he heard a splash. Senruh looked toward the rock-edged pool there. Behind it water streamed down the dusky mirrors that stretched from floor to ceiling and to each side of the cave's farthest wall. They reflected the pool's gleaming leaves and flowers, its dark water awash with green . . . A head emerged, in silhouette but for two great black eyes rimmed with green and yellow fire. They caught Senruh's gaze. Marget's question faded, replaced by a tug on his mind.

Welcome, brother, a voice whispered in Senruh's head. Senruh stared at black ripples slashed with green lapping at a noseless face. Brother! That? The grip on his mind firmed.

You and your Choices are no stranger, manling. The voice paused. The boy sensed a waiting. *Danger!* he thought. But he did not feel danger. Only strength, and a curious tentative kindness. The bazaar had whispered guesses about such a creature. Frightened, intrigued, Senruh stretched his thoughts to the other. And sinuous brown-green flowed through them to make his mind their home.

I have followed your account to our healer, the voice said. *The fears, the changes have made you brother. Look!* Alien pictures—yet familiar as seen by his doubled mind— crowded behind Senruh's eyes.

In the water dweller's skin, Senruh flirted through the water, a small sleek swimmer. As his fins and tail flipped through the water he was filled with babyhood's wonder and endless possibility. His sides ached, they itched. Lumps formed. They spread into claws, then legs and long taloned fingers. He felt an upward pull, he swam ever higher, he clambered up a rock, the water about him thinned. He met the sky's silver mirror, he thrust through it, he staggered under gravity's heavy hand. Air ripped into lungs he had never known he possessed. And in his mind, thought burst into being . . .

In a gray-shadowed cave half-in, half-out of water, he studied jeweled book scrolls. He dreamed—not of words and new fine-spun webs of thought, but of eyes and slim strong loveliness and trysts beneath the moon-washed waves . . .

Blood pounding, he stood on land. His neck frill rose. Behind him his mate crouched, dewy-eyed, awaiting the victor of the death match she had forced. The kill's fierce joy rushed through him. He raised his daggered thumbs . . .

In their grotto floored with silver pebbles, wild with victory, he coupled with his mate even as she wept for her disemboweled lover lying twitching at their feet. And later Senruh-the-water-dweller wandered the shore alone, ashamed, alarmed at this new ecstasy he had found within himself, the peace-keeping disciplined scholar . . .

He could bear no more! Senruh pulled free of the water dweller's memories. They had pried up the edges of his own unhealed wounds, his furtive knowledge.

Brother! the other whispered. In the distant pool the boy saw widening circles and, slipping beneath the surface, a long thin hand and lethal pointed thumb. Disoriented, Senruh blinked into a haze of green light. Marget was beside him still. She was speaking.

What the swimmer said is true, Senruh thought. With Marget sponsoring him, that creature in the pond, the tactile being across the room, each person in this chamber that she gave loyalty to as well as those scattered among the stars, would be his new sister, cousin, mother, father . . . He would have a family such as the bazaar had never dreamed of! How they would talk if they knew! The boy waited impatiently for Marget to finish.

". . . and the cavern's energy-saving. Cool in summer, warm in winter, protects us from your sun . . ."

"Marget?" he said when she drew breath. "When you adopt me into your tribe will a clerk from the temple take word back to the Slave Courts?" *And the bazaar?* he added to himself.

"It's not that simple," she began as he stared around the lofty chamber. Neither the green glow nor the white splashes of moonlight hinted at a secret entrance from the Temple of Sassurum. Yet Ariahnne had used it. If she could be believed. Senruh moved closer to the healer trying to recapture his feeling of homecoming and of safety. Her gold-brown eyes looked up at him with clinical detachment.

"Tired? This should be over soon if Grinelda ever appears. I'm looking forward to getting you back to your pallet!" She put her hand on his knee and squeezed. Senruh froze.

A pallet touch and a reference to one in public! In the health room, could he have misunderstood? Surely, Marget had refused him! He remembered her caress of a moment earlier. Perhaps she lied and it was not only for luck. Well, he had offered. He swallowed and stared at her small fine-boned hand, waiting for it to grope higher, displaying his availability, his worthlessness, to the assembly. He stole a glance at the little healer's face.

It was quiet. She watched Enkolo, who stood just inside the open entrance doors. He was motioning someone to hurry. Marget smiled.

"Enkolo's a good administrator," she said. "And a grade-one empath. I know of two opportunities he's refused to shuffle papers for a whole star quadrant. If anyone can handle Grinelda, he can. So don't worry." She patted his knee and put her hand back in her lap.

Senruh stared at his clenched fists, wondering when she

would handle him again. Then he began to think. Marget had seemed unmoved. Spacers showed their legs freely. Perhaps they touched another's without concern. Feeling lightened, he looked to his other side.

Moonlight spilled through the dusky green light from a jagged hole in the ceiling. Through the gap he could see the volcanoes' fire-webbed slopes and the midnight sky thick with stars. The veil's scarlet had long since set.

For a moment the boy seemed to stand again in Ariahnne's villa at sunset, staring at another sky hole and at what lay beneath it. Ras's sweat-sheened face still haunted Senruh's dreams; as did the bearer's fate. Shivering, sharing the man's joy bright with pain, Senruh followed the spill of moonbeams downward. A shadow moved from a niche into the column of greenish silver. Moonlight blazed on fair curls.

"Pell!" Senruh jerked his broad grin into a frown as the boy, unsmiling, sat beside him. Senruh glanced at him, then away. New skin like that Marget had given Senruh sheathed the boy's bare feet and one hand. The other moved naturally. It no longer hung useless at his side.

"We have to sit together," Pell said. "Enkolo told me. He's sponsoring me." In the strange light his eyes were the color of sun-lit pools overhung by ferns. They glanced toward Marget.

"I saw what she was doing. Didn't take you long to find someone to do your tricks for, did it? She pay well?"

"Better than you!" With satisfaction Senruh watched Pell flush and turn away. *Unwarranted! Wrong!* he thought, enraged. On his other side Marget stirred.

"Who are you talking to, Senruh? Is that your friend that Enkolo bandaged? The one you were so worried about?"

Pell shot Senruh a surprised glance before he stared back at his hands twisting in his lap.

"I wasn't worried!" Senruh said roughly. *Truth,* the scribe told him again in his mind. And, *Talk as you have to me,* Marget had advised.

"Yes," Senruh muttered. He found himself unable to take his eyes from the other boy. When they came in, dust had smeared Pell's face and matted the golden tangles. Now his curls glittered. So. Enkolo had a 'fresher too.

Senruh pictured the big hands guiding Pell through its steam and sprays. He felt hot then cold, found a raging echo in himself of the bearers' jealousy. He stopped short. He would not be like them! He concentrated on the spacers' leader, his shake of the head and faint smile, as a thin, determined-looking young woman shouldered by him.

Lips pursed, face hidden by dirty brown hair that fell, unbound, almost to her waist, the girl seemed to be staring at her tray. There, she balanced a pile of fat dry cakes, a steaming silver 'seq urn, and a crock of songfruit pressings. Their blue lights arced and spun above its broken seal. Stacks of ritual masculine bowls and feminine vases rattled beside them. Senruh's eyes widened as he looked from them to the girl. She moved purposefully in his direction.

A creature no higher than his chest, Senruh estimated, she wore a Rabu priestess's robe of thick shimmering spider silk, its green tinged with gold, the goddess's sacred color of growth and renewal. For a moment Senruh imagined himself at Ariahnne's side at a midnight fete, and his lady's caustic amusement at what the girl's choice did to her already sallow skin.

Beside him Pell exclaimed, "A priestess! Do the spacers worship Sassurum?"

Senruh hesitated. "I didn't think so."

"No—" Marget began, leaning around him, but the young woman, near them now, looked up.

"I can answer for myself, Marget." She had a nasal accent. "Nothing wrong with *my* hearing! No, we don't worship your goddess," she told Senruh, "but she's our sponsor. I'm making a few changes." She looked challengingly at the healer. "This is my idea—to honor her, and any Napharese visitors. Like my robe?" She looked down

at herself smugly. A splotch—it looked like a soup stain—
decorated the gold-threaded front panel.

Senruh felt a small shock. It was sacrilege for anyone
but the goddess's chosen to wear such a garment. Novices
had been known to grow into old womanhood and die without Sassurum's ever appearing to them and appointing
their color. Well, perhaps the girl did not know. "It is very
rich, lady," he said diplomatically.

She shrugged. The cups rattled, balanced, and subsided.
"I can afford it," she said as Pell let out a breath. It was
very bad luck to break a ritual cup. It was one of the reasons they were so seldom used.

The girl wavered a last man-length across the stone then
sank to her knees, tray wobbling, to offer its contents to
Senruh.

"Need help, Grinelda?" Enkolo said from behind her.

She shook her head. A long brown hair loosened and
floated down to settle on the cakes. "Let me do my job for
once, Enkolo!" The dark-faced man grinned and faded
back toward the doors. As he passed Marget, the healer
caught at his sleeve. He paused.

"Are you expecting trouble?" Marget pitched her voice
low. Senruh, watching under his lashes, saw Enkolo
shrug.

"Just staying ready. I'll leave her to you." He nodded toward the brown-haired young woman as Grinelda began
the offering ritual.

"Will thee partake of refreshment, oh honored Brother
of Nations, Defender of the Sacred Tree, Stone, and Star?"

Senruh risked shooting an amused glance at Pell. The
boy returned it, blue eyes shocked. Grinelda had coupled
the intimate pallet form of *you* with the most formal of
royal salutations. If this was an example of the Questioning, Senruh began to think the off-worlders needed his
answers. Marget interrupted.

"You might introduce yourself, first. Grinelda's our
Studier of Mankind, Senruh, our anthropologist. She was
my partner's assistant, a fine statistician and anthropome-

trist. For a cycle she's been doing Jien's work besides her own. She's a member of one of galaxy center's foremost families, the—"

"Introductions come later!" Grinelda cut in. "As you'd know if you ever read what Jien wrote instead of just endlessly transcribing it! And never mind my family. They wouldn't thank you for telling!"

Senruh straightened on the narrow shelf. He had heard that tone of belligerent pain before. Next to him Marget tightened his lips. Hastily Senruh made the proper reply to Grinelda.

"I thank you for your courtesy, noble priestess," he said, giving her the title her robe merited. He ignored Pell's disapproving stare.

Balancing an effervescing bowl of blue songfruit liquor in one hand, Senruh reached under Grinelda's dropped hair for a cake. He sipped politely, bit into the pastry's floury sweetness, and bowed. The girl's close-set eyes blinked up at him.

"You're welcome," she said. "I hope we vote to keep you and that the temple lets us. Marget's report on you was very—interesting. I'm looking forward to getting to know you better. A lot better."

Senruh choked, mouth full of crumbs. "Keep!" he wheezed. "Marget?"

Grinelda rose and nodded. The tray dipped. As she knelt before Pell she said over her shoulder to the healer, "I thought you were minimizing his chances of being Sacrificed. The priestesses almost never let us keep a runner who kills. You can't coddle these people, Marget, or they won't know when to fight. They can. Or they wouldn't have survived."

"I saw no need to frighten the child," the healer broke in. "I have some influence with the temple, our colonists. And you keep away from him, young woman, or I'll put you on report! I don't care how influential your family is, I won't have him tampered with. He's had enough of people like you!"

Senruh changed position on the uncomfortable ledge. He stared at his hands, acutely conscious of Pell listening to the two women fight over him. Behind his embarrassment, panic fluttered as he remembered his master's and the guard's threats. He could not go back! "Uh, Marget, Grinelda . . ."

"It's all right, I can wait." The young woman flashed him a tight smile. The green light glinting on her hair and teeth and eyes gave her the look of a stalking change lizard. Senruh edged closer to Marget.

"She can't keep you trussed up forever. At least I've warned you," Grinelda said. "And Marget—" She swung toward the healer. The 'seq urn tilted, dark red liquid sloshed onto the tray. Its bitter aroma teased Senruh's nostrils. "If I were you," Grinelda said, "the next time I examined my patient I'd take a good, hard look. This one hasn't been a child for a long, long time." She gave Senruh a straight-mouthed stare that encompassed him from his bare soles to his stiffening face then, still kneeling, turned to Pell.

As the Studier of Mankind and Pell went through the offering ritual—Senruh noticed that the other boy was not as careful as he to avoid the stray hair—Senruh gazed into his bowl of songfruit liquor. In the dark blue fluid shot with stars, he saw glossy curls and, between his black brows and his cheekbones' flat planes, the impenetrable shadow that was his eyes. That bright image was what Grinelda wanted, as a child might a glittering toy or even a shabby broken one, he thought. She had no interest in the qualities Marget had named that lay behind his unseen eyes.

Just this morning Senruh would have been flattered by the girl's interest, pleased at the prospect of her coin. Now he was not. He glanced at Marget. Marget, whom he had expected to give him a new life. Was Grinelda right, could freedom only be taken for oneself? Already today he had done much toward his own.

As unaccustomed pride worked in him like new white shoots pushing toward the light, Senruh heard a rippling exclamation. He glanced from his sparking bowl to Margget. She did not look at him. Instead, her startled eyes were focused over his shoulder at the cavern's end.

"By the ten thousand nonexistent gods . . . !" Pell breathed at Senruh's side. Senruh turned, fast.

Beyond the rocky vine-hung pool the mirrored wall had split to reveal a stony tunnel. In its mouth torches smoked, trailing black and yellow streamers on the passage's dark breath. Their fiery light coruscated over a tall young-old priestess; her golden hair streaked with copper seemed to blaze. High priestess of Sassurum, sister and consort to the Ensai, she sponsored the spaceport on Naphar and was its judge. Two Rabu priests flanked her; more crowded at her back. From behind her came the rich soft ring of bells.

In a low voice that carried to the chamber's farthest corners she said, "I come on behalf of the bazaar slave, Senruh," and stepped into the room.

Chapter Twenty

SENRUH STARED at the priestess. Smoking light and verdant shadow coursed through her bright hair and the shining folds of her blue-green robe. It matched her eyes: green for all that grew and changed and blue for the sea and sky that gave it life. As she paced toward the water dweller's pool, disks of fire and darkness floated on the waves, winking through the lace of rock and silhouetted flowers.

The torches flared. Shadows from the vines above the pool shot toward the tunnel's mouth. They twined about a second pair of soldier priests escorting two captives from the passage. At Senruh's knee, Grinelda lowered her tray to the floor with a crash.

"Well! They've never done that before!" she said. "Scroll! Where's that curd-eating scroll?" She fumbled in her sleeve, unrolled the paper; then stared, mouth open.

The captives had stepped from the dark. Torchlight gleamed on the swinging golden chains of royalty. They shackled the wrist of a dark-haired man, a half-breed, to that of a gaunt stately woman, a Rabu half a head taller than he. As the tall woman paced forward trailing her fellow prisoner, her amber veils bordered with red curved then straightened about golden sandals and bony hands alight with rings. Rouge gave her haggard face its only color. She did not look at the boy or his companions.

"Ariahnne," Senruh breathed. Less than a man-length from him, she stopped before the priestess. Her fellow prisoner turned his head. Senruh saw harsh features, black long-lashed eyes that stared through him, then away. Beside the boy Grinelda gave an approving growl.

"Ras! But he's—!" Feeling kicked, Senruh looked from the first head bearer to the priestess and Ariahnne. He slid off the narrow ledge; beside him, Marget's hand pulled him back.

"Don't you dare bow to that—that woman!" she hissed.

"Do you know them, Senruh? Is that the princess you . . . ?" Pell broke his narrow-eyed silence. "Don't kneel. You don't owe her loyalty. I won't, not even to the priestess. I'm no follower of her goddess! I—" Grinelda hushed him. He subsided, then bent low. "Who's that with her?" he whispered. Senruh opened his mouth to answer. He shut it.

In loud tones the muffled soldier priests told the captives to face their priestess and hear her charges. At Senruh's feet Grinelda scribbled furiously on her scroll. Senruh nodded toward Ras. "He's her servant. I thought—he should be dead!" He took a shuddering breath of the smoky air. As Ariahnne and her minion turned, their chains rang in a hush broken only by the torches' sputter, a cough, and a pulsing roar like the tread of distant marchers. The bright-haired woman took a scroll from her sleeve and read.

"Ariahnne Addiratu, First Dweller of Qaqqadum, you are accused: Of leading a bond servant into theft and illegal liaisons. Of encouraging your slaves in public lewdness. Of denying a minion his Sacred Choice in the disposal of his person and in the form and length of his servitude. Of planning his death—secret, unmourned, unsanctioned by Sassurum. And of slave murder.

"If these accusations are proved, I, the Mouth of Sassurum; I, who by right of equal birth may try you and find you guilty, will charge you with betraying the goddess's weak and helpless. As is required by law your accusers are here, your trial is now. Blessed be the swift justice of Sassurum, heavier on the privileged than on the poor.

"How do you answer, cousin, First Dweller of Qaqqadum?"

As the tall priestess spoke she beckoned. Senruh glanced over his shoulder. Two figures shuffled from the tunnel. One seemed familiar.

Beside her the muffled soldier priests had dropped their mantles. Murmurs rose from the great chamber. One man wore a butcher priest's scarlet robes, gold-bordered for royal Sacrifice. Slowly, with both hands, he raised his sword. The torches behind him sliced its imprint across Ariahnne. In the green dark someone exclaimed. Ariahnne ignored it, staring coolly at the other priest, who was enveloped in white shroud clothes. He pulled on a shapeless eye-slitted mask, took from his sleeve a cup of darkened silver, banded with black jewels. It was the Cup of Merciful Forgetfulness.

"Will—will they kill her right here?" Marget's fingers tightened on Senruh's upper arm. He nodded.

"If she's found guilty."

Marget swallowed and let him go. "Well, she must have known she couldn't get away with it forever!" Released, the boy slid to the floor and bowed over his splinted arm. Marget exclaimed and grabbed at his suit. He raised his head, lips parted to protest. No sound came. Ariahnne was turning.

Yellow eyes stared over her single face veil. They focused above his head. He whipped around, following her gaze to her two accusers. They were closer now. Abruptly, Senruh recognized the woman. In the Avenue of Precious Delights she had cried shame at the bearers' excesses and hurried away. Senruh's mouth twisted. Much good her censure had done him, then or now, either! He glanced back, fell into Ariahnne's sulfur gaze. Paralyzed, he stared upward.

Ras was a silent shadow behind his lady as she paced toward Senruh, golden sandals shushing on the stone, chains calling like lost bells. She stopped.

"My little lizard," she breathed from high above him,

"so you did escape. To accuse me. You were ever full of sur-prises."

"I didn't, lady! I wouldn't!"

Behind him Marget's voice rang out. "No. I did! Crea-tures like you should be stepped on, hard, before they do more damage!"

Ariahnne flicked the healer a single burning glance. She looked back at the boy, the blaze in her eyes a little abated. "So, my own, it seems you did not betray me after all. Yet, I must defend myself to you. When you are look-ing so very fine." Appreciatively, her gaze slid down his orange suit. Flushing, Senruh drew his legs under him. Ariahnne laid a hand on his hair. She turned back to the priestess, her husky tones smooth as thickened honey.

"I plead only goodwill," she said, "at the most an overzealous mother love toward this, my most treasured minion."

"The audacity—!" Marget hissed behind Senruh. Above him Ariahnne, ignoring the healer, straightened her back. Her voice took on the throb of anger.

"Unaccustomed as I am to justifying my actions to a nameless half-breed robe tosser so ill-bred as to spy on my most private moments . . . !" Ariahnne stopped, breathing hard.

Through smarting eyes, Senruh had seen Ras give a tiny shake of the head. The only break in the moment's quiet were the ripple and splash of the water dweller's pool and a sound like tramping soldiers and the clash of arms. *The wind*, Senruh thought. In the shadows beyond the torches he glimpsed Enkolo strolling toward the doors. Above the boy, Ariahnne continued.

"When your temple guards came to my villa, cousin, and presented me with the list of my crimes, I—persuaded—them to escort me here through the inner city. There, by Sassurum the All-Seeing's temple, we extracted this evi-dence that the last-named and most heinous of my offenses did not exist. Ras?"

The broad-shouldered head chairman bowed to the

priestess, then, chain horizontal between them, circled
Ariahnne to stand, feet apart, before Senruh. Ariahnne
nodded toward Ras.

"Is this the slave whom you saw so compromisingly
shackled to my floor?" she asked the boy.

"I—yes! But how . . . ? He died. We ate—!"

"You are not certain?" Ariahnne's tone was silky. "Perhaps he looks different, now. If he were as you last saw
him . . . ? Ras!"

At her gesture the bearer, stony-faced, unlaced his robe.
He shrugged an arm and shoulder free; he spoke in his
gravelly voice to the guard. "Unshackle her." He nodded
toward Ariahnne. "It is not seemly that she should kneel
at my side when I lie upon this stone." Half his back
emerged. Senruh caught his breath.

A multitude of scars, red and new, white and old, crossed
the strongly muscled flesh. Beside the boy Grinelda leaned
forward. He glanced at her. The small brown eyes looked
hungry. He found his voice.

"No!" he said. "Don't! It's him. But how—?"

Ariahnne bent. A jeweled hand emerged from her drifting veils. Long nails touched her servant's shoulder. Indif-
ferently he straightened, pulled his robe about him and
reknotted the laces.

"It is very simple," Ariahnne said. "Ras did not die. He
never does. Though that first time, in an excess of enthusi-
asm . . . Eh, my Ras?"

Black eyes glanced upward. They held a reminiscent
smile. Envy twisted in Senruh's loins, he felt it move his
mouth and eyes. The bearer's gaze caught him. Incredibly,
one thick-fringed lid descended in a wink. The man folded
his arms; his fetters sang a golden tenor to the outside
wind's crash and grumble. At the cavern's shadowy end,
Enkolo listened at the doors.

"As it happened," Ariahnne took up her story, "that
first time also we were seen. Entirely by chance. And when
later I offered freedom to that chairman who had observed
us—if he would enter my central chamber unforced—his

eagerness when at last he came, his terror, were so . . ." She paused, trembling, her mantles drifting uneasily about her. ". . . delicious . . ." she whispered.

She swallowed and added, "But I do not murder helpless slaves! All who come to my inner room are free! Certain of their imminent destruction, perhaps, but also by then yearning for it. For I am skilled! At the last they beg it of me as I once . . ." She stopped and bit her lips, her fingers twisting among her mantles like jointed serpents. Ras stepped forward, touched her sleeve.

"Let me, lady," he said. She took a long breath, clasped her hands until the knuckles whitened, and nodded. The man looked over his broken nose at the colonists as if they stood on a remote shore. His sculptured mouth straightened. "It is a game with her," he said. "When her chosen companion—one each cycle or two satisfies her—sees what we choose to show him, what this boy saw"—he nodded toward Senruh—"or perhaps a little more, she offers him his freedom, from her and from his debts. In exchange he must go to her and while she watches, strip, lie upon that floor, let her fasten each shackle . . . She leaves ample time between for him to cry refusal. Which she will honor but at the cost, he knows, of his newly won freedom. He allows it all. Because by doing so he gains something—freedom, ecstasy—that, however brief, he has come to love more than life." The head bearer cleared his throat.

"Iniquitous!" the healer muttered from the ledge behind Senruh. "Barbaric! And he's as much to blame as she is. To lead those children . . . ! How he could, when he himself—! I'll never understand!"

"I understand," Grinelda said from the floor where she sat cross-legged by Senruh, her bile-colored robe hitched almost to her knees. She had stopped writing on the scroll in her lap. Her gaze clung to Ras's solid shoulders.

"Senruh! Was that what you—?" Just above him, Pell's whisper was harsh. Senruh flushed and glanced covertly at Ariahnne. He shifted his knees on the stone. They were beginning to ache. In front of him Ras showed no more interest in their voices than in the wind.

"Her shackled companion's terror and despair," Ras continued after a sidewise glance at Ariahnne, "approximate as no player's could her own, when her mate and his unspeakable friend took her, a sheltered young woman deeply in love with her partner . . ." The harsh face worked, then smoothed. His rough voice steadied. "After, when he wakes, he finds himself in freedmen's housing by the Temple of Sassurum. There I or the mute offer him a choice: a gold piece for each cycle of service and transport from this city to another. Or, if he pleased her, access to himself when she wishes and two gold coins for each additional cycle of service. In either case her condition is that none of her minions see him again.

"Most leave. I stayed. I live in chambers above the warehouse that—employs me."

"That you *own*, my Ras, do you not?" Ariahnne's shaking voice held a proprietary pride. "And how many others by now supplied by your ships, your caravans . . ."

The dark face did not change, though when he looked at her it lightened into what, on another, might have been the preface of a smile.

"Periodically my lady comes to me there," he said. "And once each cycle or two we play out the mime this boy witnessed." He gestured toward Senruh. The golden fetters caroled like untaught chimes.

"I am free," Ras ended firmly. "But there is nothing I would not grant her." When he stopped, his ruined face as expressionless as when he began, the only sound in the room was the plash and drip of the water dweller's pond.

In the green darkness by the entrance Enkolo held the door. Three tall off-worlders went out; he shut and barred it behind them. Dark face thoughtful, the tall spacer drifted through the listeners to kneel by Marget. Senruh looked from the two of them, conferring, to Ras. Beside him Ariahnne swayed, caught herself, then stood firm. He touched her sleeve.

"Come, lady," Ras said. "They are answered enough. You are tired. Let us go." Looking down her thin curved nose at him, Ariahnne shook her head.

Behind Senruh, Marget's heels clacked on the floor as she bounced up. From the corner of his eye, Senruh saw the kneeling Enkolo grab for her, miss, then watch her, his eyes narrowing.

"Just like that!" Marget exclaimed before Ariahnne could speak. "Well, she doesn't get off so easily! What about this poor child, here?" She gestured toward Senruh. Enkolo's fingers closed on her other arm and jerked. She sat down with a thump.

"No interference in local politics, Marget." The spacer's murmur was soft as a manskin sheath on a dagger. "You didn't consult me on this. One more word and out you go; possibly home." As she shot him a fulminating look but shut her mouth, he lifted a neat eyebrow. "The ice is breaking up faster than I planned." Behind her, his orange-clad arm hovered by her shoulders, her waist; it dropped. The green tilted eyes intercepted Senruh's glance, grew bleak. Pointedly, Enkolo looked back at the prisoners.

Veils whispered. Chains sang their unresolved melody. One hand on Ras's arm, Ariahnne turned toward the priestess. "I would answer my other accusers! I take the stewardship of my slaves very seriously. This one, though only borrowed, has been like a dear son to me." Her knuckle rings glowed in the misty light as she reached out to ruffle Senruh's hair. Behind the boy, Pell snorted.

Senruh's scalp crawled. That same hand had pushed back his robe as he lay in the dust, had touched him, assessing his readiness to be a bearer . . . But behind his eyes torchlight flickered in a courtyard, in his mind he heard midnight laughter. Those were gentler memories; perhaps she, also, held to just one or two? His throat thickened. Within him grief wrung her hands and closed her eyes.

"Like any mother I looked forward to the day of this

boy's independence. For always he deferred to my wishes
in the solution of his boyish difficulties, even his choice of
pleasures. I hinted!" Ariahnne sighed. "To no avail. Ster-
ner methods were called for. Though my heart bled for the
pain I must cause him." A pointed tongue moistened thin
lips. "For his own good, of course," she added and glanced
down at Ras, who gave her a wary nod.

"My bearers exceeded their orders. They have been punished." Ariahnne's tongue flicked out once more. A small
sated smile crouched in the corners of her mouth. "As for
that young weed of a noble, his methods were crude. After
no more than two or three of those undisciplined lash
strokes, I sent him on his way. I could not allow him to
spoil . . . !" She stopped. Infinitesimally, Ras had shaken
his head.

"Is this true, bazaar slave Senruh?" the high priestess
broke in. The boy lowered his forehead to the floor.

"I—I don't know, lady." Shrinking, wishing Pell was not
there for he knew what he must do next, Senruh reached
around his splint to the neck opening in his orange suit.

"Marget?" Enkolo prompted from behind him. "If you
can speak on this, do so, or they'll have him stripped."

"I—it could be. If the whip had a lot of lashes. With something on them that could gouge." Shakily, Senruh lowered
his hand.

"That is in your favor then, Ariahnne Addiratu, whatever your motive," the tall bright-haired woman said.
"Continue."

Ariahnne spread her hands and smiled. In the light of
the sputtering torches her teeth looked yellow and sharp.
"That is really all. Evidently this delectable but obtuse
small scuttler here saw where his life Choices were leading him. For he has freed himself from me, has he not?"
She drew a breath and stared over the assembly's heads,
the smile gone from her thin lips. "As I would I could," she
whispered.

Senruh scarcely heard her. He shut his eyes. How she
must have despised him. Even her joy in him had been a

trick. Fool! To hope that she had cared for one small part of
him or their time together. He bit his swollen lip until it
ached. He heard a hushing of garments and was enveloped
in the scent of crumbling flowers and age.

"Look up, my heart, and listen," a husky voice murmured to him alone. Obedient, he lifted his face, scowling
to keep back the tears. Ariahnne knelt before him, Ras a
tall shadow behind her. As she looked down at Senruh, her
sulfur gaze swirled to tarnished gold. She extended an age-
spotted hand. When he did not take it she let it fall, her
chains ringing like enchanters' chimes.

"Forgive me, my treasure, for frightening you." Her intimate tones were clear. They carried beyond the priestess
to the whole assembly, Senruh thought. "I beg your indul-
gence for cultivating your dependence, for encouraging
your less decorous penchants, for leading you unknowing
into my debt, and—the crux!—for choosing such a severe
awakening." She bowed her head. The yellow mantles
edged with scarlet floated around her braids and gems and
paste-stiffened curls. When she looked up her stubby
lashes were dark with moisture.

"Can you ever pardon me, my small damaged joy?" A
tear slipped down one raddled cheek. Ariahnne never
cried. Belief struck Senruh like a fist.

"Ah, no, get up! There is nothing to forgive, you—you
were good to me!" Choking, through blurring eyes, Senruh
watched her sway to her feet. For a moment the dry hand
touched his hair. He remembered its other intimacies and
shivered. A tiny smile curved her mouth.

"You were ever a sweet-natured child." She bent toward
him. Her breath was spiced and old. "I loved you, you
know, my little caged lizard. It is as well for you that you
are free of me. Though I shall miss your heart-catching
song."

Senruh bent his head. "And I loved you, lady," he told
her for the first time. He doubted that she heard him. She
was turning, drawing Ras with her, their fetters pealing

above the grumble and cries of the wind. Husky voice controlled, she began her answers to the other accusations.

The last words said, Ariahnne leaned heavily on her bearer's arm. She stared down her curved nose at the equally tall priestess before her. "Your verdict, cousin?"

The torches' reflected flames twisted with green shadow in the priestess's bright hair. Beneath its gold and copper waves, her turquoise eyes widened, darkened; she held up a finger.

A breeze seemed to stir through the great green-lit cavern. The rumble of thunder, the cries of ghostly beleaguered armies shivered in the dimming air. Night clustered about her head and she seemed to grow. Her high piled hair, sooty with shadow, darkened into loose black curls that caught the wind, netting a myriad of stars and suns while behind her the cave's walls glimmered to midnight. She gazed at each watcher in turn, her eyes deep and black as the spaces between the worlds.

"Sassurum!" The witnesses and soldier priests whispered the goddess's name. They lowered their foreheads to the floor.

"What are they—? Why—? And what's that noise?" Pell sounded bewildered. Head still lowered, Senruh glanced behind him then followed the boy's blue gaze. Pell seemed scarcely to look at the red priest who, at the goddess's gesture, rose and lifted his sword or at the white-shrouded one, on his feet again, who held the black Cup of Merciful Forgetfulness before him in both hands, or at the goddess, tall as a cloud, standing between them.

"You have done wrong, my daughter," the presence said. Her deepened voice contained the sound of all Naphar's seas and the winds that moved on them and the grinding of the continents wandering the planet's floods of molten stone. "Your sorrow at your mischief is not complete, my child. Yet, neither is your evil. Nor do my two beloved sons—Ras, Senruh—whom you have most injured, wish for revenge. I know that you, too, have suffered grave wrong and still work out the righting of it. For these reasons, this one time, I allow you your life. But not as it was. You are banished—let it be so written!—to your estates far from the city that provided your amusements and ignorant too-young victims. Nor shall I again entrust my bound children to you. Only the free may serve you—record it!— and you shall inform your idleness with labor. Your overseer: my erring but much-loved son, Ras."

Huge black eyes gazed long at Ariahnne's bent head. "You shall drink the cup," the goddess said. "Tonight, before you begin to forget, you may choose jewels, scrolls, instruments of pleasure, for your exile. You may use them as freely as Ras, who has been your most willing tool, allows. This is your second chance, my daughter. Do not let it slip. There will not be another." The night-dark eyes gave Ariahnne a stern look of great tenderness. Their gaze turned to Senruh. His belly quaked but he could not glance away.

"As for you, Senruh, my son, I have followed your flight with grief and with joy. Without my permission and outside the Weavers' plan, you have cut short the lives of eight of my children. More hang in the balance. Still, it was my messenger that led your flight and I know both your hearts, your causes, and your repentance. You and your companion may have your lives. But only if you can win them. Your existence must become a hidden thing. Beware, my child."

Senruh tried to speak the formula of reply. No words came. The goddess smiled, teeth white as beach shells in the thickened light. For a moment a zephyr breathed around the boy's hair and throat as if she had touched him, then sighed away through the chamber. Transfixed, Senruh watched the dark-haired being expand until her amber skin and flying tresses seemed to fill the cavern. They thinned; behind her the shadows shook and paled; walls replaced the midnight sky.

Once more green radiance bathed a rocky cavern soft with ferns and murmuring water and a tall bright-haired priestess who had been, for a time, the Mouth of Sassurum. She gestured.

The red priest lowered his sword. Its blade threw the fitful torchlight in golden handfuls among the vines and stones and colonists' rapt faces. She gestured again. On her other side the masked white-robed priest stepped forward. His sleeves fell back, he proffered the cup, its black gems liquid with reflected flame. Her bony hands trembling, Ariahnne took it. Holding the chalice in both her palms, she stared into it.

"Drink deep, cousin," the bright-haired woman said. "Your respite from memory will last a cycle or perhaps a little more. May I wish you peace in your new life?"

"New life!" Marget's whisper from behind him recalled Senruh to himself. "Is that all—?"

"Hush, Marget," Enkolo's deep voice answered. "Just what do you recommend? Chopping off her head?"

"Well, I—!" Marget broke off as, before them, Ariahnne lifted the Cup of Merciful Forgetfulness. She pushed her yellow veils aside, flung back her head, and drained the chalice. Torchlight flared on its curved sides. Watching, Senruh traced their blackened filigree of leaves and flowers, named the healing herbs, memorized the light scattering, green and gold, over the gems on Ariahnne's fingers and woven through her elaborate coiffure . . . She lowered the cup. She returned it to its keeper.

"Will I—? How long?" she asked.

"Till you begin to forget?" the priestess said. "Till morning at the shortest. Certainly by tomorrow's sunset. All the persons you have known, all your feelings will be locked in the past. Only your learning will remain."

Ariahnne stole a sidewise glance at Ras then looked away from his stolid face. He seemed to stare into a hidden distance. The priestess smiled.

"Strong attachments remain but no recollection of their quality or circumstances."

"I—see." As, beside her, Ras's dark face lightened, Ariahnne released a long breath. "The goddess has not lost her gift for irony. So. My plaything is to be my keeper. And shall you treat me as I have you, my Ras?"

As the priests bent to unlock their chains, Ras looked over them to Ariahnne. In his roughened voice he said, "I do not change. If you wish me with you, lady, I will be there for you. If you do not, I will go. I will aid you in any pleasure. They are all one to me. You owned every part of me long ago. I will always belong to you whatever you do. Or become."

Ariahnne smiled into the black eyes so near her own. She laid an age-spotted hand on his strong forearm. "I know," she said. "Come. Let us choose our tools for beguiling the days ahead. Perhaps—who knows?—I will require none of them and, at least for a cycle, I will sleep freed from dreams."

The last fetter chimed to the floor like an ended song. Stepping over it, she swayed toward the tunnel. A priest accompanied her. Ras stood still, watching. His black gaze moved to Senruh's. The boy flinched from the dislike, the jealousy, he had found in the other bearers' eyes and expected to find . . . His face slackened with surprise. Ras's eyes snapped with tolerant amusement.

"Why? Aren't you angry because I—she—?" Senruh halted, face crimson. But Ras only shook his head. He glanced again at Ariahnne, awaiting him at the tunnel's entrance.

"There's no need, now. And you loved her. It meant much to her." He turned. Without a backward look he walked briskly toward his lady.

Senruh stared after him. Behind the boy Marget cleared her throat. "All right," she said. "I pity her. A little. But that poor man! Patient, faithful, loyal . . . !" Her voice was thick.

Next to Senruh, Grinelda halted her scribbling. "Pity!" she said. "Envy's closer. I wonder . . ." She gave Senruh a speculative look.

He hardly noticed. To him, her voice had blended with the roar and tramp of the wind without. His throat ached, he bent his head. Behind him Enkolo muttered to Marget; the tall man rose and started toward the entrance. The healer jumped up and caught at his orange sleeve. Senruh closed his eyes. So Marget and the scribe had been right. The loyalty, the friendship he had thought as rare as odd-colored dragons did exist, even a homecoming of sorts. Not just in the stars but everywhere if one had the courage to find it. And more, the goddess and his lady had cared. Always. Tears prickled behind the boy's eyes as deep inside him something that had been broken began to heal.

Outside the barred twin portals, heavy feet stamped to a halt. Chainmail jingled, fists and lance ends pounded the carved wood.

"We claim blood right!" a contralto called. Deeper voices laced with shrill ones clamored behind it. "Admit us!" the first voice said. "We want those guard killers for death geld!"

Chapter Twenty-one

"I WAS AFRAID of that!" Enkolo's voice came from behind Senruh. Slow with surprise, the boy, still kneeling from his encounter with Ariahnne, looked from the shaking entrance doors at one end of the cavern to Enkolo and the white-robed healer. They stood a man-length from him before the seating ledge, about halfway between the doors and the tunnel gaping at the chamber's end. Senruh watched Marget's pale hair slide, green-shadowed, over her collar.

"You won't give them up?" she asked Enkolo. "Their own priestess forgave—!" The spacer's dark hand detached her small one from his sleeve.

"I won't endanger a whole mission for a couple of native boys, Marget. Or risk civil war. The last one between temple and state lasted a hundred cycles."

"But—!" She followed, talking, as Enkolo strode toward the pool. Almost running, he rounded it, stooped, and disappeared behind the pool's rocks and trailing plants.

"Guard killers! Send out the boy!" Outside the doors, feet began to stamp in time to the calls. Senruh jumped up, heart thumping, in time to see Enkolo palm the wall beside the tunnel's mouth. The mirrors shimmered into place. Shock replaced Senruh's fear.

"How—?" Fingers stiff at his side, he looked down at Grinelda for an explanation. He would not make the averting sign! But, cross-legged at his feet, she continued writing on her scroll. Just above her, Pell's bright head tilted. He looked up at Senruh.

"What's death geld?" he asked. He shifted on the narrow ledge. "Is it, well, what it sounds like?"

"Death! Death! Death!" the guards outside chanted in unconscious explanation. They began to beat their shields with their swords. Heart pounding against the scratchy orange suit, Senruh hunkered down. He felt safer, more hidden . . . He swallowed.

"It's a death for a death," he said. At his side Grinelda glanced at him, pushed her scroll wider, and scribbled on. "Don't they—? Isn't there any death geld in the highlands?" he asked Pell. The boy shook his head, eyes wide. Forcing his gaze from the doors, Senruh explained.

"Those guards we—we killed are shadows now in Arob Shamsi. They're screaming for revenge. They won't give anyone any rest till you and I take their places. Then they can get new threads from the Weavers and be one with the goddess in the bowels of the earth until it's their turn to be reborn. Or that's what the priests say." He glanced over his shoulder. The reverberating door seemed to be holding. "Mostly death geld means we get killed, or almost killed, once for each guard."

"Fascinating!" Grinelda breathed beside him, her writing tool poised. "Even Jien never published anything like that. I may get a monograph out of this!"

Senruh looked at her with distaste. At the sound of Enkolo giving orders from his place by the reflecting wall, the boy turned. Ten colonists, most in orange suits like his and the spacer's, hurried toward the carved entrance portals. The panels shivered with a rhythmic banging.

"Senruh!" deep voices shouted from beyond the doors. "Send out the filthy robe tosser!" shrill ones elaborated.

"They know you," Pell whispered as Enkolo walked toward them. "I never thought—! Of course, it's you they want. They hardly saw me, don't know my name. But I was the one who—!"

"Glad I'm going to be flayed and sectioned and not you?"

Senruh growled. As the words brought home his peril, the hair lifted on his scalp. Just moments before he had thought himself safe, even cherished. *Fool!* He looked at the door. Through the crack he saw the yellow light of torches. If they burned down the panels—!

"No!" Pell exploded just above him. "If you go or fight, I will too! This was my idea. Besides, I ple—" He stopped.

Senruh turned. For the first time he looked hard at the wiry form perched above him. The other's fingers twisted in a divided bright-colored lap.

"Orange! You too?"

Eyes dark as a twilight sea flicked Senruh a defensive glance. The guards gave up their chanting and roared as Pell nodded toward Enkolo. The tall spacer had stopped near the pool to snap a series of orders to the remaining colonists there. "He burned my robe," Pell said. "Didn't have anything else." Squeezing his knees together, he tucked his feet against the stone ledge. Flushing, Senruh pulled his gaze from the long strong legs. He imagined them stripped of the orange suit, in the hands of the guards outside, the citizens, the inhabitants of the Slave Pens . . .

"No!" he said, and swallowed. "Don't help! Hide while I draw them off. You couldn't—couldn't cope. Just stay out of my way when I run!"

"I can so!" Pell began, blue eyes sparking with anger. Looking up, he shut his mouth. A big hand closed on Senruh's shoulder. Enkolo.

"Now! Now! Now!" united voices howled in the outer cavern.

"We have to give them an answer, boys," the tall man said. He glanced at the quivering doors. "If either of you was a ruler, you'd have a chance in court. But you're both half-breeds, right? Same caste?"

By Senruh's other side, Grinelda stopped writing. Her small brown eyes watched them intently.

"No!" both boys said at once.

"He's only a little emptyhead," Senruh blurted. He

pulled his glance from the doors and made himself look at the other end of the room. Marget was standing by the mirrors. She gave him a strained smile. Feeling a little strengthened, Senruh nodded to her and looked Enkolo in the eye. "He's impulsive," he went on. "He didn't understand what he was doing. I did. Well, look at his brain size—compared to mine, he hasn't got anything to think with!" He grinned briefly at Pell, who was glaring at him. "If we're in trouble, it's my—!"

Pell's toe banged Senruh's ribs. With a gasp Senruh ended his tumble of words.

"Close your teeth!" the fair boy hissed, and shot to his feet. "Don't listen to him!" Pell told Enkolo. "I'm the ruler. Small. Born to think, administrate. He's only a lout, a slave, brawl! Look at those arms, that chest—when would he have had time to develop a mind?" A satisfied blue glance flicked Senruh, whose mouth had tightened.

"I thought of all the killings!" Pell finished. "I'll go with the soldiers. You—you just take care of him. Get him better!" Eyes suspiciously bright, the boy took one step toward the booming portals. Enkolo's long arm hooked him back.

"Not so fast, young fellow. Before either one of you immolates himself let's see if we can't talk them out of it. And—either I missed something back there or you boys did."

Senruh looked hard at the green eyes. If the situation had been less tense he might have thought they gleamed with amusement. Then the tall man was gone, pushing through vines and flowers to the back reflecting wall where Marget waited. She moved toward him, seeming to ask a question. Enkolo shook his head.

"Take off the bar!" he called toward the entrance. As two of the off-worlders stationed beside it obeyed, Senruh looked at the small healer, bitterly regretting his not having dug out of her the Question and its answer that would have made the spacers want him enough to defend him. If he had just a little more time—!

"Unless you do something besides sit there, you're going to die," a nasal voice whispered in his ear. The boy swung around. Grinelda's close-set eyes stared into his. Behind him the doors crashed open. The stone floor seemed to shake as the city guard tramped into the room.

Beside Senruh, Grinelda kneaded her haunches as if she had a cramp in them. She yanked her gleaming robe over her knees and sidled toward the boy. She leaned near. Her dull brown locks parted into strands that caped her almost to the elbow. They gave off a feral smell. Her ribs and thin breast rubbed Senruh's arm. Only cycles of his master's discipline kept the boy from pulling away. A long brown hair drifted onto his sleeve. Senruh looked past it, over his shoulder, to the close-ranked guard. The contralto was shouting orders for quiet.

"If you had my robe you could escape and go anywhere on Naphar," Grinelda breathed into Senruh's neck. Her breath was moist. His skin crawled. "All you have to do is take it. And give me something for it." She rose. At her long slow look he felt as though unclean hands searched beneath his orange suit. Watching him over her shoulder she sauntered toward the flowers and ferns and waist-high stone surrounding the pool in the cavern's center, only a few man-lengths before the mirrors.

She knows, Senruh thought. But Marget had missed the orange suit's indecency. Well, the healer was prudish; still, Senruh wished she had offered him the robe. He didn't know with Grinelda, if he could—

Senruh heard chirrs and fingersnaps. He turned, fast. If they were coming after him—! But the soldiers were leering at the orange-suited colonists who had just stepped from the shadows. The guards' superiors ordered quiet. A square older woman with cropped gray hair and a sand-colored face pushed forward. She thumped the butt of her spear on the cavern floor.

"We've lost eight men, maybe more, to a couple of boys who shouldn't have been able to get near them," she said. "One we don't know. But the other's a half-breed robe

tosser from the bazaar's southern quarter. Senruh. No last
name, no tribe. We want him. We won't use force if we can
avoid it, but if we have to, we will." Senruh felt cold. He
recognized that voice—he had last heard it howl, "Take
careful aim—and fire!"

Behind the stocky woman a mutter rose from the troops.
Chainmail jingled. Torchlight bounced off the officers'
crested helmets and the troops' mail caps, as the men and
women banged their spears in agreement. All Rabu, they
towered over most of the colonists.

That sight and the sound of his own name catapulted
Senruh after Grinelda. He ran, bent double; skidded onto
his knees at the grotto wall. He clutched the rock, straining to see through the profusion of sweet-scented flowers.
He froze. Tiny red crystal bells lay by his hand, their
prismlike stamens winking with green and white light. If
they tinkled all alone—! The Rabu might be night blind
but there was nothing wrong with their hearing. He heard
a slithering sound, then a hand tugged at his leg casing.
Grinelda lay on the floor grinning up at him.

"Couldn't resist me, eh?" she said. "Should be novel.
I've never done it with a dead man before. Or a robe tosser.
Does it only work if I put a coin in your slot first? Let me
see . . ." Propped on one elbow, she thrust a dirty hand
into her robe's chest pocket. Senruh stared at her, wondering just how well Marget knew her co-colonists. Even in
the bazaar he had seldom been addressed this forthrightly.
He glanced up. By the mirrors, Enkolo had gestured. Behind Senruh a second colonist joined the first in talking to
the guard's leaders. At the boy's feet, Grinelda raised an
eyebrow.

"Too complicated for you? I've heard about you half-
breeds. Well, who cares if only part of you is here. It's the
part I can't wait to get my hands on!" She opened her
palm. A tiny white-metal coin brimmed with green reflected light. *Not even silver,* Senruh thought, anger beginning to simmer under his bemusement. Before him, by the
mirrors, he glimpsed Marget moving toward Enkolo. The

spacer's deep voice mixed with her liquid one. They seemed to be arguing but Senruh could not make out the words. Grinelda poked him.

"See?" she said, and held the coin under his nose. "For you. When you—I—" In the interests of utter clarity she made a very explicit gesture. "Then I—give—you—robe! Understand?" Her grin broadened. She eyed him from below as if it were the end of a bazaar festival night, she an underfed child, and he the last sticky sweet on a tray.

Abruptly, as behind him he heard an off-worlder begin the measured phrases of what sounded like a speech, Senruh's mounting fear and offended sensibilities collapsed into a laugh. He smothered it, bent, and looped a section of Grinelda's musty hair above her ear. He whispered into it, watched her pout, then whispered some more. She began to look interested. At last she nodded and began pulling her yellow-green robe over her head.

Senruh averted his eyes from her exposed lower limbs while, by the doors, a sharp contralto overrode a spacer's conciliatory tones. Stooping by the pool's wall, Senruh dragged a finger down his suit, opening it. To one side he heard a rustle.

As he stepped out of his loathed orange clothing and Grinelda's robe dropped to the floor, the ferns beside them swayed; Pell's curly head appeared. Scowling, the boy looked from Senruh to Grinelda, then stopped. He stared at the young woman's long-legged form. Her scanty undertunic hid very little. Senruh, watching, felt a twinge of jealousy.

"What are you doing here!" he asked. He glanced down. Marget's sexless bandage, his legs—! Flushing, he scrabbled for Grinelda's discarded robe, then looked up toward the mirrors. If the healer should see them after her warning! But Marget stood on tiptoe apparently looking beyond the grotto at the negotiations by the doors.

"Wait, you're going to need help getting my robe over that splint!" At the sound of the nasal voice Senruh turned. The Studier of Mankind's head was under his chin.

He took a hasty step back as, superbly unconscious of her undress, Grinelda reached for him. She eased a wide sleeve around the splint, she pulled more silken folds over his head. Senruh's embarrassment faded. If she didn't care—! Absorbed in the intricacies of the borrowed robe's inner ties and flaps, he scarcely noticed the guards' thumping spears as they stood ready to hear their sirdar's orders. Grinelda smoothed more folds over him. They were still warm. And still smelled of her, he thought, breathing with care.

"I can see why Marget's so taken with you," the spacer's anthropologist told him, ignoring the glowering Pell beside her. "It must be fun to have your own muscle-bound idiot child to dress and undress . . ." She stopped in the act of yanking the robe downward to run her hand over Senruh's bare chest and shoulders. He stopped breathing.

"He's no idiot!" Pell broke the moment. His eyes were the color of songfruit pressings and seemed as full of arcing lights. He glared from the girl to Senruh, unspoken words written all over him. Grinelda shrugged and let the spider silk ripple down Senruh's length. It stopped at his shins, he saw with dismay. Oh well, he could stoop when he mingled with the guard by the doors, pretend to be a little emptyhead helper to the priests . . . He saw Pell take another long look at Grinelda's nether regions. Behind the boy green radiance glinted beside yellow torchlight on chainmail, metal rattled on stone and clashed with other metal as the guards moved into a new formation.

Beside Senruh, the fair boy tore his gaze from Grinelda and said stiffly, "Well, if I'm interrupting something! I only thought you might need help, but I'll be glad to go back. I'd rather! She's smaller than you, Senruh! Perverted, low . . . !" Pell turned. He stumbled past twining flowers, blundering toward white moonbeams shafting the green twilight. He seemed not to see the brief silhouettes passing before them to merge with the glowing dark.

Rage flashed through Senruh. He paid no attention to the tiny crescents of reflected green or the wash of silver on chainmail, nor did he register the other tall forms advancing, single file, along the cavern's opposite wall. One-handed, he grabbed Pell's orange suit between the shoulders and yanked the boy backward.

"Stop and listen for a change!" he hissed into Pell's neck. It smelled clean. Alien herbs spiced the soft curls, he breathed in Pell's familiar warmth. For a moment Senruh felt weak. The boy twisted from his grasp and kicked his knee. As it buckled, Senruh snatched at Pell and, sitting back on the wall, gave way to the safety of anger.

"You and the purity priestesses!" he said into Pell's set face. "You're both so perfect, and you've both got minds like dung piles! So how do you know what to accuse me of? Curtain lifting? Collecting two-for-a-bit inkings of skin-to-skin companionings?"

Crouching before him, back to the doors where only a remnant of the guard waited with their sirdar, Pell answered in a shaking voice, "Dung pile! Maybe! But at least I keep my thoughts in my head! While you—!" His gesture included the sky as well as the whole of Naphar. On either side of him Senruh heard deep-voiced mutters. Fury shut them out. He grabbed both Pell's shoulders to shake him.

"You—!"

"Shhh!" Grinelda's sticky hand clamped around one of Senruh's. Pushing between the boys she straight-armed Pell away from him. "You two want to fight or live?" Her hand moved up Senruh's arm. Through the silken sleeve she pinched it. "Look! You're surrounded! Run now in any direction and they'll know you couldn't possibly have come in with them, be one of them!" Senruh looked around him. It was true. The guards encircled the room preparing to search it, each trooper two arm-lengths from the next.

"Torches!" the stocky woman called from her post by the carved entrance portals. "And look under every leaf! The scum's got to be here. Chased him in ourselves!"

Heart thudding, he hunkered down, glaring through the plants toward Marget. Surely she—! But she only stood before the great shadowy mirror, her face white. In the hush,

before the guards shouted obedience, her musical voice
came clearly.

"Ah, Enkolo, how could you! This time you've arranged
for me to watch!"

As the tall spacer winced, Senruh saw the four men and
women in front of the mirrors take fireboxes from their
sleeves. Leg muscles twitching with his desire to run,
knowing he could not, Senruh flung himself to the floor by
the water dweller's pool. Grinelda scooted toward him,
pressed her hip and shoulder firmly against his. Senruh
was suddenly conscious of the thinness of his robe.

"Your friend's right, you're no idiot child," she whispered. "I thought Marget was exaggerating! If you survive
we're going to talk. Here they come! It's up to you, now."
Senruh looked toward the cavern's end.

There, the guards and their mirrored other selves
stowed the firebox wrappings in their robes. They snapped
down the boxes' insulation locks.

Senruh peered through nodding plants to watch the soldiers lift their boxes' pierced brass lids. Pulsing flowers of
light suffused the four intent faces as each blew on the
coals. With careful fingers the guards sifted white slivers
of tinder. Flames sprang up like golden sheaves. The
guards took their unlit torches from beneath their arms;
they touched the tips to the fire. The scent of burning firecloth and pitch tinged the air, almost overpowering the
cavern's stony tang.

Yellow hands of torchlight slid across four man-lengths
of rock to search the fronds where Senruh hid by the pool.
The water splashed gently beside him. He got to his knees,
watching the guards march toward him. Haunches tense,
he sat back on his heels; he almost overbalanced into the
pond. Stems and leaves rustled; Pell shoved against him.
Senruh looked for Grinelda, but she was gone. The feet
tramped closer.

"Turn! We'll take them back to back," Pell whispered,
his body tense with excitement. "We can boost a few into
the water. When reinforcements come from the entrance,

I'll hold them. You go. If I can I'll follow." His blue eyes squinted into the now brilliant torchlight.

"I—" Senruh's voice failed him. Pell could pass for an off-worlder. He had no need to chance death this way. Senruh was hunting words of thanks and refusal when four sets of studded sandals crashed into the grotto. His knees tightened; then a splash swiveled Senruh's head toward the pond.

Framed by ripples of reflected fire, a large-eyed head and twin-daggered thumbs emerged from the water. Senruh felt Pell grab a harsh breath. The water dweller took one powerful stroke toward them. Great eyes stared into Senruh's. Long, thin fingers grasped the boy's wrist and ankle, jerked him down. Then with scarcely a splash, the hands pulled Senruh beneath the surface.

Chapter Twenty-two

SMOOTH WEBBED FINGERS brushed Senruh's face. He kicked violently, struggling upward, starved lungs burning. The creature tucked him under one cool arm, the boy's splint pressing against the large bony chest, his legs floating past the water dweller's almost nonexistent hips. The boy's mind flipped toward panic. Alien thoughts touched its edges; his heart thumped and he tried to jerk away. The thoughts withdrew. He sputtered as the creature snapped a constricting film over his face. With a powerful kick it shot them downward.

Senruh's throat convulsed. His captor squatted with him in the dark currents beneath a rocky overhang. The boy pulled a hand free. Tearing in vain at the covering on his face, he glared upward to the air.

Moonlight spread across the pool's surface like a white shield. Rays of fire streaked it. In their base, a round shadow that could have been a head appeared, then vanished.

Senruh's temples thumped, his lungs ached, he must draw breath! Was this the water dweller's friendship? An easy death that caused the spacers no embarrassment? In a last burst of strength the boy kicked and thrust at the other; it held him easily. Then, consciousness dimming, the sweet nausea of his new pleasure crept through the boy's belly to his loins. Half-horrified, half-wildly welcoming the ecstatic flood, he turned in the other's arms. Senses

232

rocketing, he drew a deliberate breath. He embraced his murderer like a lover.

Air tingled through Senruh from his scalp to his toes. The limbs entwining him gently put him away. A wide-lipped noseless face stared into his. The boy's cheeks flamed—what the other must have felt from him! He yanked his head into the current, unable to look into the great black eyes. And, in the respite, he wondered.

Was this a dream, that he breathed water? Or was the spacers' liquid a thickened air? Curiosity pricking through his shame, he drifted in the other's clasp and remembered Marget urging him into the health room 'fresher. His dressings would be all right, she had said, "They're the same semipermeable membranes we use to visit the water dwellers—let air in and keep water out."

Senruh's pleasure in solving the problem dimmed. The other knew him now. Soon, so would the rest of the spacers. They would never want one like him. His throat thickened, he refused another nudge to look at the other. A soundless voice arrowed through his mind.

Little brother, the water dweller sang. And with the words came comprehension and shared pain. Senruh rocked in the light hold. As tendrils of thought crept through him, he found the delicate probing almost perversely pleasant. At last, curious, savoring new experience, he allowed the other access to all his memories.

He stood again in the deserted bazaar, Pell behind him, struggling and defiant. Again Senruh hissed, "What sort of place is your highlands that it never taught you anyone is capable of anything!"

More images swarmed through his mind. They cleared. The scribe's seamed face turned upward to a sun he could no longer see. "A scholar does not refuse knowledge, Senruh," the old man said. The hazed eyes dimmed, faded . . .

Once more the boy knelt in the spacers' cavern, the bright-haired priestess looming high above him. She was Rabu, the co-ruler of Qaqqadum, yet she had come to him because he, Senruh, had been denied his sacred right of Choice.

The boy's life pictures faded. Those of the water dweller's silver world overlapped them. The creature whispered in Senruh's head.

"After that one exultant night, I interfered no more with my mate's choice. My mate chose freedom. I never killed again. Though I have had the chance. And the desire."

As Senruh stared at the long knives that had been born on its thumbs and shared the other's past despair, he shrank suddenly from the new shared intimacy. *Pallet talk!* his mind shouted and, pushing the other's thoughts away, he concentrated on the crystal sphere of air balanced between the water dweller's nose slits and lipless mouth. Slowly the current's surge cooled the boy's cheeks. He lifted his gaze to the creature's great black eyes. He found sadness there as he had expected, but also the spark of victory.

Brother! the voice sang in his mind as the creature pulled him into what he knew now was a sibling's clasp. As the cool webbed hands spread across his back, his robe floating above him, the boy laid his cheek against the other's sharp-boned one, inhaled the water-flavored air, and at last opened all his mind.

After a timeless period a black circle appeared in the moon-flooded surface; a spear followed, its length piercing the dark currents. It caught in Senruh's high-floating robe, tore free . . . A shout came from above.

Feeling pliant as weed in the moving currents, Senruh saw and heard those things as from a great distance. He rested on the other's wide, thin-skinned chest, at peace, mind bound with his new brother's while both of them delved freely into Senruh's own. The water-quieted shouts seemed only images of old fears until reason prodded the boy. Those terrors had had cause. The airy world above held soldiers who would rip his life from him. Could they find him here, pull him, dripping, to Sacrifice? The water dweller nodded, fathomless gaze holding Senruh's.

You have seen truly, brother. When they think to use them, their pistols' marker beams will find you in an instant. And the stored air in that mask will last only a little longer. It refills too slowly for you. You must go to safer refuge. The creature looked away, frowned, and after a pause, thought, *Those were but the initial searchers. Their sirdar calls them now to order. When they return I can protect you for a while with these.* It held up its sharp-nailed hands. *But our leader has not yet settled whether you may stay. I have sworn to follow him. If he signals me to give you up, I must!*

Caring little, Senruh waited, suspended with his friend and brother in a dream of book scrolls glowing like jewels in the watery depths of a cavern; the feasts of silver-winged insects swarming from shining rolls of fog into misty light . . . The creature interrupted the vision of its life.

Not all here fear the chaos of undiscipline as much as I do. Its thought quested through Senruh's toward the surface. The boy felt it meet an answer; their twined minds blossomed with joyful light.

The unhappy one will aid you. She likes mischief, the water dweller spoke. *She awaits you by the pond. There. Come!*

With his friend, Senruh dove upward to a surface washed with moonlight and overhung with branches and matted vines. In their shadow he clung to a projecting root; the water dweller peeled the boy's borrowed mask away. Holding his gaze, the large eyes rimmed with fire slid beneath the ripples. Then even the smooth head was gone. Alone, Senruh breathed in smoke, the scent of rotting plants, and fear.

Heavy feet trampled from the pool, spears and soldiers' huge mailed backs clashed and jingled in green light brilliant with a receding torch's flare.

"—where!" deep voices and higher ones shouted. Guards

rushed from the grotto they had been searching to the entrance portals.

"There!" Grinelda's nasal screech came from just beside the boy. He started. "I saw him, lunging toward the doors, he has a knife! Oh, save me!"

When only a lone soldier remained, his back turned to the pond, his gaze fixed on his companions milling about the doors, Grinelda—limbs gleaming like dusty moonbeams—dropped to her knees and hissed into the bushes, "Senruh! Are you here?"

"Yes, lady," he whispered. Then even the sentry hurried away. At Grinelda's sign Senruh heaved himself from the pool. Water sluiced from his robe, its coolness trickling into the pond with the thin sound of summer fountains. The sirdar's contralto blasted through it.

"Halt! Report to me tomorrow before first meal, you! and you! and you! Back to positions! Undisciplined, soft-living, slack-bellied sons of dung lizards . . ." Distance rounded the edges of her voice as she strode across to her troops at the door, her mail rattling, her handwhip swishing. Senruh got to his knees, sopping robe heavy. Grinelda pressed against his side.

"Come on, you gorgeous thing!" she said in his ear. As he rose, her small hand patted his behind. He turned to her, questioning; then heard a snapping of stems, the brush of leaves.

"Senruh! I thought you were dead." Pell's anxious face pushed through the vines at Senruh's feet.

"What are you doing here?" Grinelda snapped.

"If there's going to be a fight, I'm helping." The boy sat up, his mouth firm.

"He's not going to fight, you fool! Killing's what got you into this mess. He's going to hide!"

"But, lady, where?" Senruh squinted into the shadowed recesses of the chamber. Surely they would be the first to be searched. The Studier of Mankind grinned.

"Have faith," she said. "Go!"

As the boy opened his mouth to ask where, the stocky

sirdar began a methodical cursing of her red-faced troops. Senruh paused. She had a far-ranging imagination.

Grinelda pinched his arm. "While their eyes are on their sirdar. Now!" Jerking her head toward the mirrors at the cavern's back, she doubled over and began to run.

The boy stared. The room's end had no cover. Not so much as a floor cushion. And to make it worse, at one side of the long reflecting wall Marget and Enkolo conferred, the man's dark tight-curled head bent toward her pale smooth one. The boy swallowed.

"Can you trust her, Senruh?" Pell sidled up to him.

"I don't know. The water dweller thought so."

By the doors the sirdar began a last diatribe. As he listened, Senruh thought how soon those Rabu men and women would be searching the cavern, furious, and eager to prove their competence.

Cold oozed through his belly. He glanced toward Grinelda. She had paused in the shelter of the rocky wall beyond the pool. Ahead of her was at least three man-lengths of empty floor. The reflecting wall held not a single recess. Senruh nodded grimly. He had little chance no matter what he did. Expecting a shout at any moment, he raced toward her. The other boy pelted after him. Senruh dropped by the outer wall beside Grinelda.

"When your friend's through feeding his eyes, tell him to get down!" she snapped. "He's about as invisible as Sassurum's dome." Heart pounding, Senruh stared through the wall's cascade of flowers to Pell. Their sweet wild scent overlaid his own smell of wet silk, cold sweat, and dread.

"Pell!" he whispered, gesturing to the boy, who was staring at Grinelda's long bare legs. Pell dropped to all fours.

"I—I've never seen . . ." he said, face flushing as he crawled to Senruh's side. With a caught breath and a slither, Grinelda whisked across the open space to the mirror's edge, curled into a ball, and rolled her eyes, signalling the boys to join her. Senruh glanced toward the mirror's other end, where Marget and Enkolo still argued.

"—and now, disperse ranks!" The sirdar's voice cracked

like a handwhip from the opposite end of the cavern. Garments rustled, swords and mail clinked as the soldiers raised their fists in salute.

Senruh took a last wild look over his shoulder, tried to suck air into tight lungs, failed, and bolted toward Grinelda. Pell's bare feet splatted behind him.

As they dashed toward her, Grinelda slapped the stone wall by the mirror, leaped up, and faced them. For an instant the cavern's reflection, mysterious with green and white light and black shadow, seemed empty, with a populous phantom cavern lurking behind it. As the distance closed between him and the Studier of Mankind, Senruh tried to skid to a halt. Grinelda reached for him.

He held out a hand, expecting her to steady him. Instead she planted a palm between his shoulder blades and shoved, propelling him at full speed into the polished metal.

Chapter Twenty-three

BRACED FOR A CRASH, Senruh instead flew through light that flared on his robe, into a rough-floored dark that smelled of earth and stone. The priestess's tunnel! Arms wide as he came through, he stubbed a toe on a narrow rut, hopped, tripped over his own feet, and went sprawling. Only at the last instant did he remember to arch away from his splinted arm. He was clambering to his knees when Pell shot through the mirror and slammed on top of him.

"Uhhh!" For the third time that day Senruh fought for breath as Pell scrambled up, gasping.

". . . *pardon!* Didn't mean—!"

Senruh's first shock of pain thinned. He struggled to sit, wet robe sticking to his elbows and knees. A section of wall trundled silently along the track that had caught his toe. Air slid at last into his lungs.

"Don't—don't worry about it!" Senruh wheezed. "Routine by now. Expect it!" All he could see at first were Pell's curls as the boy took a few steps down the inclined tunnel toward the mirrors and hunkered down.

"I can't hear your grateful effusions, boys." At Grinelda's nasal voice, Senruh looked up, startled. It seemed to come from a button in the rocky wall, not an arm-length from his dripping shoulder. But she was outside the tunnel! He could see her grayed silhouette plainly, leaning against the now-solid but transparent mirror. Senruh's hand twitched. *No!*

"You should be safe in there," she went on, "unless Enkolo thinks of it and hauls you out. But that would show the city guards the temple's secret entrance, besides letting them know we off-worlders aren't as simple as we look. So I don't think he will. Though he may speak to me severely after they leave." She giggled. "Just so it's in private! I've been trying to get him alone for the last cycle. And now I'm going to prove to the local peace keepers you aren't here!"

With a flip of her short tunic, its thin cloth seeming as fragile as pond ice on a winter morning, she skimmed across the stone to the grotto's blossom and fern. Senruh scooted up the tunnel's slant until he could glimpse the top of her head. She worked her way along the back of the cavern to its side, often turning to look toward the distant entrance as if judging the distance. She also darted glances toward Marget and Enkolo, standing at the great mirror's edge. Each time they looked her way, she froze.

Senruh shook his head; his pain was creeping back. He cleared his throat. Pell, who had been gazing after Grinelda, started, and turned.

"I never knew girls were like that. Brave," Pell amplified when Senruh lifted an eyebrow: "In my highlands they mostly stay in the women's quarters or shuffle around in veils a hand thick. Because of the radiation, you know. They'd never talk to a man like she does!"

Pell broke off. Crossing in front of their transparent wall, Enkolo was moving toward the spot where the boys had entered. Marget followed, almost running.

"They can't see us or hear us in here, can they?" Pell whispered.

"Not from what Grinelda said."

"Then how can we—?"

"I've been thinking about that." Senruh nodded toward the shining grayness. "Those mirrors aren't metal, like ours. There's just a thin film of it over glass. Or whatever they use. As long as it's darker in here than out there, we can see through it, while all they get are reflections. As for the sound—" He pointed to the button he had discovered earlier. Water dripped down his sleeve to his finger and onto the stone, making a dark trickle on the chiseled brown. "I think that works like the one in the health room."

Senruh halted. He remembered what he had overheard Pell say—or had he dreamed it?—through that machine.

"Well, but even if they could make a piece of glass that big, it would have splintered when we came through," Pell objected.

"I think that was just a picture of a mirror. Remember, for an instant there were two reflections, one in front of the other? My lady has smaller images like that in her villa, only of people . . . uh." Senruh glanced at Pell. He could not know what the people did. Senruh hurried on. "Her pictures were made of light, she said, like the guards' laser beams but not strong enough to hurt. When that wall moved back in place, Grinelda probably turned off the picture-making machine."

Pell grinned. "I wondered why you didn't produce one of your averting signs."

"You make them too!"

"I don't—!" Pell began as Senruh opened his mouth to further defend himself. Both boys halted. A deep voice rumbled from the button.

". . . just check if they're in the passage before the guards get close enough to see . . ." Enkolo. The boys looked at each other, then turned to the tunnel entrance. The tall spacer, his suit's color and outline muted by the strange glass, bent in front of it, hand ready to slap the wall. "I'm sure that was Grinelda sending the guards away from here. It'd be just like her to—" His hand swung back.

Senruh looked over his shoulder into the tunnel's shadowy depths. Beyond the torches and tinder stacked ready at the entrance, he saw no curves. If Enkolo shone a light—! Well, he could try. Senruh tensed aching haunches.

Outside the mirrors, Marget hurried around the crouching spacer. She grasped his arm. "Please, Enkolo! Don't find him." The tall man paused. Tilted green eyes stared down into light brown ones.

"Don't you think you're carrying this sponsorship a little far, Marget?" he asked. "The boy's a thief and a liar and the cheapest kind of songboy. Certainly not worth hazarding a mission over, or a civil war. Ordinarily, you'd be the first to see that. He's influenced you. Played you like one of those native zangliers you're so fond of."

Marget caught her breath. Her pale face drained of all color. "I can't *believe*— Enkolo! He *hasn't*. Or if he has, I couldn't blame him! You saw my report, heard what those guards will do to him. And he's not, not only what you said. He's a fine boy! As you yourself told me when he came in."

" 'Fine'?" The hardness in his eyes belied Enkolo's lazy smile. Senruh, kneeling in the dark, shivered as water crawled down his back, making a pool under him that squelched. Studiously avoiding Pell's gaze, he willed the pair to stop talking about him. "Wasn't 'beautiful' the word you used?" Enkolo finished.

Senruh remembered the menace that had seemed to creep from the shadows when the tall man had found him with Marget outside the doors. He thought of Ariahnne's bearers. Icy hands clasped in his belly.

Quickly he searched his mind for a way to use Enkolo's weakness for Marget before it crushed him. The boy stared through the mirror over the pair's heads. Motion by the doors caught his eye: the gray-haired sirdar deploying her soldiers.

Two by two they spread toward the cavern's periphery. Three pairs marched down the center of the dim chamber, in and out of silver light toward the water dweller's pool. In the tunnel watching, Senruh edged his knees off his soggy hem. How long before the guards found his wet trail, followed it . . . ?

The boy eased to his feet. He scuffed his bare foot over the tilting floor of dirt and rock, then turned to estimate its upward slope into the dark. He nudged Pell and jerked his head toward the blackness. The other boy rolled to his knees. Pell reached for a torch; he paused. Enkolo's deep tones came clearly through the button.

"How much are you going to grieve when this one dies?" the tall spacer asked Marget. "Because if it's not the guards tonight, it'll be the life he lives tomorrow. You know the profile as well as I do, you've seen what happens to them. Boys like him in every port!

"Sure, I was willing to give him a chance when he came in. They were shooting at him! I didn't know it had been the other way around, first. Besides, I recognized . . . Well." From his vantage point behind the slick gray wall, Senruh watched Enkolo straighten. He gestured with the hand that had hovered above the stone ready to slap open the entrance. Beside the tall man Marget stood, head bowed, her pale hair falling forward to hide her face. Enkolo rounded on her.

"Yes, I told you he seemed reasonable, deserving! The key word is 'seemed'! That's how your 'beautiful boy' operates, Marget; watching you, changing his ways to use your reactions to his advantage. That, and sexual attraction. He's more comfortable seducing authority than standing up to it! And you want me to put the whole colony—your life, mine, our mission—on the line for that?"

Dust and pebbles grated between his toes as, in the passage behind the mirrors, Senruh forced his mouth into an ironic smile and carefully lowered himself to the floor. Its stale scent of trampled unturned earth and stone and old smoke filled his nose and throat until he wanted to retch. He wasn't like that! Some fellow half-breeds, perhaps, but not him! Someday . . . ! He sagged. He had no more somedays. Nor energy, he found, for a last dash for his life, but Pell . . .

"Go!" he whispered to the boy below him, squatting closer to the great reflecting wall. He could not look at him.

"No!" Pell said. At the venom in his voice Senruh glanced up. The gray-blue eyes were slitted; Pell's fists clenched on his knees. "If that's what he thinks, he's no sponsor of mine! I'm staying! I'll help you kill him—all of them!"

Senruh smiled faintly. "No, you won't," he said. "You get up that tunnel. But thanks." Out of the corner of his eye he saw, beyond the mirrors below him, a swirl of white. Marget had turned, fast. She glared up at Enkolo.

"How dare you despise Senruh for being weaker, smaller; a half-breed with no power in the courts; forbidden education, skilled work, even weapons?" She jammed her fists into her white robe's pockets. Her chin jutted. "And how dare you consign that boy to the trash heap just because he used the only armaments his government and that religion of his have left him? I think he's done wonderfully all by himself, and if we can just not get in his way, he's going to do even better!"

Flushing, Senruh blinked into the passage's darkness above and behind her, unable to decide which embarrassed him more, Enkolo's attack or Marget's defense. He stared blindly over their heads. Near the doors a glimmer of near-white and a transparent flutter caught his eye. He squinted. Concentrating on the jerky movements at the far end of the cave, he almost succeeded in blocking out Marget's forthright tones.

". . . not the first to use his charm, manipulate those in power! Unfortunately, he won't be the last . . ."

Curiosity growing, Senruh squirmed backward deeper into the passage until, looking across the cavern, he could resolve the glimmer near the doors into arms and legs. The fluttering became the transparent skirt of Grinelda's undertunic. She flitted behind a last group of spacers and unassigned guards. Between them and Senruh at the cave's end, three pairs of soldiers searched the grotto. They had almost reached the pool. On its other side Senruh's wet trail gleamed beneath the flowers.

". . . and what's this 'beautiful boy' quotation, Enkolo?" Marget's voice cracked through the button by Senruh's ear. "I knew you were listening. You set it up that way

yourself. So why are you suddenly as snide as a jealous adolescent?''

Jolted away from his worry and from Grinelda's intrigu-
ing activities, Senruh motioned for Pell to hand him an
unlit torch from the stack by the tunnel entrance—he
could club the guards with it when they came to take
him—and listened for the couple beyond the reflecting
wall. They might even yet say something he could use. He
watched the tall man face Marget, shoulders tense.

In a goaded voice Enkolo said, ''Because I *am* jealous!''
Marget's jaw dropped. The deep voice didn't pause. ''And
don't tell me you didn't know. Deaf, dumb, and blind you
may have been this whole past cycle, but you can't have
missed that! None of the other colonists have. Even your
beautiful boy saw it. I've envied Jien, then his memory,
even your work! And now this—this—*boy*—!''

Inside the tunnel Senruh winced. He looked between
Enkolo and the healer to the entrance. Grinelda was
climbing the walls by the doors, clinging to its nooks and
crannies like a lizard after a scuttler. He pointed. Pell followed the line of his arm, eyes widening.

''Enkolo!'' Marget's fluid voice vibrated in the passage's
dark air. Senruh looked through the mirror. The little
healer was staring up at the dark-faced man. She pushed
her hair back, revealing a small reddening ear. ''I—I had
no idea, or I'd never have said—!'' Her head almost ob-
scured the distant sight of Grinelda poised on hands and
knees on a shelf beside the portals. Senruh held his breath.
Then Marget moved and Enkolo blocked Senruh's view. A
smile twisted the spacer's dark face.

''Don't look so stricken, Marget,'' he said. ''I'm a big boy.
I'll survive.'' For a moment he seemed to stare into himself, tilted eyes unfocused. ''All right,'' he said. ''Maybe my
judgment is out, here.'' He glanced up at the guards
spreading out now around the pool, just a few man-lengths
from the cavern's end. ''It's probably too late now, anyway.'' He turned his gaze on the healer. ''Your protégé can
have his chance. He's fascinated you, his friend, our an-

thropologist, our right-living water dweller, even our chief of field operations. You recognized the boy from his reports, didn't you? Well, *I* liked him! He must have something. I just hope we're not too disrupted finding out what it is!"

Beside the tall man, Marget's face suffused with color. Senruh, in his hiding place, watched her snatch up Enkolo's hand, give a small gasp and drop it. "I'll go tell him!"

"Don't bother." The spacer's voice was dry. "If that young man's the boy I think he is, he's halfway up the tunnel by now and won't care, or else he already knows." He looked over Marget's pale head; a commotion had begun by the doors.

In the dim gray light above them, Senruh stared at the earthen floor. "I'll show him," he said, jaw tight. "I'll come back here so loaded with honors, knowledge . . . He'll apologize on his knees for that!" His lip shook. He bit it, hard. Without rising, Pell sidled closer. He gripped Senruh's shoulder. Senruh looked up.

"Oh, by the universal egg!" Enkolo said from just outside the mirrored wall. Senruh's attention switched to the cavern. He didn't notice when Pell took his hand away.

Before him, Enkolo's voice rose to a shout. The tall spacer strode swiftly toward the doors, snapping orders as he went. He stopped at the edge of the clot of undeployed Rabu, all as tall as he. He pushed at them; they looked at his orange suit. They ignored him. Enkolo stood lance-straight.

"Grinelda!" he shouted, looking upward. Senruh followed his glance.

Chapter Twenty-four

FROM HIS VANTAGE point higher on the tunnel's slant, Senruh stared with Pell through the mirrors and across the cavern to the entrance. There, arms out, Grinelda balanced on a shelf beside the carved doors, her mouth a circle of surprise. Her voice came clearly through the perforated button set in the rock beside the boys.

"Oooh!" she said and batted her meager lashes at the soldiers below her. "What are you doing here?"

The paralyzed guard said nothing. Behind the mirrors Senruh grinned as he watched the helmeted officers try not to eye the girl's long bare legs. Behind the tall men and women their chain-capped troops ogled the girl. On her shelf just above them, Grinelda pursed her lips, touched them with a finger, and posed, one knee coyly hiding the other.

"Oh, go ahead and look!" she urged as, belatedly, an officer ordered, "Eyes front!"

Several man lengths from the troops, Enkolo came at a fast lope. "Stand aside!" he rapped out to the colonists and soldiers in his path.

Grinelda darted a glance from him to the guards. "We don't have a leg fetish," she said kindly, her nasal tones hurried. "So much more comfortable in your climate! Well—" With a breathless laugh she looked down.

Enkolo stood just in back of the soldiers. He snapped an order at a helmeted officer. The woman glanced at him, then at his suit, grimaced, and looked back at Grinelda.

With what sounded like a curse, Enkolo shouldered past her into the ranks.

At the cavern's end behind the mirrors, Senruh watched the spacer push toward the stocky sirdar. She seemed to ask a question. He gave a curt nod. With a look of covert sympathy, Senruh thought, she gave an order. The ranks straightened. Enkolo lunged through them. He stopped, back stiff, at Grinelda's feet.

"Grinelda." Enkolo's deep voice was controlled. "Come down. Now."

From her perch, the Studier of Mankind gave him a quick look, patted her lank brown hair, and launched herself, tunic flying, into the soldiers' midst. Being short, she promptly disappeared from view but her thin tones came clearly through the button by Senruh's shoulder.

"Don't mind me!" Her voice was backed by the crunch of studded sandals and jingle of mail as the troops made space for her. "But I'm dressed for swimming and it would be so disappointing to change my plans." From the guards came a chirr and a low growl. Galvanized by the sound and the memories it brought to life, Senruh leaped to his feet in the tunnel and peered through the reflecting wall, his heart pumping faster. Just in front of him, Pell sucked in a breath and pointed.

Through soldiers' legs and robes massed by the doors, the boy glimpsed a pale arm, a flimsy skirt. With a final wriggle, Grinelda emerged into the cavern's dusky light. Behind her, the soldiers crowded out of formation, chirring and snapping their fingers, impeding Enkolo's progress as the tall spacer pushed after his anthropologist. Senruh held his breath as he saw the tall man grab a helmeted officer's arm. Green eyes blazing, Enkolo shouted over the din, "Form up your troops!"

The surprised officer jerked out an order; immediately around him, the soldiers paused. Enkolo shoved between them. Watching from behind the mirror, Senruh felt a reluctant sympathy. In the bazaar's thoroughfares, he too had struggled through tall uncooperative crowds. And the

man's errand was urgent. Didn't Grinelda realize—! Senruh ran backward, deeper into the tunnel. Squatting on its
inclined floor, he looked over Pell's head to the center of
the chamber.

There Grinelda flitted through dim green light and sudden cascades of moon silver. She neared the grotto, dodged
around a quartet of guards, brushed through fern fronds
and trailing flowers, and vanished.

"Where—?" Senruh asked. Across the cavern the soldiers ranked by the doors gave an inarticulate shout and,
as one, moved after the young woman.

"There!" Pell's voice from in front of Senruh was eager.
He stood on tiptoe, peering through the great gray trans-
parency. "She's run around the pool. Her back's to us.
She's standing where we came through the mirror!" Pell
had come close to speak. He leaned back, making sure his
voice carried. His ringlets slid across Senruh's cheek. Senruh held very still. Pell too seemed to hesitate.

"She's going to dive!" Pell's whisper was strained. Senruh stared beyond him through the hazy glass.

Between gently waving plants, he saw Grinelda curl her
toes over the pond's rocky edge and crouch. She leaped,
body horizontal to the water, arms and legs wide. She
whacked the surface, silver and green mushrooming
around her. It sloshed across the rocks, sheeting halfway
to the mirrors. Face screwed into an anguished grimace,
she sank.

"Ouch. Not too graceful, is she? But at least she's
safe . . ." Senruh broke off. Pell wasn't listening. Blue
eyes sparkling in the passage's tarnished light, he pointed.

"Look! She's erased half your trail from the pool!"

Grinelda surfaced. The guards arrived at a dead run, Enkolo drawing abreast of them.

"Grinelda. Out!" *Enkolo's tone would have frozen a vol-
canoe's fiery ooze,* Senruh thought. If the big man ever lost
control . . . Even Grinelda looked taken aback as she
heaved herself, dripping, from the water. Her soaked tunic

clung, more than transparent. The soldiers jammed around her, their comments loud and specific.

In back of the pool, behind the mirrors, Senruh glanced at Pell. The boy's gaze was welded to Grinelda. A sharp-nosed lizard seemed to gnaw in Senruh's belly. He pushed away the thought and looked past the other boy into the cavern.

Grinelda no longer dripped on the entrance side of the pool. Skidding out of Enkolo's reach, she raced around it toward the cave's end, setting the crystal bells chiming, the leaves and flowers waving. She bounded across the three man-lengths of stone and slid to a halt in front of the mirror where the boys had entered. A dusty moonbeam found her.

"Look! I'm moon bathing!" She giggled shrilly, struck an attitude, and lifted her sopping hair. With a quick movement she grasped it in both hands and twisted. Water splatted around her feet, drenching the stone in all directions. Beyond her, kept in order with difficulty by their young officer, soldiers milled beside the pool. A few lunged toward Grinelda.

"Search her!" one shouted. "Maybe she's got him under her tunic!"

"Maybe she *is* him under her tunic!" another called.

"Good thinking! Better check!"

In the tunnel's safe dark, dank with the smell of packed earth and rock and secrets, Senruh's memories revived. Nausea bulged in his throat as he watched the troopers converge on the girl, their chainmail glinting green then gold in a torch's flare. With a choked exclamation the boy jumped up, lunged toward the mirrors, then stopped, heart pounding.

"She's crazy!" he said. "Swimming! Like that! With them here! And there's nothing we can—"

"No, she isn't!" Pell was just in front of the reflecting wall, scrabbling among the unlit torches. "You saw her drip all over your trail, then wring out her hair at the place where we came in. She's brave! And she likes you. Here, catch!"

As the torch smacked into Senruh's hand, he ignored the hollow note in Pell's voice and looked again through the shining wall. "Now what's she . . . ? Oh, gods!"

For Grinelda had darted a single wide-eyed look up at her pursuers and scampered to a broken cylinder of moon and starshine. She posed there just long enough for the guards to change course, then she sped into verdant shadow, the soldiers clanking after her.

She passed a huddle of white. Marget. Face almost as pale as her robe, the healer counted glittering tools into a black case. She glanced over her shoulder, watching the young Studier of Mankind scamper toward the grotto.

"Grinelda!" Enkolo bawled, raising his voice at last. "Cover yourself or get back in that pool! Or I'll place you under arrest!" At his signal, a detachment of orange-suited colonists moved toward him, shoulder to shoulder, scattering the last staring guards by the entrance.

No longer able to see Grinelda, Senruh hurried up the passage until its incline allowed him to look down on the jostle of tall helmets and glinting caps. "Look, Pell—!" The boy hurried toward him. Together they stared as, dimmed by the glass, Grinelda's pale form broke from the soldiers. She ran behind them to the pond's edge nearest the mirrors, hesitated, aimed a lascivious wink over her shoulder at the glass wall, and dove. Black ripples edged with fire swelled about her length; it gleamed greenish white as she sank into the depths and was gone.

"Search the pool!" a soldier yelled. Volunteers charged forward.

"With the torches, you dolts! Keep your robes on!" a helmeted officer shouted.

One burly guard, ahead of the rest, yanked his sandal from the water. He flung himself backward. "Don't search it at all. She's got a big friend in there!" A smooth dark head had broken the water, reflections sheeting from it like ribbons of light. Beneath them, black eyes rimmed with fire blinked wide. And from the water before those baleful orbs, twin daggers rose.

The remaining guards scurried to form ranks. At their head Enkolo and the stocky sirdar spoke. Fragments of their conversation filtered through the button in the tunnel's wall. Beside it, Senruh carefully put down his club. After a moment Pell did the same. Lowering himself to the passage's floor, Senruh leaned toward the button and listened.

". . . temple sponsors us . . ." Enkolo rumbled. ". . . threat to one of my personnel . . . public lewdness . . . removal of the victim's Choice . . . complaint to high priestess . . ." The spacer's dark profile looked grim.

He's using the priestess's words, Senruh thought. *He must be a good commander.* Many times the boy had heard the soldiers agree, *When your position's weak, attack!* He eyed the sirdar beside the spacer. The glass darkened her sword-chopped hair to near black.

"All very fine," she said, "but nothing happened. And we want that boy."

The spacers' leader spoke again. ". . . goddess appeared . . . gave him his life . . . 'hidden thing' . . . no need to cause you trouble, allow a search . . ."

When Enkolo finished, the stocky woman frowned and slapped her handwhip against her palm. She gave a reluctant nod; she turned and directed her troops about the cavern. In the tunnel, watching the pair, Senruh thought he saw the tall man's shoulders relax a little, his chin lose some of its aggressive tilt. In his turn the boy let out a long breath.

"I think they've made a bargain," he told Pell. "The guards can search; if they don't find us they'll go. In return, Enkolo won't complain to the temple. Pell?" The boy was not beside him. Senruh stared into the dimness. He found the other near the opposite wall of the tunnel, fair head leaning on his knees, shoulders quivering.

"Pell!" Senruh hurried toward him, then dropped to the floor, hand hovering over the boy's shaking back, afraid to touch it, afraid not to. "Pell, it's all right, she's safe with the water dweller, he's got breathing masks down there . . . And so are we safe! Or—did I say something? Pell, what is it?"

Wet blue eyes lifted at last. "Sorry!" The boy's mouth trembled. "It's not what you think. I just— I was scared for her, but she was so funny! And when she winked, your expression—" He went off into another bout of silent laughter. Senruh rolled back onto his heels, affronted but relieved.

Pell caught his breath and peered up at him from beneath his tousled curls. "I was right the first time," he said. "Everybody does look at you the way I did. For a while there, I thought Grinelda was going to take a bite out of you." He wiped his eyes and wriggled across the floor of beaten earth and stone to lean against the wall. Hesitantly, Senruh followed. He hunkered down beside the boy.

"I—I've been jealous of all the people who've had slices out of you," Pell said more quietly. "Your master, that Ari-ahnne, those guards . . ." His mouth jerked and he swallowed. "But I'm beginning to see it isn't all your doing. And it isn't always much fun, is it? Or even very flattering?"

"Uh," Senruh said. He felt himself go scarlet.

"I guess," Pell said after a moment's hesitation, "now you'll have to, with Grinelda—?" The thick gold lashes flickered as, with a tight smile, the boy studied his clenched hands.

Senruh jolted away from the wall. "No!" he said. "I'm teaching her court speech and that's all! I convinced her she'd get more out of that than—than the other. Because it was that or nothing. Whatever Enkolo says, or you, I'm not for sale to everybody!"

Eyes bright with anger, Pell whipped his head up and opened his lips. Senruh braced himself. Pell shut his mouth. "Enkolo said I needed a lid for my temper," he muttered.

"I'm sorry," he said. "I didn't mean—! It's not my business. I was trying to tell you, I don't care. But I put it wrong and—and made you angry. Again. I can't ever—!" His fist thumped his orange knee.

Senruh looked away, stomach flipping. He remembered the dream conversation in the health room. What if it had been real?

"Pell, I—!"

But the other boy was still speaking. Smile crooked, he said, "You could rub dirt on your face to discourage all your admirers. Or not smile. Even I—" He stopped, face red. Then, deliberately, he said, "Even I'd take you, on any terms, when you smile."

Senruh stopped breathing. Outside the gray mirrors, the soldiers, the colonists, Marget and Enkolo seemed to fade away. Like a thin gold bubble, the silence balanced between them, ready to topple and be caught, held—or smash and crumple.

"Pell, there aren't any terms. Not with you. If you want, sometime we can finish what we started. Or not. Or—or even talk. About anything." He swallowed hard. "And if you want to try your luck with Grinelda, I won't get in your way. I just—! It's you—!" His usually ready words gone, Senruh groped for Pell's hand. A warm unbandaged one caught his in a fierce grip.

"Anything," Pell said. His fingers convulsed around Senruh's. "I've been thinking a lot—that's one thing we do well in the highlands—and Enkolo had some advice for me when I first came in . . ." Blue eyes darted a glance at Senruh, then stared at the opposite wall. It was almost black in the muted light. "But still." Pell's grin looked strained. "Telling you just now I li—! Lo—!" He shrugged, face red. "I'd rather have faced the sentries again! And even then, if I hadn't overheard you in the health room, on that voice-throwing machine, when you were telling Marget—"

"But I—" Senruh turned quickly. Close beside him, Pell's eyes were the color of the evening sea. "I heard you, too!" Senruh said. "I thought it was an accident. I—" A laugh shocked out of him. "I wonder why it's so important to them that we understand each other! Turning those switches on and off, pretending they didn't know . . . Grinelda said the colonists aren't as simple as they seem. I just hope we answer their Question right, whatever it is, so they won't have wasted all this strategy!"

Pell gave him a shaky grin. "What did you hear me—? Don't tell me." After a moment, voice a little high, he asked, "How do you think that chiming machine works?"

Senruh explained his theory about the lodestone, supplementing it with the scribe's lessons on wave motions. "Why aren't you upset about these machines, and calling them names?" he asked. "You're so upright about everything else."

Pell looked offended. His hand turned in Senruh's, relaxing companionably. "I'm no superstitious barbarian! If a thing exists, the followers of L'h believe he put it there to be understood or used. Just because it's inconvenient, they don't shut their eyes and pray for it to go away. Not that I follow L'h or any other god, but—"

"That sounds like—! And you didn't see the goddess when she appeared." Senruh stared at the boy. "You really don't believe in her at all, do you? So, we have that choice, too! Or—"

"What goddess?"

Deep in theological discussion, the boys scarcely noticed Grinelda's entrance into the tunnel. Senruh's first intimation that she stood beside him was the meaty smell of wet unscrubbed flesh and, a moment later, small fingers grasping his drying shoulder.

"You can come out now, boys!" she caroled. "And what have you been doing to amuse yourselves all alone here in the dark?"

Senruh dropped Pell's hand as if it burned him. Finding himself unable to look at the other boy, he got up and stalked out of the tunnel. After its grayness, the green radiance outside seemed very bright. No chainmail glinted, no torch flared. The guard was gone. In his vision's fringe

Senruh glimpsed a streak of white. Marget. Still in her white robe but no longer carrying her instruments, she smiled at him from across the room and beckoned. He nodded; he paused to wait for Pell.

The boy emerged, Grinelda beside him. Pell stopped, blinking, in a wash of moonbeams. They dripped like liquid silver through his curls and lashes, streaking his blue and green gaze with white. Grinelda stared up at him.

"First time I've gotten a good look at you!" she said. She tucked Pell's arm firmly under hers and fluttered her scanty lashes at him. "How friendly are you with him?" She jerked her head toward Senruh. "Enough for a three-way?"

Senruh swallowed a laugh as Pell made a gargling sound, flushed darkly, and looked aside but not, Senruh noticed, without a quick scan of Grinelda's tunic, once more plastered wetly against her. She reached up, patted the fair boy's cheek, and said not to worry, she wasn't in that much of a rush, she'd give him time to get used to the idea. She dropped his arm, looked around the chamber, and skipped toward Senruh, Pell's gaze following her with a distinctly speculative expression.

When the Studier of Mankind halted in front of him, Senruh bowed, face stiff as he fought back a hot twist of jealousy.

"Thank you, lady, for hiding me. I owe you my life." He hesitated but in the end he did not put his forehead to her bare foot as he would have only that morning in the bazaar. He was beginning to know that if he behaved like a slave he would be treated like one.

Grinelda wriggled, water sluicing from her hair and tunic, and grinned upward. "Oh, well, I expect a show of gratitude! Want to come along while I change, get started repaying me?"

And abruptly, Senruh was back in the Avenue of Precious Delights staring up at the sky's white hot zenith. Instead of small brown eyes, yellow ones seemed to burn above floating face veils and Grinelda's nasal tones were replaced by a woman's husky voice. Ariahnne. "A fine first payment," she whispered again in his memory, "and only a drop in the flood to come!"

"No!" Senruh said violently. He blinked as his towering lady and noon's dust and heat shrank to a small, nearly unclad girl standing in a dim green cave lit by shafts of silver moonlight. Grinelda ran a nervous hand through her locks. Several loose hairs wrapped around her fingers; she peeled them away. Senruh watched them drift toward the stone below.

"I will add gestures and etiquette," he said more moderately, "but not as payment. As a gift from one—one friend to another." And with the words came a glow. They were true! His startled gaze met the girl's. She blinked up at him; a shadow of a smile flicked her mouth.

"All right," she said, and for a moment the petulance and hunger smoothed from her expression. "It's a bargain, friend! But I warn you, I won't stop trying. Now I'm going to put on a robe. Or do you like me better this way?" She did a flirting turn. He grinned and shook his head.

Just a step away, Pell watched her, blue gaze shocked but intrigued. It moved, it caught Senruh's. Firmly, Senruh pushed away his resentment. He did not own Pell, after all. He had been so thoroughly possessed himself, he doubted he would ever want to own anyone. He winked. An answering smile flooded the fair boy's face, warming as winter sun on a chill afternoon.

The gods take vengeance on mortals feeling this much happiness, Senruh thought. It was then he remembered. "But lady! Grinelda!" he called after her. "What about the Question?"

She hardly paused in her flight across the cavern. "Let Enkolo ask it. You'll do fine. Friend!" From the entrance she wiggled her fingers at him then flung her whole weight against one of the great carved doors. Grudgingly, it swung open. Like a smudged moonbeam, she slipped into the yawning dark.

Enkolo. Senruh remembered the tall man's censure of him to Marget. Suddenly, he wished Grinelda back.

Chapter Twenty-five

SENRUH STARED AROUND the great green chamber. Its columns of moonlight slanted now; already Shirah, willful daughter of long-vanished L'h and the Sea Goddess, Asherah, descended the sky. Soon the girl moon would visit her mother's palace beneath the tides. When her glow vanished, where would Senruh be? His gaze caught on a slide of straight pale hair.

Between the cavern's end and the doors Marget stood, moonbeams turning her to white and silver. She beckoned him again. With an unaccustomed sense of belonging, he sloshed through the puddles before the mirrors and hurried toward her, Pell's bare feet whispering behind him.

"You survived. Congratulations." The warmth in Marget's eyes belied her terse welcome. The cavern's encircling ledge was just behind her; she sat on it and patted the space beside her. Smiling, the boy dropped onto the rough shelf. Pell squatted by his knee, bare toes gripping the floor. Senruh wriggled on the hard sharp edge, wondering if he could join him. No. He needed Marget's help and she wanted him to perch here.

"Marget?" he began. "This Question Enkolo will ask. Is it—?"

"Did I hear my name?"

Senruh looked up, startled, into intent leaf-colored eyes. The spacers' leader had appeared with the stealth of a stalking lizard. The tall man hunkered down beside Pell.

"Awhile back there," Enkolo said, looking from one boy

to the other, "we were talking about your castes. Let's see. You're not half-breeds. One of you is tall and the other short, so you're ruler and master. Is that right?"

"Yes! But it doesn't matter!" Senruh said. "Pell's no little emptyhead, he—he belongs anywhere! Because—"

"I don't care if he *is* oversized!" Pell interrupted. "He deserves—!"

Enkolo cleared his throat, his face unnaturally solemn. Getting to his feet, he motioned for them both to rise. Again his hand was upside down as he beckoned, pink palm curved upward as if to cup the sky.

"Come here, boys," he said. "I want you to see something."

He led them down the cavern past the grotto toward the reflecting wall masking the priestess's tunnel. As the smell of wet rocks and broken stalks and blossoms grew stronger, Senruh watched his yellow-green robe and Pell's orange suit approach in the mirror. Was Enkolo taking them to the temple for justice? Or Sacrifice? As he had not done since he had entered, Senruh straightened and lifted his shoulders high. Behind him, dark blue eyes narrowed, Pell slid into his highlands arrogant crouch.

When they stopped before the shining expanse of smoky green, Senruh bent his knees, gripped the stone with his toes, and glanced back. Pell gave a short nod. They would fight. Here. Now. Enkolo's heavy hand dropped onto Senruh's shoulder. He shook it.

"Look up, son, and relax." The deep voice seemed to hide a smile. "And Pell—stand straight! Now. Tell me what you see."

Confused, heart slowing, Senruh gazed into his own dark eyes. Beside his mirrored image, reflected blue ones did the same.

"But—!" the boys said in unison.

Their eyes were at the same level. Senruh's gaze slid to the reflections' shoulders, one pair broad, the other less so. They too matched. His own dark head even seemed a little lower than Pell's riot of golden, green-tinged curls.

"You—!" he said, staring at Pell in the mirror. "We were on different levels on those—those stairs when we came in . . . Never once stood barefoot, side by side . . . !"

"And before, you wore those thick sandals, wouldn't take them off! The only time we . . ." Pell stopped, face reddening.

The only time they had lined up head, hip, and toe had been in the copse. And then, neither had been concerned with height. Gaze hooded, Senruh looked at Pell. So. There had been no perversion. If, in spite of what the other boy had said, that had been Senruh's attraction . . . Pell's blue eyes looked back steadily. Senruh could not read them. Behind the boys, Enkolo tightened his grip as he turned them toward each other.

"I think," the dark-faced man said, "what we've got here is either a tall midget and a short giant without a thing in common, or a pair of friends. What do you boys say?"

Senruh lifted an eyebrow. He saw an answering gleam in Pell's shadowed eyes. Pell had spoken out in the tunnel. It was only fair . . . He swallowed.

"We're friends!" he got out as Pell wordlessly held up an arm. With his good hand, Senruh clasped the other boy's wrist; Pell's callused fingers wrapped around his.

"And that was the critical Question!" Enkolo slapped them both on their backs; "Uh! Sorry! Forgot." Enkolo's face stiffened in sympathy as Senruh winced. "If you two can overcome your own culture's strongest prejudice, there's a good chance you're flexible enough to adapt to us," the spacer finished as Senruh got his breath and the comfort Marget had given him began to return. "Welcome!"

Grinning, the spacers' leader took Pell's hand as he had in the entrance. Palm to palm, he squeezed it. When it was Senruh's turn, Enkolo's tilted eyes were quizzical. "How's your shoulder? Better?" he asked. His flashing smile held tension. Senruh hesitated. Afraid of what he might find in that green gaze, he avoided it, nodded, and thrust out his good hand. Enkolo's big dark one engulfed it.

"Sorry about the tricks," the tall man said. "But we had to know you, fast. And still give you every chance." He did not drop Senruh's hand; instead, he waited. Bracing himself to meet polite masked hate, the boy looked up.

Tilted green eyes gazed back at him, as steadily as had Pell's. Senruh scanned them, then the dark face. He could discover no trace of jealous anger, only forbearance and a willingness to trust.

He thought of the tricks that had led to Pell's standing here beside him, a friend; of Marget waiting, of the water dweller, of Grinelda . . . And on the surface of Naphar, the others he now felt free to love. Inside him a great huddled flower of joy shook its head. Uncrinkling its green and red and golden leaves and petals, it expanded to his eyes and fingertips, filling his inner darkness that only a little while ago had been a cramped and frightening place. *Tricks!* he thought. *There should be more tricks like that!*

"It's all right," he told Enkolo. "In fact, it's fine!" And he smiled.

The tall man blinked. He did not change expression but his face seemed to lighten.

"I'm beginning to see why the others were pulling for you," he said. "Glad you're with us, son." And this time, Enkolo's grin was unforced.

As Shirah slipped, a white glowing coin, into the Western Sea, Senruh lay stretched on a pallet in the anteroom of Marget's sleep chamber. Flasks and squeeze bottles of fluid surrounded him, his eyes were closed. Soft as pillows, his dreaming thoughts carried him back to the dim green chamber where he had won friendship, freedom . . . Freedom! Sharp-edged, new, he seemed to hold it in his hands and turn it, scanning its bright faces. Not to be owned, he thought, no longer to have his days ordered by another.

The boy stirred on his pallet. What would he do with this freedom still wet from the hatching? He had not thought much beyond its achievement. What other purpose could now fill his life? And would he live the whole of it here, always a stranger, forever explaining . . . ?

Like a sudden knife, yearning struck him: for the bazaar's heat and dust and smoking braziers; its certainties, even its pain, bearable because it was known; his being one of many . . . The spacers' stony silence pressed on ears aching now for the clamor of street drummers and the tootle of wormcase flutes, the cries of sausage and crisp sellers, priests' incantations, the chanting of storytellers, the scribe's singing words . . .

The scribe! The boy jerked through falling tapestries of sleep. Who would steal coals and joy smoke for the old man now? Or roam the bazaar, ears wide for the gossip, the histories, the tales the old man craved? And who would love Senruh as the old man had, as only another native of the great white and amber city could, understanding all? Or had the scribe loved? He had always required his joy smoke, after all . . .

Your fears contain some truth, my brother. The water dweller's cool thought slid into the boy's mind and his dreams. *But like all such terrors, they also lie. My brother, look!*

The water dweller nudged at the boy, freeing him . . . Senruh's consciousness seemed to rise through the antechamber's rock and the earth above it, into brilliant night. There, salt winds blew him to the great round city flickering with torchlight, a heap of shadowed amber at the plateau's edge above the luminous spume. The bazaar within its walls grew large around the boy. As, bodiless, he seemed to tumble toward it, its mud walls thinned, its flapping awnings grew transparent, he fell through them.

Senruh glimpsed the scribe's brown face, the white wisps of hair. And then, he was the old man. With the water dweller's guidance, the boy fitted his awareness into the scribe's body, he dreamed with him behind the blind eyes as the old man fingered edged metal. He squatted comfortably, spun a dial . . .

* * *

In his hollow, scooped from the clay beneath a long-vacant stall, the scribe listened to Marget's liquid accent reporting Senruh's arrival in the space colony. The old man stopped the recording now and then to correct an idiom or pronunciation; at last Marget yawned and signed off.

Setting his transmitter-receiver on RETURN, the scribe felt across the chilly dust for his bowl. He sniffed its lifeless coals; he sighed. Hooking a frail arm around it, he wriggled into the incense-laden night.

He breathed in the scent of the sea. A warm land breeze cut across it, redolent of the fire mountains' sulfur and the nearer lamp oil and smoke. They worked late in the Street of the Weavers, the old man thought; the palace's commission of new thick tapestries must not yet be finished. Pain gnawed at his belly. He stared into his unchanging dark, wondering where to go for ease.

There had been a child at his storytelling this morning; a girl child and quite a young one, judging by her voice and the shape of her little hand in his. She had asked questions. Extraordinary questions, given her age and her owners' neglect. He felt again the ragged sleeve that had brushed his palm, the tiny callused finger and thumb. A weaver, he thought and nodded. Yes, he had heard whispers of a new girl slave there, bought by a childless couple for her lack of appetite and her tying of small exquisite knots.

The old man nodded once more; his face turned one way then another, sniffing among the currents of air for warmth and burning oil and the scent of new fiber. Sensitive fingers traced rough walls, old feet shuffled along familiar ruts; soon he pulled aside a door curtain and felt the heat of a meager fire on his cheeks, smelled the stuffiness of a room too full of work and cooking and unwashed occupants.

"Who's there?" The woman's voice was sharp. The

scribe cringed into a squatting heap and gathered his rags
around him. He lifted his bowl.

"Joy smoke?" he quavered. "It is blessed by the goddess
to give, and to hear in return the doings of the great ones of
old."

"Oh, give it to him," a man growled. "If nothing else, a
tale will keep the brat quiet. I'm tired of listening to her
snivel. Give him bread, too, and curd. Make him stay and
talk awhile, keep us awake while we work."

The old man clutched the bowl to his chest as the coals
glowed to life, starting the joy smoke rising. It drifted over
his hands, rich, warm, satisfying. He bent, breathed deep.
He tingled with the heightening of sensation that reached
from his soles to his nails' ends and that undid the ravages
of Naphar's fierce sun on his withered cells. Surely the
sight that the smoke took from him was little enough payment for the joy of living in this vigorous enticing city and
among its people. He had loved them from the moment he
stepped onto Naphar's hot, arid soil. And even then he had
not been a young man.

He heard a stifled sob from the slaves' nook behind the
clacking looms. He took up the hunk of dry bread and
hard-edged curd the woman had dropped in his lap, and
scuttled toward the child's pallet. Squatting by it, his bowl
on his knees, he heard a rustle and a sniff and then a wondering silence.

"Are you awake, oh new small daughter of my heart?"
he whispered, and proffered the bread. After a moment the
hand took it, returning a meticulous half. The old man
smiled and at the sound of eager chewing, held out the remainder and also the curd. This was a good little one, he
thought, as promising in her way as that other.

He had not gone quite blind yet in those older days. He
remembered the small boy's great dark eyes, as remark-
able as those of all the other children the scribe had helped
to dream and to find their way. That boy had freed himself
now, a thing the scribe had wanted for him, but the old
man would miss him as he missed them all. The scribe's

rheumy eyes filled with the easy tears of age. A sigh and a rustle from the pallet recalled him to the child before him; he sorted through his mind for tales.

They could not all be saved, these lost lovely children of Naphar. Direct interference was forbidden, but Naphar's own myths and histories and science were not, and one or two children helped to a brighter future were better than none at all. On the scribe's own dying, sparsely settled planet, only individuals mattered. His language had no word for majority or masses or statistical probabilities. He held out the last of the bread and curd.

"And would you hear a tale of marvels before you sleep, little one?" he asked softly as the weaver grumbled behind him and shouted to the girl not to forget to build up the fire when the dawn trumpets sounded.

"Oh, yes. Please!" she whispered to the scribe.

"Have you heard the story of the bazaar boy who, with his companion from the fabled highlands, challenged an ancient city, its soldiers and its gods, to gain the freedom of the stars?"

"No!" the child breathed. Shyly, the small hand took the remainder of the crust.

The old man smiled and nodded, bent over his pottery bowl to inhale deeply of its vapors, and began.

As dawn's first shadowless light brushed the fire mountains behind the dreaming city, Senruh drifted, soft as a breath, from the blind scribe's presence and fell deeper into sleep. In his mind the water dweller whispered, *You are never alone, my brother, not once we have made the siblings' link. And you know, now, you have brothers and sisters among the stars where you may, one day, take your teacher's purpose as your own.* The whisper thinned; only a touch, a fragrance remained.

The boy's mouth curved. In his mind he flew companioned through his world's hot and windy skies, the orange flying lizard's beauty swooping joyously before him. Below them lay the spaceport—rooted in Naphar, built for the stars—his home.

He looked over his shoulder and laughed aloud. For behind him, grinning, green wings thrashing, puffed a very real, very pudgy, pink-spotted dragon.

Acknowledgments

I would like to thank all those who patiently answered my questions, especially Gordon Baker, M.D., Seattle, Washington; Debra Boyer, Ph.C., Department of Anthropology, University of Washington, Seattle, Washington; Robert Fitzgerald, M.D., orthopedic surgeon, Mayo Clinic, Rochester, Minnesota; Cyrus H. Gordon, Ph.D., Director, Center for Ebla Research, New York University, New York, New York; hustlers past and present who agreed to interviews; Virginia Sawin, Ph.D., Supervisor—Biochemical/Genetic Toxicology, Shell Development Company, Houston, Texas; Seattle City Police Department, Vice and Narcotics Division; and the U.S. Marine Corps Recruiting Office, Burien, Washington.

For editorial suggestions, I am grateful to Jean Bryant and The Class, to Don McQuinn, and to Gene Wolfe.